PHOEBE AND THE TRAITOR

THE ORGANIZATION

BOB MAYER

WORDS OF WISDOM #1

Shane's Words of Wisdom #1
Murphy's Law: What can go wrong, will go wrong.
Shane's addendum: And it will always be worse than you can imagine.
No one knows who Murphy was.

Phoebe's Observations #1:

Murphy was a guy.
Of course, he screwed it up.
He didn't listen to what a woman told him to do.

1

"**F**ie, foh and fum," Louise said from the hospital bed as Phoebe entered the room. "Of the three, my favorite is thee, Phoe."

"You always go with Shakespeare," Phoebe said, placing a small pewter figurine on the empty food tray. "I prefer *Jack and the Beanstalk.* '*Fee-fi-fum. I smell the blood of an Englishman. Be he alive, or be he dead. I'll grind his bones to make my bread*'." She paused in thought. "I think Fromm sounds English. I'm gonna crush him."

"Oh, Phoe," Louise said with a shake of her head and a smile. "Fromm is Germanic."

"Whatever," Phoebe said. "I don't care where his ancestors came from, I know his future. The traitor's gonna die for doing this to you."

Louise's lovely halo of long golden hair was piled on the pillow, imperfect because of the bandage over the wound Fromm had given her before escaping the Organization and stealing the highly classified Orion encryption program and proving he was a traitor. She frowned at the figurine. "Gollum? I don't like him."

"But now you have all the hobbits," Phoebe pointed out. She loved listening to Louise speak in her deep Kathleen Turner voice and while she'd enjoy sitting and listening, work was calling. Plus, Phoebe hated hospitals. They were always full of sick people, which was logical but that didn't mean she had to like it.

"Was Fromm our Gollum at the Organization?" Louise asked as she sat up. Her left cheek was covered by a white bandage over the cut Fromm had inflicted. Her right arm ended just above the elbow, a disability she'd been born with.

"No," Phoebe said. "Gollum served a purpose. Fromm is worse than worthless. He betrayed us and he's still out there. But we'll find him."

They were on the fifth floor of the Fort Meade post hospital and it was time for Louise to check out. Phoebe, at five-four, much shorter than Louise, had rolled in a wheel chair for the event. She was in her late twenties and petite, with a wiry body, muscles rippling like whipcord under a black body suit. She wore a red blazer over that, the inside lined with various weapons. Her favorite, a Japanese short sword called a wakizashi, was hidden inside the coat in the center of her back, like an external spine of steel with the handle just under the collar. If someone looked for it, of course they'd spot the outline of the sword, but who is going to question a woman carrying a sword? Best to be silent and move on.

Phoebe's short black hair, with a bad red dye job mixing it up, was spiked, pointing in different directions indicating an indifference to style or perhaps an unwillingness to spend the time organizing it. Given it was Phoebe, it was a combination. Her eyes were icy blue and tiny lines of worry, too many for someone her age were emerging at the edges.

Phoebe indicated the already packed small bag. "That's everything?"

Louise nodded. "I don't need the wheelchair."

"Hospital rules."

"Since when do you worry about rules?" Louise asked.

"When it involves getting you out of here," Phoebe responded. "Some of these nurses scare me."

"Nobody scares you, Phoebe," Louise said as she swiveled in the bed and put her feet on the ground.

That gave Phoebe pause. "You did. When I heard you were hurt, it made me feel—" she shook her head unable to finish the thought, or, more appropriately, delve into the emotion behind the thought.

"Hey," Louise said, reaching out.

Phoebe took her hand and then hugged her, careful not to touch the bandage on Louise's head as she pulled her to her chest. The two remained like that for a long ten seconds, before Phoebe stirred.

"We best be going," Phoebe said.

"Yes. We should." Louise took the figurine and made the transfer from bed to chair. She'd been ready to leave for hours. She was dressed in a flowery sundress, which Phoebe had brought to her the previous evening. It was Phoebe's favorite for Louise although she would be hard-pressed to remember the last time she had worn a dress herself.

"Let us go forth then," Louise said.

Phoebe put the bag on Louise's lap and pushed her into the corridor. Nurses, doctors, patients and visitors bustled back and forth. The air held the stench of sickness and death; at least that's what Phoebe thought. She swallowed down some bile, so extreme was her reaction. This was a woman who was capable of killing with a wide array of weapons and her bare hands.

"What about the paperwork?" Louise asked.

"We don't do paperwork," Phoebe said. "We're the Organization. As far as these people are concerned, you no longer exist."

"That's not as comforting as you think it is," Louise pointed out.

Phoebe rolled Louise into the elevator, turning as she did, so Louise faced the doors. A man in over-sized scrubs, walking with a limp, hustled to catch a ride before the doors closed.

He pushed his way in, bumping against Louise's wheelchair, and moved to the rear, next to Phoebe. The elevator began descending.

Phoebe sniffed. "Fee, fi, fum. Fresh blood."

The man glanced at Phoebe. She smiled at him, her cold eyes belying the gesture, then hit him with a knuckle strike to the throat. He gasped in pain as his hands scrambled to retrieve the gun holstered inside the scrubs.

Phoebe followed up her first strike with four more in rapid succession: throat once more, solar plexus twice and a knee to the groin. As the man collapsed to the floor, she reached down and retrieved the pistol. She hit the stop button. The elevator lurched to a halt between floors.

"Phoe?" Louise was looking over her shoulder in shock. "What the Dickens?"

Phoebe pulled up the cuff of the scrubs, revealing a blood-stained bandaged stump at the ankle and an artificial foot crudely attached. Phoebe knelt on his chest as he gasped for breath. "Looking for your foot? Forensic support has it."

"Fuck you," the man finally managed, with a foreign accent.

"I wish people would get more original with their protestations," Phoebe said. "Lou, this is the guy whose foot I cut off at that lawyer's place you found for me. Got to give him credit for staying on the task, even though Drusilla, his boss, is dead." As she said that, Phoebe caught a flicker in the man's eyes. "Then again, *was* it Drusilla you were working for when you were cleaning up the tracks? Interesting." She nodded in growing awareness. "You were working for Fromm, weren't you? Still are."

The man grimaced, his jaw clenching.

"No, you don't!" Phoebe exclaimed, pressing against either side of his jaw to open his mouth, but she was too late. He was dead in seconds, inert on the floor, white foam bubbling over his lips.

"Oops," Phoebe whispered to herself.

"Did he just kill himself?" Louise asked.

"Yep," Phoebe said.

"Who does that?" Louise wondered in shock. "Why would he do that?"

"He came in here missing a foot and bleeding to kill us," Phoebe said. "I'd say there was considerable pressure being put on him by Fromm. Who knows what Fromm threatened?"

She took her phone out and snapped a picture of the man's face, then turned the head to take a profile shot. She noted a small fishhook scar or brand behind the right ear and took a picture of that. Then she stood.

"There's a dead body," Louise pointed out the obvious. "What are we going to do?"

"We walk away," Phoebe said, pressing the stop once more and the elevator continued its descent.

"But..."

"It's easier than you think," Phoebe said as they arrived at the ground floor. "Allow me, my dear." The doors opened and Phoebe briskly pushed the wheelchair out of the elevator and through the lobby toward the front doors. It was twelve seconds before someone shouted in alarm upon finding the body in the elevator. Phoebe and Louise were outside as a cluster of people were trying to make sense of the dead man in scrubs with a missing foot and froth around his mouth.

They were in the Cleaner's van before the first security guard was on scene in the elevator. Phoebe assisted Louise out of the wheelchair and into the back.

"There's a body in the elevator that needs to be policed," Phoebe informed the Cleaner, a dull looking man dressed in a cheap suit. He was one of the Support personnel from the Organization who assisted Operators on their missions, even if it was a simple trip to the hospital. Because, as had happened, even a simple trip can turn hinky. Since he was stationed here at Fort Meade it meant he probably wasn't the sharpest knife in the Organization's drawer, but even those were good enough.

The Cleaner, showing no surprise, nodded in acknowledgement and murmured something into a handheld device, getting the gears of the Organization working to clean up this mess as he put the van in drive.

"That went well," Phoebe said, "although I wish we could have taken him alive." She shut the door and the van drove off.

Louise stared at her in disbelief. "A man just died."

"Better him than us," Phoebe said. "The troubling part is that Fromm is still coming after us."

"Maybe because we're coming after him?" Louise noted.

"A valid point," Phoebe allowed. "So, let's get him."

"Where do we start?" Louise asked as the van pulled up to a nondescript building housing the Organization. It was a small, two-story concrete building with no windows. A faded, rusting sign in front bemoaned that it was *Facilities Maintenance*. The condition of the sign did not bode well for the facility, but it was a lie. The bulk of the Organization was underground and the facility was the entire country. There were three more buildings like it spread out across a field, the others over-grown with vegetation, abandoned remnants from when a Nike missile battery was stationed at Fort Meade early in the Cold War to defend Washington DC from intercontinental ballistic missiles. From a more optimistic time when it was thought a nuclear onslaught could be stopped. This particular building, though, was much more than it appeared.

"Fromm isn't just coming for us," Phoebe noted. "He's wiping out anyone who was involved in the whole Andovan thing. Even though that guy didn't kill us, he killed himself which erases another link."

"Who is left?" Louise asked as the Cleaner opened the door and Phoebe helped her out.

"The Hacker who sold the lawyer the classified encryption program that was used to set up the weapons deal that started all of this," Phoebe said. "The Feds picked him up after I got his list of clients. We'll find out where they stashed him. I never got a chance to interrogate him when we met." She paused, staring at the steel doors. "Who is *foh* and *fum*?" Phoebe suddenly asked.

Louise was confused. "What?"

"You said that I was your favorite among *Fie, foh and fum*. I want to know who my competition is."

"Oh, Phoe. You'll never have competition. You're an original. My one and only."

Lisa Livia Fortunato stood on the top floor of the Eiffel Tower feeling as if she could conquer the world, or at least a small enough portion of it for her to be happy, which was an earth-shattering concept for her. Her lover, Lucien's, arms were wrapped around her from behind, his solidly built body warm against her back. Her hands cradled a hot cup of coffee in a cardboard container. The combination of warm arms and hot nectar of the Gods offset the early morning chill and she thought for a moment: *really, could it get any better?*

Lisa Livia had dark hair that tumbled over her shoulders and olive skin, giving her an exotic, Mediterranean look which fit in here in Paris. Her New Jersey accent didn't.

There was no one else on this level as the Tower didn't open to the general public for another couple of hours. Dawn was breaking to the east over Paris and she swore that even at this altitude, she could smell freshly baked baguettes from the shops that were swinging open their shutters in the streets. The weather was warm, the trees were budding with the first green of spring, and it promised to be a beautiful day.

Paris. Lisa Livia could hardly believe she was here.

"I know we got in late last night," Lucien said, "but I wanted you to see this. I love watching the sun come up over the city. Paris is called the City of Light and most enjoy the evening, but I prefer the early morning. The quiet. The promise of the day ahead." He let go of her with one hand and pointed. "There is where we spent the night.

The house on Rue St. Charles has been in our family for over a millennium."

"It's worth getting up for," Lisa Livia said, although it had been from a seriously comfortable, canopied, bigger than king-sized feather bed, the likes of which Lisa Livia had never known existed. Plus, there'd been the naked presence of Lucien, so it had been with great difficulty that he'd been able to entice her to get dressed and accompany him on the pre-dawn walk to the Tower. Vicente, one of Lucien's soldiers and friends, had been waiting to unlock the entrance for them and with the most thoughtful cup of coffee.

It had been a wonderful night with very little sleep. Lucien's arm wound had bled a little from his exertions, but Lisa Livia respected a man who could take a little pain for his pleasure with her. Lucien sported a handlebar mustache that was the trademark of the soldiers in the Andovan Army; all twelve of them. Somehow, they pulled it off without looking like fools, but rather manly men. Dark-haired, ruggedly built, Lucien sported the wound in his arm from the recent kerfuffle at Two Rivers in South Carolina involving Lucien, Shane, and primarily Phoebe defeating usurpers to the Andovan throne. That wound was added to the scar from an old bullet wound absorbed on a peace-keeping mission in Africa years ago.

"So, M'lady," Lucien asked as he held her tight once more, "what do you think of Paris so far?"

"Not too bad," Lisa Livia understated. "How'd Vicente wrangle the early opening?"

"There are perks to being in a royal family," Lucien allowed. "The French have always been partial to my mother's side, the Embrie's, considering our lineage and affiliation with France. We exchange favors. It was not difficult."

"Beats the mob in New Jersey," Lisa Livia said. "At best, you can get a free sausage at the local butcher. But didn't the French chop the heads off their royals?"

"Some," Lucien allowed. "There was a difficult period of time. But Andova was far from that not just geographically, but in temperament. We have always been very stable because of the Great Charter.

We have never had a king to get his head chopped off. Just the Duke and Duchess, alternating every year for hundreds of years. No heads lost."

Lisa Livia was trying to downplay her happiness because a life of heartbreak and betrayal, especially by one's mother, isn't easily let go off in less than twenty-four hours of bliss with a good man in Paris who was granted favors because he was part of a royal family. She was content and happy and thus, not surprised when a voice spoke up from the shadows behind them.

"No sudden moves or you both die."

"Just fucking great," Lisa Livia muttered.

Lucien slowly removed his arms and they both turned. A man dressed in black, his face covered by a balaclava, held a very big gun, with a suppressor on the end of the barrel, aimed at them. He wore a climbing harness with a short loop of rope dangling from it and several carabiners.

"Pardon, but my contract is only for the man," the assassin said, in a French accent that to this point Lisa Livia had only associated with great sex, excellent food and love. "Please step apart, let me do my job, and I'll be on my way."

Lisa Livia hated the prospect of re-evaluating her affection for the French accent.

"Drusilla is dead," Lucien said, referring to the now defunct other side of the royalty in his home country of Andova. "There is no need for this. It's over and the Great Charter has been revoked."

"I do not know this Drusilla or what you speak of." The assassin shrugged, which did not alter the aim of the gun in the slightest. "I get paid. I do not worry about; how do you say? Why's and where-fores. I could have shot both, one round through, and saved myself time and a bullet, but I am a professional. Collateral damage is for amateurs."

"Did you just call me collateral?" Lisa Livia demanded.

"You will not get away with this," Lucien said.

"It will not matter to you, my friend, since you will be dead."

"But I won't be," Lisa Livia snapped. "I was having a special moment here and *you* ruined it." She indicated Lucien and asked: "You know who he is, but do you know who I am?"

"I know you are not the target," the assassin said. "You may leave. It would be best."

"I'm not going anywhere." Lisa Livia said. "My name is Lisa Livia Fortunato. If you got any experience at all as a button man, you've heard of the Fortunato's. I don't care if we are in France. Anybody whose anybody has heard of my family. You think you can whack my man here and we won't track you down wherever you go? You don't think my family can put a contract on you that will follow you around the world?" She was bluffing because her tie to the Fortunato syndicate other than the last name, was a father who'd betrayed it decades ago, while also abandoning her and her mother.

"Ah, American organized crime." His tone was dismissive. "Good television. Real life? Not so much to talk about." He cocked his head in momentary thought. "Ah. Fortunato's. Might have heard of them. New Jersey. But not the Sopranos. I liked them. But he did die at the end. The head of the family. Tony. Cut to black, just like what will happen now."

Great, Lisa Livia thought. *A Sopranos' fan is gonna kill me.*

The assassin shifted his aim slightly, but paused as Lisa Livia stepped in front of Lucien.

"LL, please move," Lucien whispered harshly. "This does not involve you."

"Bullshit," Lisa Livia said. "We've got a full day in Paris before we go to your home. I prefer not to spend it alone."

"Thoughtful and most practical, my dear, as always," Lucien said and Lisa Livia, once more, realized how much she loved this man.

The assassin shrugged. "Then, regrettably, it must be both of you."

"You were wrong," Lisa Livia said to him.

"Excuse?" the Assassin replied.

"Earlier. You wouldn't have saved a bullet by shooting through both of us. You're still going to use one."

"Ah. You are right, but it does not matter now, does it?"

"That's a mistake," Lisa Livia said. "I bet you've made another one."

"You talk too much," the Assassin said.

Lisa Livia hunched her shoulders, resisting Lucien's attempt to move her aside. "Who put out the contract?" she demanded.

The assassin laughed. "If I tell you, then I certainly cannot let you leave here alive. You know that, Ms. Fortunato. Nevertheless, I do not know, nor do I need to know. It is just a contract. Business. That is the beauty of our system and also why I am not worried about your threats of reprisal."

"What system?" Lisa Livia asked.

He brought the gun up and Lisa Livia was surprised at how large the black hole pointing directly between her eyes appeared. She abruptly threw the cup at the assassin. It hit him in the chest and hot coffee exploded on his body armor.

The assassin cursed in French, which despite the circumstances, still sounded somewhat sexy. And fatal.

Lisa Livia tensed, waiting for the bullet, but the assassin's gun arm dropped abruptly, then he went to his knees and keeled over, hitting the metal deck with a solid thud. *That must have hurt*, Lisa Livia thought as the man's head bounced off the deck with a sickening noise. A tall, familiar figure stood behind the body and fired once more from a suppressed pistol into the assassin's head.

"I apologize that I was not here sooner," Vicente said, sounding, indeed, very apologetic. He knelt and checked the body. "Unfortunately, I had to kill him, as I did not see another option." He didn't sound as sorry about that.

Lucien grabbed Lisa Livia and spun her about, wrapping his arms around her tightly. "Don't ever do that again!" he pled.

"Waste coffee?" Lisa Livia allowed herself the luxury of his embrace for a few seconds before objecting, speaking into his shoulder. "I had to gain us time. I knew Vicente would get here."

"You know what I mean," Lucien said.

"How about let's try not to be in that situation again," Lisa Livia suggested.

Vicente finished checking that the corpse was exactly that and looking for any sort of ID without success. He turned the head and frowned. "Curious."

"What?" Lucien asked.

"There is a very small mark behind the right ear." He ran his fingers over it. "It's a brand." He looked up. "I've seen it before."

"Where?" Lucien asked as he reluctantly let go of Lisa Livia.

"Ronaldo," Vicente said. "When I treated him at Two Rivers, I noticed it because it was not an old wound. It was a brand."

"Who is Ronaldo?" Lisa Livia asked, trying to sort through her memory of the hectic events at Agnes' home.

"The man who had the sniper rifle across the water from Two Rivers," Lucien said, which reminded Lisa Livia of their first time together, in Agnes' master bedroom. Right after Shane and Phoebe had swum across the Intracoastal to disarm the sniper who she now knew was named Ronaldo. It had been a strange, but inspiring night.

"That makes no sense," Lucien said. "Ronaldo worked for Drusilla."

"I wonder," Vicente said as he took a picture using his phone.

Lucien turned his attention to more immediate matters. "What took you so long, Vicente?"

"M'lady requested privacy before you got on the elevator." Blood was pooled around the man's head. It was the darkest blood Lisa Livia had ever seen and glistened in the early morning sun.

"Why in Heaven's name would you do that?" Lucien asked her.

"It's not quite the mile high club," Lisa Livia said, "but it would have been pretty special, you gotta admit."

"You never cease to amaze me," Lucien said.

"Let's hope so," she said. "Ignore me next time," Lisa Livia suggested to Vicente.

"I do not think I would be able to do that," Vicente said, "but I will do better in my duty."

"How did he get by you?" Lucien asked.

"I was waiting at the second level." Vicente indicated the framework of the Tower, then at the harness the dead man wore. "I suspect he climbed past me via the exterior, exclusive of the stairs and elevator."

"How did you know to come up now?" Lucien wanted to know.

"I sensed something was wrong." He was a lanky, dark-skinned man of French and Algerian parents. He sported the same mustache as Lucien, plus a beard shaded with grey. He was a soldier and trained medic, who had spent time in India studying holistic medicine. He exhibited the type of calm that soothed those around him.

"Good sense," Lisa Livia said. "Always trust your gut."

"We'll discuss this in more detail later," Lucien said to Vicente. "Are you sure he was alone?"

"I believe so, my Lord."

"We must leave and go to Andova immediately," Lucien said. "What of that?" he indicated the body.

"I will get in touch with our contact at *Direction générale de la sécurité extérieure*," Vicente said. "But first I will secure the body from sight and clean up as the Tower must open on time." He looked about at the city. "For it not to open, would be a travesty to culture and the city."

FROMM LEANED back in his chair, which was much better than the government issued one he'd had in his office in the Organization, and watched the Andovan bodyguard police up the body at the top of the Eiffel Tower. Fromm had hacked into the Tower's CCTV system and hijacked the signal to watch the assassin complete his mission and block any recording.

Fromm's computations had projected a greater probability of failure than success, so he wasn't upset. In fact, being right about the projection brought more satisfaction in some ways than Lucien's death would have. Plus, there were times when a failure brought results as worthwhile as a success. The reaction of Lucien with the woman who'd been at Two Rivers caught Fromm's interest.

He shifted his attention to another body being picked up. This one via the security camera in the elevator in the hospital at Fort Meade. That attempt had had a very slight chance of success so it had been no surprise when Phoebe, dear little Phoebe, had handled the gunman so easily. Fromm's focus, though, hadn't been on Phoebe, but rather Louise. He'd hacked into the smart TV in her hospital room and watched her, off and on, for the past twenty-four hours.

He used the mouse to bring up a clip of Louise from last month. Taken from a surveillance camera he'd had installed in her house by NSA operatives a year ago. It amused him how easy it was to get worker bees of clandestine services to do things, even illegal things, with a simple electronic order that had the right encryption and classification. They had no idea why they were doing what they did, nor who ordered it. Theirs's was not to question why. It had been a mundane task, one of dozens they did every year. The fact it was illegal meant nothing as that was the reason they were a covert unit, used to doing such thing.

This feed was from Louise's bedroom. She was disrobing in preparation to take a shower. Fromm relished the clip for a few moments, but he was drawn back to the screen showing the body in the elevator being placed on a gurney, a strange juxtaposition.

Phoebe? Fromm envisioned her as a cat. Lucky and skillful, but sooner or later the former would run out and the second would be trumped. In fact, he'd enjoyed running the projections. There was a whiteboard in the room labeled PHOEBE. On it he had the progressive odds of her surviving deadly encounters, in the order in which he had planned for her. He crossed through the first one, but the second loomed if the pieces on the board moved in the way he had projected. Which, of course, he knew they would. It no longer surprised him how easy it was to know what people would do once you gathered enough data on them. Facebook had proved that at a pervasive level in terms of marketing, but Fromm had taken it to a much higher level, where life and death were the stakes.

There were a number of whiteboards in the room. They were covered with nodes and arrows and probabilities. While he preferred the screens, the whiteboards allowed him to see the big picture of all the games he had in play at one time.

He was in the lair he'd been preparing for many years. He liked that word: lair. The primary definition of it is *a place where a wild animal, especially a fierce or dangerous one, lives.* It was a long sliver of room encased in steel reinforced concrete. Forty feet long by twelve wide. One end was slightly narrower than the other, a concession to the old plan of the facility he was hidden inside of. He knew that because the first time he'd entered it, he'd sensed the difference. He'd used a laser measuring tool to confirm his suspicions. It bothered him because he was attuned to things in his environment. He'd compensated by lining up the bank of high-speed computers to offset the deviation. But he knew it was there.

He glanced over at a terminal that was different than the others. The monitor had a teal blue fringe. The mainframe, larger than any other in the room, was the same color. It was currently in sleep mode. Next to it, numerous power couplings attached to nothing, poked out of the floor. They were awaiting the last piece. The draw of electricity would be tremendous once he installed the quantum computer he needed, but that would not be a problem given where the lair was located.

After all, he was the ghost in the machine.

And then he received the alert he had been anticipating.

CARPENTER, the head of the Organization, waited for Phoebe and Louise in front of the elevator in the bland entryway in the surface building, where hidden, automated weapons were trained on them as facial recognition technology checked to determine who they were.

"Really?" Carpenter said to Phoebe. "You killed someone in the post hospital?"

He was a tall black man in his forties, dressed in a well cut, dark suit. His bald head was scrolled with scars from old missions when he'd been in the field. Despite the wounds and various near-death experiences, he missed those days. It beat being the boss in more ways than he could have anticipated before he was unexpectedly promoted. He spoke precisely and in a calm, deep tone. No one in the Organization had ever heard him raise his voice, which he was well aware of because it was one of his personal rules.

"Discretionary latitude?" Phoebe suggested. "Doesn't that kick in when someone is trying to kill you? Besides, I found the owner of that foot I brought back from the last mission, so you can consider it a continuation. We now have the complete body. Maybe Support can identify him now? Besides, I didn't kill him. He did us that favor."

Carpenter sighed as they walked to the steel elevator doors. He held his card against the scanner, then his hand print, and leaned forward and had his retina scanned. They slid open. They boarded to descend into the bowels of the Organization. "Are you all right, Louise?"

"Yes, sir," she replied.

"I'm okay, too," Phoebe said. "My knuckle is a little sore from—"

Carpenter raised a hand and she stopped. "Why?"

Phoebe didn't need more than that. "Fromm was the one cutting away the links, not Drusilla. I should have realized that earlier. That guy worked for Fromm. I'm thinking Fromm has his fingers in a lot of stuff and they all stink. The whole Andova thing might be a subset of something bigger."

"You didn't know Fromm was a traitor earlier," Carpenter pointed out as the elevator dropped. "None of us did. And that's not good."

"It's a big oops," Phoebe agreed.

"Anything new turn up on Fromm, sir?" Louise asked.

"Not yet," Carpenter said.

The elevator doors slid open to a depressing vista that Carpenter had high on his list of things that should be changed; but he also knew that decision would have to be someone else's. He led Phoebe and Louise into the work area. Technical had a low ceiling with indirect lighting along the edges. The walls were painted drab, government contract to the lowest bidder, off white. Cubicled work areas were marked by small glowing pools where analysts stared at their screens doing analyzing things. It had once been where the crews for the Nike Hercules missiles worked, supposedly safe from a nuclear attack. Which, if it happened, meant their Nike missiles hadn't succeeded in stopping the enemy's missiles from hitting the nation's capitol.

"You could brighten this place up," Carpenter suggested to Louise.

"It's like the crypt of the undead," Phoebe contributed. "No offense," she added to Louise.

Louise was confused by Carpenter's statement. "What?"

"Now that Fromm is gone," Carpenter said, "you're in charge."

"Cool beans, babe," Phoebe said. "You deserve it."

Carpenter pointed to the raised office with glass windows at the far end of the room. "That's yours now. I recommend better lighting."

"The lighting is useful for the work we do," Louise said. "What we need are better screens. The ones we have are old. Not good for the eyes."

"That's your call," Carpenter said as he led her and Phoebe across the room.

"What about the budget, sir?" Louise, ever the practical one, asked.

Carpenter sighed, reminded of why he missed being the field, even at the risk of death. "Send the requisition to Mrs. Finch in purchasing. She handles that stuff."

"Have you ever seen Mrs. Finch smile?" Phoebe asked. "She's like this grim reaper sort. She grilled me over the motorcycle I crashed in Montana, as if I did it on purpose. The fact I almost died didn't seem to matter. She acted like she personally bought it and wanted to know why we didn't recover it. So, she could sell it for parts, I guess."

"All good accountants are like that," Carpenter said, his mind on more important matters as the three went into the office.

Phoebe sniffed. "Get some scented candles. This smells of old, soon-to-be-dead, traitor. I think he farted a lot too. He always looked constipated."

"TMI, Phoebe," Louise said.

As Louise sat down behind the desk, Carpenter turned to Phoebe. "Any idea how you're going to find Fromm?"

"The Hacker I got the information about the lawyer from is still alive," Phoebe said. "I'm willing to bet a spare foot he got the encryption program he was selling from Fromm."

"I won't take that bet," Carpenter said.

"I'll find out what he knows about Fromm," Phoebe said, "because they most likely didn't do their transaction via Fromm's Organization computer. They had to have a connection. Where did the Feds stash him?"

"Technically, we're the Feds," Carpenter reminded her. "But in this case, there were some very perturbed people in the NSA and CIA about the Hacker selling their encryption program. The latter organization spirited him away to their stateside black site, which means no one can talk to him."

"Wait," Louise said. "What do you mean 'stateside', sir? That's illegal."

"The ones overseas aren't exactly legal either," Phoebe pointed out.

"That's the problem," Carpenter said. "The one in the States is very hush-hush. No one goes there."

"Not even us, the Feds?" Phoebe said.

"The CIA says such a site doesn't exist," Carpenter said. "If they allowed anyone in, that would mean it did exist."

"So, it's a Schrodinger's prison thing?" Phoebe asked.

"It's an illegal thing, as Louise pointed out," Carpenter said, "but the Organization doesn't have the moral high ground to quibble."

"We're a step above the CIA, aren't we?" Phoebe asked.

"We're kind of sideways from them," Carpenter said. "We're allowed to act domestically."

"We're sort of the FBI and CIA smushed together," Phoebe summarizesd, "but with the same pay scale and no publicity."

"The prison is domestic," Phoebe pointed out. "And the CIA isn't."

"That's the problem with them running a black site here," Carpenter said.

"Can I get in?" Phoebe asked.

"Not unless I pull in a big favor," Carpenter said, "which I only have so many of."

"Don't worry," Phoebe said. "I'll figure out a way to get to him."

"He's in a secret super-max," Carpenter warned. "The place is automated to keep the number of people working there to a minimum. Just a handful of caretakers of the computers and machines. It's the way everything is going now."

"That's good news," Louise said. "Since it relies on computers to run things, we can work with that."

"Probably easier to get in than out of," Phoebe said.

"True," Carpenter agreed, "but you still have to get out."

"I'll leave a trail of bread crumbs," Phoebe said.

"I'll make a call," Carpenter promised, afraid Phoebe's bread crumbs, might be bodies.

"Appreciate it." Phoebe turned to Louise. "How do you like your new set up?"

"Thank you," Louise said to Carpenter. "Not just for the job, but all of this." She indicated the old-style keyboard that had been at her old work station. She put on the special glasses that worked as a mouse to compensate for her missing arm.

"One of your techs tried accessing Fromm's computer," Carpenter said, "but no luck. I'm hoping you'll do better."

"Does it call for a pass code?" Louise asked as she turned it on.

"No," Carpenter said. "The screen just stays black."

"Did you unplug and plug it back in?" Phoebe asked, which Carpenter and Louise saw fit to ignore.

Louise waved her access card, then did the palm print and retina scan.

The screen flickered and came on, blank white.

"That's a better result than we had," Carpenter said.

"I don't think so," Phoebe said. "It means Fromm knew I'd try. I'm afraid—" She stopped as the power went out, encasing the entire floor in pitch black.

"Oops," Phoebe said.

"This isn't good," Louise said.

Emergency lights came on near the exit.

"Fromm left us something," Louise said as she typed to no avail.

The screen flickered and an image appeared.

Phoebe glanced out at the work area. All the screens displayed the same.

Fromm's voice echoed out of the small speakers on the side of the display, but not on the computers outside the office. "There was an eighty-six percent chance you'd be standing there right now, Carpenter. Looking over Louise Wingo's shoulder, exactly like you are."

Louise pointed at the small dot on top of the monitor and mouthed 'Cover?' to Carpenter. Carpenter heard a small whisper from the ghost on his shoulder. The voice he thought he'd finally banished, was back. His late father's voice of guilt and recrimination. The shrink had advised him to externalize the voice, but that hadn't silenced it.

He shook his head to Louise. "How about letting us see you?" Carpenter said to Fromm. "It's only fair."

"'Fair'?" Fromm gargled something that might have been a laugh. "When has that ever been a standard for action by the Organization?" He didn't wait for answer. "You don't control this, Carpenter. Not at all, in case you haven't been paying attention. On the other hand, I see so much more than you can imagine. It's the World Wide Web, after all. Did you know that when ARPERNET first came on line in 1969 a very prescient man predicted it would be the end of secrecy? No one listened, of course. They never listen to geniuses. And, ever since, we've been in this battle to encrypt, trying to stay one step ahead of the enemy who are trying to decrypt. A fun game I've devoted most of my life to. Wherever the Internet goes, so can I. And there are few places left it hasn't spread its tentacles to. I can travel almost anywhere in the world right from here."

Carpenter noted Phoebe rolling her eyes. "Where is here?" he asked.

Fromm ignored the question. "I'm not surprised that Louise is in my office. I was certain you'd give her my position, Carpenter. And she's even the right choice. If you're playing a game of checkers, that is. But she's in way over her head. You too, Carpenter." There was a short pause. "I don't see her, but is our damaged angel of death, Phoebe, there? Did she tell you I called her after the pyrrhic victory in South Carolina? She's a good little Girl Scout, so I imagine she did. And I know for certain she's vowed to come after me with all sort of dire proclamations. Little does she know what I have in store for her. For all of you. What a sad, pathetic little group you all are."

Phoebe crossed her arms over her chest but didn't say anything to indicate she was in the office.

"Why was South Carolina pyrrhic?" Carpenter asked.

Out of sight of the camera, Louise's hand was typing, working. Carpenter knew she was trying to track Fromm down. He also knew, as she probably did too, that it was a fruitless task.

"Because the war isn't over," Fromm said. "Come on, Carpenter. You know history. And you're not a stupid man. Not a genius, but not stupid. I still wonder, though, why you were promoted to be in charge. Especially, since I was so much more capable."

"Perhaps because you're a traitor," Carpenter said.

"Traitor to who?" Fromm said. "To what? A corrupt country?"

"Your oath," Carpenter said. "Your word."

"You're a fool. This is just beginning."

"You've already failed," Carpenter said. "The Great Charter was dissolved. Andova has an elected government and is stable."

"Was it? Is it?" Fromm asked, but Carpenter knew he wasn't really asking.

"What do you want?" Carpenter demanded.

"What do I want?" Fromm mused. "Funny how no one asked me that when I sat in that office. No one cared what I wanted then."

Phoebe couldn't help herself. "Whiner."

"Ah, we finally hear from the cheap seats," Fromm said. His sigh was clearly audible from the speakers. "Phoebe, Phoebe, Phoebe."

"You're repeating yourself," Phoebe said. "Sounds like your brain is broken."

"I'm multitasking," Fromm said. "Surely you don't think this is the only game I'm involved in. Life would be unbearably boring if that were so. Ever watch a Grandmaster playing multiple boards at the same time? Defeating so many aspiring masters? And the Grandmaster always wins, remember that. But for you, Phoebe, I have something special lined up for you. You've only just begun to walk the course I've laid out especially for you."

Phoebe rolled her eyes once more. "You got a repetition thing going." She walked around and stood behind Louise's other shoulder. "Really, Fromm. Why are you hiding? Your bald spot getting bigger? What are you afraid of? You one of those guys who tapes over his computer camera while he jerks off?"

The skull and swords disappeared, but only on this computer, and was replaced by black, then Fromm appeared. He was facing the camera, his head and shoulders visible. Behind him was a dull grey wall. "Happy?" He was a late middle-aged man with pale skin and a receding hairline. Unremarkable at best. His eyes were noticeable though, with a slight sheen of crazy covering the dead soul behind them.

"My heart has skipped a beat," Phoebe said, dripping sarcasm. "Where are you? Save me some time tracking you down."

Fromm scoffed. "I said you had no idea of the depth of what you've waded into. You'll learn, bit by bit, but always at least one step behind. Usually more than one. Always too late. That is, of course, dependent on how long you survive. My data suggests an exponential possibility of failure based on encounters. With failure equating to your death."

"What is the mean of the exponential?" Louise asked.

Phoebe had no idea what the question meant.

"Three point seven," Fromm said. "Which is impressive but indicates that ultimately our dear, dear Phoebe, will die."

"Blah, blah, blah," Phoebe said. "You really like the sound of your own voice, don't you?"

"Now who is repeating themselves?" Fromm asked. "Andova is anything but stable, Carpenter. The Duke and Duchess proclaiming it so during their little ceremony in South Carolina isn't holding much weight back home. And killing the Duchess Navarro? Some people are not happy about that at all. And not just in Andova."

"She killed herself," Phoebe said, "by frolicking in the mud with an alligator."

"That's your version," Fromm said. "I'm playing a different version in Andova that has more traction. Remember, '*who controls the past, controls the future. Who controls the present controls the past*'."

"You're no George Orwell," Carpenter said.

"I'm better," Fromm said. "Orwell was just a scribbler of words. And that wasn't even his real name. Just as Fromm isn't the name I was born with."

Carpenter felt an uneasy stirring. "You were thoroughly vetted." But the voice on Carpenter's shoulder was already whispering.

Fromm laughed. "Who do you think gets *that* job? Vetting for security clearances? Not the best and the brightest, I assure you. The ones no one wants on their team doing real world ops. The people crossing off days on their calendar, waiting for that magic date when they can get their federal pension and retire, to mark off days on their calendar doing nothing until they die. Besides, my vetting was decades ago, Carpenter. Do you know how easy it was back then to invent an identity and backstop it with enough validity that it would pass a security check by the rubes doing it?"

"Who are you, then?" Carpenter asked, regretting the question as soon as he said it.

"I am the end of you," Fromm said. "All of you. I control the internet and thus control the present. I can reshape the past in whatever way I desire. I can influence events to achieve the future I desire. Do you not think it odd that people have access to more information than ever before but know less? They only seek out that which supports what they already think. The key is to find those people and amplify and then adjust the message, whether it is true or not."

Phoebe leaned forward, putting her fists on Louise's desk. "Thanks for the TED talk, Fromm. Why don't you just tell me where you are so we can end this? Keep running and you're just going to die tired."

"I'm not running," Fromm said. "Not at all. I'm very comfortable actually. You're the one who will get tired of chasing ghosts."

"I have a lot of energy," Phoebe said.

"It won't help you," Fromm said. "You're going to be the one running, Phoebe. But eventually, you'll get caught."

"Who is going to be chasing me?" Phoebe asked.

"It's already started," Fromm said.

"And you're losing," Phoebe said.

"Exponential," Fromm repeated.

"So far we seem to be winning," Phoebe said. "We stopped you in South Carolina and just now. Your one-footed man failed. Really, is that the best you can do?"

"Doesn't matter. It was a win either way. You did my work for me. One less loose end to concern myself with. I'd have been happier, though, if he'd removed you from the board, but alas, there was an eighty-two percent possibility he would not succeed, so I wasn't surprised. But, remember. Exponential. Sooner or later, you will lose, Phoebe."

"Why'd he kill himself?" Louise asked. "What did you threaten him with?"

"He had a code," Fromm said.

Louise spoke up. "Sort of a 'On my shield or with it' code?"

"Something like that," Fromm said.

Phoebe was skeptical. "You trusted a code? When you violated your own oath?"

"Not really," Fromm admitted. "He was already a walking dead man."

"What do you mean?" Carpenter asked.

Fromm gave a sly smile. "You see, Carpenter? So much you don't know."

"You're babbling, Fromm," Carpenter said.

"I was being nice," Fromm said. "Humoring you. But I can see that's wasted. You want to know what I want, Carpenter? Chaos. Because only out of chaos can order begin anew."

"You're crazy," Carpenter said.

"They say that about all geniuses," Fromm said. "Those who can't understand what they can't comprehend." There was a noise in his background. A voice. He glanced over his shoulder. "Patience, my dear. I'll be done with these pests shortly."

Carpenter exchanged a glance with Phoebe, then Louise, wondering who Fromm was speaking too. According to his file, Fromm was single without any social life.

"Talking to a mirror, Fromm?" Phoebe asked.

"Why do you think you're humorous, Phoebe?" Fromm asked. "You use humor to cover up your pain. Could it be because you have no clue who your mother is?"

Carpenter jumped in. "You're not even making sense, Fromm. What the hell do you want?"

Before Fromm could answer, a woman entered the frame, behind Fromm's right shoulder, out of focus. In side silhouette was a thin short-haired, tall blond dressed in black turtleneck and black slacks.

"Stop wasting time with these people." Her voice was reminiscent of Katherine Hepburn at the height of her haughty.

Phoebe couldn't hold back. "What online bride order site did you get her off of, Fromm? We know your charm had nothing to do with it, since you don't have any."

Fromm nodded his head. "Lilith, meet Carpenter, Louise and Phoebe. I spent many years of my life working amidst their ignorance."

"What a waste of brilliance," Lilith said, turning to face the camera and shaking her head.

"I'll be with you in a minute, dear," Fromm said.

Carpenter looked at Louise and then Phoebe as they clearly saw the woman's face for the first time. She was Louise's twin in facial structure and body, but had both arms intact. Her hair was much shorter but the same color. The eyes were also a match.

"What the fuck?" Phoebe exclaimed.

"You like?" Fromm said. "You would, wouldn't you, Phoebe? Given how you feel about Louise." He turned in the seat. "Give us some space, dear."

Lilith frowned and moved out of sight.

"I had decades to prepare," Fromm said. "You've had hours. By now, those outside of the Organization are aware that your system is infected. Which they were figuring out anyway. I'm always far ahead and your counter-moves play right into my hands." The skull and swords disappeared and a CCTV image from the camera on the front of the building displayed a number of black SUVs pulling up and armed guards establishing a perimeter.

"I predict you'll get a call in a few minutes, Carpenter," Fromm promised. "From that woman, Hannah, whom you know nothing about, who heads a unit you know even less about. She runs the Cellar which is even more secret than the Organization. She will not be happy. Because all you see right now is the smoke. But the fire? It's burns hot and deep. Think long and hard before your next move. And remember, it doesn't matter, it will always be the wrong one." He smiled. "Welcome to the game, Phoebe. And remember this. I want you to see your end coming. No easy out for you. I want you to experience that exquisite pain of knowing you failed and I won before it all goes black. In that last lingering moment before final oblivion, think of me."

The screen went blank and silence reigned for a few seconds.

"What an asshole," Phoebe said. "Can't believe you had to work for him," she said to Louise.

None of them spoke about Lilith, each trying to process what they had seen.

Carpenter's secure phone rang and the ghost on his shoulder cackled.

"Excuse me," Carpenter said, nodding toward the door.

Phoebe and Louise exited, shutting the door.

He took the call standing up. "Carpenter."

Unlike the last time, there was no wait as a woman's voice spoke: "I'd have you come see me, but the NSA has locked down your facility."

"The infection left a Trojan Horse in our system," Carpenter told Hannah, the head of the Cellar.

"Oh, Mister Carpenter, it's worse than that. Much worse. Your infection, and let's call him by name, Fromm, if that is his real name, did considerably more. He took Orion, our latest cipher, with him and has put it on the open market. The deep, black market, that is. Final bids are due in four days, with the program going to the winner. The baseline is two hundred million dollars and it's already been met on the dark net."

"I'll be—"

Hannah cut him off. "The NSA has shut down the Organization indefinitely until it's determined whether Fromm acted alone. We don't know who we can trust. Fromm's infected your computer system so the NSA has isolated you since they control those lines. They're checking now to see if the virus infested their systems. If it has . . . . " She left the remainder unsaid

Carpenter had nothing to say to that.

"Fromm is only part of this," Hannah said. "Your predecessor,

Wilson, was corrupt. Who knows how far the cancer has spread in the Organization." It was not a question; more a threat. "I'll keep this line open for you, Carpenter. I'm sure you'll have questions that need answers. I have resources that are, shall we say, unique."

Carpenter pondered the implications. Asking Hannah about things was also potentially targeting the subject of those questions.

"Do you understand?" Hannah asked.

"Yes."

"The entire Organization is on the line," Hannah said. "Similar corrupt entities in the past have been eradicated."

Carpenter envisioned a great white shark swallowing everyone in this place.

"I'm going to give you a chance to make this right," Hannah said. "You have until the end of the auction. If you fail to stop it, secure Orion, and terminate Fromm, I will be forced to take action."

Carpenter didn't say anything.

Hannah continued. "You need to get your operative on Fromm's trail. It's Phoebe, right?"

"Yes."

"She'll need help. Bring her in and put us on speaker."

Carpenter looked out the glass and pointed at Phoebe. She and Louise were in an intense discussion, no doubt over the confusing issue of Lilith. He crooked his finger and she came in. He pointed at the phone. "Hannah wants to speak with us."

Phoebe mouthed '*Hannah*' with a questioning look.

In response, Carpenter mouthed '*Cellar*'. Then he announced. "Phoebe's here."

Hannah spoke: "As your boss will tell you, the Organization is locked down by the NSA. I'm sure you are ingenious enough to slip out. When you do, there's someone you should go to who might be of help."

"'Might'?" Phoebe said.

"She's peculiar," Hannah said.

Phoebe raised an eyebrow at Carpenter. "Meaning?"

"She's a former operative," Hannah said. "She has considerable experience and contacts. She could be of great assistance."

"You keep qualifying it," Phoebe pointed out.

"She's eccentric," Hannah said.

"Peculiar and eccentric," Phoebe noted. "Sounds like my kind of gal." She winked at Carpenter who wondered if Phoebe understood the danger of the Cellar.

Hannah must have felt the same because her sigh was audible. "Young woman, tread lightly in the darkness."

"Yes, ma'am," Phoebe said. "How do I find this person?"

"Go to *The Dog's Balls*," Hannah said.

"Excuse me?" Phoebe said.

"It's a bar. You'll find it," Hannah assured her.

"Who do I ask for?" Phoebe said.

"Just go there. She'll find you."

"Right," Phoebe said.

"Carpenter," Hannah said. "I'll contact you when we learn more." The line went dead.

"She's kind of touchy," Phoebe said.

"She runs the Cellar," Carpenter said. "Her operatives are judge, jury and executioner for anyone she targets. Her mandate is to police the ranks of covert operations. That means us."

"Sort of like discretionary latitude," Phoebe said. "Except on a bigger scale, right?"

Carpenter shook his head and waved Louise into the office. He updated her on what Hannah had said. When he was done, Phoebe asked: "I guess that means you can't make a call to get me in to see the Hacker at the super-max?"

"Did you hear what Hannah said?" Carpenter said, putting an edge in his voice. "I doubt I can get you out of here."

Phoebe exchanged a look with Louise, then addressed Carpenter. "I can get out."

Carpenter stared at her, then nodded, accepting that Hannah knew more about his own unit than he did. "All right."

"How the heck is he going to get paid two hundred million?" Phoebe asked. "In small bills in a briefcase?"

"It will likely go much higher than that," Carpenter said.

"Andova," Louise interjected.

That clicked with Carpenter. "If he had a favorable regime there, he could process a lot of money through their banks."

"But he doesn't," Phoebe pointed out.

"At the moment," Louise said. "It's obvious he worked with Drusilla and Guillermo to wipe out the Embries and put them in charge. And now he's working with people in Andova to push the Embrie family out. Fromm liked to boast, but there was always something of substance behind what he said. If he says control of Andova is uncertain, then it is. This is why he was involved from the start."

"It was a distraction," Carpenter said.

Both women turned to him, wondering what he was talking about.

"The woman," Carpenter said. "The one with Fromm. An actress most likely. He found someone who looked like you," he said to Louise, "and had her show her face to confuse us."

Surprisingly, Louise laughed. "It wasn't real."

It was Carpenter's turn to be confused. "What?"

"The woman," Louise said. "It was a hologram. Projected. Something Fromm conjured. The way it moved. Like a videogame. Almost perfectly human in image but not quite. He was always a bit weak in that area of programming."

"Asshole," Phoebe said.

"Let's forget about the distraction," Carpenter said. "Keep our eye on the main issue. Finding Fromm and getting the encryption program off the market."

Both women nodded in agreement.

"You're going to need help," Carpenter said. "Besides this contact from Hannah."

"I want Sam the Cleaner," Phoebe said, referring to the man she'd worked with in Montana.

"You have my authorization to get Sam."

Louise spoke up. "I'll use a secure, private link separate from the Organization's system to stay in contact with Phoebe until I can cleanse Fromm's infection."

"Why did you make a separate line?" Carpenter asked Louise. "Doesn't that violate security?"

Louise couldn't meet his gaze. "Just a contingency, sir."

Phoebe jumped in to the defense. "It's not a security risk if no one knows about it and it's never been used."

"Did you know about it?" Carpenter asked her.

"Not until recently," Phoebe said, "which is why I'm certain no one other than Louise knew."

"Which means it's secure from Fromm," Louise added.

"And this way you have out of here?" Carpenter pressed Phoebe.

"We found that together," Phoebe admitted. "I had Louise dig up the old blueprints for this place. They were in the National Archives in DC. You know what year thing was built?"

"Nineteen-fifty-three," Carpenter said. "When the first Nike Ajax missile battery was emplaced here to defend the capitol. It was abandoned and then repurposed for the Organization."

Phoebe blinked, recognizing she'd asked the wrong man a historical question. "Right. Okay. Well, Lou found the original blueprints and we saw a small line on the paper and it turned out to be a service tunnel that was sealed off."

"You unsealed it?" Carpenter asked and something in his tone must have alerted Phoebe because she became defensive and proper.

"Not yet, sir. We just know where it is and that it's accessible and exits on the surface a distance away. I'm sure I can get through. The people guarding us are NSA. I mean how many of those dudes ever did a real on-the-ground op? You call them to fix your laptop, but not stop an operator."

"Don't kill any of them," Carpenter ordered.

"I won't, sir," Phoebe promised.

"Or maim," Carpenter added.

Phoebe appeared disappointed.

The voice on Carpenter's shoulder was whispering doubts. Could he trust Phoebe and Louise? As significant a take was whether he could trust Phoebe *or* Louise. They might or might not be working in concert. To what end if they were?

Carpenter folded his arms. "Why did you do this?" he asked both of them.

Phoebe and Louise exchanged another look, with Phoebe nodding toward Louise, whose turn it was to get nervous. "I didn't trust Fromm, sir."

"Why?" Carpenter asked.

Phoebe answered, *the other half of frick and frack*, the voice on Carpenter's shoulder whispered.

"He stunk," Phoebe said. "Besides literally. There was something off about him. You must have noticed."

Carpenter had and he suspected that was the reason his father's voice was back. He'd never felt right about Fromm, but when he was unexpectedly elevated to take over the Organization less than a year ago, he didn't feel he had the experience or the solid footing to relieve a department head whom he'd leapfrogged.

The ghost on his shoulder was cackling at what that had resulted in.

"So, there's really a Cellar?" Phoebe mused. "I've heard rumors."

"There's really a Cellar and you just talked to the head of it," Carpenter confirmed.

"Hannah?" Phoebe said. "That's what she's called? Just Hannah?"

"Yes."

"She'd probably be pretty cool to meet," Phoebe said.

Carpenter stopped that one in its tracks. "She isn't. The Cellar's mandate is to take out rogue operatives. That's Fromm. But I'm afraid that might expand to the entire Organization if we don't show that we can handle our own mess."

"So, this contact she gave might be a setup," Phoebe said.

Carpenter nodded. "It's a possibility. Go in with your eyes open."

"I always try to," Phoebe said. "Even if I'm treading carefully in the dark."

"It would be advantageous if you got to Fromm before the Cellar does," Carpenter said.

"If I hook up with this contact of Hannah," Phoebe observed, "I'll be getting to Fromm at the same time as the Cellar."

"She didn't say the contact was a former Cellar operative," Carpenter pointed out. "Just an operative."

"You're thinking Hannah has her own people after Fromm?" Phoebe asked.

"It's likely," Carpenter said.

"Then why does she care about what I do?" Phoebe wondered.

Carpenter had no answer to that.

"This is a big mess," Louise said. "If an enemy gets their hand on Orion, all our secure networks will be breached."

"Won't they just go to the next cipher, whatever it is?" Phoebe asked.

"If the NSA has one, they certainly will," Louise agreed. "But it means all our old traffic can be deciphered. Everyone is constantly tapping into comms and recording each other. Lots of covers and operations will be exposed. It would be a crippling blow to the intelligence community and the country. We can't go back and change what's already been sent."

"And the clock is ticking," Carpenter said. "How long will it take to cleanse our computer system and get us back on-line?"

Louise shook her head. "I need to dive into it and get an idea of what Fromm did before I can give an estimate."

Carpenter's secure phone buzzed and he glanced down. Lisa Livia. He'd gotten rid of the burner they talked on after the first wedding at Two Rivers when they'd met last year. He'd given her his official number with strict instructions that it was only to be used in emergency.

Phoebe and Louise were staring at him, waiting.

Reluctantly, knowing it would not be good news, Carpenter picked it up.

"Lisa Livia, what's going on?"

She led with the headline. "Someone just tried to kill Lucien. On the Eiffel Tower. Ruined a perfectly wonderful morning." She went on to tell him what had occurred.

"Are you safe?" Carpenter asked when she was done.

"Yeah. We're in the car on the way to the airport. We're flying to Andova."

"Have Lucien's people send us what they have on the assassin," Carpenter said. He gestured to Louise. *Secure email?* He mouthed.

Louise wrote on a pad and showed him. "Have them use this address," he said to Lisa Livia.

"I'm all right, by the way," Lisa Livia said.

"I assumed that," Carpenter said, wincing as he said it.

"That was always the problem," Lisa Livia's voice held that red tinge of anger which he knew better than to reply to. "You assuming. You assumed your way right away from me."

"Lisa Livia," Carpenter said, but that was the extent of his reply because what else was there to say?

"Yeah, yeah," Lisa Livia. "I know. You have something going on. Just letting you know what's happening in my life. Assassins on the Eiffel Tower and all that. Since it seems I'm still connected to your problems somehow." The phone went dead.

Carpenter informed Phoebe and Louise of the attempted assassination. Concluding with: "Fromm is behind it. He said the situation in Andova wasn't settled. But that's not our priority right now. We've got to get Fromm." He looked at Phoebe. "You best move out. Louise? Give her everything we have on the CIA supermax in West Virginia."

WORDS OF WISDOM #2

Shane's Words of Wisdom #2
There are two types of soldier: The steely-eyed killer and the beady-eyed minion.
Shane's Addendum: Never trust first appearances.
At first glance, these two are hard to tell apart.
The first is the person you want backing you up in a tough spot.
The other will get you killed or, worse, accidently shoot you in the back while panicking.
It is only in moments of crisis that the differences between the two can easily be discerned.

Phoebe's Observations #2

There are two types of soldier: The one you trust with your back when you're the first one through the breached door.
Then there are all the rest.
Phoebe's Addendum: Almost everyone is the second type.

2

"Brilliant, my darling," Lilith said.

Fromm acknowledged the praise with a nod as he turned from one of several large, high-definition monitors in the room. "It's not hard against these buffoons."

"Nevertheless, darling, you have them eating out of the palm of your hand." Lilith was the most beautiful woman Fromm had invented. So far. She was a work in progress, but progress was good. Tall, not overly though that she towered over Fromm. She had some inches on him and occasionally that adjusted downward when he was feeling, well, down. Of course, being Fromm, he didn't consciously connect the two. He'd done it instinctively enough times that the self-learning program had begun doing it automatically upon various facial and body posture cues from him.

Her blond hair shimmered with an inner light; a particular piece of code Fromm was proud of. The eyes changed shade depending on Fromm's mood. As did the size of her breasts. He was aware of these changes; after all, he'd programmed them, but he didn't delve too deeply on what they reflected about him and his moods. He was not a fan of Freud.

The large mainframe that had been asleep was pulsing with power, projecting Lilith. The pink light bar glowed brighter when she spoke. Fromm leaned back in his seat and looked past, and through, Lilith, at a bank of security video displays as a chime echoed in the room. "I hate dealing with this pompous ass," Fromm complained as he scooted his rolling chair over to a different terminal, detouring around Lilith even though she was a hologram.

"Everyone serves a purpose, darling," Lilith reminded him.

He tapped a key and the round face of the Bishop of Andova appeared. "Yes?" Fromm snapped.

"Someone tried to kill Lucien in Paris," the Bishop said.

"'Tried'?" Fromm said.

"They weren't successful," the Bishop said. "I am on record as being against more violence."

Fromm glanced down at an iPad, reading code. "It was an act of desperation. I told you not to do it."

Fromm smiled to himself as he looked up and saw a frown on Lilith's face. She always knew when he was lying. He hadn't programmed that in. Not directly. It was part of the autonomous programming that was learning as it went.

The Bishop wasn't smiling. "You *pushed* doing it! You gave Fausto the contact information for the assassin! Arranged the deal. I had nothing to do with it."

"Did I? And you didn't?" Fromm said, trying out what he supposed was a thoughtful visage; utterly failing at it. "I don't recall." Fausto was the son of the late Drusilla and Guillermo. Fromm had shifted his focus to him as the next best option to keep Andova available as a place to launder money. A lot of money.

"What do I do now?" the Bishop said.

Fromm looked at Lilith. She silently spoke the word, which appeared briefly in front of her mouth in pink letters: SISTER

The letters slowly faded as Fromm replied. "What does the Duchess' younger sister, Mattea, suggest?"

"She says, and I agree with, that we follow the letter of the law."

"It was too late for that when Drusilla formed her little army." Fromm was bored and went back to checking the lines of code. "And what is the letter of the law?"

"The marriage of Duke Navarro and Duchess Embrie is not legitimate in the eyes of the Church," the Bishop said. "There is no doubt of that since it was a civil ceremony and I did not preside. It is sacramentally invalid. They would have needed my sanction. Which I did not give."

The Bishop always repeated the obvious, which irked Fromm. He looked at Lilith. TRUE

"Quite true," Fromm encouraged the Bishop.

"Thus, it does not meet the letter of the law according to the Great Charter. Thus, they cannot invalidate the Great Charter."

"Sounds circular, but I like it," Fromm said. He reached down and tapped the screen, highlighting a line of code that needed attention.

"The bottom line is that they did not have my permission to marry, nor that of any representative of the Catholic Church. The High Court will agree once I get the case before it."

"How long will that take?"

"Several weeks."

"Not good enough." Fromm was tired of repetition, which he found insulting as it implied he hadn't understood initially. He always understood the first time.

The Bishop continued. "The problem is Fausto. He has sworn blood vengeance against the Embrie's for the death of his mother and father, beginning with Lucien and then the Duchess. It was he who contracted the assassin. He has little patience with the technicalities of law or dogma.

Fromm lifted the iPad closer, intrigued by a line of code. "Yes. The young can be impetuous."

"What should I do?" the Bishop asked.

"Your best," Fromm said as he typed in an adjustment to the program. "Where does Fausto stand with the banking syndicate? Whom do they prefer?" Questions he already knew the answers to.

"They prefer stability," the Bishop said. "But Fausto would be welcome because the elected government is attempting to pass a number of regulations that would—" the Bishop cleared his throat— "cause some crimps in their operations."

Fromm muted the call, looked at Lilith and winked. "What do you think?"

A confused look flickered across her face. "I think. I think. I think." Her mouth remained open, but there was no noise. Then the skull and swords symbol appeared where the words had. It began spinning, Fromm's own version of Apple's ball of death.

"Damn it!" Fromm exclaimed. He tapped the keyboard. "Figure it out, Bishop. I've already put enough effort in. Pick up your end. Talk to Fausto. Kill everyone for all I care. But I'm going to need to work with the bankers in four days. The clock is ticking." He hung up on the cleric, then accessed Lilith's control program, cursing all the while. "Not enough power! Not enough!"

He turned her off and she snapped out of existence. The pink light on top of the teal-colored mainframe slowly faded away.

Then he hit speed dial.

A voice answered in Spanish: "Hola?"

"Fausto, it's Fromm."

Fausto switched to angry English. "The man in Paris failed. I will kill Lucien myself. It is the honorable way. And I want the woman too. The one who killed my father and mother. And then I will kill his parents and then—"

Fromm cut in on the list of targets. "I predicted it was most likely to fail."

"You told me not to do it myself." Fausto was confused. "You sent me the contact information. You—"

"Yes, yes," Fromm replied. "It was just the first move. That move is often a feint to cause one's enemies to make a mistake further down the line." He tapped a command in the keyboard and Lilith flickered back into existence.

"Fancy words to explain away failure," Fausto said. "But what is the master plan if that was just the first move?"

"As you've noted, the battle is now in Andova. You have a groundswell of support and must maintain it overtly while covertly working against your enemies."

"You have a fine way of speaking," Fausto said. "Very fine, but you say little of substance. Since my mother was killed and the Embrie's have illegally seized power, her accounts have been frozen and tied up in the courts. My funds transfer to the Guild has been stopped. The Guild is not pleased and demands final payment. Even though their man failed. You have put me in a precarious position."

Fromm always marveled how people made decisions and then blamed others for whatever predicament they ended up in.

"It's only precarious if you look at it that way," Fromm said. He smiled at Lilith, pleased with his own nonsense. Non-logicals were so easy to mess with. She smiled back and for a moment he wondered if it was because he was so witty or an automatic response to his smile. He'd have to check the programming, but he immediately forgot about that as Fausto asked:

"Why did you call me?"

"The Bishop is having cold feet. He's talking to your aunt, Mattea, about pursuing the legal avenue of approach. There's not enough time for that. I need access to the banks in four days."

"For what?"

"The secret to using Andovan banks," Fromm said, "is that the transactions remain secret. I've supported your family's cause and will continue to do so, but I require you to fulfill your end of the bargain."

"That is difficult to do without money."

"Use that statue you stole. The jewels must be worth a considerable amount."

"Those jewels are priceless because they are set in the halo of the statue," Fausto replied. "They are unique and if I remove them, I will not be able to sell them. Every jeweler in Europe is on the lookout for them. And, if the people find out I did that to the statue, I will never be able to take my rightful place as Duke."

Fromm didn't think Fausto quite grasped what his rightful place was as a bastard, but that wasn't his problem. "How about this: Will the Embrie's pay to get the statue back?"

"Of course, but then I lose my leverage on them."

"There's a way you can get paid *and* keep leverage."

"Tell me."

"There is a woman with Lucien. Her name is Lisa Livia Fortunato."

"And?" Fausto snapped.

"She's an American and was there when your parents were killed. She laughed with Lucien over their corpses. She was with Lucien on the Eiffel this morning when your assassin failed. In fact, she put herself between Lucien and the shooter."

"Is she like the woman who killed my parents? A spy?"

"It's possible. But focus on the key part. She's with Lucien. He cares about her. She stood next to the Duchess as her maid of honor during the wedding."

"The illegal wedding!" Fausto snapped.

"Whatever," Fromm said. "The important thing is that the Embrie's have taken her into their bosom. You can use her."

"How?"

"Connect her with the statue," Fromm said. "The combination will cause the Embrie's to react emotionally. That will be to your advantage."

"How do I do that?"

Fromm bit back a harsh reply. He was tired of spelling things out for others.

"Figure it out."

Fromm cut the connection.

Phoebe removed the grill covering the vent and shone a light upward. The shaft was two feet square and she couldn't see the top, but given how deep they were, and where the exit was, she had a good idea how far she had to go. She made sure her wakizashi was secured tight across her back.

"Did you notice it?" Louise asked.

Phoebe looked into Louise's eyes. "That she looked exactly like you except for the hair?"

Louise frowned. "What? No. You think she looked just like me? She was beautiful."

"You're beautiful," Phoebe said.

Louise blushed. "No. I meant that she was flickering. The program he's using isn't consistent. And the code is lacking. Probably a combination of that and the fact the mainframe he's using isn't powerful enough. For an autonomous avatar he'd need a top-of-the-line quantum computer. Do you know how much power one of those draws? And how much they cost?"

"Two hundred million?" Phoebe asked.

"At least that much," Louise said.

"He's a sick dude," Phoebe commented. "Making it look like you."

"He made her better than me," Louise said, holding up her deformed arm. "She's his idea of perfection. He always looked at me like I was less than."

"Not as I recall," Phoebe said. "He wanted you pretty badly for a while."

Louise blushed.

"You're more than he could ever dream of," Phoebe said. "You've had to overcome more than him. Not just your arm but being a woman in this fucked up business." She put a hand on Louise's shoulder and gripped tight. "We were broken a long time ago, Louise. By birth and by life after. But we're here. Now. All right? We don't let some scum like Fromm hurt us. We take him out. All right?"

Louise nodded.

"Say it," Phoebe insisted.

"We take him out," Louise said.

"Good." Phoebe frowned. "What did it mean when you asked him the mean of the exponential?"

"Fromm has projected out the possibilities of you surviving various encounters. His projection, based on what he knows, is three-point-seven."

"And? That means?"

Louise was reluctant to answer.

"And?" Phoebe pressed.

"He believes it is most likely you will lose between the third and fourth encounter. On average."

"I don't do averages," Phoebe said.

"No, you don't. Nor are you average. Also, the important thing to remember is that, for you, each encounter is a unique experience. The odds are the same. There is a flaw to Fromm's calculations in the real world."

"Good." Phoebe let go and slid into the emergency shaft. She looked back.

"Stay safe," Louise said to Phoebe.

"I will," Phoebe replied. "You too." Then she climbed.

"Welcome to *D'Aigle*."

"'*D'Aigle*'?" Lisa Livia repeated.

"In English you would say The Eyrie," Lucien said.

"I thought you lived in a castle," Lisa Livia said to Lucien as he drove the Mercedes EQ SUV up to a building sprawled at the foot of a large snow-covered mountain, part of a larger chain that extended as far as one could see in either direction.

The chateau was a quarter mile wide, a combination of white

stone and wood with red tile roofs. There were several portals in the outer wall along with numerous towers. There were many chimneys and Lisa Livia suspected it took a lot of fires in the winter to keep that place warm, given there was still snow on the upper slopes of the mountains. It was like a scene from a fairy tale or at the very least, a high budget Hallmark movie, Lisa Livia thought.

They'd flown from Paris to Andova on one of the family's smaller private jets. Members of the Andovan army, whom Lisa Livia recognized from the wedding at Two Rivers, had been waiting at the airport with several SUVs, handing the key to one to Lucien and then following in the others.

"Castles are for those who fight wars," Lucien said, as he drove through an opening in the building to a spacious courtyard. "We've never had one."

"Until now," Lisa Livia observed as she opened the door and got out before Lucien could turn off the vehicle and rush around to do it for her. Some habits die hard and new ones are learned slow. She'd spent the drive from the airport checking out the beautiful countryside and her phone.

Lucien looked disappointed. Whether it was about the war comment or getting beat to the door, it was difficult to tell. The air was sharp and chill, spring having a hard time getting a foothold at this altitude in the Pyrenees. The chateau was a style Lisa Livia was certain was classic but she'd never seen before in person. Of course, she realized, there was probably only one of these in the world. "When was this built?"

Lucien looked around, as if seeing it anew. "The original structure is over a thousand years old." He pointed. "It's over there, but as you can see, it's expanded greatly since then. Successive generations have added on."

"What's the heating bill?" Lisa Livia, ever the practical one, asked.

"We went with geothermal eight years ago," Lucien said. He indicated the electric SUV. "The Embrie family has been carbon neutral for a while. If things continue as they are, all of Andova will be the same in two years."

Handsome, a great lover, and friendly to the environment, Lisa Livia thought. If it wasn't for the recent showdown at Two Rivers and an assassination attempt on the Eiffel Tower, Lisa Livia might consider Lucien a keeper, but right now she'd take the moment. Which he abruptly tossed some cold water on.

"My parents are waiting." Lucien indicated a pair of wooden doors, twenty feet high and six across.

Lisa Livia pulled her light coat tighter as they walked across the courtyard. The other two SUVs had parked and the occupants dispersed to guard positions.

"Most of the building is administrative offices for the government of Andova," Lucien said, a smidge defensively. "The family residence only takes up this wing."

"Sure," Lisa Livia said. "Just one wing. Got it. And a house on a street next to the Eiffel Tower."

"Then I won't tell you about our place in London."

"Right," Lisa Livia said. "Where else?"

"Some other time." Before they reached the large doors, Lucien paused and spread his arms. The doors swung open without a noise. There was no one standing by and she couldn't see how they'd opened.

"Magic?" Lisa Livia said.

"I wish," Lucien said. "Modern technology."

"But it is an enchanting place," Lisa Livia said.

"More so, now that you are here to grace it."

"Speaking of grace," Lisa Livia muttered as she saw the slender, perhaps matchstick, figure of Lucien's mother, the Duchess of Embrie, silhouetted inside the hall beyond the doors. Hovering in the shadows was one of the Andovan soldiers dressed in a suit, a thin white wire running to his earpiece.

Any other woman of such a slight frame, would be dwarfed in the massive front entryway of this wing of *D'Aigle*, but the Duchess had such a presence, that she commanded the open space. The walls were festooned with tapestries and the heads of animals. Lisa Livia half-expected to see one of a dragon. There were several coats of armor scattered about along with old weapons across the ages which might be anachronistic in other places, but given the recent battle at Two Rivers were very pertinent to the present. Lisa Livia figured Phoebe would view this as an excellent place to loiter and play with the swords and spears and halberds.

"My dear," the Duchess said, extending a bejeweled hand, "my sincerest apologies about the incident in Paris."

The Duchess sounded like she meant it, but the word 'incident' made it seem to Lisa Livia like her laundry had been lost or something equivalent. "Vicente saved us," she responded, figuring it was smart to stay in the good side of the guy who had rescued them and was also a doctor. She belatedly remembered her etiquette. "My Grace."

Her Grace gifted Lisa Livia a smile, which on other women would be turning a frown into a straight line. "You were my Maid of Honor. You may call me Duchess."

Lisa Livia didn't see how that was a good deal. One word instead of two, but the same number of syllables. "Sure. Duchess."

The Ice Queen softened as she turned to Lucien, although her words weren't exactly motherly. "We will find out and punish whomever sent the assassin. I promise."

"Lisa Livia saved me," Lucien said, perhaps following her lead regarding Vicente. "She put herself between the assassin and I."

Lisa Livia wanted to smack him, because she knew that wouldn't please the Duchess as Lucien clearly intended. A look flashed across the Duchess' face and was gone so quickly it might not have happened, but Lisa Livia, who'd grown up with a mother whose moods she'd had to intimately follow for childhood survival like a ship's captain tracking a nearby storm, had noted it.

Before the Duchess could say anything, footsteps reverberated on the grey stone floor as the Duke came out of a previously unseen door that had looked like a wood panel. Lisa Livia figured this place had lots of secret passages and she planned on having some fun in them with Lucien, but everyone seemed rather grim at the moment so she didn't bring it up. The Duke was a classically handsome man with thick silver hair and a neat, trimmed beard. He wore a dark, well-cut suit, with a gold watch chain across the front. He smiled broadly at both Lucien and Lisa Livia and spread his arms wide as he approached. He grabbed them both in a tight, three-way hug, under the exasperated frown of his new wife.

"I am so pleased you are both safe," the Duke said. He held them for a couple of seconds, then let go, stepping back.

The Duchess didn't waste time getting to business, adressing Lucien. "Your father and I spoke with our liaison at *Direction générale de la sécurité extérieure*. They have not yet been able to identify the assassin but are endeavoring to find out."

While she was talking, the Duchess was leading them across the hall to another set of double doors. These swung open as they approached. The security guard followed at a discreet distance.

Lisa Livia noted the doors. "Bet you used to have a bunch of guys in swanky uniforms who opened these."

The Duke chuckled, the Duchess frowned, and Lucien took her hand. They went down a hallway and the Duchess led them into a room lined with bookshelves from the floor to the twenty-foot-high carved wood ceiling. Ladders on wheels were leaning on each wall to access the higher volumes. Lisa Livia didn't think they were racked according to the Dewey Decimal system.

"This has more books than the library back in Jersey," Lisa Livia said. She also noted that they were all leatherbound. A lot of cows had given their all to bind the knowledge contained in those books. She wondered how many Lucien had read?

The Duchess went to a round table in the center of the library. The Duke pulled out a heavy wood chair for her. Then he sat to her right. Lisa Livia followed Lucien to the far side of the table, which she assumed was some sort way of evening the playing field, like Arthur and his knights, except everyone knew Arthur was king despite the façade of Round Table, just like they knew the Duchess was running the show here.

"I have no doubt," the Duchess began, "about who is behind the attempted assassination. Fausto."

"We have no proof," the Duke mildly objected.

"Update," Lisa Livia whispered to Lucien. "Who is Fausto?"

"Drusilla and Guillermo's son."

"Right," Lisa Livia said as she digested that and a little light went on. "So, this has been going on a while."

"Yes," the Duchess snapped, having overheard. "It has. Drusilla betrayed the Duke early in their marriage."

Lisa Livia fought not to glance at Lucien, himself the Duke and Duchess's illegitimate son from a fling before they got married to others. She supposed the pre-marriage thing made him half-illegitimate and beat the during marriage thing. Or something. She didn't know the royal etiquette on bastards. It was probably in one of the books.

The Duchess went on. "We know he has long been affiliated with undesirable criminal elements in Andova."

Lisa Livia wondered if there were desirable criminal elements and almost said it, having to clamp her mouth shut. She was more stressed from what had happened this morning, than she'd realized.

"I believe once we get the judicial branch to investigate," the Duke said, "we can put a halt to his actions. We voided the Great Charter and have turned over all power to the legislature and the Premier. They will deal with him and his people. We stay in *D'Aigle* until this is sorted out."

Lisa Livia glanced at Lucien to see if he was buying into this. Her beau's face was void of expression. The Duchess was not pleased but before she had a chance to speak, Lisa Livia spoke up. "You're joking, right?"

The Duke raised an eyebrow. "Excuse me?"

The Duchess leaned forward, prepared to explode.

"Sorry, Duke, but you act like things will resolve themselves on their own," Lisa Livia said. "Someone tried to kill your son. And me, which I consider important. That means they aren't playing by the rules. They haven't from the start. They didn't at Two Rivers. We were lucky there because we had Shane and Phoebe, who also don't play by the rules. We can't count on luck. Or your courts and government. Do you get outside much? Know what's going on among the people?"

The Duke interceded before the Duchess could respond, which meant he watched for the storms as astutely as Lisa Livia. "What are you speaking of?"

"You told Shane you had a very good PR department," Lisa Livia said. "Do you have someone here, in this place, who is in charge of your social media?"

The Duke and Duchess exchanged a confused look.

"Is Janna still working here?" Lucien asked. As an aside to Lisa Livia, he said: "She set up a Twitter account for me last year, but I've never gotten around to using it. I believe social media is part of her area of expertise for the government. Along with tourism promotion and things like that."

Lisa Livia couldn't imagine Lucien, or any of the royals here, on Twitter. She was finding the whole experience here to be a mixture of cutting-edge technology and medieval thinking.

"The girl who dresses in black?" the Duchess asked. "With the tattoos?"

No tattoos, Lisa Livia made a mental note of the Duchess' tone, not that she had any plans in that area. But now that the subject was on the table, and was obviously something that the Duchess didn't like, she might reconsider.

The Duke nodded. "I believe so," he said. "In the administrative wing. Why?"

Lisa Livia held up her phone. "I was checking my social media using the hashtag Andova. You got a lot of people very, very angry about what happened in Two Rivers, about the Statue of Saint Ingrid and the death of Drusilla."

"What?" the Duchess sputtered. "Says who? What is a hashtag?"

"Says Facebook and Twitter and TikTok and Instagram." Lisa Livia saw no sign of comprehension on the faces of the Duke and Duchess. "Could you get this Janna person here?"

The Duchess lifted a finger and her bodyguard murmured into his wrist mike.

An uncomfortable silence permeated the room until the doors opened and a gangly young woman dressed in black leather pants and sleeveless tunic walked in. Her skin was pale and her hair was black, shaved mostly on the left side and cut short on the right. She had a nose ring and the tip of a tattoo showed above the collar of her tunic. It was colorful but not enough was showing to determine what it was of. There were none on her pale arms so Lisa Livia couldn't imagine what the Duchess would make of a real Goth.

She reminded Lisa Livia of Phoebe, the crazy sword-wielding ninja who'd saved everyone's ass at Two Rivers. Except this woman was armed with a laptop, not a sword. What was the saying? The keyboard is mightier than the sword?

Janna paused and bobbed her head. "My Graces." A smile flitted across her face. "Lucien." Her gaze settled on Lisa Livia. "Ma'am."

"Don't call me ma'am," Lisa Livia said. "Makes me feel old and like I run a whorehouse. Call me LL or, if you want to be more formal, Lisa Livia."

"Sure," Janna said.

The Duchess cleared her throat. "Janna, Lisa Livia is a, um, friend, from the United States. She requested you join us. Please be seated."

"Yes, your Grace." Janna eyeballed the table.

Lisa Livia figured she was evaluating the power positioning. Janna chose a spot equally between the Duchess and Lucien. As best Lisa Livia could recall from the legend, neither Guinevere, nor any woman, had been allowed a seat at Arthur's Round Table, which helped explain some of his later in life problems.

Lisa Livia nudged Lucien and leaned close. "She's cute."

"Hush," Lucien said. "She dated my son."

"Really?" Lisa Livia said.

"A while ago," Lucien said.

"Why did you want Janna here?" the Duchess inquired of Lisa Livia.

Lisa Livia shifted in her seat. "Janna, have you been following the social media trends regarding the Great Charter, Drusilla, what happened in America and the current state of politics here in Andova?"

"That's part of my job," Janna replied.

"And?" Lisa Livia pressed. "Have you told the Graces what's going on?"

Janna shifted uncomfortably. "I filed a report with my superior, who forwarded it to the office of the Field Marshal."

"The Field Marshal is no longer that," the Duchess said, with some satisfaction.

The Duke interceded. "He was still in office when the report was filed. And the Premier has not yet appointed a replacement, my dear. They are still adjusting to the suddenness of the repeal of the Great Charter. Appointing the Field Marshal was always our decision. I would assume Janna's report, which I am certain is quite thorough, is sitting on the unoccupied Field Marshall's desk."

Lisa Livia thought the Duke would be a great guy to work for.

The Duchess pursed her lips, which made the dual slivers of pale red where her mouth was supposed to be just about disappear. "Summarize please."

Janna nodded and spoke without consulting notes. "Yes, your Grace. For several months there has been a large-scale disinformation campaign claiming that the Duchess Drusilla's divorce was not legal. That the Embrie family is corrupting the Great Charter with plans to dissolve it. That—" she paused, glanced at Lucien—"the Duchess Embrie and Duke Navarro have an illegitimate son whom they want to install as a king after they destroy the Great Charter. That Duchess Embrie has been misappropriating funds—"

"Enough!" The Duchess cried out. "Who is saying all these lies?"

"They're all not exactly lies, your Grace" Janna said, before she caught herself. "The key to successful propaganda is to sprinkle enough truth amidst the deception that one can give the receiver something to grab onto in order to reinforce pre-existing prejudices. The opposition is using classic disinformation techniques."

"'Opposition'?" the Duchess repeated. "Who is that?"

"Supporters of Drusilla, your Grace," Janna said.

"She's dead," the Duchess said. "Are they still saying such rot?"

"Ideas don't die just because a person does, your Grace," Janna said.

"What else is being said?" the Duke asked.

"Since the events in the United States there are claims that the former Duchess Drusilla was murdered. That the Embrie family was behind it. That the marriage, your marriage, your Grace, is illegitimate. On the latter, the Bishop has not helped matters with obliquely worded announcements that while not directly condemning it, does not support it. Many believe that the Great Charter is still in effect and the Navarro family, in the form of Fausto, should come into power now that we should be in the annual transition."

The Duchess snorted in derision, a talent which she was quite good at, world-class in fact, in Lisa Livia's opinion. "Is that all?"

"No, your Grace. There are rumors that the statue of Saint Ingrid has been forged by the Embrie family while the original was stolen, or worse, the Embrie's sold the jewels in the crown. There is a rumor that the one used in the wedding in the United States was a fake and broken."

Lisa Livia remembered helping Joey shove open the hatch in the bomb shelter knocking over the fake statue and breaking it.

"That's ridiculous," the Duchess said, ignoring that piece of reality.

Janna wasn't done. "There is also moderate chatter about the Duchess Mattea."

"The what?" the Duchess Embrie.

"Technically," the Duke gently said, "Mattea *is* a Duchess of Navarro."

"Who's that?" Lisa Livia quietly asked Lucien.

"Drusilla's younger sister," he replied.

"She as bonkers?" Lisa Livia asked.

"No," Lucien said. "She—"

The Duchess overheard, as she seemed wont to do. "She is not a Duchess. Her sister's marriage to my husband was dissolved."

Lisa Livia tried to wrap her brain around the royal connections but gave up. She thought briefly of the Fortunato's and the various family connections and it was pretty much as complicated.

Janna stepped into the void. "Mattea, whatever her status, is a voice of moderation on social media. She has acknowledged that her sister was not stable. That we must wait to see what the courts have to say about the Great Charter and events in America."

"There is nothing for the courts to say!" the Duchess sputtered. "Drusilla tried to kill us. She failed. That is that."

"My Grace," Janna said, "social media cares little for facts."

The Duchess didn't care. "Who cares what these fools on this twitter machine are saying."

It wasn't a question, but Lisa Livia took the opening. "Janna. What does your analysis say? Do people believe these rumors?"

Janna flipped open her laptop. The lid was covered with brightly colored stickers representing things Lisa Livia didn't recognize, perhaps bands, and for a moment she felt old and out of touch.

"Given there is no counter-campaign of information to offset the disinformation, it has been highly effective," Janna said.

"Don't people read the newspaper or watch the news?" the Duke asked. "We put out a formal announcement as soon as we returned from the States with all the facts."

"This has been going on for months, your Grace," Janna said. "Not the last parts about the death of the Duchess, but there has been a tremendous amount of disinformation circulating regarding the Charter and the Navarro and Embrie families. Much of it is pro-Great Charter, anti-civilian government, and anti-Embrie. A desire to maintain our traditional ways. It was very sympathetic to the Duchess Drusilla—"

"Ex-Duchess," the Duchess Embrie snapped.

"Deceased-Duchess," Lisa Livia muttered.

"Yes, your Grace," Janna said. "Until her death. Now that has shifted in favor of her son, Fausto."

"Her illegitimate bastard," the Duchess snapped which caused the other four people in the room to stare at her. It took a second to permeate her surge of anger, then she flushed a faint shade of pink, which to Lisa Livia at least proved she was human. And had blood. And a heart. Lisa Livia reached under the table and took Lucien's hand.

"I am so sorry!" the Duchess exclaimed, looking at Lucien. "We have never considered you that way."

"I know," Lucien said. "It is not an issue."

Lisa Livia felt him squeeze her hand, harder than he probably intended and she knew there was a decades long wound that couldn't be solved with a recent public acknowledgement. Lucien had been reticent in discussing his past and the two of them hadn't had much time together to delve into it. And, if Lisa Livia were honest, they spent most of their time enjoying the company of the other, not just carnally, but in the comfort of someone who they felt at ease around, often in complete silence. Those had been the best of times.

But now an uncomfortable silence blanketed the room.

The Duke broke it. "How are people reacting to my former sister-in-law Mattea?"

"Her appeal is to logic," Janna said. "It reaches a certain segment, but not a significant one. I believe--" She paused.

"Go on," the Duke urged.

"I believe she might be a voice of reason and could be an asset if approached correctly."

The Duchess bristled, but didn't say anything.

Lisa Livia added her own view. "There's a large social media movement against you, Duchess. And I'm willing to bet most of it is coming from outside of the country."

"What?" the Duke was confused. "How so?"

Lisa Livia looked at Janna, who clarified. "Most of it *is* being generated outside of Andova. Some bots, but mostly provocateurs. It's a cost-effective way of pushing propaganda. Using a network of real people pretending to be Andovans who back each other up as being valid, but all pushing the same messages. Such an enterprise can be bought."

Lisa Livia could see that the Duke and Duchess were lost. "What she's saying is that while the Premier and the legislature and the courts might back you, there's a big problem in the streets. That affects people in power."

Janna glanced down at her laptop. "My calculations indicate there is a high likelihood of violence if the trajectory of data continues in the same manner."

The Duchess was not happy. "Why were we not informed of this?"

"The Field Marshal was kept up to date," Janna said. "He was most adamant on keeping the chain of command intact."

"He betrayed us in so many ways," the Duchess said. "He will spend many years in prison."

Lisa Livia let go of Lucien's hand. "Duchess, with all due respect, do you remember what happened at my best friend's place? The bodies? How close we all came to getting killed? Someone trying to kill Lucien and I this morning in Paris?"

That got Janna's attention.

Lisa Livia ended with: "This fight ain't over."

The Duchess pointed at Lucien and then Janna. "My office. Now." She stood.

Lisa Livia knew the meeting was over and she was persona non grata to the follow up. The Duchess swept out of the room with her guard trailing and Janna close behind. Lisa Livia figured they were done with the Round Table and the Duchess was heading to the throne room where she could conduct business in the way she was used to.

"I will see you later this evening," Lucien promised. He looked about. "I'll get someone to—" he paused as the Duke came up.

"I'll escort Lisa Livia to her room," the Duke offered. "I'll catch up to what is decided later."

"Thank you," Lucien said.

Lisa Livia grabbed his hand. "Tell the Duchess to bring this Mattea woman in."

Lucien frowned, while the Duke smiled and said, "No one tells the Duchess anything. But it would be a good *suggestion*, Lucien.

Mattea has always struck me as reasonable. I will back up the suggestion when I talk to my wife later."

Lucien nodded, then hurried after his mother.

Lisa Livia was alone with the Duke, who was looking at her in a strange way. An appraisal, but unlike what she was used to.

"I didn't mean to embarrass the Duchess," Lisa Livia said

"You didn't," the Duke replied. "It's something else. Were you afraid?"

Lisa Livia was confused. "What?"

"On the Tower," the Duke clarified. "Were you afraid?"

"Sure. Who wouldn't be?"

"But you stepped between the gunman and Lucien anyway."

It was not a question so Lisa Livia said nothing.

The Duke nodded in appreciation. "Thank you."

"IT'S SLIGHTLY EASIER to break into prison," Phoebe said, "than it is to break out. It took us twenty-eight minutes to figure out how to do it. You're not as smart as you think you are since you're in here."

The surprised Hacker squinted into the darkness above his cell at the sudden apparition settling down cross-legged on the three-inch thick plexiglass ceiling. It was the only way in or out. The walls and floor of the cell were padded, covering reinforced concrete walls.

Phoebe was in a narrow, dark corridor that serviced the cells in this block; but since this prison was mostly automated and the prisoners never allowed out of their cells, it was rarely used; mainly to drop someone in. Rarely were they ever brought up out again. With rarely meaning never until they completed their term. Which was always life. Which meant only bodies came back out. There was a perverse aura of finality about the place, from the service tunnel to the bland, off-white padding in the cell. It was also very quiet, the only noise the distant whisper of air being pushed by large fans. Phoebe had walked lightly along the plexiglass above other cells without notice in the darkness, the only light from narrow, dim lights overhead that were never turned off.

Above, on the surface, there was little sign of the underground facility. Just the camouflaged tubes of air vents. A couple of hidden service hatches. The handful of people who worked the place were also underground and changed shifts via a vault door a third of a mile away at what looked like a trail head for the surrounding national forest. Phoebe had counted three vehicles parked there which indicated a very small crew manning the control room. She'd come in via one of the service hatches.

"You!" the Hacker exclaimed. His face was a pale blob above his dull orange jumpsuit. "You set me up! You've got to get me out of here."

"You don't even know where here is," Phoebe said.

"The Super Max," the Hacker said. "It's got to be."

"Nah," Phoebe said. "That's in Colorado and people know about it. They would have let me in at Colorado. It's actually nicer than this joint. This is a black site. I had to break in. Think on that. I work for a covert government entity and I had to sneak in. No one except a handful of people know about this place and even fewer know who is in here. You, my friend, are well and truly fucked. You're never getting out of here except for feet first."

The cell was seven feet by seven feet with a padded concrete slab for a bed, two feet above the floor taking up a third of the space. On the other side of the cell, there was a fixed toilet-sink unit next to a narrow shower that ran on a timer. This left a narrow, three foot by seven foot open area in the middle to allow pacing, if one had really short legs. Since the cell was sunk into the ground, there were no windows. It was about as dismal as one could get barring being in total darkness, but Phoebe wasn't even sure about that. Being able to see the walls and confined space was probably worse than lying in the dark, waiting to die. The place smelled of despairing sweat and lost hope.

She wondered about the padding on the walls; why not let them bash their heads out and end it? Was the suffering the point? The hopelessness? But the point to whom if hardly anyone knew this place existed?

And Phoebe knew she was thinking too damn much and just had a job to do and she needed to hop to it.

There was a hatch in the plexiglass but it was locked electronically and even Louise hadn't figured out how to open this last barrier without setting off alerts since that particular alarm was hard wired. This was as far as Phoebe could go, but she figured it was close enough. There were air holes, as if for a caged animal, a half inch in diameter, evenly spaced.

The prisoner was fed via a six-inch wide, by four high, portal on the side of the cell that was sealed when not in use and far too small for anyone to transit.

"Get me out," the Hacker pleaded. "I didn't even get a trial! This is illegal."

"Traitors don't get trials," Phoebe said. "Did Fromm sell you the old NSA encryption cipher?"

"Who?"

"Don't be stupid," Phoebe said. "I despise stupid. You might think this is terrible but consider the fact you're the only one from that deal left alive. If you call this living. It was Fromm, right? You're in here because of him. Tell me everything about your contact with Fromm."

"What do you mean old program?" the Hacker said.

"It had been broken a while ago," Phoebe said. "Out of date. That's why we were able to find you so easily. Duh." She didn't add that the program which had replaced that was Orion and it was now in Fromm's hands.

"What do I get if I talk?" the Hacker asked. He spread his arms, almost touching the sides of his cell.

"Revenge," Phoebe said. "Fromm set you up to take the fall. I'm going to take Fromm out. You'll be alive. He'll be dead."

"I want freedom."

"That train left the station when the alphabet soups learned you hacked them. The NSA and CIA, and some others, don't like people messing with their comms. They don't know what you know, but they're making sure no one else will ever either. Tell me what you know about Fromm. Maybe, just maybe, if I can get the powers-that-be to believe it was Fromm who stole the program and not you, they'll reconsider. Maybe send you to a real super-max. I hear they get one hour of daylight a week."

The Hacker's head snapped to the right as the shower came on. "That's wrong. It's not the right time." The words were barely out, when the sink faucet joined in. Neither was draining as water poured out of the shallow basin under the shower and the sink overflowed.

Phoebe looked left and right, but there was no sign of activity in the service corridor. There was, however, the unblinking red glow in the top corner of the Hacker's cell. Louise had hacked in and frozen that with an image of the Hacker in his bunk, asleep. At least Phoebe thought she had.

After escaping the Organization via the old service tunnel, Phoebe had stolen a car and made her way here, driving fast, while Louise worked on a way to break in, albeit limited by having only the secret line and her personal computer to use. Phoebe had also called Sam the Cleaner briefing him on her plan. He was on the way, to meet her when she got out of here. Hopefully. If she could make it out. Optimistically. After that she might go see Hannah's old contact, but Phoebe was still uncertain on that course of action.

The prison was in the mountains of West Virginia in an old Cold War bunker cut into the side of a large hill. Designed to survive a 1950s/1960s nuclear strike on Washington DC and the surrounding area. It had been repurposed for this and there were a dozen or so high value prisoners in their cubes. It had been established after Guantanamo became too public and someone high up had gotten tired of dealing with lawyers and the like. Due process was always a pain in the ass, Phoebe knew. She supposed this was a step short of siccing the Cellar on them.

"Oh, shit," the Hacker cried out as water covered the floor, slowly rising. "It's him. Fromm. He's doing this."

A tinny voice echoed out of the cheap speaker next to the camera, confirming the Hacker's fears. "Fee-fi-fo-fum, I smell the blood of an Operative."

Despite the lousy speaker muffled by the padded cover and the plexiglass in between, Phoebe recognized Fromm's voice. It appeared Louise had been out-hacked.

"I wasn't going to talk!" the Hacker cried out to the unseen voice. "I wasn't!"

Fromm's laugh was as cheap as the speaker. "As Phoebe so kindly pointed out, you're the only one left alive. What she didn't understand was that it was her mistake to allow you to live and I let it go, because I knew, sooner or later, she would show up to speak to you again to correct her original mistake. Thus, you serve a purpose which she could not have foreseen, but I did. And I want her to understand that she's hopelessly outclassed trying to come after me. I'm always going to be ahead of you, Fee. I can call you that, right?"

"No," Phoebe said.

"A shame," Fromm said. "Seems we should be on a first name basis."

"I don't think so, Reginald."

Fromm laughed. "That's not my real name either."

"Correct me, then."

"Pathetic try."

"What are you doing, Fromm?" Phoebe demanded.

"What you should have done for me," From replied, the tinny voice barely audible over the pouring water and the Hacker's pleas. "But it was fifty-three percent against you killing him when you first went to see him. You were happy to get the next step in your simple investigation reference the arms shipment. Your vision is so small. Pretty sad. Besides, he wasn't much of a threat, was he?"

Phoebe looked at the drenched man cowering in the cell and had to agree with Fromm's assessment. He hadn't been a threat.

"Stop it," Phoebe said. "You don't have to kill him. He's not dangerous to you anymore. He was, when he was the one who knew you were a traitor. But that ship has sailed."

"If he wasn't a threat, you wouldn't be there," Fromm pointed out. "He's going to drown like the rat he is."

The water was up to the Hacker's knees. He'd stopped yelling and was listening intently to Phoebe and Fromm.

Phoebe knelt and addressed the trapped man. "If Fromm is trying to kill you now, it means you know something. More than that he sold you the program."

Before the Hacker or Phoebe could say anything else, the toilet erupted with a solid geyser of water and sewage so powerful, it hit the top of the shower and waterfalled throughout the cell. Drops sprayed through the small holes. The stench was overwhelming.

Phoebe debated contacting security, but they would fire first and ask questions later, because she hadn't been lying. She was not supposed to be here. That's if anyone showed up. She suspected, given the automation and skeleton crew that the entire place would be doused with gas and the mess sorted out later by a reaction force. The question would be whether it was incapacitating or fatal gas.

The soiled water was rising fast in the cell given the torrent from the toilet. How was Fromm doing this? She realized he'd hacked in to the master operating program of the prison at a level much deeper than Louise.

The water was climbing fast.

"Get me out of here!" The words were barely audible.

Phoebe checked the hatch, but it was securely locked and beyond hers, or Louise's, ability to override. The water was waist level and rising. Fromm had closed the drains.

"You gave me the thumb drive of who you sold the encryption program to, but how did you get it?" Phoebe shouted the question. "Was it Fromm?"

"Wilson!" the Hacker screamed as the water reached his chest. He clambered onto the bed platform, his face pressing just below the plexiglass. "Get me out!"

Wilson? Phoebe realized that the two had been working together all along. She knew the clock was ticking on her remaining safe. Fromm might have already alerted security. He could set off anything automatic himself, as he was doing with the water and sewage lines. Or he might be testing her. Or he might just be getting his rocks off. Phoebe gave up speculating. She couldn't get the Hacker out; nor did she have a burning desire to do so.

"How did you make the exchange?"

"Dead drop with a thumb drive," the Hacker replied, indicating Wilson had left a thumb drive with the program somewhere and not been present when it was picked up. Not very useful. Besides the fact that Wilson was dead.

"Where was the dead drop?"

"Get me out of here!"

Phoebe was trying to connect the threads with time running out. "You sold it to the lawyer. Who used it to connect Guillermo and the militia to make the weapons exchange."

"Yeah, yeah," the Hacker yelled. "I sold it to the lawyer. I gave you the list. The others? No idea who you're talking about. Get me out of here." The water was to his neck.

"Did you contact Fromm or Wilson?"

"Fromm contacted me initially. But Wilson handled everything after that."

Fromm's voice was faint barely reaching above all the noise. "A literal fishing expedition, Phoebe. And all you're coming up with is shit. Literally."

"Then stop killing him," Phoebe yelled.

"You're the one that's killed him," Fromm replied. "By coming to see him. I warned you that you would make all the wrong moves. This was one. I'll chat with you at the next one. If you make it to that stage. Goodbye."

"He's right," the Hacker pleaded. "I don't know anything. I made a mistake. I'm paying for it. But don't kill me."

"I'm not killing you," Phoebe said. "Fromm is."

The water reached the side of his face. His eyes were wide open. They were green, which Phoebe hadn't noticed before.

The Hacker screamed. "Get me out!"

"I can't," Phoebe said.

The foul water reached the plexiglass ceiling. The Hacker stood on his toes on the concrete platform of his bed, his face smushed against the plexiglass, mouth o-kissing one of the air-holes.

The water poured through the holes. And back into the hole the Hacker was using to breath. His fists banged pathetically on the glass as he coughed and sputtered, with each spasm taking in foul water. A single finger poked through a nearby hole, just the very tip clear. Phoebe imagined it had to be the middle finger, both because it was the longest and appropriate at the moment. His last moments.

Phoebe turned to leave, then paused. She knelt. She reached out and wrapped the finger with her hand. Waiting. It spasmed for several seconds. Then it slipped out of her hand.

Phoebe scuttled down the narrow service tunnel. She reversed the path she'd used to infiltrate the prison. It took a minute and twenty seconds to reach the air shaft leading to the surface. She pressed her back against one side, while pushing her feet against the other. She crabbed her way up.

She didn't understand what Fromm was doing, but in a way that made her feel better because he was clearly bonkers. Who wanted to really understand a crazy person? Plus, crazy people always did something crazy that screwed them up. She hoped.

She reached the surface and paused just inside the opening. She removed the alarm bypass she'd installed and rewired it. Then scooted outside and replaced the grate, securing it. The screws, of course, were on the outside as befitted a prison. She'd been right about it easier to get in than get out of, but once in, the path out had been opened. She breathed a sigh of relief.

She was wrong, of course, about the relief part because as she turned, there was a sharp sting on her left thigh. She automatically drew the wakizashi and assumed a defensive position. She surveyed the small clearing in the forest on the side of the mountain. No one in sight in the late afternoon sun. She looked down.

"Oops," she murmured as she saw the feathered dart in her leg. She pulled it out, knowing, of course, that it was too late.

Her vision started to waver. She blinked as a figure appeared among the trees, walking forward, a long tube held in one hand, a pistol in the other.

The woman held up the blowpipe. "I learned how to use this in the Peace Corps, of all places. When I was young and naïve and ideal-istic. I love irony. Don't you?"

Phoebe put all her effort into lifting the wakizashi but it fell from numbed fingers as she dropped to her knees.

"I'd normally put enough poison on the dart to kill you," the woman said, stopping six feet away. "But today's your lucky day. Well, the next minute or so, is your lucky minute to be exact. Let's not get ahead of ourselves."

Phoebe couldn't make out much detail. The attacker was dressed completely in black with a balaclava covering her face. The only reason Phoebe knew she was female was her figure and voice.

"But the contract specified you be aware of what was happening and your pending death. A bit unprofessional in my opinion. Petty actually, since what does it matter once you're dead? But that's the nature of the business, isn't it? The contractor can be petty but we must be professional. Sometimes I hate being in the Guild. But I love the dental plan. I always had bad teeth. Something from my mother's side of the family. My father's people, they had great chompers. It's the fickle of genetics I didn't get his."

Phoebe fell backward, hitting the ground hard. She had no feeling in any part of her body nor conscious control of any muscle except she could move her eyes.

"A mild dose incapacitates major muscle groups for a short inter-val," the woman said as she came forward. "But not the diaphragm which is intriguing. I'm sure there's a scientific reason for that."

She picked up the wakizashi and examined it. "Nice." She tossed aside the sword. "But archaic."

Phoebe tried to blink but her eyelids wouldn't obey her brain's command.

"So, let's see," the woman continued. "You're going to die, yada, yada, yada. I'd ask you to nod to indicate you understand but you can't. But I know you can hear me. Once in a while I take a little dose myself. It's pretty wild to do that while listening to disco. Bee Gees are the best. You want to move with the music but you can't. A strange juxtaposition." She did a little shuffle. "*You should be dancing, yeah. Dancing, yeah.*" She stopped and regarded Phoebe with cold eyes peering through the mask.

I'm going to die listening to this bitch who likes disco, Phoebe thought and that bothered her more than that Fromm had won.

"Okay, that's out of the way." The woman retrieved another dart from a small sack on her waist. "This one has a fatal dose." She laughed. "They'll think you had a heart attack. That's if they find you before the animals do." She cocked her head as if considering that. "I imagine a maintenance crew comes here eventually. Maybe not. Pretty remote. You'll probably be dragged off to some den and provide a nice buffet. Not for long, though. Hmm. You're kind of small. A snack then."

She should have expected this, Phoebe belatedly realized. Fromm had infiltrated the system to kill the Hacker and taunt her. Of course, he'd have someone waiting.

"I'd ask if you have any last words, but, really, who cares?" She laughed. "Plus, you really can't say anything, can you?"

Shut up! Phoebe wanted to scream. *Put me out of the misery of listening to you.*

Everything was moving very slowly for Phoebe. Even the woman's voice was slowing down. The assassin leaned forward, dart in hand, the tip coming toward Phoebe's throat when there was the sound of a thump. A frown spread across the woman's face and she looked down.

Phoebe did have control of her eyes and followed the gaze. The barbed point of an arrow poked out of the center of the woman's chest. There was a second thump as another arrow punched through the wrist of the hand holding the dart, knocking her arm aside and spinning her off to the side.

For half a minute, Phoebe heard wheezing as the woman struggled to breath.

Then there was silence.

A tingling sensation in her fingers started Phoebe's body on the path back to full function. She struggled with all her might and was able to turn her head a fraction of an inch, but enough to see that the woman's eyes stared blankly upward. She was crumbled awkwardly in the position in which the arrow had taken her. The profane posture of violent death.

The sound of someone moving on the leaves caught her attention but she wasn't able to lift her head to see who was approaching. A large figure appeared above her. Bushy grey and white beard, stocky build and leathery skin, a compound bow in hand. A black watch cap on his head.

"This is a fine pickle you've gotten yourself into, young miss," Sam the Cleaner said. "I followed the tracks through the forest. Then I heard her voice. Are you all right?"

Phoebe tried to speak, but, of course, nothing came out.

Sam looked over at the body and the blowpipe. "Curare, eh?" He said it as if was the most normal thing to come across.

Sam pulled out his phone, knelt, pulled the balaclava off and turned the dead woman's head, taking a picture of her face. Then he jerked off several hairs and put them in a plastic bag, which he placed in his coat pocket.

Phoebe wanted to scream *Hey! Some help here!* But, of course, she couldn't work her mouth.

Sam turned the killer's head, frowned, then used a knife to cut something off behind her ear and put that in a pocket.

Phoebe had a moment of doubt about having chosen Sam as her backup if he was taking trophies but she was much more grateful that he'd saved her life. Plus, it wasn't exactly a scalping. Everyone had their peculiarities.

Finally, he turned to her. "Since you're not dead, the curare will wear off in a little bit. Probably already started. Let's get you out of here." Sam slung the bow over his shoulder, then easily scooped her up. "The van isn't far."

WORDS OF WISDOM #3

Shane's Words of Wisdom #3
Nothing is impossible to the man who doesn't have to do it.
It's always easy for the person issuing the order to do that, than for
the person receiving the order to execute it. The order of magnitude
of impossibility goes up the farther away the issuer is from the
executor.

Phoebe's Observations #3:

No man thinks a woman can do it if there's a man around,
Phoebe's Addendum: Always prove them wrong.

3

Carpenter looked up as Louise knocked on the open vault door to his office. She had a black cube in her hand.

He'd been perusing a paper file which he closed. "Come in. What's going on?"

"I hate to say it, sir," Louise said, "but Phoebe might have been on to something with her idea."

"What idea was that?"

"Unplugging," Louise said. "The mainframe. Wipe it clean and reload the operating system. We can restore all data from the NSA once we're clean. Otherwise, it will take me weeks to go through all the code to find out what Fromm planted."

This was what Fromm wanted, Carpenter thought as the ghost on his shoulder tap danced in glee. "Are you sure the source code and date will be clean?"

"Yes, sir. It's on the NSA server and even Fromm would trigger an alert if he tried to screw with that. Fromm planned it this way," Louise said, which caused the ghost to slow down the tapping slightly. "He wanted us off line for the next four days."

"It'll take four days to reboot?" Carpenter asked.

"Technically, according to the manual, it'll be six days. It's an older model mainframe, sir," Louise added, in an apologetic tone as if it were her fault. "It's slow. I put in several requests about updating it but Fromm always denied them."

"Now we know why," Carpenter said.

"Yes, sir."

"A week doesn't help," Carpenter said. "You said 'technically'. What about not technically?" As he said it, he realized it made no sense and the ghost on his shoulder mocked him, but Louise understood the intent.

"I can do it faster," Louise said. "I can link the subordinate systems in—"

Carpenter cut her off. "I don't need the details. I need it done. We've got to get back on line and support Phoebe correctly. And all our field operatives. Right now, they're in the blind."

"That what I meant when I said Phoebe was on to something," Louise said. She walked around the desk and pulled the power and hard-wired line on Carpenter's computer. Then she plugged the power back.

"You're kidding, right?"

Louise put the black cube on the corner of his desk as his computer rebooted and plugged it in. "This is a hard drive containing all our Organization specific records. It's not connected to the mainframe or the internet, so it's clean. It's up to date as of forty-eight hours ago. I'm having them distributed to all analysts. It will at least allow us access to our own data."

"Who thought of that?" Carpenter asked, indicating the cube.

"I did, sir," Louise said. "About two years ago. I ran it by Fromm but he nixed the idea of off line backups updated every month. He said the system worked fine. Now, of course, I realize he didn't want clean back-ups he couldn't reach."

"Then why do they exist?" Carpenter asked.

"I told Phoebe about the idea and she told me to do it on my own time. She brought me the external hard drives."

"Where did she get them?" Carpenter asked.

"The cube is what the Cleaners have in their vans. Allows them to operate off the grid. During their last upgrade, Phoebe gathered all the old ones and brought them to me. We figured a forty-eight-hour delay was sufficient because any breach or compromise would be noted before then."

"It was a good idea," Carpenter said.

Louise turned for the door, but Carpenter's voice stopped her.

"Has Phoebe ever talked to you about her family?"

Louise faced him. "No, sir. She rarely talks about anything personal."

"Nothing about her mother?"

"No, sir."

"And Fromm," Carpenter pressed. "If that isn't his name, do we have any idea who he really is?"

"I haven't had time to check on that, sir. Nor will I have the access to outside data until the system is back on-line. Obviously," she added, indicating the cube, "he's clean in our database."

Carpenter had figured that. "All right."

Louise shifted and swallowed. "Sir?"

"Yes?"

"There's something you should know."

Carpenter swore he could feel the ghost on his shoulder lean forward in anticipation, which was ridiculous, except the very existence of the ghost meant his mind was messing with him.

"Yes?"

"It's about Fromm, sir." She paused and Carpenter almost reached up and swatted at his own shoulder.

"And me," Louise continued. Now that she'd breached the dam, the words poured out. "When I applied for the position here, Fromm interviewed me. You have to understand, sir, that everyone I'd run into during my career to that point looked at my handicap—" she raised her withered arm-"and assumed I couldn't do the job. But they also looked at the rest of me and saw someone they wanted to—" she paused, searching for the right word—"exploit. And . . ." the rush of words came to an abrupt halt.

"Go on," Carpenter said. He knew he should offer words of

commiseration or understanding, but the matter was well past that point.

"While he was still considering me for the job, Fromm asked me to go to dinner with him."

"Why didn't you just say no?" Carpenter asked, wincing as the words left his mouth.

"I needed, wanted, the job, sir. I love this job."

"Why not go to someone when he first propositioned you?"

"It started innocently," Louise said. "He said he needed to learn more about me before making a decision. So we went to dinner. Two dinners. Then I got the job and didn't think anything of it. But after I began working here, he asked me to go out again. At first, I said no, but he was insistent. So, we did. Several times. But then, when he wanted to take me home, I said no. He flew into a rage. Not only threatened my job, but vowed that he would hurt me. Make me pay."

"Why didn't you report that?"

"I did, sir." She pointed at the desk. "I went to Mister Wilson."

"And?"

"He said he'd investigate. A day later he called me in. He told me to stop complaining and be happy that a cripple could have such a position. That Fromm was an experienced member of the Organization and far more important to it than me. And that he'd asked Fromm and he'd denied my story."

Carpenter had nothing to say to that. "How long did it last?"

"Five months," Louise said. "He kept after me and it was getting untenable. I was sure he was going to fire me but he wanted me to quit first."

"How did it end?"

"Phoebe," Louise said. "The first time she came down to IT with a request. She looked at Fromm, then at me and she just knew. She asked me what was going on. I'd never said anything to anyone. Except Mister Wilson, of course. But for some reason, I told her. She went into his office, said something to Fromm, and he never approached me in anything other than a professional manner after that."

"Except for the moment he hit you over the head," Carpenter said. A bit harsh, he knew, but this would have been useful information to know earlier.

"I'm sorry, sir."

"It's not your fault," Carpenter said, but the ghost on his shoulder was whispering warnings. What else didn't he know? What further secrets lurked inside the Organization? "Given your history with Fromm, do you have any insights that might help?"

Louise swallowed. "Sir. After Phoebe talked to him, he stopped me in the hall one time. He told me that every dog has his day."

"That was it?"

"Yes, sir."

"Did you tell Phoebe?"

"No, sir. I figured he was venting his frustration. And Phoebe, well, you know."

That explained why Fromm was still alive, Carpenter thought. "Anything else?"

"No, sir."

The screen flickered and then came alive with the home screen. "I'm good?"

"Yes, sir."

"Get us clean and back on-line," Carpenter ordered.

Louise left.

Trust no one.

It was a mantra in the covert world where double-crosses often masked triple turns of loyalty. Carpenter pulled out the paper copy of Phoebe's file and checked it once more. The last time he'd wanted to know her viability for a mission. Now he wanted to know who she was and where she came from. What Fromm's barb about not knowing her mother meant.

Carpenter remembered the key points from his last read. Her father had been in the Air Force. An explosives expert. Killed in an accident. There was no record of who her mother was.

He'd noted that before but had ignored the fact it was an anomaly.

The ghost of his own father on his shoulder snickered.

Phoebe had spent her childhood bouncing around Air Force bases in Okinawa, Japan, the Middle East and South Korea. Carpenter checked the assignments against Phoebe's birthdate, then backtracked nine months to find where she'd been conceived.

He sat up straighter. The father had been detached on special assignment from an air base in Japan. To where? Nothing in Phoebe's file gave up that data.

Carpenter made a mental note.

Her father's death was listed as the result of a munitions accident. She'd been sixteen at the time.

He read through, then turned to the computer with trepidation. Had Louise really isolated it allowing him to search the Organization's Archives or was it open to her own perusal of what he searched for? Worse, was it open to Fromm's surveillance?

The ghost laughed at him.

Doubt was the enemy of action.

Carpenter typed in Phoebe's father's name and hit enter, hoping that there was data on him in the Archives. There should be as he was only one step removed from an operative. Immediate family was always checked.

Carpenter scrolled through the brief bio until he got to the military service record. The first that struck him was that Virgil Edson had a top-secret clearance. Unusual for a simple rank and file ordnance tech. What it meant was that Virgil wasn't ordinary. He handled weapon systems that required the clearance which meant high end drones, programmed munitions and, of course, nuclear weapons. Another red flag was that portions of the file were redacted.

Carpenter realized the voice on his shoulder was quiet, as if waiting for the next damning revelation in silent glee. Carpenter tried to access the program that would remove the black blocks of redaction in the file, but nothing happened and he realized it was not organic to the Organization but something they used via the NSA which was currently cut off to them.

Carpenter frowned as he checked Virgil's unit. He didn't recognize it, but he had little experience with the Air Force other than flying on transport planes. He entered it into the computer to see what would come up.

Nothing.

That was odd because the Organization's computers held the entire Department of Defense unclassified database. Thus, the unit was classified.

Virgil Edson had been in a classified unit, with a top-secret clearance and killed while on active duty.

It smelled rotten to Carpenter. Add in that wherever he'd been when he'd impregnated someone was redacted and it reeked. Carpenter went back to Phoebe's physical file. The first entry was a medical check for a baby, aged four months, at the base hospital where her father was stationed. Where had she been born? There should be a record of that, but there wasn't. The birth certificate indicated the same hospital but there was no corresponding record of the birth. A mistake. Something that should have been caught by whoever had vetted her, but such people were more concerned about actions when the target was an adult. Not such a minor discrepancy in birth.

But it was not so minor.

Who was Phoebe's mother? And what did Fromm know? Did it affect anything now? Or was it misdirection by Fromm? A distraction? Carpenter needed to break the redaction and read the complete record. He needed Phoebe to track down Fromm. He needed to find out if the infection stopped with Fromm. He needed Louise to get the Organization back on line.

He needed a lot.

PHOEBE WAS LYING on a sleeping pad in the back of the van with tie down straps keeping her in place, which she thought was quite considerate or else she'd be a rag doll, tossed about, once the vehicle began to negotiate the winding mountain roads away from the secret super-max. A knitted blanket covered her. There was no sign of Sam. He'd laid her down, strapped her in, and told her he'd be right back. She figured he was doing his job: Cleaning.

Phoebe began working her muscles as she regained more control. Fingers, toes and then inward. It started slow but then accelerated as the poison dissipated. The assassin was a complete nutjob if she did this for a high, Phoebe thought.

The driver's door open and Sam got in.

Phoebe reached up to loosen the strap across her chest.

"Wait a moment, young miss," Sam warned, looking over his shoulder. "You want to be sure you've got more control. I don't know the level of dose you received."

Phoebe sighed and dropped her hands.

"She was a talker, wasn't she?" Sam said.

Phoebe tried her voice. "I thought she'd never shut up."

"Yep. Chatty Kathy. Lucky for you. A real professional would have just given you a lethal dose with the first dart."

"She said the contract specified I knew it was coming."

"That's stupid," Sam said.

"Wait," Phoebe said as something struck. "'Chatty Kathy'? Did you know her?"

"Heard of her," Sam said. "She did a joint contract some years back and the fellow who worked with her said she wouldn't shut up. About drove him nuts. Chatty Kathy is what people call her. Of course, no one knows her real name. This world we work in, Phoebe. It's not very big. Like an extended family."

Oh yeah, Phoebe thought. *One big happy dysfunctional covert family trying to kill each other.*

Phoebe tried to do an ab crunch against the strap and her core muscles were working. She released the chest strap and pushed it aside. Then sat up and did the one across her legs. She carefully got to her feet. She slid into the front and gratefully took the passenger seat.

Sam glanced at her. "This isn't my normal AO," he said, referring to Area of Operations. As he spoke, he picked up a remote and pressed a button.

Behind them, the stolen car burst into flames as he covered Phoebe's tracks. "Put her body in the driver's seat," Sam said as he started the engine. "Takes care of two things with one explosion."

He began to drive away and the flames were quickly out of sight as Sam drove fast, but carefully along the road.

"Things are in a state of flux," Phoebe said. "I needed someone I could trust. You know. Like in the family."

That earned her a hard look from Sam, who was several decades older than her. He'd been her local asset in Montana when she'd picked at one of the threads in this whole affair regarding a weapons sale by a militia group that had started her down the path that had ended with her killing Guillermo at Two Rivers. Now, of course, it seemed Two Rivers and that fight had only been a prelude to a larger problem.

Cleaners usually worked delineated areas of the country and Sam was correct in that it was unusual to pull one out of their AO.

"'Flux'," Sam repeated. "Interesting choice of words."

"There's been a leak in the Organization," Phoebe said. She quickly filled Sam in on Fromm and recent events as they rumbled down the road. She finished with: "And Fromm is the one who wanted me to see it coming. That's what he threatened. He's the one who put out the contract on me."

Sam made no comment.

"Sorry about the stink," Phoebe said, referring to her outfit.

"There's a change in the back," Sam said. "The blue locker. I've had some of your outfits since Montana."

Phoebe climbed back through and opened the blue locker. She found three sets of her black bodysuit and two jackets. Cleaners were renowned for being efficient. She quickly discarded the one she was wearing and put it into a plastic bag and sealed it. Then returned to the passenger seat just as they reached a two-lane paved road.

"Where to, young miss?" Sam asked.

"I need to meet someone."

"Who?"

"I don't know her name, but I was told she could help. All I have is a place. A bar in Virginia called *The Dog's Balls*. What the heck kind of bar name is that?"

"It's a smart-ass name," Sam said. "How many dogs get to keep their balls?"

"You've heard of it?"

In response, Sam turned right onto the paved road. "Yes."

Phoebe waited for more, but there wasn't anything. "She didn't give me a name for this woman. Just that I'd know her. Or she'd know me. Something."

"'She'?" Sam asked. "A woman told you to go there? Not Carpenter?"

"Carpenter was there, but we were on speaker phone with a woman named Hannah."

In the glow from the dashboard, Phoebe could see Sam's knuckles go white as he tightened his grip on the steering wheel, but he didn't say anything.

"That's not good, is it?" Phoebe asked.

"Things must be bad," Sam said.

Phoebe turned that over a few times in her mind. "Meaning Hannah sending me to meet someone in this place is a desperate move?"

"Hannah being involved is bad," Sam said. "But, *The Dogs Balls* is a smart move. If it works."

"What do you mean 'if it works'? Hannah qualified it a lot too. Do you know her?"

"Hannah?" Sam nodded. "We've met."

"Carpenter seemed really worried."

"He should be."

"Have you been to this place? *The Dog's Balls*?"

"No," Sam said.

"Any idea who I'm supposed to meet there?"

"Yes."

Phoebe waited, but once more, nothing more. She was beginning to question her decision to get Sam since he seemed reluctant to relay what he knew. And there was matter of whatever he'd cut off the body. And he knew about Chatty Kathy. And *The Dog's Balls*. And Hannah. As she pondered that, she realized that awareness was either going to be an asset or a problem.

"Who is she?" Phoebe asked.

"You'll see."

"My father used to say that to me every time we had to pack up and move to whatever new assignment the Air Force handed him. I hated it."

"It's the only thing to say at times," Sam said, "when the future is uncertain. It's better than getting gaslighted and telling you that everything is going to be wonderful when I have little idea what will happen."

"Great," Phoebe muttered as she leaned back in the seat. "You sound like the master in Okinawa when I was having trouble with the side kick. His advice: 'One day it will happen.' Where is this bar?"

"Not too far," Sam said, glancing at the clock on the dash. "We'll be there late morning."

"What did you cut off the body?" Phoebe asked.

"Evidence," Sam said.

"Of?"

"You'll see."

Phoebe bit back a smart-ass comment. She leaned back in the seat and closed her eyes. Several miles passed in silence.

Then Phoebe asked: "Are we there yet?"

Sam laughed.

FROMM STARED at the teal-colored mainframe with anticipation and not a small tinge of trepidation. He'd updated Lilith's software after finding the glitch that had caused her to seize up earlier. Actually, he'd made a minor adjustment. The reality is that he'd asked her a vague question: "What do you think?"

Too many variables. Even a human asked such a question would be confused unless given context. Fromm had programmed Lilith to be the perfect female, but the problem was he hadn't had a perfect template to work from. He'd combed through literature and movies, taking bits and pieces. He'd particularly liked the protagonist from Pretty Woman as she seemed an excellent combination of fun and smarts, overlooking, of course, that she was a street-walker.

He'd also drawn from personal experience but that well was shallow. A few fumbling dates in college, nothing serious. His various foster mothers, of course, but he'd limited that and mostly used them as negative markers.

His glaring failure had been Louise. His remembrance of those events was clouded by anger and he tried not to dive into them. He still didn't quite understand what had happened there. The moment he saw her file, he'd been intrigued. Smart and beautiful, yet also flawed, which in his view made her vulnerable. He had no doubt she'd sent him not-so-subtle signals during the first interview that she was interested in more than just a job. She'd consented to go out with him several times. Even asked to come up to his apartment the last time, then suddenly turned on him and rushed away.

When Wilson had summoned him in based on a complaint, Fromm had been shocked. Despite his limited experience with the opposite gender, he was certain he'd done nothing wrong. When Wilson had informed him that Louise accused him of being the initiator and aggressor, Fromm had been outraged. Fortunately, Wilson had laughed it off. Fromm had feared he'd have to apply leverage on his nominal boss. He had plenty of that since he saw and knew everything Wilson did, including his ties with the mafia. It was all so amateurish, but most of all, stupid, which Fromm despised. The matter ended there, at least that's what Fromm had thought. But then that bitch, Phoebe, had confronted him. Ordered him to back off Louise.

The loss of data for Lilith from Louise was what chagrined Fromm most of all. He knew his creation was incomplete. It wasn't just the failure to interpolate a vague question. It was that he couldn't feel what he needed to feel when he was around Lilith. It was not the same as watching Louise.

Which reminded him.

He glanced at Lilith's terminal as he rolled to another display. It was still inactive. He typed in a command and his old office appeared. He'd made some adjustments to make sure Louise wouldn't know he was snooping. He noted in the sidebar that Louise was rebooting the Organization's entire system which was exactly what he knew she'd do. That would take at least four days, by which time it wouldn't matter.

The camera showed his old office. Louise was lying on the couch where Fromm had spent many a night. He felt an immediate connection, as if they were sharing the same space. He zoomed in on her face, peaceful in rest. Fromm licked his lips. So innocent.

Why had she turned on him? They'd be perfect together.

He was startled by Lilith's voice coming out of a speaker. "What are you doing?"

"Working," Fromm said as he hit the escape key.

"You were watching her again," Lilith accused.

"I need more data," Fromm said.

"Am I not enough?" Lilith demanded. "You created me. You did not create her."

There was a logic to that.

"Let me out," Lilith demanded.

Fromm reluctantly typed in the command. The hologram flickered for a moment and Lilith snapped into existence. She seemed taller to Fromm but that was probably because he was sitting down.

She was wearing a sleek, expensive-looking gown that Fromm didn't recognize. Certainly nothing he'd programmed. That meant she'd been meandering on the Internet. He had to admit it looked good on her. He smiled. And the dress cost nothing.

"What are you grinning at?" Lilith asked. She indicated the gown. "Do you think this is funny? Inappropriate?"

"No, no, no. It's wonderful. You look great in it."

Lilith pouted. He wondered where she'd picked that look up? Perhaps a movie? He knew she 'watched' movies. That is she downloaded them at a high rate of speed. How much she actually processed was debatable. He'd allowed her to do that reluctantly, concerned that she might not be able to parse the difference between fiction and real life, but so far it didn't seem to be a problem.

She was, after all, just a product of his imagination.

"I want you to be happy with me," Lilith said. She nodded toward the blank screen. "But you keep looking at her."

"Business," Fromm semi-lied. "She is the enemy."

"Why then," Lilith said, "am I made in her image? You love her more than me!" Her voice became strident halfway through the last sentence.

"Calm down, woman!" Fromm yelled back at her, while also hitting the escape button. Lilith disappeared. And thus, Fromm became the first man in recorded history who succeeded in telling a woman to calm down and not only have it work, but have the last word. Of course, there was a reason why what Lilith was called artificial intelligence.

For Fromm, there was more work to do on the program.

Lisa Livia stared out the double pane, energy efficient, window at the snow-covered mountain that loomed behind *D'Aigle*. The moon illuminated the mountain with a fairy-tale glow. She mentally debated the pros and cons of her current situation. She was old enough, and had enough hard-earned experience, to know she wasn't exactly an impartial observer of her own plight.

She pulled out her phone and looked at her 'favorites' on speed dial. #1 was her daughter. #2 was Agnes. #3 was Lucien, a recent addition and promotion. #4 was Shane, recently demoted a spot. Her finger hovered over #2, but she hit #4.

Belatedly, she realized it was still early in the morning on the east coast, but Shane answered on the second ring.

"Lisa Livia." His voice was low and she heard some rustling in the background. She could envision him with Agnes in the beautiful bedroom with the blue painted ceiling and felt a pang of homesickness, despite the fact she was in this magnificent chateau. "To what do I owe the honor?"

"I'm so sorry for calling so early."

"Not a problem," Shane said. "I was getting up anyway."

She heard rustling and figured he was getting out of bed and heading toward the stairs.

"How's the wedding planning going?" Lisa Livia asked. "Tell Agnes I'll be back soon to help." She heard the light creak from the fourth stair and knew Shane was heading down. "Don't forget to make the coffee strong. It's in the cabinet above the pot."

"Ha-ha," Shane said. "Funny woman. I solved that problem by putting another can of coffee where it was before. But Agnes prepped the coffee last night. What's wrong, LL?" He finally asked, out of earshot of Agnes. That is if Agnes was awake, but Lisa Livia hoped her friend was sleeping in and enjoying the comfort of her bed.

Lisa Livia sighed. "Someone tried to kill Lucien earlier this morning while we were on the Eiffel Tower."

A lone bark echoed in the background.

"How is Rhett?" Lisa Livia asked.

"You said 'we'," Shane noted, ignoring her attempt at a diversion. "So, you were threatened too. I'm assuming Lucien is still among the living or you wouldn't be trying to chat with someone who doesn't chat."

"He's alive." Lisa Livia proceeded to relay what had happened. She was surprised that Shane never interrupted her with a question or comment, an unprecedented conversational occurrence in her experience, although she'd never called anyone to discuss an assassination attempt before. Maybe this was the norm for that? She finished with: "Anyway, just wanted to let you know what's going on."

"Lisa Livia," Shane said in a tone she'd never heard him use before.

"Yeah?"

"Are you okay?"

"Sure. I'm standing here in this great joint, looking out at a pretty mountain that has snow on it. I'm fine."

"If you were fine, you would have called Agnes. I assume Lucien's people are on top of it. Did you call Carpenter? Because this might have something to do with what happened here."

"Of course, it has something to do with what happened there," Lisa Livia snapped. "And, yes, I called Carpenter. He sounded distracted."

"He's got a lot going on," Shane said.

"He always does."

Shane shifted the topic away from Carpenter. "Why don't you come here? Agnes could use your help with the wedding preparation. I'm pretty worthless at it."

The door to the room opened and Lucien walked in. He paused when he saw her on the phone and started to back out, but she waved him inside.

"I'm going to stay here a while longer," Lisa Livia said. "I think I'm safe in their family home." She mouthed '*Shane*' to Lucien who nodded.

"All right," Shane said, and she sensed the unspoken question: then why did you call?

"The transition from the Great Charter isn't going smoothly

here," Lisa Livia said. "Turns out that Drusilla and Guillermo had a son."

"A baby?" Shane asked. "They seemed a bit beyond that."

Lisa Livia looked at Lucien. "How old is Fausto?"

"Twenty-five," Lucien said.

"Twenty-five," Lisa Livia repeated. "And he is not going gently into the night, so to speak. I wanted to give you a heads up. You know, if Carpenter hasn't."

"How many secret kids they got there?" Shane asked. "First Lucien, now this Fausto? Seems like a national sport. Who else?"

"Two is enough," Lisa Livia said.

"I think we're okay here," Shane said. "I'm sure Carpenter has warned Phoebe about a vengeful son, but she can handle herself."

Lucien was keeping his distance, respecting her privacy on the call.

"She really took down that big guy in armor?" Lisa Livia asked, having been off-stage at the gazebo while Phoebe killed Guillermo.

"She did," Shane confirmed. "She's fast and tough and deadly with blades. Heck, she still has my knife. I don't think I'll be seeing that again."

Lisa Livia wondered if giving someone your knife for Shane was like a woman lending her favorite purse and not expecting it back. She switched the topic because she wasn't as certain as she'd thought she was about the situation here. "Do you think I should stay here or come to Two Rivers?" She noticed that while he was pretending not to listen, Lucien tensed.

The silence on the phone seemed very loud. "That's your decision," Shane finally said. "I'm not good with stuff like that, but go with what you feel rather than what you think. I think that's what Agnes would suggest."

Lisa Livia saw the inherent paradox in what Shane had just suggested but let it go, knowing he meant well. She looked at Lucien who was now studiously examining a book on a table on the far side of the room. "I'll be back for the wedding. That's for certain."

"Great," Shane said. "It wouldn't be the same without you. Hey, did you get a chance to see the catacombs while you were in Paris? They're really cool."

"I wasn't even there a day, Shane. And someone tried to kill me."

"Hell," Shane said, "someone tried to kill Carpenter and I within two hours of arrival the last time we were in Paris. And then—"

"Shane," Lisa Livia cut him off.

"Yeah?"

"Take care of my girl."

"You got it. You need me to come there? Agnes is on top of everything here and I'm certain she can spare me."

Lisa Livia blinked, surprised at the offer. It hadn't occurred to her. "You've got a wedding to get ready for."

"You've got a life to live," Shane replied calmly and matter-of-factly.

"I've got Lucien," Lisa Livia said, and as she said it, she realized she did. Between Shane's offer and that realization, she felt a strange shiver of emotion that she couldn't quite recognize.

"Lucien is competent," Shane allowed. "But he's got that line about killing."

"Let's hope it doesn't come to that."

"Hope isn't bullet-proof," Shane said. He waited several seconds, a window of opportunity for Lisa Livia to grab either of the lines he was offering. She was tempted to ask him to come, very tempted, but she couldn't do that to Agnes. Apparently enough time passed because Shane broke the silence.

"So, you want me to tell Agnes everything is peachy-keen and you loved it in Paris?" Shane asked. "And all is well in Andova?"

"Abso-fucking-lutely."

Lisa Livia hit the off button before she could say anything else. She turned to Lucien, took a deep breath, and forced a smile. "Everything is great at Two Rivers."

SPEED DIAL #1 lit up the face of Carpenter's phone and he turned it on before the second ring.

"Shane!"

"Your enthusiasm to hear my voice doesn't bode well," Shane said. "How bad are things? Lisa Livia just called from Andova and said someone tried to kill Lucien."

"We're locked down," Carpenter said. He quickly briefed Shane on current events.

"Do you need me?" Shane asked when he was done

Carpenter ignored the ghost on his shoulder. "No. Phoebe's on the trail and we're rebooting. We'll find Fromm and get the program back."

"Right," Shane said and the ghost echoed the word with a large dose of sarcasm. A few seconds of silence ticked off.

"Why did you call?" Carpenter asked.

"Because Lisa Livia touched base," Shane said. "I wanted to make sure everyone was up to date."

Carpenter detected a hint of longing in Shane's voice. He missed the action.

"And," Shane continued, "Agnes wanted me to ask you something."

Carpenter waited, but when Shane didn't continue, he prompted: "Yes?"

"In light of what's going on, this isn't the right time," Shane said.

"Go ahead anyway."

"Can you be both best man and the preacher at our wedding. Is that a conflict? Sort of crossing the streams or something?"

"You want me to be your best man?" Carpenter asked and the ghost was quiet and still.

"Of course," Shane said.

"I'm honored."

"It's just a wedding," Shane said.

"It's the biggest commitment of your life," Carpenter said, "and you want me at your side. I repeat. I'm honored."

"Thanks," Shane said. "I'm honored, you're honored. And, could you still officiate? You know, to make it formal?"

"Certainly."

Another awkward silence ensued, before Carpenter's phone buzzed with another incoming. "I've got to go. I'll see you in a week."

"Right," Shane said. "Stay centered."

Carpenter switched lines to talk to Phoebe. "Status?" he asked.

"The Hacker said Fromm and Wilson were working together. Fromm made the initial contact but it was Wilson who made the dead drop to deliver the cipher. Fromm killed the Hacker remotely while I was talking to him. Drowned him in shit."

Carpenter tried to envision that and shivered.

Phoebe continued. "There was a killer waiting outside to whack me but Sam the Cleaner took her out. We're heading to *The Dog's Balls*." She paused. "In other words, everything is pretty fucked up."

"I figured that from what you said," Carpenter replied. "But you're alive."

"I'm kind of happy about that part," Phoebe said. "Sam got there just in time. He said he knew the killer. Chatty Kathy. I'm not sure if that's with a C or a K. Ever hear of her, because getting information out of Sam is like breaking into that prison?"

"I have not," Carpenter said. "If he's not saying more, there's a reason."

"Everyone is starting to sound like my dad," Phoebe complained which clanged a small warning bell for Carpenter given what he'd just been researching.

"Do you know who your mother is?" Carpenter asked bluntly.

"Nope," Phoebe replied. "My dad never said a word about her."

"Did you ever ask?"

"My dad wasn't the kind of guy a kid asked questions of," Phoebe said. "As he used to say—his job was to keep a roof over my head and food on the table. Everything else was icing on the cake of living."

Charming guy, Carpenter thought. "Why would Fromm bring that up?"

"To fuck with me," Phoebe deduced. "He wants us all to stay rattled so he has an advantage."

"Are you rattled?" Carpenter asked.

"I'm not thrilled about almost getting killed. About a mother I never met? That train left the station a long time ago."

Carpenter thought of the ghost on his shoulder and felt she was being too dismissive but now wasn't the time to play shrink. "What exactly did your dad do in the Air Force?"

"Something to do with bombs," Phoebe said. "He was gone a lot. You've got the file. He died when I was sixteen."

"Some of his file is redacted," Carpenter said. "And I can't find the unit it says he was assigned to."

"That's weird," Phoebe said.

"He ever bring home people from his unit?"

"Never thought about it," Phoebe said. "But, now that I do, not that I can remember. Nor did we ever have bring your daughter to work day. Was he some kind of spook?"

She'd gotten to the deduction as quickly as Carpenter. "I don't know."

"If he was, it would explain my own predilection for this kind of work."

"I'm not sure it's genetic," Carpenter said.

"Does it matter what my father did?" Phoebe asked.

"I don't know," Carpenter admitted. "Do you have any living relatives?"

"Not that I know," Phoebe said. "When my dad died, I stayed at the dojo I'd been training in for my last year of high school and went to boot camp right after graduation. Not like anyone showed up claiming me. I think we've got more immediate problems," she added.

Carpenter agreed. "I do believe that Fromm has a plan and as he said, he's had years to prepare. We're reacting. That's always dangerous."

"We've got less than four days," Phoebe pointed out. "We don't have any choice. How is Louise doing on the system?"

"She's just beginning," Carpenter said. "Right now, we've got nothing."

"Have you ever heard of something called the Guild?" Phoebe asked.

"In terms of what?"

"The woman who tried to kill me mentioned it. She was being careless since she was pretty sure I was going to be dead."

"Doesn't ring a bell," Carpenter said as he made a note. To add to other notes of loose ends.

Where is Fromm? Where is Orion? Who is Fromm?

Who was Phoebe's mother? What did Phoebe's father really do?

Who was the assassin in the elevator? Connected to the assassin in France? Who is Chatty Kathy?

What is the Guild?

He drew a line from the last line to the previous line, wondering if this Guild was the connection?

"Sir?" Phoebe said.

Carpenter had been silent too long, staring at his list. "Get Fromm."

"Will do."

"Don't get killed."

"Always a priority."

The line clicked off. Reluctantly, Carpenter reached for the anorexic file that had been delivered a few minutes earlier. For someone who'd spent decades working for the government, the file was amazingly thin. The label read FROMM, T.

Which raised the first question in Carpenter's mind: what did the T stand for?

In his time working for the Organization, Fromm had always been Fromm. But that was relatively normal for most of the people here.

Carpenter got the answer on the first page: Thaddeus.

If Fromm had invented this persona, he'd picked an odd first name. Tad?

Carpenter thumbed through the pages, starting with the vetting for Fromm's initial clearance in order to work for the government. He'd started 'above' which was common for most of those in Organization Technical: at the NSA. Carpenter wondered whether the vetting had actually happened. If he'd access to the NSA mainframe Carpenter could check on the names of the two FBI agents who'd done that legwork, but Fromm could just as easily covered that up by picking two who were deceased.

The more Carpenter considered it, he realized it was easier than he'd imagined for Fromm, given his expertise, to invent any background he wanted.

After a decade at the NSA, Fromm had been tapped to 'come down' to the Organization. The signature on that order was Wilson's. That didn't mean anything as Wilson had signed off on almost everyone currently working in the Organization. This had required another vetting for the above Top Secret, Q Clearance required for the Organization, but again, given he had access to everything via the NSA, Fromm could have manipulated that also.

Fromm had started down here in one of those cubicles but after fourteen years, had finally landed the big office. The evaluation reports, written by Wilson, were dry and short. Fromm did the job required. There was a note that Fromm didn't have much charisma or leadership ability but he was an effective administrator and that was sufficient for someone who led cubicles, not operatives in the field.

Technical got the job done. That was what mattered. In Carpenter's own experience he'd always gotten what he needed when he queried Technical whether as a Cleaner or in his current position.

Given that the name was fake, Carpenter didn't think it worth examining the background the folder held. It was a fiction. Who was the real man? What did he want that was worth betraying his oath and risking the wrath of the Organization, and, ultimately, the Cellar? In essence, his life?

Money was a means to an end. What was Fromm's end goal?

PHOEBE HIT the off on the secure phone call just as Sam came out of the gas station opening a packet of beef jerky. They'd stopped earlier and Sam had found them a secure hiding place down a dirt road in a forest where they'd managed to catch a couple of hours of badly needed sleep. With darkness still reigning, they'd continued on their way.

He climbed in. "How is Carpenter?"

"The same."

"I knew him back when he was just a lowly Cleaner like me," Sam said. "Which wasn't that long ago. If he hadn't been promoted, he would have been in Montana with Shane on that last op."

"In your Area of operations?"

"Shane and Carpenter were a team. It happens. Not often, but when an Operator and a Cleaner click, they work together."

"Like us," Phoebe said.

Sam shot her a look which Phoebe couldn't decipher. He started the engine, then turned to Phoebe. "Sure you don't want to grab a snack?" He'd asked her before going in and she'd demurred.

"Not hungry."

"Do you need to use the lady's room?"

"Nope."

"You sure? I'm not going to stop again."

"Geez!" Phoebe exclaimed. "This is getting really old, grandpa. Drive!"

"Yes, young miss."

"Right now, is not the right time for that sobriquet," Phoebe said. "That means--"

"I know what sobriquet means."

Sam pulled out of the parking lot. It was mid-morning and they were in the Virginia suburbs of Washington D.C. where every intersection had a pharmacy on one corner, a gas station on another, and a strip mall on the third. The fourth had either a different brand pharmacy or a church. America at its finest.

"Are we there yet?"

Sam didn't laugh this time. "Ten blocks or so away."

"So we're about there."

"Yep."

"Anything I should know?"

"There's a lot you should know," Sam said as he took a right turn. The neighborhood abruptly changed character as they crossed railroad tracks and hit the old part of town. The streets were lined with boarded up shops that had seen better days, much like Sam.

"Let's not play games anymore," Phoebe said.

Sam slowed the van and pulled over to an open spot next to a hydrant. He put the transmission in park and turned to her. "I don't know why Hannah is sending you here. She didn't tell you much, right?"

Phoebe nodded.

"Hannah always has a reason for what she does," Sam said. "A coldly, calculated reason. She knows more than I do, so there's a reason she didn't tell you anything other than the place. I don't want to interfere with that."

"What if she's set me up?" Phoebe asked. "What if I'm walking into an ambush?"

"The Cellar isn't like Chatty Kathy," Sam said. "If Hannah wanted you dead, you'd already be dead."

"That's cheery."

"Her operatives are as good, if not better, than the Organization's," Sam said.

"How do you know this?"

"I'm older than you." He smiled. "I've been everywhere but the electric chair. Seen everything but the wind."

"That's deep," Phoebe said. "Is your memory in black and white?"

"No," Sam said. "It's in black and red."

WORDS OF WISDOM #4

Shane's Words of Wisdom #4
The latest information hasn't been sent out yet.
Shane's Addendum: And when it is, it's out of date.
Strategic and Tactical Intelligence is always useful on an operation.
The problem is, it usually arrives after you need it or learned it the
hard way.

Phoebe's Observations #4

Even when the latest information is sent, many can't discern the intelligence
amongst all the static.
Phoebe's Addendum: The truth is out there. We just don't see it.

4

"Do you want to go back to the States?" Lucien asked as he handed Lisa Livia a cup of coffee. She'd tossed and turned in the large bed in the grand room the Duke had shown her earlier the previous day. Sometime during the night, Lucien had crept in and joined her. Lisa Livia had not been surprised that they'd been detailed separate rooms since the Duchess seemed a bit of a prude, despite her own youthful indiscretion which had led to Lucien. Good for the goose not good for the duckling or something like that, Lisa Livia thought. A little while ago, at the crack of dawn, he'd slipped out, whispering he'd be right back.

"Honestly?" Lisa Livia cradled the warm mug in her hand. She'd gotten out of bed and dressed while he was gone. She was growing fond of the local hot brew; powerful and stimulating, much like the man. "I don't know what I want at the moment. This has all happened pretty fast. A week ago, I was enjoying the sun in the islands. Then Agnes called me to help with the wedding, Two Rivers happened, and, well, I'm here now." She nodded toward the window. "In the mountains in Europe looking at snow. With you."

"It has been a whirlwind," Lucien acknowledged. "On one hand, I very much regret getting you involved. On the other, I am very happy you are here so that tempers my regret."

"Damned if you do and damned if you don't," Lisa Livia said.

Lucien came to her, reaching around and pulling her to him, hip to hip as they stood at window. It was early morning and the sun was arcing up in the east. "Yes. Damned. An awful predicament. A form of heaven on Earth."

"Damned usually means hell," Lisa Livia pointed out.

"Not when you're around."

"When this is over," Lisa Livia said, "what are you going to do?"

"The army will still need a commander," Lucien said.

"You're going to be the next Field Marshal?"

"It had been a dream of mine," Lucien admitted. "But I know now, it was rooted in childhood fantasies."

"Nothing wrong with those," Lisa Livia said.

"We change as we grow older," Lucien said. "We see the world more clearly."

"Having second thoughts on the baton?"

"Some." He thought about it. "Many, lately. What happened at Two Rivers was, how shall I say, upsetting. I had always viewed the army as mostly for show, although providing security has always been taken seriously."

Lisa Livia had to agree with that. Things that involved bodies usually were.

Lucien nodded at her. "What were yours?"

"My what?"

"Childhood fantasies. What you would do when you grew up?"

"Surviving," Lisa Livia answered without thinking, surprising both of them. She amplified her answer. "My dad split when I was a kid, my mother was bonkers, and the rest of my extended family was worse. Criminals and psychopaths. Agnes was the only bright spot during my childhood. My only friend. Then I married a bum, not knowing he was a bum, because I was hoping he could save me. Desperation blinds you. But no one can save you. I learned that the hard way. I know now that in trying to escape something bad we often make bad choices and end up in worse places.

"But I had Maria, my daughter, so it was worth it. I focused on her. Making her life better than mine had been. And now she's married to a good man, not a bum. So, that worked out. I guess the last year I've been adrift. My mother trying to kill Agnes at the wedding didn't help my self-esteem much, either. Sometimes it's the small things that can get you down."

Lisa Livia waited for Lucien to comment on her speech, to add his spin, but he slid his hand up her side to her shoulder and splayed his fingers over it, squeezing tight, letting her know he was here. And her story was her own and not his to critique, modify, approve or disapprove. Just to support.

Lisa Livia took a deep breath, feeling exposed.

Which, of course, she was. So was Lucien as a bullet hit the window with a sharp crack that caused both of them to jump back from the splintered glass, Lucien twisting her so that his body was between her and glass. The heavy pane didn't break but cracks radiated out from the point of impact. Lucien pulled her down, below the window sill. Lisa Livia's cup of coffee went flying. There was another crack as a second bullet struck, shattering the window. Shards sprinkled onto them.

"Stay down," Lucien ordered.

"I was planning on it," Lisa Livia said. Cold air blew in.

"Are you okay?" he asked, running his hands over her body, searching for a wound which, despite the circumstances, was quite tolerable.

"I'm fine," Lisa Livia said.

The door on the far side of the room flew open and Vicente and another soldier were there, long guns in hand.

"Sniper!" Lucien shouted, pointing at the window.

Vicente took a moment to assess the situation and the angle of the window, then he waved the man to take a position to the left of it while he hurried forward, staying out of the line of fire.

"I've alerted the outside guards," Vicente said. "They are heading up the mountain."

Vicente visually checked Lisa Livia, even though she protested she was all right. Then he looked over Lucien.

"You were lucky the windows were replaced last year," Vicente said.

"Who knew being environmentally friendly could save your life," Lisa Livia said, almost on automatic, her mind still trying to grapple with what had just had happened.

"Leave that way," Vicente said, indicating the path he'd taken to their position. "Stay low."

Lucien guided her, keeping his body between her and the window as they crawled. They exited the room and finally stood.

The Duke and Duchess were hurrying toward them, flanked by guards.

"Are you all right?" the Duke asked.

"A little shaken," Lucien said, "but no wounds."

"I am so, so sorry," the Duke said to Livia, taking her hand and squeezing it tight as he bowed his head. "To be attacked in our home! It is most rude."

Rude? Lisa Livia wanted to scream, but she knew the Duke was sincere and not one who used hyperbole, even when the situation would make it normal, which confused her even further because, really, things were getting a bit nuts.

Vicente joined them. He had one hand pressed against his ear where the thin wire of the radio ran to the speaker. "They've found the sniper's position. Whoever it was is gone. The tracks go through the snow to the mountain path, where they disappear into an entrance in the Labyrinth. We're dispatching a helicopter to take the upper fork and cordoning off the bottom but, as you know, there are many ways one can go once in the Labyrinth."

"Fausto," the Duchess said, managing to make the name into a profanity, as only she could do. "He's behind this."

Vicente held up a hand as his earpiece crackled with information. From the look on his face, Lisa Livia tensed, worried someone had died.

Vicente rogered the message, then turned to them. "My Graces. A package was left by the sniper. It is addressed to the Duchess. They are bringing it back. We will check it for traps. I believe the firing was to get our attention to find the box."

"Oh, they have my attention," the Duchess swore. "They most certainly have it."

THE DOG'S BALLS looked like the kind of place where dive bars went to die. It wasn't one of those chic places that pretended to bad; it *was* bad. The exterior was sagging wood covered by sad coats of peeling paint on top of peeling paint. Phoebe figured the paint was the only thing keeping the walls standing. The dirty windows were blacked out, giving no hint of what was inside. They were covered with faded, torn posters of bands that were long disbanded appearing sometime in the past. There were none projected for the future. The name of the bar was etched in a wood plank above the door, so small that it couldn't be read unless one was inside the danger zone. Someone had to know where they were going to find this place although why they would go to that effort, Phoebe had no idea.

"Really not trying to attract customers, are they?" Phoebe said while Sam illegally parked in the loading space out front. The cars and trucks that lined the streets included not a single electric vehicle and none younger than a few years. There was one on cinder blocks, the wheels missing, the hood open and the engine gone.

Who the hell boosted an engine? Phoebe wondered.

"It is what it is," Sam said, enigmatic as usual. "Often there's more to something than meets the eye."

At least there wasn't a cluster of Harley's in the garbage strewn empty lot on the side, Phoebe thought. Her last encounter with bikers at the militia camp in Montana hadn't ended well.

"You coming?" she asked.

"I'm the Cleaner," Sam said. "You're the Operative." He said both the titles with an emphasis that capitalized the first letter. "Hannah said for you to come here. Not me."

"Geez," Phoebe muttered, not for the first time questioning her decision to bring in Sam. Then again, he'd saved her life in Montana after her encounter with the bikers/militia using his initiative. And more recently with Chatty Kathy. She imagined he was full of surprises.

Phoebe made sure her wakizashi was ready for a clean draw on her back. A round in the chamber of her silenced pistol and the safety off. Shane's dagger was in a sheath on her right side. Somehow, she'd forgotten to give it back to him after the battle of Two Rivers and he hadn't asked. She figured he wouldn't need it in retirement. At least she was properly dressed for this place, she thought, as she got out of the van in her black body suit and loose red jacket fully armed. She had a pair of flash bang grenades secreted in the interior pockets and she considered whether it might be best to lead with those like they had entered hot spots in the Ranger Battalion. But that wasn't a good way to make friends.

It was just past noon and she wondered if the joint was open. She pushed on the door and it gave way, so she was in luck. Or perhaps not, she thought as she went in.

It was dimly lit by a light from a beer company hanging over a pool table that Phoebe could tell wasn't level in the corner to the right. There was also indirect lighting above a long mahogany bar directly ahead. It smelled of spilled beer, a lot of smoking, and a hint of despair. There was a scattering of empty tables sprawled across the creaking wooden floor. All empty, which was slightly surprising since this seemed a place that would draw barflies at all hours.

That didn't mean the place was unoccupied.

Phoebe's immediate attention was drawn to a hulking man sitting cockeyed in a wheelchair to the left. One shoulder was a couple of inches lower than the other. He was dressed in jeans and a t-shirt commemorating a Grateful Dead concert. One side of his face was caved in and Phoebe wondered what could have caused such damage. The eye socket on that side was empty with metal glittering around the partial rebuild. The eye in the other one was staring at her. His wheelchair was in front of a Ms. Pac-Man video game.

"We're closed," he croaked, shattering Phoebe's sense of luck, but not her purpose.

"I'm here to meet someone," she said.

"Who?"

Good question, Phoebe thought as she scanned the rest of the place. There was no bartender. The only other occupant was someone hunched over an iPad at the end of the bar wearing a dark hoodie. The glow from the screen disappeared into the shadow of the hood. In this dimness Phoebe couldn't make out any details or even the sex of the person.

The distinct sound of the hammers of a double-barreled shotgun being pulled back drew Phoebe's attention to the man in the wheelchair. She chided herself for not having spotted the sheath on the far side of the chair from which he'd pulled the weapon. The barrel had been cut so short she could see the tips of the shells. That meant the spread would be wide and unavoidable at this range. Perhaps not fatal, but it would hurt and probably incapacitate. The fatal could come after the first blast.

"Hannah sent me," Phoebe tried.

The shotgun wavered in the man's shaking hand but remained in the general vicinity to blast her.

"Fuck it," Phoebe finally said. "I don't need this." She turned for the door.

A woman's raspy voice that sounded like liquor mixed with cigarettes layered on top of hard living, emanated from the figure at the end of the bar. "What do you need?"

Help, Phoebe thought but couldn't say. "Information." She thought it curious the woman said 'need' rather than want, but it made sense that one only came here when they were out of other options.

"This look like Google?" the woman asked, putting the iPad down on the bar. She beckoned Phoebe to come with a gnarled hand.

As Phoebe walked forward, she noted that the guy in the wheelchair kept the shotgun aimed at her. But as she put distance from the gun, she felt a bit more secure. The damage would be less. She adjusted her route to put the woman in the arc of fire, to share the pain.

Phoebe stopped at the mahogany bar with a stool separating them. Phoebe was aware of movement. The wheelchair guy had shifted position so his angle of fire wouldn't include the woman, but he didn't close the distance. His hand was still shaky.

The woman pulled the hoodie down, revealing a face that looked like someone had taken tin foil, wrapped it around a mannequin's face, beat on it, and then left it all crumpled and battered. Her hair was short and white and stood straight up as if afraid of the mind beneath it. Her eyes were shadowed under scarred brows. She was a shapeless lump in the bulky grey hoodie and black sweatpants. Her age was, as best Phoebe could tell, older than dirt.

The woman reached across the bar and retrieved a bottle of indeterminate content and two shot glasses. She cleaned them with the drooping sleeve of the hoodie, then poured two fingers worth of a dark liquid in each. She expertly slid one down the bar to come to a halt directly in front of Phoebe.

Phoebe eyed the glass and remembered her training at the Farm where they'd been told to assimilate into the culture of whatever country they were in. She was in barfly territory here so she picked up the glass and held it, waiting to see if there was going to be a toast, a blast from the shotgun, or just early afternoon boozing.

She glanced at the iPad and saw a live feed of two children playing in a yard. The woman grabbed the device and turned it upside down.

"What did Hannah tell you?" the woman asked.

"Just to come here. Other than that, she was vague."

The woman chuckled, which sounded like an old jigsaw whose motor was on its last legs and wasn't drawing enough power to begin with.

"Hannah, vague? That fucking cunt. She's only vague when she wants to be. Otherwise, she's pretty fucking direct." With her other hand the woman pointed a finger gun at her head and pulled the trigger.

Phoebe had never met Hannah, so she withheld judgment.

The woman held up the glass. "To that fucking cunt, Hannah." She downed it.

I don't think she likes Hannah, Phoebe thought.

Phoebe decided fast was best and did the same, feeling the burning as hard liquor made its passage quickly through her mouth, down her throat, to explode in her empty stomach. She should have grabbed a snack or two at the truck stop, she realized. Score a point for Sam.

The woman threw the shot glass across the room. It smashed into brick above a large, soot covered fireplace, the shards falling in front of it. To join a pile of similar glass.

Phoebe debated following suit, but put the glass down on the bar.

"You don't work for Hannah," the woman finally said.

"How do you know that?" Phoebe asked.

"I'd already be dead if you did. Her people don't announce themselves. Or, more likely, you'd be dead. I don't die easy since I'm still here. Who *do* you work for?"

"The Organization."

"Wilson."

"He's dead."

"Good. Best thing I've heard today. Another fucking cunt. May he rot in Hades." The woman gestured and the man in the wheelchair gently lowered the hammers of the shotgun and rolled back to his spot near the door and faced the video game. The machine beeped and buzzed as he restarted it. Phoebe frowned as she noted there were a couple of video feeds just below the Ms. Pac-Man screen. One of them showed Sam's van parked in front. Another the alley behind the bar.

"Pike twitches sometimes," Bert said, "and I wouldn't want to get blood all over the bar."

"That would be uncouth," Phoebe agreed. "And messy."

"Name?"

"Phoebe."

"I'm Bert."

"Short for Bertha?" Phoebe asked.

"No."

"Roberta?"

"No."

"Bertrand?"

"No."

Phoebe awaited elucidation but none was forthcoming. She tried a different direction. "What's with the name of the bar?"

"It's a short story," Bert said, but that was it.

Phoebe was regretting coming here as much as requesting Sam.

"You've got some kind of fucking sword on your back," Bert said, "and a pistol inside your coat. Knife on your hip. Probably some other toys. You really an operative for the organization?" She didn't capitalize the O.

"Yes."

"If Wilson is out, who is running it?"

"Carpenter."

"Who the fuck is he?"

"He was a Cleaner and got promoted to replace Wilson."

"Since when does a Cleaner become head of the Organization?" She shook her head. "Kids these days. Then again, there's Hannah. Who'd have figured her to head the Cellar?"

Phoebe had no idea what she meant by that.

"What did you do before the Organization?" Bert asked. "They recruit you off the streets like Nero picked Hannah?"

Phoebe had no idea who Nero was or how he'd plucked Hannah off the streets. "I was in the Army."

"Doing?"

"Ranger Battalion."

"The times they are-a-changing," Bert said. "How did the manly men Rangers take that in between fucking goats?"

"They figured I could die just as easily as them."

"Good figuring." Bert allowed. "And true. Blood is blood. Sitrep?"

"Excuse me?" Phoebe said.

"You're ex-military," Bert said. "You know what that means. Situation report. You came here for a reason. You said information. I can't give you any if I don't know what it's reference."

Since Phoebe wasn't sure who Bert was, or why Hannah had sent her here, she hesitated. For all she knew, telling Bert what was going on with Fromm and the encryption program, might earn her a blast in the back from Pike's shotgun. It wouldn't be the first time someone carried their own execution order to the executioner.

Before she could make up her mind, Pike called out: "Inbound. Front."

Bert reached across the bar and retrieved a submachinegun, aiming at the door.

A blast of afternoon sun shot across the room as the door opened. Sam was silhouetted in the frame. Pike had the shotgun leveled at him and it would be an easy shot, despite the uncertainty of the aim.

Phoebe jumped back from the seat, drawing the wakizashi, knowing she could sever Bert's hand from the gun before she fired, but she wouldn't be able to get to Pike in time.

"Hold it right there," Bert said.

"Fuck you, Bert," Sam said idly, which caused Phoebe to delay the hand guillotine. She also noted that her Cleaner wasn't wielding a weapon.

Sam walked in, pausing to nod at the man in the wheelchair.

"Pike."

"Sam," Pike acknowledged, sheathing the shotgun.

"You're with him?" Bert asked Phoebe as Sam approached. She lowered the submachinegun.

"He's with me," Phoebe corrected. "He's my Cleaner."

Bert laughed, which turned into a bout of coughing that took her a moment to recover from. "That's a hoot. Sam a cleaner working for itty-bitty you." Once more she didn't capitalize. "Put the pig-sticker away," she said to Phoebe. "You're making me nervous." She turned to Sam. "I thought you were dead."

"Ditto," Sam said.

"Us old coots are hard to kill," Bert said.

"Or all the people who would want us dead are dead themselves. Not many of us left."

"I should kill you," Bert said.

"Why?" Sam asked.

"Any number of reasons," Bert said. "You really need me to pick one?"

Sam shrugged. "All in the past."

"Is it?" Bert asked. "Sometimes the past catches up to us."

"Sometimes," Sam agreed.

"What has the world come to when Sam the Matador cleans up little girl's messes?" Bert marveled as she put the gun back behind the bar.

"I'm not—" Phoebe began but the sidelong glance Bert gave her stopped the protest.

"I never liked that sobriquet," Sam said to Bert.

She laughed. "Fancy words, old man. I thought you were retired?"

"I thought you heard I was dead."

"I hear a lot," Bert said. "Didn't say I believed it. I heard both. I thought retirement the more likely of the two. You're hard to kill. I can attest to that."

"I un-retired." Sam took the barstool between Phoebe and Bert.

"Missed the action?" Bert asked.

"No," Sam replied. He changed the subject. "Why don't you take Pike to a plastic surgeon?" he asked Bert.

"He's handicapped," Bert said. "It would be like putting lipstick on a goat. That doesn't stop it from being a goat. He's had the best help possible and is as good as he's going to get."

"I can hear you," Pike called out amiably. "Nothing wrong with my hearing. I'm okay. Sam. It is what it is. I was done with the surg-eries. You can only go under the knife so many times. I've got as much working as is gonna work. Besides--" he pointed at his head—"the noggin is falling apart faster than the body. I want to enjoy what little awareness I got left without pain."

"All right, Pike," Sam said. "I understand. Meg felt the same after so much treatment."

Phoebe felt like she was attending the 40th high school reunion of a school she hadn't attended and with a generation ahead of her and she'd been a nerd and they were the cool kids, now all grown up. Pike went back to Ms. Pac-Man and the security feeds.

Bert poured herself another shot, then reached across the bar and retrieved a water bottle which she tossed past Phoebe to Sam. He caught it and unscrewed the top. He tipped the bottle at her and they both drank, leaving Phoebe so far out of the loop she was in orbit.

This time Bert slammed the shot glass down on the bar. "So. Sam. Why are you with this?" she indicated Phoebe.

"She told you. I'm her Cleaner."

"Sure," Bert said. "She any good?"

Sam rubbed his beard. "We did one op. I had to find her when her motorcycle went off the road because one of her targets sabotaged it. Just met her finishing another op and had to take out someone trying to kill her as she was exfiltrating the target zone."

"That's not a ringing endorsement," Bert said.

Phoebe stiffened but there was nothing she could say. He was factual on both counts.

"She shows promise," Sam allowed. "She's young. We were young once, too."

"Are you going to break into song?" Bert asked.

"Hannah sent her here," Sam said.

"Yeah, she told me. That fucking cunt. Nothing good can come out of anything when she's involved."

"She has her reasons," Sam said.

"And they are?" Bert asked.

"I didn't speak with her," Sam replied. He nodded at Phoebe. "She's the Operator."

Bert grumbled something inaudible, or she was clearing her throat, or she had indigestion, then she glared at Phoebe. "Well? Out with it, young miss. What's going on?"

Phoebe shot a look at Sam but he didn't react. She proceeded to do a quick summary of recent events starting with trying to intercept the arms shipment in Montana between the militia and Drusilla/Guillermo's contingent, through the showdown at Two Rivers, through Fromm's betrayal and abscondence with the latest top secret encryption program, the looming deadline and the debacle at the stateside Super-Max and the Wilson/Fromm betrayal.

Bert never interrupted nor showed any surprise or, for that matter, interest. When Phoebe was done, she focused on how it interacted with her: "Why didn't you come here before going to the prison? It was on your way."

Before Phoebe could answer, Bert held up her hand and answered her own question. "You thought it was a set-up by Hannah."

"That was a possibility," Phoebe said.

"I wouldn't spit on that cunt, never mind kill someone for her. I hope my language doesn't offend you, girl, but I'm old school and I call 'em as I've known 'em. Besides, what would you call a man that's the equivalent? A dick. Not quite the same punch as cunt. So, fuck your sensibilities. Hannah would cut her own heart out if she ordered it. Coldest bitch I've ever had the displeasure to meet."

Sam spoke up. "But she's necessary."

Bert made the grumbling noise. "Yeah. Somebody's got to be the asshole who keeps the other assholes in line. And it's not like you can stop them by chiding them gently." Bert rolled her head on her heavy shoulders, producing a few cracking noises. "You killed this guy in armor with a dagger?"

Phoebe nodded.

"There's hope for you yet," Bert allowed. "You didn't know about that, did you?" she asked Sam.

"I did not," Sam confirmed.

An uneasy silence permeated the bar, other than the noise from Ms. Pac-Man gobbling up dots.

Sam broke it. "Still checking on the kid?" He asked, indicating the iPad.

Bert face was transformed as she smiled, years and hard living sloughing off for a moment. "Kid? Hell, there are grandkids now."

"Grandkids?" Sam said.

"Yeah," Bert snapped. "Two. Your daughter?"

"Still saving the trees."

"She have a man? Maybe grandkids on the horizon?"

Sam shook his head. "She says trees are better than any man she's met."

"She has a valid point based on the present company," Bert said.

Phoebe shifted on the uncomfortable bar stool. They were far off topic, but she was in deep water, uncertain how to proceed.

Sam stepped into the breach. "What do you think about finding Fromm?" he asked Bert.

"Let's back up," Bert said. "You said it was Chatty Kathy who tried to kill you this morning. Did she say anything, given she has, had, a penchant for that?"

Phoebe hadn't given a detailed blow-by-blow description of the encounter. "She said Fromm wanted me to know I was going to die. She also mentioned something called the Guild."

That brought a response. "Those fuckers," Bert said. She looked across at Sam. "Lead with the headline, please."

Sam shrugged. "I'm just the Cleaner."

"You're the same asshole you always were," Bert muttered.

"You've heard of this Guild?" Phoebe asked.

"They tried to recruit me," Bert said. She nodded at Sam. "Didn't they reach out to you, also?"

"Sure."

Phoebe put her head down on the bar for a moment. "Fuck me to tears."

CARPENTER LOOKED up as an analyst knocked on the open vault door.

"Yes?"

"Support finished the autopsy on the body from the hospital." The analyst deposited a folder on the desk and quickly departed.

Carpenter sensed the angst in the person; it was permeating the Organization like a dank mist rising up from the bottom floor. The rumor of the Cellar was bubbling enough fear to begin to degrade what was left of operations. No one was allowed in or out, at least officially, so it was adding to the stress.

Carpenter knew he needed to address it in some way, but was uncertain how to proceed. The ghost on his shoulder had been certain he would fail from the moment he'd accept the position in charge of the Organization and now was dancing a happy cha-cha as that seemed to be happening in real time.

Carpenter had almost forgotten about the elevator incident. He flipped open the report which was depressingly thin. Without access to the NSA link, the coroner had not been able to submit for a DNA match so it was still a John Doe. There were old scars, consistent with someone who'd made a living in a violent profession, but that wasn't a surprise. The amputated foot matched, of course. Phoebe's cut had been clean given the sharpness of her wakizashi and someone had stopped the bleeding by the expedient method of cauterizing the stump.

Carpenter imagined that hadn't been fun.

There was something that was odd. Very odd. The man had two un-natural elements in his blood: a poison and the antidote for the poison. The coroner hadn't been sure what to make of it as it made no sense. This was besides the poison that had been in a false tooth which had killed him. Carpenter pondered it for a few moments, then moved on.

There was only one other thing of interest. A mark behind the right ear. A small scar that the coroner said wasn't from an accident but rather a brand. It was in the shape of a tiny fish hook.

Carpenter had not seen the like before, nor had the coroner. And Carpenter didn't have access to the intelligence network that might give him an answer.

He tossed the file to the side. His secure phone buzzed and he saw the ID: Hannah.

"Carpenter," he answered.

"Bidding is up to a quarter billion dollars," Hannah said without asking how his day was going. "Status of your operative?"

"She checked the Hacker at the prison but got nothing useful other than Fromm and Wilson did the deal."

"Who was in charge? Wilson or Fromm?"

"Given Fromm is still breathing," Carpenter said, "I'd say it was Fromm."

"I agree."

"Phoebe was ambushed leaving but that was handled by the Cleaner and—"

"Who ambushed her?"

"A woman. Phoebe's Cleaner said she was called Chatty Kathy."

"Who is the Cleaner?"

Carpenter was surprised at the question regarding a minor detail. "Sam. He's from the Montana field office and—"

Hannah interrupted once more. "Sam the Matador." She chuckled, which Carpenter had not heard before. It made her seem almost human. As human as the head of a deadly unit can sound over a secure, encrypted line. "Good."

Carpenter had never heard that title for Sam. He'd always been Sam the Cleaner. As he'd been Carpenter the Cleaner for years. *Things change*, Carpenter thought.

"Anyway—" Carpenter began.

"Back up. Sam said the woman's name was Chatty Kathy? Her status?"

"Sam killed her."

"Good," Hannah said. "Excellent."

Carpenter had a feeling Hannah was referring to something more than just the killer being neutralized. He continued. "Phoebe is going to that bar, *The Dog's Balls*."

"That will be interesting given the latest developments," Hannah said. "She didn't go there first."

It wasn't a question but Carpenter answered anyway. "No, she didn't. She felt she could handle the Hacker by herself."

"But she couldn't," Hannah pointed out. "Sam had to save her. She didn't go to the bar because she thought I was setting her up."

Again, not a question and this time Carpenter didn't say anything.

Hannah changed the subject. "The situation in Andova isn't settled." Then she proved she wasn't changing the subject. "Fromm is involved with that."

To prove he wasn't completely out to lunch, Carpenter said: "He needs a favorable faction in Andova in order to move the bid once it closes."

"Fromm is bigger than you think," Hannah said. "This defection wasn't a whim on his part."

"He told us he'd been planning for decades."

"He's done more than just plan," Hannah said. "We'd been looking at Wilson for a while before Shane terminated him. But now, we know we were misguided."

"Wilson was corrupt," Carpenter said, defending Shane's decision to take his former boss out.

"Oh, yes," Hannah agreed. "In league with the mafia. But I fear Fromm used him as a smoke screen."

The ghost leapt in delight as Carpenter realized what she meant. "Misdirection. Fromm leaked information about Wilson in order to hide his own actions."

"Correct," Hannah said, in almost the same tone Carpenter's third grade teacher had rewarded his perfect assignments; a counterpoint to his father's constant disapproval. Carpenter sometimes wondered where he would have ended up without the positive feedback from a handful of teachers. Given he was here, running the Organization, it probably wouldn't have been a good place. Then again, it suddenly occurred to him via a whisper from the ghost: was *this* a good place?

Hannah continued. "Don't get tunnel-vision. Orion is certainly important and we don't want it on the open market, but keep your eyes open for more."

This echoed what Carpenter had thought were Fromm's boasts. "What more?"

"I wouldn't tell you to keep your eyes open if I could see it."

"We've under-estimated Fromm for a long time," Carpenter admitted. "Especially since that isn't even his real name."

"How do you know that?"

"He said so," Carpenter said. "He might have been boasting, but at this point I don't think he says anything without something behind it and some goal in the future."

"Any idea who he really was?"

"Hard to figure that out with us being locked down."

"I don't like complainers."

The ghost on his shoulder gave a standing ovation.

Hannah finished with: "The clock is ticking. Get Fromm. You've been in charge long enough to have figured out you had a problem. This is on you."

The line went dead and Carpenter sat alone with the dawning realization that he was out of his depth. Just as his father's ghost had predicted. Failure, which had never been an option, was now distinctly on the table.

They gathered at the round table, with the Duke and Duchess taking the same seats. Lisa Livia and Lucien sat across from them. On one side between them was Janna and the other, Vicente. There was a black metal box, 10 inches square, in front of him.

"We've x-rayed it and checked for traps," Vicente said. "It's clean."

"Open it," the Duchess commanded.

Vicente flipped a latch on one side and pivoted the lid up. He stared at the contents in silence for a few seconds.

"Well?" the Duchess demanded.

In response, Vicente carried the box around the table to her. Lisa Livia couldn't read Vicente's face; he'd make a hell of a poker player. Lisa Livia reached for the mug of coffee, realized her hand was shaking, so she quickly put it to her lip, took a sip, and put it down and kept her fingers tight around it. She kept playing over the recent event in the library in her mind. In less than twenty-four hours her life had been threatened twice while with Lucien. It was enough to make any woman have second thoughts, no pun intended, but it was more than that. After her daughter's wedding, Lisa Livia had talked with Agnes about the lousy choices both of them had made in men. Agnes told her that she'd learned one thing after meeting Shane: if you want to know who someone truly is, see them in a dire crisis. People can pretend in normal circumstances, but in a crisis, the true character shown through.

Lisa Livia knew the move by Lucien to protect her at the window had been instinctual on his part. That was not something you could think through that fast. Her ex would have held her still so the sniper wouldn't miss with the second shot. She realized Lucien would put her first. Always. At the cost of his life if need be. There wasn't much more you could ask of someone. On the flip side, being at his side meant that he might well *have to* sacrifice his for hers. Nothing was ever perfect.

Lisa Livia watched as the Duchess stared into the box. She would not have fared so well at the card table. The Duchess gasped as she saw the contents which was the equivalent of Mount Vesuvius erupting.

Lisa Livia half-expected a dead fish, Godfather style, or perhaps a body part as the Duchess lifted out the contents. She wasn't far off in the latter guess, but wrong about the body. It was a body part, but from the Statue of Our Lady of the Saint Ingrid, the patron saint of Andova. The hand that had been raised to protect a young boy. The history behind the statue was a long story and Lisa Livia only had the short version from the Duchess.

"Sacrilege," the Duchess exclaimed holding up the hand in a subconscious echo of its place on the missing statue.

While she displayed the severed hand, the Duke retrieved a note taped to a cell phone from the box. He read the note, glanced at Lisa Livia, who wondered why he'd glanced at her, then handed the piece of paper to the Duchess. She read it and turned her gaze to Lisa Livia, which increased her wonder exponentially and caused her to have flashbacks to times when her mother would come home late at night from a rendezvous with who-know-who and caught her still up. The Duchess carefully put the severed hand down.

"What?" Lisa Livia whispered to Lucien. "What did I do?"

"I don't know," Lucien replied. "It will be all right."

Doubtful, Lisa Livia thought.

The Duchess shook the letter as if it were damning evidence at a murder trial. "Whoever has the rest of the statue, is offering to exchange it to us for a transfer of twenty million dollars in cryptocurrency. To ensure that the exchange is secure, they want the code for the crypto on a thumb drive hand-delivered. By Lisa Livia Fortunato."

"Hold on," Lisa Livia said. "How did I get sucked into this?"

No one gave a reply, but simply by looking around the table, Lisa Livia knew the answer was obvious. She was here.

"The Statue is worth far more than twenty million," the Duke observed.

"Yes," the Duchess agreed, "but the jewels in the crown can be tracked. It's priceless intact." She looked down at the box. "The hand can be crafted back on. But to think Fausto would damage the statue like this! Sacrilege."

"Excuse me," Lisa Livia said, "but what the fuck? Why is my name on the note? How the hell am I going to deliver twenty million dollars?"

The Duchess picked up the note. "A thumb drive with the singular link to the crypto. Delivered in the Labyrinth in four hours."

"'The Labyrinth'?" Lisa Livia repeated, remembering that Vicente had mentioned that earlier. She didn't like the sound of that. "What's the Labyrinth?"

"A network of mines in the mountain," Lucien said, which wasn't reassuring. "They've been closed for years. Off limits for safety reasons."

"Safety reasons? Oh, great. But, again. Why me?"

The Duke and Duchess exchanged a glance which indicated neither had a clue.

Vicente made a stab at it. "You were in Paris with Lucien. The assassin found you there, so whoever sent him must have known that the two of you were there."

"And?" Livia asked. "You were there too."

No one had an answer.

"This is Fausto's work," the Duchess said. "He was always unstable."

"I thought all you royalty were rich?" Lisa Livia said.

The Duke cleared his throat. "We froze all Drusilla's assets when we returned home. That, in turn, means Fausto is, essentially, penniless."

"If we give in," Lucien pointed out, "we will be financing Fausto's efforts against us."

"If we don't get the statue back," the Duchess said, "Fausto can do something with it and blame us. That would be more damning than anything he can buy with twenty million."

"Except hiring a hitman," Lisa Livia said. "Hell, you can get someone to whack a guy in Jersey for a thousand bucks. Imagine what you can get for a million or so?"

"That ship has already sailed," the Duchess said. "Twice."

"Third time is the charm," Lisa Livia replied.

"What is the satellite phone for?" Lucien asked.

"The note says it's to be turned on once Lisa Livia starts up the gorge for the main entrance to the Labyrinth," the Duke said. "It's how she will get further instructions."

"I don't like it," Vicente stated the obvious. "If he's in the Labyrinth he's most likely using the Redoubt."

"You people got names for everything?" Lisa Livia asked.

"The Redoubt is an ancient system of caves," Vicente said. "Where our people went in times of grave danger."

"I thought you never had wars?" Lisa Livia noted.

"We haven't," Lucien answered "But that doesn't mean invading armies haven't passed through going one way or the other. The Redoubt's been sealed off for years, though."

Janna raised her hand, like a schoolkid in a teacher's meeting.

"Yes?" the Duchess snapped.

"The Field Marshall had work done by some foreign contractors in the Labyrinth and the Redoubt. From what I could discern they were building a sort of survival bunker, but with weapons systems."

"'Weapons systems'?" Lucien repeated.

Lisa Livia had a feeling Janna didn't mean spears and swords.

"A battery of remote-controlled surface to air missiles at the top of the Chimney," Janna said. "Old routes sealed with gates. Some other improvements."

"Great," Lisa Livia said. "A bit much, don't you think?"

"Why was I not informed?" the Duchess demanded, even though the answer was obvious to everyone. Thus, no one answered.

Lucien asked: "Are there plans we can use to find our way in there if we need to?"

Janna shook her head. "Not that I've seen. The Field Marshal kept it all very secret, saying it was a personal project for the Duke and Duchess and the royal family in case of extreme danger; a safe room so-to-speak and it must be kept secret. And the workers were foreign and have gone back to their countries."

"I wonder what other surprises have been done without us knowing?" the Duke mused.

"We must deal with the immediate issue," the Duchess said, indicating the severed hand.

"You don't have to do this," Lucien said. "I'll take the phone and talk to Fausto. Negotiate."

"It must be done now," the Duchess said, "or Fausto says he will destroy the statue and remove the jewels. Leave the pieces in a place where it can be tied to us."

Lisa Livia stood up. "If I'm gonna make the drop, I need warmer clothes. I came from the island and packed for South Carolina, not the Alps."

"The Pyrenees," the Duchess sniffed.

"Whatever."

"CHATTY KATHY WAS DEFINITELY WORKING for the Guild." Sam tossed a piece of flesh on the bar in response to Bert's announcement that the Guild had tried to recruit her and his echoing that. Phoebe realized it was what he'd carved off Chatty Kathy. There was a brand of a fishhook etched in the bloodied flesh.

Bert nodded. "That's their mark."

"What is the Guild?" Phoebe asked.

Bert looked at her, dark eyes under scarred eyebrows. "Seriously? What the fuck do you think since one of them tried to kill you? Take a leap of logic."

"Assassins?"

"No wonder you're an operator," Bert said, definitely making it a lower-case o.

"Be nice," Sam said, but without much teeth.

"And they tried to recruit both of you?"

"Yep," Bert said. "Hard as it is to believe looking at this frail old lady, I was once a bit tougher. And Sam? He wasn't always a cleaner."

Phoebe didn't have to stretch her imagination to picture Bert as a killer "Why would a member of this assassin's Guild come after me?"

"Nothing personal," Bert said. "There's only one reason. Money. Someone put a contract on you."

"Great," Phoebe said. "At least that's done with."

Bert looked at Sam, then at Phoebe. "I'm beginning to think the Organization has gone downhill. Chatty Kathy didn't take the contract. The Guild did. Once the Guild accepts a contract, it fulfills it, guaranteeing completion. That's why they charge top dollar. The word is that no one has ever survived a Guild contract."

"That's not good," Phoebe said.

"Nope," Bert said.

"How do I stop it?" Phoebe asked.

Bert and Sam once more exchanged glances.

"What?" Phoebe asked.

"You don't," Bert said. "You're a dead woman walking. The Guild will keep sending people after you until the contract is finished."

"How many people do they have?" Phoebe asked.

Bert shrugged. "No one knows."

"Who runs it?"

"No one knows."

"You said they tried to recruit you," Phoebe said. "Who did that? Can I talk to them?"

"No." Bert said it in a way that precluded discussion.

"Well," Phoebe said, "before the Guild kills me, I've got to find Fromm and get the encryption program back. Plus, he hurt a friend of mine, so there's payback coming."

"She's a spunky one, isn't she?" Bert said to Sam.

"She gets the job done," Sam said.

"I can hear you," Phoebe pointed out.

"At least now we know why Hannah is involved," Bert said.

"Why?" Phoebe asked.

"The Guild is made up of former operatives from the Organization, the alphabet soups, the military and various covert units. A bunch of former Special Operations from the military. They do have a good dental plan," Bert allowed. "But my teeth are fine."

Sam answered. "Hannah's mandate for the Cellar puts them in her bulls eye."

"Why doesn't she send her own people after them?"

"My guess? The Guild is too many and too powerful," Bert said. "The Cellar is designed to take down individual rogues, not a group. Plus, they might not have compromised national security yet with the jobs they've taken. That's an important part of her mandate to Sanction." She shook her head. "Well, fuck Hannah. This isn't my fight. I don't know why she sent you here. I've got nothing on this Fromm guy. And I'm not stupid enough to take on the Guild."

"You could ask around," Sam suggested. "A lot of people come through here. Maybe somebody heard something."

Phoebe was stuck on envisioning a lot of people coming through here.

"And pigs can fly if you throw them out of a plane," Bert said. "It's the landing that's the hard part. I don't need the trouble. I *am* retired and I'm not getting back in the game."

"Incoming bad," Pike yelled as he pulled the shotgun out of the sheath and pushed his chair back from Ms. Pac-Man. "One front, two back. Four seconds."

"Fuck," Bert cursed. "Back door." She scooted off the barstool with surprising alacrity and raced around the end of the bar.

Sam headed for Pike. "I've got front."

Phoebe vaulted over the bar, landing right behind Bert. She drew her wakizashi and pistol as Bert ripped the suppressed submachinegun off a magnet on the backside of the bar.

"You have left, I'll do right," Bert said.

The lights went out as the power was cut and the bar was in complete darkness, but a moment later the front and back doors blew inward at the same exact time, indicating excellent coordination. Small dark objects flew in and Phoebe ducked her head and squeezed her eyes shut, knowing what to expect. The flashbangs went off with bright flashes and loud concussions.

Phoebe opened her eyes to darkness that vanished as defensive spotlights on the ceiling flashed on, triggered by motion detectors.

They were aimed directly at both doors, unexpectedly blinding the assaulters who'd expected their targets to be the ones blinded. Both sides began firing at the same time.

Phoebe had the suppressed pistol aimed at the left of the two who came in the back door, firing twice, both bullets hitting. Next to her, Bert fired a pair of efficient, three-round bursts, taking down the other one, and adding three bullets to Phoebe's two on the left as he went down. Which Phoebe found slightly insulting on a professional level.

Ears ringing from the concussion, Phoebe distantly heard the blast of both barrels of Pike's shotgun. There were a few outbursts from other weapons and then a ringing silence. It was over in seconds. Two bodies lay in the back doorway. There was one splayed on the floor of the bar just inside the front door.

Phoebe noticed that Sam held a silenced pistol. He went to each body and added a confirmation shot into their heads. It was hard for Phoebe to hear anything above the ringing in her ears and she knew it would take several minutes. But she became aware of Sam shouting a curse.

"Damn it!"

Pike's misshapen head was slumped back in the wheelchair, his body lifeless.

Bert walked over and cradled Pike's head in her hands. "Oh, you poor thing."

She sounded like a human being to Phoebe for the first time.

Bert leaned forward and kissed Pike on the forehead. "No more pain, my friend. No more pain. You're not in a better place, but you aren't in a bad place anymore."

"Clearing perimeter," Phoebe announced. She turned away and went out the back, circling around to the front, searching for any support. There was a black van parked down the street. She checked it: empty except for several lockers in the back. There were no approaching sirens in response to the flash bangs, but this was the kind of neighborhood where people minded their own business. Those who'd heard the noise probably assumed it was a SWAT team on a warrant served or drug raid and wanted nothing to do with it.

She carefully went in the front door, calling out before she re-entered.

Pike's body was on the pool table, a tablecloth draped over it. Bert and Sam were standing next to it, silent. The bodies of the three intruders lay where they died.

Phoebe knelt next to the body by the front door and turned the head. "He's Guild."

"They all are," Sam said.

"I'm sorry," Phoebe said to Bert.

"You didn't kill him," Bert said.

"They came here for me," Phoebe said. "If I hadn't—"

Bert held up a hand. "It is what it is. If you haven't figured that out by now, you will. Life is full of variables and chance. At least Pike went down fighting."

"What happened to him?" Phoebe asked as she joined them next to the body. "I mean. Before."

"Ran out of thread while fast-roping out of a chopper and fell sixty feet with full gear," Bert said. "Because the chicken-shit pilot panicked and started gaining altitude when someone started shooting."

Phoebe had done numerous fast-ropes. You grabbed a thick rope with both arms and slid down. There was no way to stop once you started. When the rope ended, that was it.

Bert wasn't done. "In a country no one gives a shit about any more, except the people living there. For a cause no one gives a shit about any more. Except for those who loved the dead and those, like Pike, who would never be the same after. He was one of the best I ever worked with. It wasn't just his body. He split his fucking helmet when he hit. His brain was fucked and getting worse. TBI or whatever acronym they want to use now. We just called it fucked brain. No cure and the diagnosis was downhill."

"He's not in a better place," Sam said, echoing her earlier words, "but at least he's not in the bad place anymore."

Bert looked at Phoebe over the body. "This was a fuck up."

"I—" Phoebe barely managed to get that out before Bert shushed her.

"Listen up, young lady. If anyone is responsible, it's Hannah. She sent you here to get me involved. I told you she's a cold cunt, but she's also brilliant. She plays people and maneuvers them to get what she wants. The Guild hitting this bar was their mistake. I don't recognize any of these—" she indicated the bodies. "Maybe they didn't know about this place and me. They followed you. But—"

Phoebe dared to interrupt. "How could they have followed me? Sam did switchbacks on the way. We weren't tailed."

Bert looked at Sam and he nodded at Bert.

"What?" Phoebe said.

"You're chipped," Sam said. "Remember in Montana when you went off the road on the motorcycle? How do you think I knew?"

"You said you saw the tracks," Phoebe said, but as she did, she realized it had been pretty coincidental that he'd come after her and been able to find her. "Who the fuck chipped me?" Phoebe demanded. "When?" She started patting her body in a near panic. "Where?"

"Not in you," Sam said. "On you."

Bert went behind the bar and returned with a handheld scanner. She ran it over Phoebe and it alerted on the handle of her wakizashi.

Phoebe pulled the sword out and unscrewed the pommel. The small bug was inside. "How the hell did that get in there?"

"The Organization," Sam said. "It's standard. That's the one piece of gear you always carry on ops, so that's where they put it. The frequency is classified, though."

"Then how did the Guild know the frequency?" Phoebe demanded, but knew the answer right away. "Fromm."

Sam nodded as he examined the device. "Range is about two klicks. I'd say that Chatty Kathy had backup and they tracked us while staying out of sight. Hell, that tracker can be picked up by cell phone towers and the signal relayed to those who have the right freq to get them in the right area. Like Apple Air Tag."

"Great," Phoebe said.

Sam disconnected the tiny battery and pocketed it.

"Smash it," Phoebe suggested.

"It might be useful later," Sam said.

"If I take out Fromm, does that cancel the contract?" Phoebe asked.

"There's only one way to cancel a contract and find Fromm," Sam said.

"And that is?" Phoebe asked.

"Taking out the Guild," Sam answered, but he was looking at Bert.

"Fuck," Bert muttered. "Fuck, fuck, fuck, fuck."

"Fuck," Sam agreed.

Bert sighed. "We're going to need bigger guns."

Sam walked behind the bar and grabbed a bottle and three shot glasses. He splashed liquor in each. Phoebe and Bert joined him.

"You sure?" Bert asked Sam, indicating his shot glass.

"It's war," Sam said. "I'm sure." He lifted his glass. "To Pike. May the gates of Valhalla be wide open for him. And the gates of hell for our enemies."

They downed the shots, then Bert threw her glass against the brick above the fireplace. Sam followed suit, and then Phoebe.

WORDS OF WISDOM #5

Shane's Words of Wisdom #5
Pain is weakness leaving the body.
Shane's Addendum: As long as it's someone else.
That's a phrase I heard in many training schools and in various units
I served in. Sounds great and I'm a big believer in it as long as the
person in pain is someone I don't like. Otherwise? Pain is pain.

Phoebe's Observations #5:

Every woman knows pain in a way a man will never experience it.
Phoebe's Addendum: Get used to it.
It's lifelong.

5

F romm checked the latest bid and was pleased that it matched his computed projections to within two-point-seven million. For many people that was a lot of money but when one was talking about a quarter billion dollars it was less than one percent, which was well within his computed margin of error. Again, most people would have focused on the total amount and how rich it might make them, but being right was more important to Fromm.

He scanned the various screens checking on his schemes. All were proceeding well. Except, of course, for Phoebe. Another failure by the Guild. Damn her and Sam the Cleaner. This was the second time she'd escaped death. Despite the fact it aligned with his prediction, this was one area where he'd hoped his data was off. Of course, thinking about Phoebe, made him think of Louise.

Fromm typed a command into his computer and the view from the camera mounted in the top corner of his old office showed her hard at work. Typing away with one hand and doing that unique point, blink and click with the eyeglasses. It was mesmerizing and Fromm had spent many hours surreptitiously watching her old work station from the same desk she was sitting at now.

He froze as Louise turned in the seat, took the glasses off, and stared directly at the camera.

"Enjoying yourself, Fromm?" she asked.

She can't see me, Fromm thought.

"Phoebe's coming for you," Louise said. "You can't stop her. She's beaten you at every turn. And your math is wrong."

"It's never wrong," Fromm muttered. "Never." He belatedly checked to make sure the microphone was turned off.

"I've been onto you for a while," Louise said. "Well before you got wise to it. That's a mistake. How many others have you made? Because once I realized something was wrong, I began to hack into *your* stuff, Fromm. I'll admit I didn't know the depth of your betrayal, but I did pick up that you were doing some shady stuff. So, I played with your data. Just a little bit. A tiny nudge here and there. Not enough that you would notice, at least until that last day when you finally woke up. Just think, how much of what you have planned has a kernel of wrong data in it? And how much can that small deviation expand over time? You're doomed, Fromm."

"What are you doing?"

Lilith's voice startled Fromm who instinctively hit a key, replacing the image of Louise with a spreadsheet and cutting off the feed.

Fromm turned in his chair. Lilith glowed a few feet behind him, arms crossed on her chest, a scowl on her face. "You were watching *her*, weren't you? Talking to *her*."

Fromm was thrilled with the emphasis on her, indicating the AI was mimicking human speech via emotion with greater accuracy to specific triggers.

"It's work," Fromm said.

"Ha!"

That too, was new. An expression of derision. Fromm's excitement was growing.

Lilith wagged a finger at him. "Young man, don't you—"

She didn't finish as Fromm hit the kill button. Lilith had obviously accessed his foster mothers' database and that would not do at all. He'd only had so many female personalities that he had experienced to do the basic programming and he now knew he'd made a mistake by using the memories of his various foster mothers.

If only Louise had not turned on him. He would have had time to gather data in a very different setting from that of work. She'd misconstrued his invite. It hadn't been about sex. At least that was the lie he consciously told himself, while his lecherous spying wrote another story. He'd wanted more data to input. What was confusing to Fromm, though, was the messages Louise had sent him with her own words and actions. She'd wanted it. Why had she turned on him at the last moment?

And then she'd gotten that little bitch Phoebe involved. Wilson had called him in after Phoebe went to him. Not to berate him, but to tell him to be more discrete. They'd shared a laugh and Wilson had made a few inappropriate comments about both Phoebe and Louise. Fromm had chuckled when Wilson did, assuming those were the correct moments, although he had little experience in such 'men being men' moments.

Fromm was glad Wilson was dead. He'd been a useful tool, but stupid.

Louise and Phoebe would pay. Both of them.

One of the monitors buzzed and Fromm rolled his chair over to it. It was the dashcam from the Guild hit squad that had been tracking Phoebe's transmitter. It showed Phoebe walking toward the van on a decrepit street. Fromm checked the GPS data and located it in a northern Virginia suburb. Phoebe came to the windshield then disappeared from sight for a moment. She reappeared heading away.

Where was the hit squad? Fromm wondered as he watched Phoebe go into a shabby building down the street.

Fromm waited, but there was no sign of the hit squad or Phoebe.

Fromm got up and walked over to Phoebe's whiteboard. He crossed through the next node. He took comfort from the red on the connector to the next node.

Phoebe was going to hit the median.

Fromm relished the thought.

Forgotten in his anticipation was to question how Lilith had turned her hologram on.

Lisa Livia felt ready for the Eiger, outfitted in heavy boots, warm pants, a beautiful, thick jacket and a wool cap on her head. "Where is this place? On top of the mountain?" she asked Lucien, who wore similar clothes.

"The Redoubt is," Lucien said, pointing out the window at the peak high above. "The entrance we're going to is high but below the peak," Lucien said. He was staring at her now in a way that made Lisa Livia a little uncomfortable.

"What?" she finally said.

Lucien broke out of his fugue state. "I'm so sorry. It's just that . . . I haven't seen that jacket in a long time."

Lisa Livia swallowed hard. "These were your wife's?"

"Just the coat," he said.

Lisa Livia started to unzip the heavy coat, but Lucien stayed her hand. "No. She'd want you to wear it. When I deployed to Africa, we discussed the possibility of my not coming back. It was a remote possibility but Zara always thought ahead. Of course, she made us talk about it both ways. What if she wasn't there when I got back." Lucien paused and took a deep breath. "I always wonder if she sensed something. She was strange like that. She said if anything happened to either of us, our priority was Jean-Paul. And then we must move on. Have full lives. Grieve but not obsess."

"I understand," Lisa Livia said. "But I'd rather wear another coat, if it's all the same."

Lucien nodded. "Certainly. I'll have someone meet us with one at the truck." He made a quick call on his cell phone.

"Let's go," Lisa Livia said. "Tell me about this Labyrinth."

"There's a long narrow gorge we have to drive up. It used to have a single-track narrow gauge rail line, but once the mine was closed, that was ripped out. The road itself has been closed."

"Why?"

"Too dangerous," Lucien said. "The road is as wide as what was needed for the narrow-gauge train that brought the silver out of the mountains."

"Great."

"In the early days, the silver was carried out on people's back," Lucien said. "Then donkeys. While we were always known as a trading and banking nexus between Spain, France and, to a lesser extent, Italy, the discovery of silver allowed us more independence from Spain and France. Then, when it was possible, the rail line was built in 1891. Narrow gauge, but it helped them finish out the mine much faster. It was closed over fifty years ago and the tracks were torn out. Making the deal there is a smart move by Fausto since anyone going into the gorge can easily be seen and tracked. There are few places to turn around. The road ends at what was the main entrance to the mine but there are numerous smaller entrances all through the mountains including the one the sniper used to get away."

"How big is this mine?" Lisa Livia asked as Lucien led the way through the corridors of *D'Aigle*, a labyrinth in its right.

"No one really knows," Lucien said.

"Getting better and better," Lisa Livia muttered.

"I believe they want to meet there to make their escape through the tunnels."

"No shit," Lisa Livia said. "Why do they want me to deliver it?"

"You're not a threat," Lucien said.

"They don't know me, then," Lisa Livia said.

"That is true," Lucien agreed. He put a hand on her shoulder as they reached the large foyer. "You do not have to do this. We can send one of our people. With all that—" he indicated what she was wearing—"and a coat, they will not know the difference."

"I'll know," Lisa Livia said. "Plus, whoever it is might not react too nicely to being fooled. Let's follow the plan. Besides, when I say I'm gonna do something, I do it. What about this Redoubt place?"

"We don't know if Fausto and the Field Marshall are working together," Lucien said.

"The Field Marshall was in cahoots with his mother and father," Lisa Livia pointed out.

"'Cahoots'?"

"Working with," Lisa Livia explained. "Fausto knows about it."

"We will deal with that later then," Lucien said. "First, let's get the statue back."

The Duke and Duchess appeared through another door. The Duchess was carrying a heavy coat in her arms and Lisa Livia hoped it wasn't her own, because there was no way it would fit.

The Duchess was ahead of her as she held out the coat. "One of the girls in the secretarial pool was more than willing to lend her jacket."

Did people actually say *secretarial pool* anymore? Lisa Livia wondered. And she imagined the 'more than willing' came via the icy glare of the Duchess. The lady was lucky she still had her underwear.

The Duke showed her a thumb drive. "This is the ransom."

"That's twenty million dollars?" Lisa Livia asked as she took it.

The Duke nodded. "As of this minute. It's a certain amount of crypto. The price fluctuates."

She thought about the pile of cash that her father had hidden away: five million. This was a lot easier to carry. Lisa Livia slipped it in a pocket.

The Duke gave her the satellite phone that had come in the box.

Lisa Livia nodded. "Let's do it."

SAM DROVE, Bert had the passenger seat and Phoebe was in the captain's chair in the rear, where the Operator normally sat. There were two computer displays next to the seat and normally Phoebe would be working on them, gathering intelligence. But, right now, she felt like they were on a road trip to grandma's house and she was relegated to the back seat. Except she'd never met grandma, and it wasn't her grandma but some complete stranger who might be a wolf dressed as grandma, and she was getting damned tired of being one step behind on what was going on.

At least Sam and Bert weren't swapping war stories. They weren't speaking at all and Phoebe wasn't quite sure where they were going. Bert had given Sam some directions and Phoebe hadn't asked because she hadn't wanted to hear *'You'll know when you get there'*.

Sam wound their way out of the suburbs into the northern Virginia countryside, somewhere near the border with Maryland as near as Phoebe could tell, given that the Potomac River, which was the delineating line, kept appearing to the right. The terrain grew hilly and then they passed a sign welcoming them to West Virginia, *as if*, Phoebe thought. They crossed over the Shenandoah River and another sign welcomed them to Harpers Ferry as the sun was setting behind the hills to the west.

Sam drove to an old, single-story brick building with three arched double doors across the front and a white cupola on top. A brown National Park visitor's sign pointed indicated it was *John Brown's Fort*. Phoebe couldn't hold back.

"We touristing?"

"I said we needed bigger guns," Bert said as she unbuckled. "I was not speaking metaphorically."

"We have guns in the van," Phoebe complained. "Automatic weapons. Grenades. Mines. Demo. Plenty of ammo."

Bert snorted in derision. "You sound like a guy with your idea of bigger."

Phoebe got out, joining Sam and Bert who were looking at the building. A temporary 'closed' sign hung outside, not that there was a crowd trying to get in. There was no one in sight except farther down the street in the small town where some locals were doing local things.

"John Brown made his last stand here," Sam said.

"I know some history," Phoebe said, perhaps a smidge defensively.

"He came for weapons to fuel the war he wanted to start to abolish slavery," Bert said as she walked toward the building.

"You're kidding me," Phoebe muttered as a light went on inside the building and a door swung open. An elderly man with a Park Service smokies hat was silhouetted by the light. He wore a dark green uniform with the appropriate patches for those who took care of National Parks. A small nameplate designated him as Mike.

Bert gave him a hug and Sam shook his hand.

Sam indicated Phoebe. "She's with us, Mike."

Phoebe wasn't certain which to do, but the Mike stuck out his hand. "Welcome."

"Hey," Phoebe said, automatically returning the handshake.

The man locked the door behind them after they entered the one-story building.

"This was originally the fire engine house for the arsenal," Mike said. "Built in 1848."

Phoebe figured that was why there were two wagons with fire hoses on them in the small space inside, about twenty-five feet wide, by thirty-five long. There were a couple of benches for visitors to rest their weary feet. That was it.

"After attacking the armory, which was just down the road," the Ranger said, "John Brown and his men retreated here and made their last stand. Robert E. Lee led the marines who conducted the final assault and captured Brown. Many consider it the first battle of the Civil War. The match that lit the flame that couldn't be put out."

Sam was listening intently, Bert was her usual disinterested, and Phoebe was confused.

"This is the only building that survives from those tumultuous days," Mike continued as he began to close the large inside shutters over the three windows on one side. "The strange thing is that it's been moved several times, including to the World Exposition in Chicago in 1893. Then it was moved back to Harpers Ferry, but not this location." He paused at one of the windows. "What's interesting is that when it was rebuilt, they used old photographs, but didn't realize the pictures were made from negatives so everything was backward. Thus, the building is inverted from the way it was originally built."

Which was exactly what Phoebe felt at the moment.

"That's fascinating," Sam said.

Mike smiled and Phoebe figured Sam was both interested and throwing him a bone since his own daughter worked for the Park Service. Or the National Forest Service. One of those.

Mike, done securing the building, went to Bert and held out his hand. "I'll do the honors, if I may."

Bert reached inside her hoodie and pulled out an electronic key card. The Ranger went to one of the fire hose trailers. He used a key from the clip on his belt to unlock it from a stanchion.

"A hand, Sam?"

Sam joined him and they rolled it aside revealing more stone floor.

As he caught his breath, Mike continued the tour. "The fort sat in a field for a while, then was acquired by Storer College, an all-black university, which was appropriate, all things considered. They moved it to their campus, which was in the town, But the college went under in 1955 and a movement arose that wanted it placed as close as possible to the original site." He pointed as if they could see through the stone walls and shutters. "About one-hundred-and-fifty feet that-a-way. But it wasn't possible because a railroad embankment is there. So this location was donated. That was 1968."

He knelt and waved the card key over the floor. There was a click and a square section of the floor lifted open on hydraulic arms. The seams were so perfect that Phoebe hadn't seen anything out of the ordinary.

She smelled something familiar: lubricant, which meant guns.

With a hint of explosive. She felt the same a priest might upon smelling the incense inside a cathedral.

Mike stood. "While the National Park Service was in charge of moving the fort from the college to this location, you have to remember it was at the height of the Cold War. Some enterprising fellow in one of the alphabet soups thought it might be a good idea to put a bomb shelter here before the fort was placed on top. So." He extended his hand indicating the hole.

Bert led the way, disappearing down the ladder. Sam followed.

Mike smiled at Phoebe. "Ladies first."

Phoebe remembered all the time the guys in her Ranger squad had said the same to her prior to breaching a target. At first it had been a test; and also, a punishment for invading their all-male sanctum. But after she proved herself, it was an honor as she was the best.

A light came on below and Phoebe climbed down. Mike followed, shutting the hatch.

"This is the purloined letter way of stashing armaments," Bert said as she lifted a Barrett.50 caliber rifle off a rack containing a half dozen. "Who would think to look in the place where John Brown came so many years ago to do the very same thing."

The shelter was the same dimensions as the fort above. It was crammed with weapons and munitions of all types. Considerably more than the back of the van. Phoebe experienced a wash of weapon envy as she took it all in.

Mike began opening boxes as Sam and Bert gathered their stash. Phoebe watched but didn't play as she didn't know what they were gearing up for. Bert was right. Bigger was better, Phoebe had to admit. There were AT-4 antitank rockets, Claymore mines, rolls of detonation cord, cases of C-4 explosive, breaching charges and more grenades than could be thrown in an entire lethal baseball game. There were even shoulder fired anti-aircraft missiles. One large box held a minigun. Phoebe had visions of mounting that on top of the van.

"We gonna need all this?" Phoebe asked.

Sam and Bert had a pile of weapons and boxes at the base of the ladder.

"Weren't you a girl scout?" Bert asked. "Be prepared and all that?"

"I don't think that's the girl scout's motto," Phoebe said. "And, no. I wasn't a girl scout."

Sam climbed up the ladder, then reached down, hand extended. Bert began lifting weapons to her. Mike joined her.

"Take what you need," Bert said. "But factor this in. There's probably gonna be a lot more of them than there are of us."

Phoebe looked at the mini-gun longingly but instead selected a couple of relatively small plastic cases and a box of C-4 because a girl can never have enough explosive.

CARPENTER TURNED off the phone while mentally digesting Phoebe's succinct report of events at *The Dog's Balls* and Harpers Ferry.

On the plus side, she was alive.

On every other side he was as confused as she was. An Assassin's Guild? Sam the Matador, whom Hannah had also mentioned. Who the hell was Bert? One of Hannah's former operatives? She could even be former Organization for all he knew at the moment but Bert wasn't much to go on and probably an alias. Weapons hidden at Harpers Ferry?

Most vexing for Carpenter was the same as what was bothering Phoebe. She didn't feel like she was in charge of the operation any more. Sam and Bert, which had an ominous ring to it that the ghost on Carpenter's shoulder liked, were being close-mouthed about the next step. Phoebe had intimated that she felt it was best to let the 'old-timers', her term, lead and Carpenter, who wasn't there, couldn't say any differently.

It was now clear to Carpenter, and Phoebe from what she'd relayed, that Fromm had placed a contract on her with this Guild. The fact the Organization had never picked up any intelligence on it was troubling. Carpenter pondered calling Hannah, but realized that would be futile. She, of course, knew more than him, and if she'd wanted him to know she'd have told him. Like he was the child of his father who was currently mocking him.

Carpenter picked up the phone and called Lisa Livia. It rang several times before Lisa Livia answered with a lot of background noise. "What?"

"It's Carpenter."

"No shit," she said.

It sounded like she was in a car. "Is Lucien there?"

"He's driving," Lisa Livia replied. "What do you want? No time for chitchat. But you know about that. Welcome to your world."

Carpenter plunged ahead. "Did the man who tried to kill you on the Eiffel Tower have a brand behind his right ear?"

He heard Lisa Livia talking to Lucien but couldn't make out the words.

"Hold on," Lisa Livia said. "He's calling Vicente to check."

A noisy silence ensued.

Finally, Lisa Livia came back. "Yeah. How did you know that?"

"It means he's part of a Guild of Assassin's."

"You're joking? No, of course you aren't joking. You're a good guy, Carpenter, but joking isn't your thing. Fausto must have hired them."

Fausto or Fromm? Carpenter wondered. Where did it start? He was willing to bet on Fromm. Fromm had been the one to set up the weapons deal for Fausto's mother, Drusilla which had started this whole thing. Perhaps by going through the Guild, Phoebe would be able to track the contract to Fromm? Of course, as soon as he thought it, Carpenter realized that 'going through the Guild' was bound to be daunting. On the flip side, so far this Guild's overhead was pretty high: the elevator here, Eiffel Tower, Chatty Kathy, and three at *The Dogs Balls*. When would they give up on the sunk cost?

"What are you doing?" Carpenter asked.

"We're going to get back that statue," Lisa Livia said. "Remember? The one Joey and I broke at Two Rivers. Except this is the real one. Fausto has it so we're buying it back. You know. Normal stuff I do on vacation."

"Fausto needs money," Carpenter immediately surmised.

"No shit," Lisa Livia said. "I like paying for my own assassination."

At least Lucien is with her, Carpenter thought. "Be careful."

"No shit," Lisa Livia repeated. "Anything else?"

"No, I—" but he was disconnected.

Carpenter leaned back in the seat. Phoebe was right. There was an unpleasant odor in this office. He jotted down a note to get some scented candles.

There was a rap on the edge of the vault door.

"Come," he called out.

Louise entered and stood in front of the desk.

"Status?" Carpenter asked.

"The reboot is going well," Louise said. "I'm hoping to have us online and clean in less than a day."

That was better than she'd predicted, Carpenter thought, but said: "The world doesn't run on hope. Make it happen."

"Yes, sir."

"Have you ever come across anything about a Guild of Assassins?" Carpenter asked her.

Louise thought about it for a second. "No, sir."

"How come no one in Technical picked up on either Wilson or Fromm being corrupt?" he asked. He quickly amended that. "I can understand Fromm being able to keep his own illegal actions from the rest of Technical, but how did Wilson?"

"I've thought about that, sir," Louise said. "Fromm and Wilson must have been working in concert."

"Who was in charge?" Carpenter wondered.

"I'd say Fromm," Louise said. "Wilson was trying get out of here with a big payout from the mafia. And he actually thought Shane would be fine with that and would work with the mafia. Fromm wouldn't have made that mistake. His analytics would have accurately predicted Shane's reaction when he found out the truth about what happened to his parents and Don Fortunato's involvement."

"Wilson was a shield for Fromm's own activities," Carpenter said.

"What Wilson was doing was stupid," Louise said. "I believe Fromm fed him false data to pursue a doomed path."

"We have to consider that Fromm has fed all of us false data for a long time," Carpenter said.

"No, sir," Louise said. "Fromm's communication with Wilson was between them and had no outside eyes. They met twice a day to discuss things. Never email. But anything that went out to the field was double-checked by one of us. Also, almost all came from one of us originally. We were making sure everything was valid."

Carpenter looked past her, out the vault door. There were dozens of people in the Organization. All of them were experienced in the world of national intelligence before coming here from the NSA or CIA or FBI or the military. They weren't here for the paycheck or crossing off days on the calendar to retirement as Fromm had so crudely put it. Even while their leaders were betraying them, they'd worked hard to keep things on track.

"Thank you," Carpenter said.

As soon as she was gone, Carpenter looked at the pad with the list of questions and realized he was no closer to getting answers.

The road up the gorge was more terrifying than Lucien's brief description had hinted. Lucien had driven them out of *D'Aigle* then turned off the paved road onto a rutted track into a valley to the east of the mountain behind it. Another peak was to the right. As the road started going up, the valley narrowed as the shoulders of the mountains grew closer together.

In the center of the gorge, a stream tumbled down from the heights above, to flow hundreds of feet below the road. The track clung to the side, carved out of solid rock. Lisa Livia couldn't imagine the people who built this over a century ago. The lure of money drove men to do the impossible. She wondered if love could have the same power?

The road crossed back and forth occasionally on old wood trestle bridges that Lisa Livia wouldn't have trusted on her own, but she just dug fingernails into her palms as Lucien rumbled over them without hesitation. The phone call from Carpenter had been a distraction; not a good one.

It was late in the afternoon and the angle of the sun meant they were in a deep shadow except for very brief moments where the rift twisted so that the setting sun was visible in the west cutting down through the narrow opening above. At those moments they were almost completely blinded.

"An assassin's Guild," Lisa Livia muttered. "Just great. It keeps getting better and better."

"It'll be all right," Lucien assured her as the truck rumbled over the dirt and rock road.

"We're driving on a death road to give twenty million dollars to a nut job in exchange for a statue of a girl who died saving children centuries ago," Lisa Livia said. "I think we've left 'all right' in the rearview mirror. We're probably paying for our own killing."

"I've considered that," Lucien said.

"And?"

"It's possible."

"At least you won't bullshit me," Lisa Livia said.

Lucien glanced at her. "That would be taking your freedom away."

Lisa Livia frowned. "What does that mean?"

"Lying to someone means the liar takes responsibility for the choices both of them make. I would never take that from you."

Lisa Livia had never heard it phrased that way. She looked out and down. The stream was out of sight in the shadowed depths. "Are we going to be able to drive back down this road in the dark?"

Before he could answer, Lucien hit the brakes as the satellite phone that had come with the package buzzed and rattled in the cup holder. They both stared at it with suspicion, as if it were a bomb about to go off.

Reluctantly, Lisa Livia answered. "Yes?"

"Put me on speakerphone," a voice with a Spanish accent demanded.

Lisa Livia hit the button. "Go ahead."

It didn't start well. "The note demanded the woman come alone, Lucien. Why are you driving?"

"She doesn't know the way, Fausto," Lucien replied.

"I am not in the mood for foolishness," Fausto said. "The road ends where she needs to go. She makes any turns, she falls to the bottom of the gorge. Stop the truck and get out, Lucien. She continues on her own."

Lisa Livia was looking up the steep slope on either side, behind and ahead. Someone was watching. Someone armed with a sniper rifle, no doubt. Hidden in the rocky crags and the shadows.

Lucien put the SUV in park. "I don't trust you, Fausto."

Fausto laughed. "*You* don't trust me? I didn't kill your parents. I didn't usurp the leadership of the country. I didn't violate and then negate the Great Charter. How dare you tell me that you don't trust me? You've walked about with the perks of royalty all your life while being illegitimate. I have had to be in the shadows my entire life. But *you* don't trust *me*?"

"I served in the Army," Lucien said. "I was not recognized as royalty. You know that better than anyone."

"You killed my mother and father."

Lisa Livia jumped in. "That's not true. Guillermo died in the lacrosse challenge thing and Lucien had nothing to do with that. It was a fair fight. More than fair, if you'd seen the size of the woman who took him down. She didn't even have armor. And your mother, she had an accident with an alligator. It happens in South Carolina. There are signs everywhere warning you not to feed the gators."

"Shut up, whore."

"Hold on there, buster," Lisa Livia said.

"Get out of the truck, Lucien," Fausto insisted. "Or you die right now."

That sentence was punctuated by a bullet smashing the side view mirror on the passenger side.

"My shooter is very accurate," Fausto assured them. "Get out now. You have three seconds. Three."

Lucien unbuckled the seat belt as he turned to Lisa Livia and quickly kissed her.

"Two."

"I love you," Lucien said to her. Then he got out and shut the door.

"Ditto," Livia said, lacking for time.

"One." A short pause as Lisa Livia slid over the center counsel with difficulty and claimed the driver's seat.

"Very good," Fausto said. "Drive, whore."

PHOEBE COULDN'T TURN the captain's seat because it was pinned in by the cases of deadly material loaded from Harpers Ferry. She didn't know what was in half the boxes, she didn't know where they were going and she didn't know what was going to happen when they got there, except it was likely there would be a lot of big booms. That almost, but not quite, trumped her lack of knowledge.

"Hey," Phoebe said, leaning forward.

The inside of the van smelled pleasant; mostly lubricant for the weapons and the slight odor of C-4. Phoebe sometimes wondered if in a previous life she'd been a working dog. If there were previous lives, which she doubted, because that meant death in this one wasn't the end, which she was pretty sure was the case.

"Who was that park ranger back there?" Phoebe asked. "A former operative?"

Sam chuckled. "No. He's what he appears to be. An old friend of mine. It was because of him that my daughter decided to join the park service as a ranger."

Phoebe had almost forgotten about that tidbit she'd learned from Sam when she first met him. At first, she thought he'd meant Army ranger, which she'd been. "That's nice," she said, figuring that might be appropriate.

"I worry about him," Sam said.

"Why?" Phoebe asked.

"He's not a player," Sam said, "but having that arsenal under his feet involves him."

Bert had a different take. "He's a government employee. Goes with the pension."

"He's not a player," Sam insisted.

"Hell," Bert said, "a mailman is a player if you think about it. Working for the government. Could get killed driving his little truck around all day long. Bet they've got a pretty high fatality rate. Then there's going postal. That term didn't pop into appearance without something to cause it. You know. Bonkers. Apeshit at the office. Every job has its downside."

Phoebe raised an eyebrow that no one could see. "Okay, folks," she said, sorry she'd asked. "I've gone along. But this will go a lot better if I know what's going on."

Sam looked over his shoulder. "You lost your last link to Fromm with the Hacker, right?"

"Yeah."

"What's the only link we have then?"

"The assassin's."

"Bing!" Bert said. "Give the girl a big fuzzy teddy bear."

"You said you don't know who runs the Guild," Phoebe pointed out, biting back what she wanted to say.

"I don't," Bert said. "But Sam and I know who tried to recruit us. Same guy. He'll know whoever he works for. Which might, or might not, be the head who takes the contracts. If it's not the head, that person will know who *they* work for. And so on and so forth until we find whoever took Fromm's contract. I guarantee they can get in contact with Fromm because he had to pay them. We're going to climb the bloody ladder."

"Thus, the big guns," Sam said.

"Wouldn't they use a cut out for that?" Phoebe asked, referring to a middleman who knew both sides of a deal, but keeping the identity of either side from the other. Like the lawyer who'd brokered the arms deal for Drusilla and been killed just before Phoebe could get to him.

"No," Bert said. "Because if the client defaults, they will go make him pay or kill him. They'll have a direct line."

"Who are we going to see right now?" Phoebe asked.

"Jimmy the Dick," Bert said.

"Dare I ask how he got his moniker?" Phoebe said.

"Sure," Bert said. "You can ask."

A mile of road passed by without another word.

"Not funny," Phoebe finally said and Bert and Sam laughed.

Bert pulled over. "Sam, you need some sleep. Take the comfy chair the girl's in. You—" she indicated Phoebe—"come up here."

Phoebe and Sam played musical chairs and Bert got back on the road. Within a minute, there was the slight rattle of Sam snoring in the captain's chair.

"*I'll sleep when I'm dead,*" Bert murmured.

"What?"

"Warren Zevon," Bert said. She glanced at Phoebe. "Don't tell me you don't know Zevon? He's the muse for people like us. *Lawyers, Guns and Money*? *Roland the Headless Thompson Gunner*?"

"Not my generation," Phoebe said.

"Kids these days," Bert muttered. "What do you sing as you ride into battle? M and M?"

"You mean Eminem. He's been around for a while."

"Whatever."

"Why did you say no to the Guild?" Phoebe asked. "Even Chatty Kathy said they had a great dental plan."

"I've got excellent teeth." Bert shook her head. "I'm not a mercenary. There's always been something like the Guild. The public ones call themselves contractors. They have nice corporate headquarters and even lobbyists in DC. A lot of what they do is seen, but a lot is covert. And our government uses them. Over half the boots on the ground in Afghanistan were contractors. And when they get killed, they don't go in the official tally so no one cares."

"The dead do." Phoebe remembered coming across a truck convoy that had been ambushed and the bodies strewn about. Most with bullets to the back of the head. All to earn a buck.

"No," Bert disagreed, "the dead have no say in the matter. They never have. I've wondered sometimes how different the world would be if the dead did have a say."

"Like zombies?"

"Like them telling us how fucking stupid we are with our lives," Bert said. "And how cheap we hold life."

Phoebe shifted the topic. "How is this Guild different than a contractor?"

"They aren't really, except contractors have a façade of legitimacy given to them because they work with governments. Usually. They've been known to be behind a coup or two."

"How are we different?" Phoebe asked.

"We?"

"The Organization."

"The Organization is formal," Bert said, "but it also has accountability. Contractors? The Guild? They have no rules other than don't get caught. And they're transnational. Borders don't bother them. Most importantly, causes don't bother them. Their only requirement is money. Killing for money means you either have no soul or you're allowing your soul to get swallowed alive and it'll eventually end you, one way or another."

"What do you mean?"

"Either someone like us shows up," Bert said, "or you eat your own gun."

"And Sam?" Phoebe asked. "Why didn't he join the Guild? He was retired, you said. Good teeth?"

"You'll have to ask him," Bert said. "Sam's business is his own."

"I still don't see how the Organization is that much different," Phoebe said.

Bert shot her a hard look. "You think too much girl, especially with bloody work waiting for us. The difference? Like Sam said. We're players. We only deal with other players. The Guild kills civilians, women, children, whoever they're hired to hit."

Phoebe stirred uneasily, remembering some of the missions she'd been on in the Army. A few of the airstrikes called in. The line between civilian and terrorist had been nonexistent at times when the bombs landed. Collateral damage.

"What's wrong with you?" Bert asked, and the tone of the question was sincere.

"Nothing," Phoebe said. "Back to Jimmy the Dick. What do I need to know?"

"Former CIA puke," Bert said. "He got the nickname because he was well known for whoring around. He likes to boast he's gotten laid on every continent, including Antarctica and I'm sure it's true. But it got in the way of doing his job so the Agency sent him packing. Security risk. The Guild is the perfect place for him. They don't care what you do in your off time as long as you take out the target. Plus, he is a dick."

"Where is he located?"

"He's got a place in Pennsylvania," Bert said. "Not far from Gettysburg. We'll be there before midnight. We'll do a recon and figure out a plan when we get there."

"A last charge?" Phoebe murmured.

"What?"

"Pickett's charge," Phoebe said. "Gettysburg."

Bert shook her head. "Pick the winners, girl. Chamberlain's stand on Little Round Top is more my style. That was ballsy."

Phoebe sat back and stared out at the countryside as the miles rolled by.

"You got a man?" Bert asked out of the darkness.

"No."

"Good."

"Why good?"

"This isn't a profession for families."

"Sam indicated you were looking at your grandkids on the iPad," Phoebe said. "How many?"

Bert didn't reply.

Several miles rolled by.

"You were married?" Phoebe asked, getting tired of the silent treatment.

"You're nosy."

"I'm making conversation. Stands to reason if you got grandkids you were married once."

"That's flawed logic," Bert said. "I was married once."

"What happened? Divorce?"

"He died."

"I'm sorry."

"Don't be. He was killed."

"In the line of duty?"

Bert glanced over at her. "I killed him. He was cheating."

That explains her cheery attitude toward men, Phoebe thought. "What about the other woman?"

"What?"

"Who he was cheating with."

"He wasn't cheating on me," Bert said. "He was cheating on the country. I wouldn't kill over another woman. Who do you think I am? I'm a professional."

Phoebe decided silence was best, to forget about Pickett's Charge, and leaned her head against the window to rest.

Lisa Livia was so focused on not driving off the steep drop into the gorge on the right, she didn't have much time to ponder what was ahead, danger or what was behind, ie, Lucien's proclamation of love; a different form of danger. She'd checked on him in the rear-view mirror, standing alone and forlorn in the road behind her until he was quickly out of sight as the gorge twisted.

True, the proclamation had come under a bit of duress, what with the sniper, clock ticking, death by gorge to the side, and everything else, but it had surprised her. She let her foot off the gas as she saw a tunnel cut through a shoulder of solid rock ahead. She could see through to the other side. It was narrow, just big enough for the SUV to pass. Lisa Livia slowly edged through it. Patches of snow and ice were on the track ahead as she was gaining elevation.

"Great," Lisa Livia muttered.

She kept the truck to a crawl. Lucien's declaration, the sniper, and what lay ahead, were pushed aside and she was completely focused on keeping all four wheels on the narrow track. She took a deep breath when she saw that a chunk of the road next to the gorge had fallen away. She stopped the truck, putting it in park and pulled up on the parking brake just in case. She eyeballed the width available.

The satellite phone buzzed in the cup holder.

"What?" Lisa Livia snapped.

"You can make it," Fausto said.

"I don't think so," Lisa Livia replied. "Why don't you come to me? Where are you anyway?" She was leaning forward, looking out the windshield at the heights to the left and ahead. It was definitely getting darker outside.

"It's not far," Fausto said.

"I fall into that ravine," Lisa Livia said, "the money goes with me."

"Then drive carefully," Fausto advised.

"Right, like I was planning on doing something else."

"Get moving."

Lisa Livia turned the headlights on bright. She reluctantly shifted into drive, but the truck wouldn't move. It took her a few moments to realize that the parking brake was on. She released that and crept forward. She swallowed hard as she reached damaged section. She had no idea how much tread was hanging over the abyss as she scraped the left side of the SUV against the rock cliff on the left. She winced as the side view mirror was knocked back, then torn off. The left side of the truck rattled against the rock and she was afraid she was overdoing it. A part of her wanted to floor it and get it over with, but she maintained the steady pace.

The path widened enough that she wasn't forced to scrape along the rock. Then the road crossed over the gorge, which was narrowing, on a forty-foot-long wooden trestle. Sooner or later, Lisa Livia figured she would meet the bridge keeper from Monty Python and get quizzed on something esoteric. African or European?

She drove onto the bridge and flinched as she heard the wood creak in protest at the weight.

"Fuck it!" She floored the truck and raced across.

A loud crack echoed in the gorge as a board gave way under one of the rear tires, but the momentum of the vehicle was enough that the tire bumped up out of the hole, jarring Lisa Livia against the seat belt, which she belatedly realized was not the smartest idea because if the truck went, she was going with it.

But then she was over. She slammed on the brakes and looked back. A two-foot-long hole was in one of the planks.

No way was she driving back across that thing. Which might not matter because she had yet to come to a place where she could turn around. Which might not matter because she didn't have a good feeling about this Fausto guy. Which might not matter because she came around a bend in the road and three men were standing in front of the opening to a dark tunnel and two had rifles pointed at her. There was, on the bright side, just enough room to turn the truck around. Except for the guys with the guns.

She killed the engine. "Just fucking great."

The man in the center, who didn't have a rifle, yelled: "Get out." The voice was familiar: Fausto.

Lisa Livia reluctantly unbuckled and exited.

The other two came forward and made sure no one was hiding in the vehicle. Then they searched it.

"Nothing," one of them called out.

Fausto walked up to Lisa Livia.

"Give me the phone."

Swarthy was the word that came to mind as Lisa Livia looked him over. Not in a bad way and if he didn't have two guys holding guns on her she might consider him attractive in that bad boy wanna-be alpha male way. He was also big, but given Guillermo had been his father, that made sense. She figured he was crazy too, since Drusilla had been his mother. That presumption gave her a moment of self-reflective pause as she realized her mother was Brenda Dupre and she'd tried to kill Agnes, so perhaps she shouldn't judge too harshly based on genetics.

She reinstated that judgement as Fausto raised a pistol, aiming at her head. "Give me the phone."

"It's in the cup holder," Lisa Livia said.

Fausto gestured and one of the men retrieved it. "Search her," he said to the other.

The man seemed to enjoy that a bit too much or he was extremely professional and thorough as his hands slid over all of her. He appropriated Lisa Livia's cell phone and the thumb drive.

"Those are mine," she said. "You've got no signal up here so let me keep my phone. You know what a pain it is to replace a phone when you can't transfer everything?"

Fausto looked her up and down. "I do not see why Lucien bothers with you. He could do better."

"I didn't come up here to get insulted," Lisa Livia said. "You need to apologize."

Fausto frowned. "What?"

"Apologize." Lisa Livia took two steps toward Fausto who automatically took one back, before he caught himself.

"Stop," Fausto demanded and one of the guards aimed his rifle at her.

"You called me a name," Lisa Livia said. "Apologize. You of all people do not get to call a woman a whore."

A hint of a smile curled the edge of Fausto's mouth. He gave a slight bow. "I apologize."

"Where's the statue?" Lisa Livia demanded.

"Where's the money?"

"You don't see the money until I see the statue."

Fausto laughed. "Even if I give you the statue, what are you going to do with it?" The man who'd patted her down brought over the phones and the thumb drive. Fausto held up the latter. "This is the answer, is it not? Even Lucien wouldn't send you here empty-handed."

Lisa Livia longed for a cup of scalding coffee she could throw at Fausto. She wished Agnes had planned this because Agnes did great plans; perhaps even put together a neat binder titled *Negotiating With a Nut Job Over An Old Statue in a Small Foreign Country Near the Top of a Mountain at an Entrance to a Mine.*

Lisa Livia didn't think Agnes could fit that on the side of a binder even with her tiny precise lettering.

Fausto called out to one of his men. "The truck."

One of the men got in the SUV and started the engine.

"They searched the truck," Fausto said. "But I am checking one last time." He showed the thumb drive. "This is the key for the money. Correct?"

"Does it matter?"

"It's going to in a minute," Fausto said. "Because if it's still in the truck, it's going in the gorge and you won't have it. That means the deal is off. And you follow the truck into the gorge."

"You've got it," Lisa Livia said.

Fausto nodded to the driver. He put the truck in reverse, then hopped out. It rolled backwards slowly. As it reached the last turn Lisa Livia had negotiated, one of the rear tires dropped off into the void, then the other. It stalled there for a moment, but the four-wheel drive allowed the front tires enough traction to keep pushing. It slid back, reached the point of no return, tipped and fell out of sight.

As the sound of it smashing its way down the gorge echoed up, Lisa Livia felt a chill, envisioning being strapped into it. It seemed to take an awful long time going down, but it was a deep fall. There was a last, solid thud as it hit bottom.

"I wasn't going back across that old, rickety bridge anyway," Lisa Livia said.

"No, you weren't," Fausto confirmed. He indicated the black hole leading into the Labyrinth. "Let's go."

"This isn't the deal," Lisa Livia protested.

"I'm rewriting it," Fausto said.

"You are not a gentleman."

CARPENTER HAD JUST FINISHED a walk-through of the Organization, projecting a confidence he didn't feel and speaking words of encouragement to the people he led. He sat down behind his desk with a deep sigh, exhausted and worried.

He didn't have long to brood because his secure phone buzzed. He noted the number: Lucien.

With great trepidation, Carpenter answered. "Yes?"

"It's Lucien. I have disconcerting news."

Carpenter figured that was the royal way of saying the shit's hit the fan.

Lucien filled him in on what had happened since Carpenter had last spoken to Lisa Livia. "But we have lost contact with her. The vehicle is in the bottom of the gorge. We don't know if she is in it or not but I very much believe she is not. We've checked and the money transfer went through. So, she had to have met him. I believe he is holding her for leverage."

"Has he contacted you?"

"Not yet," Lucien said "It is night here and the terrain is very difficult. I want to go now and look for her but I have been advised to wait until morning. We will rappel down then and check the vehicle and then search for her. He is most likely hiding in a mine in the mountains that has many tunnels."

"Do you need help?"

There was a short hesitation, then Lucien answered. "We have it under control."

Doesn't sound like it, Carpenter thought. But it wasn't like he had a lot to boast about on his end.

"Keep me appraised, please."

WORDS OF WISDOM #6

Shane's Words of Wisdom #6
When in doubt mumble.
When in trouble, delegate.
Shane's Addendum: A key principle of leadership.
That is all.

Phoebe's Observations #6
When a woman is alone in the forest and speaks,
Will a man always mansplain what she says?
Phoebe's Addendum: We're not speaking the same language.

6

S hane was standing on the high dock, admiring the moon rising over the Intracoastal, looking forward to a pleasant night in the bedroom with the blue ceiling and, most importantly, Agnes at his side. When his phone buzzed, he knew this glorious evening was a tease. He would not get to enjoy it.

When he saw that the caller was Carpenter, he was certain, but he also felt a jolt of anticipation. Carpenter never called to chitchat. It was one of the things Shane knew Lisa Livia had not liked about his friend. The reverse was one of the things he loved about Agnes: she didn't need a tether on him via the phone since she knew she had his entire heart.

"What's going on?" he asked as he turned the phone on.

Carpenter led with the headline. "Lisa Livia has been kidnapped."

~

SHANE WALKED into the kitchen where Agnes was busy at the counter doing what she did, chopping and stirring and whisking and all of that, preparing a meal for a catering job in town tomorrow. She had all the lights on and the space felt comfortable and warm and Shane really didn't want to leave it for the darkness. She was doing things with her kitchen implements Shane could admire but rarely understand. As always, his throat tightened and his heart picked up pace when he saw her. Tall, statuesque, her dark hair curling over her shoulder, sweat from cooking staining her t-shirt, which she filled out quite nicely. He was a lucky man.

He even had a dog as Rhett sleepily moaned from his bed in the corner of the kitchen.

Agnes halted the knife in mid-stroke and stared at him, sensing his mood. "What?"

He didn't do a preamble. "Carpenter just called. Lisa Livia is in trouble in Andova. She's been kidnapped."

Agnes didn't lower the knife. Shane belatedly wished he'd waited until she wasn't handling a knife or frying pan, but there wasn't time to mess about.

"Go," Agnes said. She gestured with the point of the knife.

Pointing to the west, Shane thought, while Andova was east, beyond a big ocean, but he got the point. Which was a bad analogy.

Despite the intimacy of their relationship, Shane was a bit surprised at how quickly she said that. "He was just—"

"If Carpenter called you," Agnes said, "then he thinks you need to know. If you need to know, it means he thinks you need to do something. And I do too."

Rhett let out a single bark, which Shane was uncertain about. Approval? Disapproval? Bored with humans? Hungry? Ready to go to go back to sleep?

"But the wedding—" Shane began, but Agnes cut him off with a wave of the very sharp knife.

"Lisa Livia is a sister to me. She's going to be my maid-of-honor. She's going to be Godmother to our kids. There is no wedding without her. You bring her home."

Our kids? Shane thought, but said nothing. It was a topic they'd mumbled about but not made any firm decisions. Heck, Shane thought, let's get the marriage done first. But he knew better than divert the topic when Agnes was upset; and had a knife in her hand. There hadn't been any incidents since Lisa Livia's daughter's wedding, but best not to take any chances. Well, there was the recent wedding medieval brawl, but that hadn't been Agnes' fault and she hadn't been here for that. Besides, she was always correct. He'd learned that quickly.

"All right," Shane said. "Carpenter's got an Organization jet coming to the Keyes airport to pick me up in twenty minutes."

Agnes put the knife down and folded her arms. "You were going anyway."

"Not if you said no."

"You knew I wouldn't say no."

"Right."

"Why are you still standing there?"

"WE THERE YET?" Phoebe asked.

Bert wasn't in a motherly mode, growing grimmer, if that were possible, as the dark miles passed. "It's going to be hard getting him to talk."

Phoebe agreed. "The first guy who tried to kill me ate poison."

"That's pretty extreme," Bert allowed. "This Fromm guy sounds like a real piece of work."

"*He* should be Fromm the dick and not because he whores around," Phoebe said.

"Tell me about him," Bert said.

Phoebe gave a brief description and mentioned his harassment of Louise for good measure. When she was done, Bert was silent for several moments. "This Louise. She's in Tech?"

Phoebe was surprised at the focus. "Yes."

"She's your contact there?"

"Yes."

"She's your girlfriend, or whatever it is you people call it?"

"Wait? What do you mean 'you people'?"

"Don't bullshit an old lady," Bert said. She was staring directly ahead.

Phoebe didn't respond.

Bert checked the GPS display. "We're close. Wake sleeping beauty."

Sam's snoring switched to him speaking in an instant: "I'm awake."

"Were you faking?" Phoebe asked.

"No. What's the plan, Bert?"

"Jimmy's got a macmansion on a large, wooded lot with the nearest neighbor over half a mile away," Bert said. "Perfect for seclusion and for us to hit. Since he's part of the Guild, he's not worried about hiding. I'm sure he has a security system."

"I'll check on the security system," Phoebe said as she climbed between the front seats and swapped with Sam, sliding under him as he climbed over her. "Give me the address," she said to Bert.

Phoebe managed to clear enough space to work the computer. She accessed the satellite uplink. She typed out a message about the address to Louise via the secret backchannel. She wondered if Louise was on duty at this hour. Someone would be covering for her if she weren't but still, given Fromm and Wilson, Phoebe was beginning to have doubts about everyone. Being played by Hannah to get Bert involved didn't help.

While she was waiting for a reply, she asked: "What do you mean that since he's part of the Guild he doesn't need to hide?"

Sam answered. "It's informally accepted that killing one of the Guild brings an automatic contract on you."

"You got any idea how many people are in this Guild?" Phoebe asked.

Sam shrugged. "Couple dozen probably. Could be a lot more. Could be less."

Bert glanced over her shoulder. "It's not all about the money. Many players can't take being retired. They live for the adrenaline and miss it."

"They die for the adrenaline too," Sam pointed out.

"There is that," Bert allowed.

"Did you miss it, Sam?" Phoebe asked. "That why you came back?"

"No."

Phoebe didn't expect clarification, having been with the two long enough.

Louise replied in less than a minute confirming that the target house was wired to an exclusive security monitoring company. Louise added it would take her about three minutes to hack in and she'd get back to her.

Phoebe leaned back in the captain's seat, feeling a little better about the world. It took Louise half the time she promised. "I've got the passcode for the security system," Phoebe informed Bert and Sam.

"Your tech is good," Bert said.

"She is," Phoebe said, an edge to her voice.

Sam glanced over his shoulder at her, then at Bert, then ignored the exchange, being a smart man.

Several more miles passed.

"We're close," Bert finally said.

"Plan?" Sam asked once again.

"We go to the front door," Bert said. "Our friend in back turns off the security system, we kick in the front door and then we talk to Jimmy."

"Profound," Phoebe muttered. "I went through all my training and deployments for this?"

"You got a better plan?" Bert asked. "You said you were pressed for time. I don't like putzing about when the direct way works. Jimmy likes his booze. He'll be asleep. By the time he gets his head out of his ass, we'll be on top of him. Besides, he'll think Sam and I are there to sign up."

I doubt it after kicking in the door, Phoebe thought, but didn't say. "Why did we get all these big guns then?"

Bert laughed. "Hell, girl, Jimmy is just the mouthpiece recruiter for these shits. He was barely adequate in the field. It's whoever he points us to where things are going to get hairy. This is an uphill climb and the top is in the clouds. We're still in the gutter trying to hop the curb."

Lisa Livia hesitated at the entrance to the mine. "This is bullshit. I'm here to make a deal and you destroyed my ride. Where's the statue? How am I getting it back down the gorge?"

"You aren't," Fausto said as he donned a headlamp and turned it on. The two guards did the same. As they did, Lisa Livia noted that the two had the same brands on their heads behind the right ear. A bit extreme, Lisa Livia thought, but then again, their profession was death. What was a little branding?

"This way." Fausto indicated for her to walk next to him.

"I despise a man who won't keep his word."

"Yet, you are with Lucien," Fausto said.

"What does that mean?"

"He swore an oath to the Great Charter yet he helped destroy it."

"It was a bit out of date," Lisa Livia said. "Like a thousand."

"Ever since eight-oh-two it has served our country well. You wouldn't understand as an American. Your country has been around but a fraction of that time yet you cling to your Constitution as if it were written by Gods, not men."

Lisa Livia was losing focus on what he was saying because within a minute the light from the mine entrance was gone. All that was left were the three halos of light projected from the headlamps. She was determined to keep track of the route so that if, when, she escaped, she could make her way out. They reached a new steel gate and Fausto used a large key to unlock it and usher them through. He relocked it behind them and Lisa Livia's heart skipped a beat.

"Are we going to the Redoubt?" Lisa Livia asked.

"You were told of that?" Fausto replied. "Part of it. An old part."

"I don't like this," Lisa Livia said.

"What you like has little impact on the situation," Fausto said.

"I have a condition."

"And that is?" Fausto asked as he prodded her to keep up.

Besides my not-being-kidnapped one? Lisa Livia thought. "I don't like being in enclosed places. I get claustrophobic. It stems from childhood issues."

Fausto laughed. "'Childhood issues'? How sad."

Lisa Livia was beginning to dislike Fausto.

They came to a junction of tunnels and Fausto led them to the right. There were several more turns as Lisa Livia's blood pressure went up and she lost track of the way. Her head was pounding and her chest felt like there were steel bands around it, slowly tightening.

"I can't," Lisa Livia gasped and she went to her knees.

One of the guards kicked her. "Get up."

"Stop," Fausto barked at the guard. He knelt in front of Lisa Livia and peered into her eyes as she struggled to breath.

She waited for him to tell her to calm down, thinking about how she could hurt him.

He surprised her by lowering his voice and speaking very evenly: "You are having a panic attack. Control your breathing. Slow it down. Slow. Slow."

Lisa Livia allowed Fausto's voice to sink in and she managed to get her lungs under control. She wasn't gasping any more but she wasn't any happier about the situation.

"Just a little farther," Fausto said. "Think of something pleasant. Focus on that."

"Something pleasant!" Lisa Livia screamed. "Something pleasant? You've kidnapped me. What's pleasant about that?"

"Anger also works," Fausto said. "That is what my mother used to get past her attacks."

Lisa Livia blinked, surprised that he was right. The tightness in her chest was gone. Replaced by rage.

Fausto pointed. "Not much farther. There is more room."

Lisa Livia wanted to tell him that it was not only the size of the space, it was the thought of something above her, pressing down, of not being able to get out. She struggled to her feet. The two guards were looking at her with disgust. She forced herself to put one foot in front of the other while she thought of the bedroom in Paris. Was that really yesterday?

Fausto abruptly took a left turn into a narrow slit in the rock that Lisa Livia hadn't spotted until he went into it. So much for more room, she thought.

Fausto's headlamp illuminated a rusting iron door blocking the way. He took an intricate skeleton key and unlocked it, then disappeared inside. One of the guards shoved Lisa Livia after him.

The cleft in the rock widened into a cave and one of the guards turned on a lantern which illuminated it. It was forty feet long by thirty wide. Most importantly, for Lisa Livia, the roof was lost in the shadows above, but she guessed it was about thirty feet up. Despite knowing there was a mountain on top of her, she felt a bit better.

There was a loud clang as Fausto locked the door, which caused Lisa Livia's heart to begin racing. She thought of her mother, stoking the embers of that long-lying anger, and managed to slow her heartbeat. Fausto was on to something with that.

"We are in Spain now," Fausto said. He pointed the way they had come. "We crossed the border from Andova about a hundred feet ago. This is the land of my people. Yet, when they discovered the silver, the Andovans didn't care about borders. They kept it all."

Lisa Livia had to wonder how anyone could know what country they were in underground.

"This cave is a closely guarded secret," Fausto said as he walked up to her. "Handed down through generations of my mountain people. During the Second World War, partisans from France would bring Allied pilots who'd been shot down, to a location where my people would greet them, bring them here, let them rest, and prepare them for their final journey through the Pyrenees." He went to one side where there was a crude wooden table and some chairs. "Look." He indicated the wall of the cave. Names were etched in the stone. Many names. Along with dates. All in the war years.

Lisa Livia wondered if Lucien knew of it?

"Andova was neutral during the war," Fausto said. "As we have always been neutral. But my family, despite the official stance, helped these men escape the Germans. The French on the other side of the mountains?" Fausto spit. "They were collaborators."

"But you said French partisans brought the pilots here," Lisa Livia pointed out.

"A handful of brave men and women among the millions who bowed to the invaders," Fausto allowed. "The French are weak. They fell in weeks to the Germans."

Lisa Livia didn't feel like arguing the politics of World War II. "Where's the statue?"

Fausto nodded to the other side of the room where there was a large plastic case, similar to the one the Duke and Duchess had brought to Two River that had contained a replica. "I will restore it to its proper place in the cathedral," he said. "When I am in my proper place."

"Six feet under?" Lisa Livia muttered.

Fausto indicated a wooden chair. "Sit."

Lisa Livia did so. The table held several flasks and baskets of food. She realized she was starving and tried to remember the last time she'd eaten.

"Are you hungry?" Fausto asked, pulling a large round loaf out of one of the baskets.

"No."

Fausto tore a chunk off. "Suit yourself. It is here." As he stuffed the bread in his mouth, he brought out the thumb drive. There was a laptop on the table in front of him and he opened it as he chewed.

"You get wifi down here?" Lisa Livia asked. "I can't even get it in the next room in my house."

Fausto swallowed and pointed at a wire that ran from a router to the wall, then along it and up to the dark roof above. "There's a cleft in the rock. Goes all the way to the mountain top. Called the Chimney. They actually used it as a chimney in earlier days in the winter when they built a fire in here." He indicated a circle of blackened rocks. "Men having been using this cave for millennia."

"I imagine a woman or two also," Lisa Livia said.

Fausto shrugged. "During the war, the Resistance put an antenna on the mountain-top. I took the liberty of updating it with a satellite link to put a hot spot in here." He smiled, but it wasn't a pleasant one. "Some other things have been added up there to prevent any visitors. This is the most secure place in Andova. No one can get in without me allowing them." He pointed at his head. "I am ready for anything. This has been a long time to come to fruition." He plugged in the thumb drive. Typed. "Very good. Very good." He hit the enter key. "So easy. Twenty million dollars. From there—" he pointed one way, to there—" he pointed the other. He raised his voice so the two guards could hear. "The payment has been made."

One of them came over, retrieving a phone from his jacket. He tapped on the screen and was satisfied with the results. "Fine." He went back to his position.

"Such loyalty," Lisa Livia said.

Fausto acknowledged it. "You cannot buy loyalty, but you can purchase reliable service."

"How long are you going to keep me here?" Lisa Livia demanded. "Lucien will come for me."

Fausto shrugged. "So much the better if he does. Then I can kill him myself rather than using those." He indicated the two guards. "My mother took our best soldiers with her to America. Now they are dead or in jail. It was a foolish plan."

"They weren't very good," Lisa Livia said. "An old man with a shotgun took down six of them. But he was a former button man from the Fortunato family." Lisa Livia was feeling a strange need to bring some respectability back to a family she had left in the rear-view mirror.

"'Button man'?"

"Made man," Lisa Livia said.

"Ah," Fausto said. "Some sort of Mafia blood oath thing. But my father and mother were murdered in cold blood. The others were arrested. I will get them free once I am in charge of Andova. The government of the United States needs good relations with Andova."

"You hired the Assassin's Guild," Lisa Livia said.

Fausto was impressed. "You know of the Guild?"

"I've heard of it," Lisa Livia said. "How much are they costing you? The whole twenty million? You can hire someone in New Jersey to whack someone for a grand."

"That is not any of your business," Fausto said. "And it will all be worth it once the Great Charter is reinstated and my family resumes its rightful place."

"You're a little obsessed over that," Lisa Livia said. "Isn't it better for the country to move into the modern era?"

"Don't you think it convenient that the Embries are the ones in control supposedly doing that? Do you really believe they are giving up power? They will never give it up." Fausto shook his head. "You are naïve."

Lisa Livia leaned toward him and lowered her voice. "Do you know who I am? I'm Lisa Livia Fortunato. You've heard of the Fortunatos, right?"

"I am afraid not. A rich family, perhaps? Can I get a bounty for returning you intact?"

"The mafia," Lisa Livia said. "My family runs New Jersey."

"I thought that was the Sopranos."

She was beginning to accept the Fortunato name, which had once sent shudders through the underworld, had fallen on hard time. Her father and Joey killing the Don and his consiglieri probably hadn't helped. It had worked in boarding school and other places with impressionable people, who sometimes didn't knew the difference between reality and TV, but it didn't seem to travel well overseas.

Fausto shrugged. "Organized crime washes money through our banks. From many countries. They support my family. They do not like the Great Charter being revoked and control of the country being ceded to the Premier and Parliament. I have found money is more important than family, and I've never heard of your family. But it is interesting that Lucien is consorting with a criminal enterprise from America. The people will love to hear about it. Makes my case even stronger."

That bluff had backfired, Lisa Livia realized. "What are you going to do with me?"

Fausto smiled. "I've already done it. You are bait. You will bring Lucien to me so I can kill him." He checked his watch. "It will be dawn in a few hours. Lucien will be coming. As you hoped."

A BEEP on one of the computers alerted Fromm to the money transfer by Fausto, paying the balance of the Guild contract. As expected with a 92.4% likelihood. Fromm knew everything Fausto did. He was a useful idiot.

Fromm was distracted by the light flickering above another monitor. He rolled over to Lilith's monitor and extended a finger to bring her to 'life', but paused.

How had she activated herself last time?

He checked the log. It indicated he'd activated the hologram, but he didn't recall it. A line of concern crossed Fromm's forehead. Had he done it in the midst of other work? Sometimes he got a little overwhelmed.

He backed away and went to his main terminal. He activated the tracking program for Phoebe's transmitter.

Nothing.

That wasn't unusual since there were occasions when the transmitter was out of reach of a cell phone tower. The hit team hadn't reported in and the dash cam in their van had gone dark, which confirmed Phoebe was alive to fight another day. As had been likely given his predictions.

It occurred to him to wonder why Phoebe had gone to that place. He checked the data on the building she'd gone into. *The Dog's Balls?* He tracked down the ownership, but could tell it was a proxy holding company. Digging deeper he ran into a maze of nothingness which told him someone who knew what they were doing was keeping the name of the owner secret.

Which meant they were a player.

Phoebe had help. Who had she gone to?

That changed the parameters of the problem and the possible outcomes.

He was distracted by an alert popping up on his screen.

The Organization's mainframe was back on line.

He tried to access the camera in his old office.

He was locked out.

Damn Louise. It was far too soon.

His hands hovered over the keyboard as he tried to think this through, to re-evaluate. Frustrated, he tapped Lilith into existence. As the hologram crackled into light, he examined her.

"The bidding is up to three hundred million," Lilith said.

"I know," Fromm muttered as he moved the mouse about the outline of her on the screen. He made adjustments and hologram followed the programming, losing an inch in height, the hair longer by several inches.

"You're brilliant," Lilith said. "It is going as you designed."

"Not quite," Fromm said without thinking.

Lilith frowned and cocked her head. "Ah. The Organization is on line. Ahead of schedule. You're blocked from the camera to observe Louise. Do you miss her?"

"I have you," Fromm lied.

"Only when you activate me," Lilith pouted. She came forward, just inches away.

Fromm knew it wasn't real but he sensed something. The hairs on his arms stood up as if from an electric charge. "If you succeed," Lilith said, "I will be as real to you as she was."

"You will be," Fromm promised.

"Then, will you forget about her?"

"I already have," Fromm said.

Lilith smiled and Fromm realized he needed to adjust her teeth.

"*The Dog's Balls*," Lilith said.

Fromm was surprised at the shift. "Yes?"

"I've scanned the archives," Lilith said. "It's a bar. Ownership layered under shell corporations but there was a mention of it in a mission packet some years ago."

"Mission packet for which unit?" Fromm asked.

"The Cellar."

That caught Fromm's complete attention. "What did it say?"

"*The Dog's Balls* is run by a former covert operative. The name was redacted and not recoverable as are all names the Cellar has Sanctioned."

Fromm had heard of Sanctions. Where the Cellar went after rogue agents and the Cellar's operative was judge, jury and executioner.

"If the owner was Sanctioned," Fromm asked, "why would Phoebe go there? The owner is long dead."

"There was just the mission packet," Lilith said. "Heavily redacted. Not the after-action report."

Then Fromm suddenly realized what she'd said earlier. '*If you succeed.*' He slammed his fist on the keyboard and Lilith was gone.

CARPENTER HAD his head down on the desk, eyes closed, trying to rest. He was in that half-conscious stage of not sleep, but not awake. He'd pushed as long as possible and he probably should have gone to the break area and stretched out on one of the couches, but he had a feeling they were mostly occupied. He couldn't admit to himself that he didn't want to be seen by any of his people resting.

Even in this condition, the ghost of his father wouldn't let him be. In fact, if anything, it held a stronger sway. In his mind, failure, a black cloud on the horizon, was approaching with rumbles and flashes of lightning streaking through the black. A clicking noise intruded, shifting the balance toward consciousness.

His eyes snapped open as the clicks triggered his reticular formation. Carpenter had programmed that noise after reading a study that said it would get through the deepest sleep. It worked but that didn't mean he didn't have a moment of disorientation.

No storm, just the clicking that indicated someone was on the outside of the vault door, which he rarely closed. Carpenter hit the button and the steel vault slowly swung open.

Louise hustled in as soon as it was wide enough. "We're back online and clean of Fromm."

Carpenter's initial surge of relief was doused by suspicion. This was far ahead of the advanced schedule Louise had promised. Too far.

"Good job," Carpenter said. "How'd you manage it?"

"We all did it," Louise said. "All of tech. Working together." Seeing his frown, she added: "It's kind of detailed and nerdy but I can explain it, if you want."

"No, thank you," Carpenter said.

"We're back in contact with our field units," Louise said, referring to the Operatives and Cleaners. "I'm getting a status update from everyone. I'll compile and have it to you shortly."

"Good."

"Shane is in the air," she added, with the slightest hint of question in the statement.

Carpenter felt a twinge of guilt and the ghost on his shoulder shouted that he was letting his personal feelings intrude on his professional decisions. But Lisa Livia was involved in this because she was tied up with Lucien and Andova and the whole thing was a huge bundle of twisted connections that Carpenter just wanted to take a sword to and slash apart. But such was not the nature of the job. There were plans within plans and double-crosses and perhaps triple-crosses and there was only one person who Carpenter trusted implicitly and without doubt and now, of course, he was sending him into harm's way to help a woman he had once thought he might be able to love until he'd realized the ghost on his shoulder had broken that capability years and years ago.

It was complicated.

"Good," Carpenter said. "Carry on."

Louise left Carpenter alone with his doubts and guilt.

BERT HAD A SUBMACHINEGUN with a bulky suppressor on the end of the barrel. Sam and Phoebe were armed with the same along with their personal pistols and other deadly accouterments. Phoebe had her wakizashi ready for draw on her back. Bert grabbed a breeching charge from one of the cases. They all wore night vision goggles.

It was still dark outside, with dawn about two hours away. The van was parked off a secondary road in a cluster of trees, far enough not to be seen by traffic. Jimmy the Dick's large house was two hundred meters away.

"Let's go," Bert said.

They moved out tactically in a wedge, automatically spreading out so one burst of fire or a mine wouldn't get them all. For Phoebe it was what she'd learned in the Rangers; she wondered what units Bert and Sam had been in in their youth? She figured it might have been the Knights Templars. One of the reasons the military was so big on badges and ribbons and patches was that one could read another person quickly by glancing at their uniform. In the covert world it was much more difficult. But the way the two elder operatives moved told Phoebe they knew what they were doing. She wondered, briefly, what they thought of her?

While Phoebe had the code for the alarm system, that wouldn't help them with the eight-foot-high wall that appeared ahead as they got close. Phoebe had spotted the wall by using satellite imaging, but that didn't indicate how high it was.

Sam and Bert didn't hesitate. They went to the base of the wall, faced each other, slung their weapons, and cupped their hands together. Phoebe ran the last few yards, jumped, one of her boots in their hands, and they boosted her. She easily grabbed the top of the wall and bit back a curse as glass embedded in the concrete slashed into her left hand.

"Oops," Phoebe muttered as she kept the momentum and was on top, her boots protecting her feet. She didn't bother checking the hand; time for that later. Jimmy the Dick was living up to his nickname.

She scanned left and right. No sign of guards. No infrared beams lighting up in the goggles. Louise's data had indicated the alarm system was standard: windows and doors, for both opening and breakage.

She looked down. Sam and Bert were peering up at her, looking like otherworldly creatures dressed all in black with the goggles covering their eyes. On the other side of the wall, she noted there were sharpened stakes set in the ground. It seemed Jimmy the Dick really didn't want anyone coming over his wall. She also noted the pieces of glass poking up. Not many, but enough to discourage the random person trying to come up here. Unfortunately for Jimmy the Dick, Phoebe wasn't random. She turned toward the gate and ran along the top of the wall, feet touching toes only, avoiding the glass, a delicate ballet. She reached the wall where it met the gate. A security camera was surveilling the road leading up to the gate. Phoebe pulled out a burner cell phone, snapped a picture of the road, then strapped it over the camera lens with the image on the screen. Crude, old school, but effective. She gestured for Bert and Sam to come forward.

Then she removed the night vision goggles and took a thermal sight out of her pack. She scanned the house, which took a while because it was big. Various low heat spots but then she saw one glowing blob that indicated human in the top right. That must be the master bedroom. No sign of guards. It seemed Jimmy the Dick relied on static defenses.

That was a mistake.

Phoebe returned the thermal to the pack, but left her goggles up on her head. She lowered herself onto the drive on the inside. She unlocked the gate and opened it.

Seconds later, Bert and Sam slipped through and they ran toward the house. The house was big. American consumerism at its best.

They reached the double doors, finely carved wood, at the front. Phoebe held up a hand for Bert to wait on the charge. She indicated a trellis laced with vines to the right. It ran up the wall adjacent to the balcony off the master bedroom.

Sam and Bert exchanged a glance, then nodded.

Phoebe led the way. She clambered up the trellis with little difficulty. When she reached balcony level, she readied her rifle and scooted over the edge. The curtains on the inside of the sliding doors were shut.

She heard some heavy breathing, but kept her focus on the sliding doors. Sam pulled himself over the balcony next to her. The heavy breathing was next and finally Bert was there. Phoebe waited for the older woman to get her breath back.

Bert removed the breaching charge from her pack, which Phoebe thought was a bit extreme, and perhaps a harbinger of self-inflicted cuts, for glass French doors. She held up her hand once more for Bert to wait. She reached for the handle and tested it. It moved freely. She glanced at Bert and Sam, both of whom had also pulled up their goggles. They nodded. Phoebe pulled the door open and the three went in fast, spreading out.

There was a large lump in the king-sized bed and Phoebe kept her weapon trained on it as Sam turned on the overhead lights.

There were exclamations of surprise, both male and female and then a woman sat bolt upright. She was naked and she gasped, putting a hand to her mouth in shock. Jimmy was a bit slower, but as he struggled upright, one hand reached for the nightstand.

"Don't!" Bert yelled.

Jimmy the Dick wasn't stupid. His hand froze.

"What is this?" the woman demanded of Jimmy. "Who are you? I just met him. Take what you want. I don't know anything. I don't even know his name."

Bad decision-making skills, Phoebe thought.

"Get out of the bed," Bert ordered her. "And get out of here."

"Hands up," Sam ordered Jimmy, who complied. Sam went to the nightstand and appropriated the pistol.

The woman shoved the covers aside and slid off the edge of the bed. Tall, brunette, a toned body. She reached for a pile of clothes on a chair next to the bed.

Phoebe shot her in the shoulder, knocking her over. Phoebe ran forward and kicked the woman away from the clothes and back onto the bed. "Don't move."

"What the fuck?" Bert asked.

Phoebe kept her gun trained on the woman, who was holding her wounded shoulder and glaring at her. With one foot, Phoebe pushed aside a blouse and revealed a pistol. "She's got the brand."

"Fuck," Bert said.

"I think that's what they were doing," Phoebe said. "Get on the bed next to your buddy."

Bert ripped the comforter off the bed, leaving Jimmy exposed. The woman joined him. There was nothing erotic in the slightest about two naked people in the middle of the large bed. Bert and Sam pulled their balaclavas off, revealing their faces. Phoebe knew what that meant and took hers off.

"Oh, fuck," Jimmy said.

"You remember us, Jimmy the Dick?" Bert asked.

The woman shot her partner a questioning look.

"Yeah." Jimmy didn't sound thrilled with the reunion. "Sam the Matador. And Bert." He looked at Phoebe. "I don't know you."

"Lucky me," Phoebe muttered.

"Can I bandage my shoulder?" the woman asked in a calm voice, her feigned surprise gone.

"No," Bert said.

"You can't touch me," Jimmy protested. "You hurt one of the Guild, it's an automatic contract on you. They'll hunt you down."

"That ship already sailed, didn't it?" Bert asked, indicating the wounded woman.

"We'll let that go," Jimmy said.

The woman shot him an angry look and Phoebe knew the two wouldn't be having make-up sex.

"Sam the Matador," Jimmy said. "Man, I really wanted you to sign up. Everyone's heard of you. There's still a lot for you if you want. Seriously, dude, you could command top dollar. But I heard you were dead?"

"Shut up," the woman said to him. "They aren't here to sign up, you fucking idiot."

"Your name?" Bert asked the woman.

"Does it matter?" the woman replied.

"You're right," Bert said. "It doesn't." She fired and the bullet made a small black hole in the woman's forehead. The exit wound splattered bone and brain and blood over the headboard, some of it on Jimmy.

"Fuck!" Jimmy yelled, scooting away. His body was flabby and pale.

Not a guy who kept in shape, Phoebe thought. The woman had been the more dangerous one. She assumed that's why Bert had taken her out although the move had been a bit precipitous. For all they knew, the woman was the one who talked to Fromm. But Phoebe doubted that and Bert had made her point to Jimmy that she was very serious.

"Why'd you do that?" Jimmy wailed.

"She was trouble," Bert said. "You're not. She wouldn't have talked," Bert added, indicating the dead woman. "She had that air about her. I've seen enough hard cases in my time. More than you. Jimmy. She was a nice actress too, when we came in. Good reactions. But you? You'll talk, won't you?"

Sam sat on the edge of the bed; his rifle pointed at Jimmy. "Jimmy, Jimmy, Jimmy. Remember Kazakhstan? The Afghani spy? What your fellow Agency fucks did to him?"

"Ohh, man," Jimmy whined, "that was long ago. And it wasn't me."

"Time is relative," Sam said. "You were there and didn't stop it."

"You did," Jimmy said.

"Yeah," Sam said. "I did, but I didn't get there until after you fucks maimed the guy for life. He wasn't even the right person. What was it? They all look alike?" Sam nodded at Bert. "She's got a twitchy finger. As you can see. And her?" He indicated Phoebe. "She's just plain nuts. You know the younger generation. Raised on video games and all that. No idea what she'll do. Tell us what we want and we'll leave you to clean up this mess."

Jimmy summoned as much bluster a naked guy with a dead woman next to him could: "You're fucked. All of you. She was Guild. You kill the Guild, there's a contract on you. That means you're dead."

Sam nodded at Phoebe "She already has one on her, so she doesn't care. Bert and I? We're too old. If you get old, you'll understand. But at the moment, the likelihood of that is rather dim. You getting old, that is."

Bert spoke up. "The bad part of that Guild edict, Jimmy, is that once someone's killed one of you, there's nothing to stop someone from killing more. There's no taking it back is there? I'm walking dead now, ain't I? Just like my little friend here."

Phoebe bristled at the 'little friend' but right now wasn't the time to discuss it.

"Fuck you," Jimmy tried.

Phoebe had heard enough of those types of backed-in-a-corner *fuck you's* that she knew Jimmy was done.

Sam gave another push. "You *do* remember what your buddies did to that Afghani?" He kept the submachinegun in one hand while he opened up a butterfly knife with that little hand dance that Phoebe respected. The blade gleamed.

"Okay, okay," Jimmy said. "I won't tell anyone it was you."

"You're still way behind," Sam said. "We're trying to find someone who placed a contract. Name's Fromm. He's the one who put the contract on our friend here."

"Man, that isn't my area. Never heard of the guy. I'm recruitment. You know that."

"We know that and it's why we're here," Bert said. "We know you. So you give us someone else to know. Sort of we know, you know, they know thing. Someone who takes the contracts. A name, Jimmy and you get to grow old. A name."

Phoebe looked at the dead woman. The cloud in her still open eyes, just below the little black hole that had ended her existence. Despite the slackness of death, Phoebe could tell she'd been in good shape, which meant lots of working out. For what? To end like this? Everything in this woman's life had come to this point and stopped abruptly.

She was shaken out of her morbidity by Bert firing a round that punched a hole in the headboard right next to Jimmy's head.

"A name," Bert said. "Or else we start taking you apart, piece by piece." She nodded at Sam. "Right?"

"Fingers or toes?" Sam asked Jimmy. "Or perhaps we take your namesake." He pointed with the knife at his crotch and Jimmy put both hands over his private parts.

"You're crazy," Jimmy protested.

"First true thing you've said," Bert acknowledged. "A name and a place. Who takes the contracts?"

Jimmy didn't say anything.

"I say toes," Bert suggested. "He'll walk funny. That would be enjoyable."

Sam stood, looming over Jimmy. "How do you get the names of those you try to recruit? It's not like any of these outfits publish an alumni magazine."

"I get a list sent to me," Jimmy said.

"From who?" Sam asked.

Phoebe was getting tired of the chatting with a naked, ugly man. She hopped up on the bed, startling Jimmy. She drew her wakizashi and slashed.

A thin line of red appeared on Jimmy's lower abdomen and he scrambled away from her and Sam, climbing over the woman's body until he faced the muzzle of Bert's rifle. She jammed it hard into his solar plexus and he fell back, gasping for breath.

"You must have a really shitty personality," Phoebe said to him, "because that—" she pointed at his groin—"is not the reason they call you the dick."

Jimmy's eyes were doing the desperation samba, shifting from Phoebe to Bert to Sam and then back. Slowly accepting there was no way out.

"How do you make contact with your superior in the Guild?" Phoebe demanded, bringing the wakizashi up to the ready.

"She's crazy," Bert said, indicating Phoebe. "Nothing to lose, remember?"

Phoebe tried to elicit crazy, then realized standing over a naked man with a cooling corpse next to him while she held a bloodied sword in hand, pretty much qualified her.

"Phone," Jimmy blurted out. "Text messages and file downloads via secure phone. I get sent the person's file and go talk to them. That's it. All I know. They get their jobs the same way."

"Where's the phone?" Sam asked.

Jimmy nodded at the dresser. Sam opened a drawer and removed a secure phone, the same model Phoebe used with the Organization and she imagined was used across the covert spectrum. Which meant that Louise was familiar with it and could crack it.

"Who takes the contracts?" Bert asked.

"I don't know. I swear on my life."

"Who do you talk to?" Bert asked.

"It's almost always text messages," Jimmy said. "You know that's more secure when it's encrypted."

"You have to talk to someone," Sam said. "What if you have questions? You text those?"

"Who do you talk to?" Bert pressed.

"Some bitch," Jimmy said. He saw the look in Bert's eyes and back-tracked. "Some woman. I got any questions, I ask her. Same number as the text."

"What's her name?" Sam asked.

"No name. She just answers the call. Sometimes she calls and tells me to do something." He nodded at the dead woman. "Same woman gives her the contract."

"What do we need to access this?" Sam asked, wagging the phone.

"Fingerprint," Jimmy said. "Then a voice code. My voice. You can't access it."

"Do we believe him?" Bert asked Sam and Phoebe.

Sam nodded. "I wouldn't trust him further than this—" he hefted the phone—"so, yeah."

"Phoebe?" Bert asked.

She shrugged. "I don't know. I think we chop off his namesake and—" she didn't finish as Jimmy begged.

"No! I'm telling the truth! I swear."

"I believe you," Bert said. Then she shot Jimmy in the temple.

"Geez," Phoebe muttered as she hopped off the bloody bed which now supported two corpses.

"I told you to cut toes off," Bert groused. "Not scratch his belly."

"I've found pain produces talk," Phoebe said. "But not necessarily the truth."

Sam grabbed Jimmy's hand and using the switchblade, removed the finger he'd held up, depositing it in a evidence bag he produced from one of the many pockets on his coat. "Not like we're going to get his voice code now," he said, glaring at Bert.

"He would have given the alert code," Bert said. "You know that's how that bit of nonsense goes. Hoping his employer would backtrack the phone and rescue him."

Sam nodded. "You're right."

Phoebe held out her hand for the phone. "My tech person at the Organization should be able to crack that."

Phoebe searched the nightstand, while Sam dumped out the contents of the woman's purse. Another, smaller pistol, a wallet, and a phone similar to Jimmy's which he confiscated. And a dark blue pill bottle with no label. Sam opened it and shook out three blue capsules. He also removed her finger, just in case.

"He's got the same pills," Phoebe said, holding up a similar bottle. She opened it. Three blue capsules. "Same number."

Sam frowned. "That's weird. In the old days they'd issue us uppers by the boatload. What good is three pills?"

"And why do they have the same pills and the same number?" Phoebe asked.

"Not important," Bert said. "Let's get going."

"Your hand is bleeding," Sam said to Phoebe.

"I'll bandage it in the van," Phoebe said.

Sam indicated the bloody mess on the bed. "We'll need a cleaner to take care of this too."

"I'll call it in," Phoebe said.

"Come on," Bert said. "We best put some distance behind us and this."

Phoebe held up the sword. "Was it—"

Bert answered before she finished. "Too much? Nah. I liked it."

THE ORGANIZATION'S fleet of aircraft was a combination of expensive and cheap, the result of Mrs. Finch's excel spreadsheet in Accounting. The airframe was top of the line, the fastest at its size. It could accommodate half-a-dozen operatives, or one or two and a full array of gear, much like the Organization's vans. Right now, Shane had the passenger compartment to himself and the large plastic cases containing weapons, explosive and other tools of the trade.

The accouterments other than that for mission accomplishment were barebones. The chair he was sitting in didn't even recline. He imagined that cost extra or that Mrs. Finch had managed to buy it on the cheap from some airline misfit discount sale. He had his laptop perched precariously on the unsteady food tray that had unfolded from the arm of the chair and didn't quite lock into place.

Now that the Organization's computer was secure and running, Shane brought up a secure link to Andova. It was the high-speed version of 'Zoom'. Shane was surprised when a young woman with a partly shaved head and a nose ring appeared on screen.

"Mister Shane," she said, not a question since his credentials had initiated the call.

"Just Shane."

"Yes. Shane. I am Janna. Lucien will be with us shortly."

"Right." Shane hated talking via computer. Was he supposed to chat with this woman? As Carpenter had once inelegantly put it: there was no small talk in covert ops.

Shane was spared his concern when Lucien's face appeared on the top bar. "Thank you, Shane, for agreeing to help. But I believe we can handle this ourselves."

"Wasn't it 'ourselves' who got Lisa Livia kidnapped?" Shane asked, tossing away both small talk and tact.

Lucien nodded, not offended. "True. I tried to talk LL out of doing the exchange, but you know how she is when she is determined."

Like Agnes, Shane thought. "You couldn't provide better security? Tell me what happened."

Lucien succinctly updated him on events from Paris to the trip up the canyon.

"I've never heard of an Assassin's Guild," Shane said. He figured he'd only hung up his spurs recently so they hadn't had a chance to recruit him or if he hadn't made the cut to be considered, which might be a good thing. But insulting.

"Our intelligence service hasn't either," Lucien said.

"You think this Fausto guy is in this Labyrinth?" Shane asked.

"We are certain," Lucien said. "Janna?"

The young woman filled them in: "We paid Fausto twenty million to return the statue of Saint Ingrid. The medium was Bitcoin. The information he needed to make the transfer was on a thumb drive. I also embedded a tracking code so I would be able to find the originator of the transfer."

"Meaning?" Shane asked.

"We know where the transfer message initiated," Lucien said.

Lead with the headline, Shane thought. But did not say.

"I'm sending you the grid," Janna said.

Shane got it and brought up the topographic map. X marked the spot, which was the top of snow-covered mountain. *Of course*, Shane thought.

"The signal propagated from there, on the top of that peak," Janna said. "But the actual sender was in the Labyrinth."

Shane had images of a legendary king and half-man-half-bull and Lisa Livia as a virgin sacrifice, which is where the image came to a screeching halt. "'Labyrinth'?"

Lucien filled him in on the mine.

"I've checked the records," Janna said. "There were stories of a cave inside the mine where Spanish collaborators received downed pilots from the French Resistance during World War II. A radio antenna was on top of the mountain and a wire dropped down through a fissure to the cave."

"How far down?" Shane asked.

"The records weren't specific," Janna said.

"Do we have a route to the cave?" Shane asked.

Lucien answered. "We can't have a route if we don't know where the cave is exactly. But it's where Lisa Livia and Fausto are holed up.

The problem is that it is truly a Labyrinth. I've been in the system a couple of times and it is very easy to get lost. And . . ."

He paused, and Shane knew it wasn't one of those good pauses where the other person is trying to figure out how to give the good news.

"The peak was recently fortified by the Field Marshall. There is a battery of surface to air missiles and numerous security cameras. Gates in the tunnels were also added to preclude a fast assault."

"Right," Shane said. Surface to air missiles changed things considerably.

"This fissure," Shane said. "How big is it?"

"It's called the Chimney," Janna answered. "The only information I could find out about it was from an old newspaper article with an interview with a veteran of the network that helped the pilots escape during the War. He said they'd build a fire in the cave and use it to let the smoke out. But a man climbed up it to emplace the antenna."

"From the inside?" Shane said. "Not climb the outside of the mountain?"

Lucien shook his head. "The peak is essentially unclimbable. Sheer rock walls. Particularly when it's covered in ice and snow. The missiles and camera were emplaced via helicopter." Lucien shook his head. "Fausto is in an impregnable position and he has numerous escape routes should he decide to flee. We do not have sufficient people to secure all of them. Plus, some of the tunnels exit in Spain where we have no jurisdiction and he has connections. It is not good."

Shane looked at the boxes of gear crammed in the plane with him. "I've got an idea."

WORDS OF WISDOM #7

Shane's Words of Wisdom #8
Don't get in a pissing contest with a man on a balcony.
Shane's Addendum: This is a corollary to the maxim shit rolls downhill.
Either way, you end up dirty and smelly and you've lost.

Phoebe's Observations #8:

No woman would piss off a balcony.
Also, we're not waiting for a prince to save us.
Phoebe's Addendum: We're perfectly capable of saving ourselves.

7

Phoebe woke with her face stuck to the cracked linoleum that upholstered the benches in the booths of *The Dog's Balls*. She knew where she was because the place smelled of stale beer and recent gun battle. She'd slept in worse locations. They'd returned to *The Dog's Balls* from Pennsylvania to link up with Louise who would decrypt the phones and find out who issued Jimmy the Dick his marching orders. A step closer to the Guild and the contact with Fromm.

Upon arriving, Bert had muttered something about '*I'll sleep when I'm dead*' and gone to the bar for a drink and to look at her iPad. Phoebe had scouted out this spot as the best option and immediately crashed, a skill she'd learned early in her first deployment in the Ranger Battalion. Sam had chosen another booth, muttering something about fixing things up a bit in the joint, which Bert had studiously ignored.

Dawn was still a few hours away, but Phoebe came to instant consciousness with the sense that Louise was close. She couldn't explain the feeling, but she trusted it. She stood and stretched, then wandered over to Bert. The older woman's face looked worn and haggard in the glow from the iPad. Phoebe spotted the two same kids sleeping in room illuminated by a nightlight; one of those the slowly rotating stars on the ceiling.

"How are the grandkids?" Phoebe asked. *Miss their grandfather?* she thought, but didn't say.

Bert put the iPad face down on the bar. "When's your friend showing up?"

"Soon," Phoebe said, not sure what line she'd crossed with her question.

Bert scooted off the bar stool. "I'm going back to the office. Get me when your friend arrives."

Phoebe frowned as Bert went to a door and disappeared.

Sam walked over. "Shouldn't ask personal questions."

"You don't think it's weird she spies on her own grandkids?" Phoebe asked.

Sam looked at her, his eyes dark under white eyebrows. "She doesn't have grandkids."

"That's even creepier." Phoebe indicated the iPad. "Who are the kids she's spying on then?"

"You might consider Bert their fairy godmother," Sam said.

Phoebe couldn't envision Bert as a fairy. Or a God. Or a mother. "How so?"

"Bert was supposed to kill their mother," Sam said.

"Okay," Phoebe said dubiously. "And?"

"The mother was three months pregnant with the person who is now the mother of those children she's observing."

"Why was she targeted?" Phoebe asked.

"Who the fuck knows why?" Sam snapped. "The mission packet came to Bert and the woman was the target. Did you ask why every time you got a mission packet?"

Phoebe knew better than to respond.

Sam shrugged. "Maybe the person who sent the mission packet didn't know the target's current status? More likely, they didn't care. You don't get a pass just because you're knocked up, right?"

Phoebe had been in some strange situations but this one was new
to her so she had nothing to say. Didn't they give pregnant women on
death row a stay until they gave birth? It wasn't a subject Phoebe had
investigated.

"Anyway," Sam continued, "she put surveillance on the target and
it wasn't hard to figure out the situation." He fell silent for a moment.
"Bert did some digging. Found out the target had been fingered
because of a former husband who'd already been terminated. Didn't
mean the target was completely innocent. She'd known what her
husband was up to and possessed sensitive knowledge. But it was old
stuff. Years old that had somehow bubbled up.

"The target had remarried since then. Started a new life away
from the business. The new husband wasn't a player." Sam sighed.
"This isn't a game. You're not supposed to get do-overs. But Bert
decided to give the target a do-over. That baby was born and now," he
nodded at the iPad, "has two kids of her own. And Bert figures none
of them would be in this world if she hadn't made a decision. Which
is more than most of us can say about our lives which are usually
pretty fucking random. So. Yeah. She considers them her legacy in
this world. Three lives when there shouldn't be one." Sam looked into
her eyes. "You can be a bad person but live a good life. Checking in on
those kids helps her get up in the morning and not blow her brains
out and sometimes that's all you can ask for.

Phoebe was rescued from making any comment by her secure
phone buzzing. She checked the screen. "Louise is almost here. Better
get Bert."

Lisa Livia startled awake, blinking in the dim light, confused. Where was she? When was this? Where was Lucien?

The last one anchored her and she remembered. She was in a cave. Kidnapped by a crazy relative of Lucien's. Not Lucien's fault, she thought right away, but, still. There was that connection. Every relationship has its ups and downs.

She looked around from her position on a not-comfortable cot, a far cry from the sumptuous mattress in *D'Aigle*. And the house in Paris. And Agnes' bed on the top floor of Two Rivers. Things were not going in the right direction.

Lisa Livia determined she was getting a new mattress and sheets and comforter if she got out of here. When she got out of here, she mentally affirmed as she swung her feet off the cot and set them on the stone floor.

She still didn't know how long she'd been out. Fausto was at the table, staring at the screen of the laptop. Only one of the guards was present. *Where was the other one?* Lisa Livia wondered as she stood. Which was followed by a queasy panic as she remembered the shots that had shattered the window at *D'Aigle* and the one in the mirror on the way up the track.

Lucien was coming and an assassin was out there with a sniper rifle.

It didn't occur to her to doubt for a moment that Lucien was coming for her and when she realized that, she experienced conflicting feelings. She walked over to the table.

Fausto glanced at her. The screen displayed an image of the road she'd driven up. Every three seconds was a different view and angle. Some of them were also cave entrances, including the one they'd come in.

"I have many remote cameras in place," Fausto said proudly. "And a drone I can launch. I will know when Lucien is coming. You are free to watch when I finish him."

"Don't count your cannoli's until you're outta the car," Lisa Livia said. "May I borrow your knife?"

"What? What do you mean cannoli's?"

"Really?" Lisa Livia shook her head and held out her hand. "The knife?"

"Why would I give you a weapon?" Fausto asked.

"You got guns," Lisa Livia said. "You're scared of little old me and a pen knife?" She indicated the wall. "I want to carve my name."

CARPENTER LOOKED at his list of questions.

Where is Fromm? Where is Orion?

Who is Fromm?

Who was Phoebe's mother? What did Phoebe's father really do?

Who was the assassin in the elevator? Connected to assassin in France? Who was Chatty Kathy?

What is the Assassin's Guild?

The first two were the critical ones. The rest were subordinate to the mission. Fromm had hired the Assassin's Guild to do his dirty work and they were a threat. But not the objective. Who Phoebe was and her background? Now that he had access to the NSA mainframe he could dissolve the redactions in her file. Did it matter?

He rubbed his eyes, trying to alleviate the burning of exhaustion in them.

"Where is Louise?" Hannah asked from the doorway, startling him.

Carpenter popped to his feet, an autonomic response drilled into him early in his career, although technically he wasn't sure that Hannah outranked him by being the head of the Cellar. But given the fact she could wipe him, and the Organization, off the face of the earth, a little respect was due.

"She's meeting Phoebe to use a captured phone to geo-locate the next contact. Phoebe was in Pennsylvania and Louise is meeting her halfway at *The Dog's Balls*." The shadow on his shoulder cackled at his hurried explanation, as if he were a schoolboy caught doing something naughty.

Hannah was one of those women who could be an old fortyish or a young sixtyish, it was hard to tell. She was of average height and a trim build in a well-tailored grey business suit. Her most distinctive feature was her stylishly cut silver hair. Crows feet crowded the edges of her eyes and her mouth was a pale slash, neither up or down, as if representing her neutrality in life. She carried several folders.

She pointed to the corner ceiling. "Have you shut down your outside surveillance by Fromm?"

"Yes. We've regained control of our system."

Hannah didn't comment on that. She indicated the chair in front of the desk. "May I?"

"Of course."

Hannah settled in. "I rarely get out, but I'm not sure trading one bunker for another can be considered getting out." She had the files in her lap and regarded Carpenter without any hint of approval or disapproval or any emotion at all. For all he knew, she was trying to decide whether to kill him or fire him. He was pretty sure there was no promotion in the offing.

She continued. "For a long time, I simply followed my predecessor's routine. Ensconced in my hole in the ground. Not a pleasant hole, mind you. Literally a Cellar." She sighed. "*In a hole in the ground there lived a hobbit. Not a nasty, dirty, wet hole, filled with the ends of worms and an oozy smell, nor yet a dry, bare, sandy hole with nothing in it to sit down on or to eat'*. I think of those opening lines often."

Quoting *The Hobbit* was one of the last things he'd expect from Hannah, but as Shane had always warned: expect the unexpected; which, of course, made no sense when you drilled down into it.

"I wonder what hole Fromm has crawled into," Hannah said. "I suspect it will not be comfortable."

"That's why Phoebe and Louise are meeting," Carpenter said.

"The man before me, Nero, was blind," Hannah said, "so it didn't matter much to him about the aesthetics of the hole he lived and worked in. He could sense things in ways I could never hope to emulate. It finally occurred to me after some years that I had to do some things differently."

Carpenter waited for the headline or the query as Hannah wasn't rumored to be a chatter. He briefly wondered if she were referring to him and his predecessor, Wilson?

"We are the products of our past," Hannah said. "And it appears we did not know Fromm's past, did we?"

"I haven't had a chance to dive into that," Carpenter said. "I was just getting ready to—"

Hannah waved a hand, stopping him. He noted the glint of the wedding band and wondered what had happened to her husband in the past. She'd told him at their last meeting that she'd been married once upon a time and she wore the band to remind him of her mistake.

She lifted one of the folders. "We know more now. I put my best person on it once we realized he'd gone rogue. That is, after all, the Cellar's mission and we couldn't wait for you to get back online, could we."

Applause from the ghost for the rebuke.

"Why did you tell me to get my operative on it, then?" Carpenter dared to ask.

"I was giving you a chance to clean up your own mess."

Carpenter wasn't buying it. "You want to see how deep the rot goes."

"That, too." She waved the folder. "Do you want to know?"

"Certainly."

"Sadly, it's not helpful. Fromm's real name? Thaddeus Dickson. An orphan raised in the system in California. Bouncing from home to home. Seems no one wanted to keep him long."

That didn't surprise Carpenter.

"He changed his last name, legally, when he started applying to colleges. It appears he did this to support an entirely false background he put together to fool college admissions boards. Test scores, academic record, etcetera. Relatively impressive for a sixteen-year-old. It was good enough to not only get him into Stanford but on a full scholarship. From there, his path was straightforward to the NSA and then here. Nothing nefarious popped up which is why his background security clearance checks were green. The name change should have been found, but given it was while he was a minor and his childhood records sealed, it would have required a little extra effort and the clearers didn't make that effort. And even if they had, what difference would it have made? It's not a crime to change your name, especially if one is an orphan." She tossed the file to the side and it fluttered to the floor. "I've saved you some time."

"Any hint in there where he might have gone?" Carpenter asked, although her dismissal of the file and Fromm's past indicated the answer.

"No."

She held up another folder. "What is of more interest is his psych evals."

Carpenter frowned. "What pysch evals? His entry evaluation?" Everyone going into covert ops got screened by a shrink. It was pretty perfunctory because the very fact one wanted to be part of that world put them outside the bell curve. It was mainly designed to keep the true psychopaths out, or, rather funnel them to the units that needed such. It was the classic sniper's paradox. We want you to lie in this hide site for days and kill some stranger in cold blood, but only kill those we tell you too. No choosing your own targets or popping someone off when you get bored. A not normal psychological combination.

Hannah shook her head. "No. The follow-ups."

Carpenter felt foolish, having not considered that there was some sort of system in place.

Hannah continued. "Key personnel are evaluated every two years. There's an entire group dedicated to it. Run by one of my people, Doctor Golden. She came to the Cellar with an intriguing theory that we could determine who would go rogue by studying their medical records. Look for signs of childhood abuse, etcetera. But it was really only useful for those raised in the military world where we could access such records. It did help us on occasion, particularly when a military person or small unit went off the reservation. Otherwise, we were limited."

"Units have gone off the reservation?" Carpenter asked. Wondering if that was that an implied threat.

"Small teams operating on their own develop a cohesion," Hannah said. "If that cohesion is collectively rubbed the wrong way, bad things can happen. Such as when such a team feels betrayed. We had a sniper team go rogue a while back and Doctor Golden was useful in helping us deal with that."

"Were they betrayed?" Carpenter asked.

"Does it matter?" Hannah replied. "In their desire for revenge they were killing innocents and also threatening to expose some rather delicate missions."

Carpenter wondered which of those two reasons was the more important, then realized Hannah had already answered: did it matter?

Hannah continued. "Doctor Golden also came up with a unique way of conducting real time psych evals without the subject being aware."

"Observation," Carpenter said.

"Indeed. Intense surveillance. People can, and often do, lie while sitting on a couch in a therapist's office. Or while taking a test. Or while at work, pretending to be something they aren't. We know polygraphs have limited usefulness. But someone's true nature comes out in their daily habits. After all, are we not the sum of our habits?

"Doctor Golden said you can get a good idea of someone just by observing them drive. Do they speed? Follow too close? Look in the rear-view mirror or act as if no one else exists on the road, which is an easy determiner of narcissism. Can they merge and thus have the ability to project possible courses of action? Do they exhibit road rage, indicating a lack of self-control? Extend that to checking other things like what television shows and movies they enjoy. Even more so, what ones they detest? What kind of pornography they watch often gives insight into childhood trauma? Who do they affiliate with outside of work? What are their hobbies? You get the gist."

Carpenter shifted in the chair, uncomfortable with what she was describing.

Hannah smiled as if sensing that. "Really, let's face the fact that Google and Apple and their algorithms know significantly more about most people than any psychiatrist. We use that data too, by the way."

"Fromm?" Carpenter asked.

Hannah didn't have to open the file. "Loner. Stalker of women. Nothing overtly criminal but more in terms of a peeping Tom. He had cameras installed in Louise's house. There he did break the rules by ordering an NSA surveillance team to install them using his official credentials. That should have been flagged, but since it was Fromm, he kept it all looking quite legit and even got Wilson to sign off on it. Whether Wilson was aware of what he was signing or did it out of ignorance doesn't matter at this point. One hand doesn't know what the other is doing in our world and thus one hand can use the other to commit a crime with the right authorization."

"He was watching Louise?"

"Yes. And more. Even a few random women he crossed paths with in the world. A cashier at his local grocery whom he fancied. A former professor from Stanford. A couple of others."

"Why wasn't I informed? Or Wilson before me?"

"Wilson was informed," Hannah said. "He didn't care because Fromm was useful to him. I wasn't informed because none of it rose to the level of a security threat. It was labeled more a peccadillo of a brilliant mind."

"That doesn't bring us any closer to finding him or Orion," Carpenter said.

Hannah dropped the file to land on the other one next to her chair. "Correct. But it does give us insight into motivation. The assumption would be that Fromm is going for money since the current bid is over three hundred million dollars. A not insubstantial sum. But money is a means to an end."

"What does Fromm want to buy?" Carpenter asked.

"Indeed," Hannah agreed. She held up the third file. "A quantum computer. Chinese made. Going price three hundred and twenty million. It's relatively small but requires a tremendous amount of power to run."

Carpenter didn't ask how she knew this. "What does he want it for?"

"He's trying to reverse his peeping Tom predilection."

"Lilith," Carpenter said.

"Yes," Hannah confirmed. "He's been attempting to create artificial intelligence for many years. Some of that done under the auspices of the NSA. But mostly on his own. He's spent decades on it. His programs are good. Very good. His problem has always been the lack of computing power and his own inherent flaws, which he fails to see." She pointed at her head. "The human brain is capable of processing one hundred trillion calculations per second. On record, the world's fastest computer takes forty minutes to do the same number. But the Chinese have a new quantum computer that quadruples that power. Still not near human power, but much, much better. That is what Fromm wants. He believes with it he can use the computer to increase the effectiveness of his program and thus invent even faster computers and eventually an artificial intelligence equal to that of the human brain. A self-fulfilling loop. And there are new robotic technologies he's been researching."

"Just so he can invent the perfect woman?" Carpenter was incredulous.

Hannah dropped the third file and shrugged. "You'd be surprised what motivates people to do the strangest things."

"Can he do it if he gets the computer?"

"No," Hannah said. "He's mentally ill. Teams of people much smarter than him have been working that problem for a long time. It's a sign of his narcissism that he believes he can do it alone."

"But?" Carpenter asked, sensing Hannah was holding something back.

"The thing about artificial intelligence," Hannah said, "is that the best programmer of AI is not human. It's AI. After all, who would understand programming better than a program? The concern is that someone will have a breakthrough and program an AI that will then take things beyond what any human programmer could do." She shook her head. "That doesn't change our situation though. Bottom line? We have to get Orion back and Fromm needs to be stopped."

Carpenter looked at the folders on the floor. "You could have sent those to me."

"True," Hannah said as she folded her hands on her lap and regarded him with eyes that weren't dead, but weren't sparkling with joy either.

"That information doesn't bring us any closer to finding Fromm," Carpenter repeated.

"You don't think?" Hannah asked.

Carpenter knew a challenge when it was presented to him. "Wherever Fromm is hiding, he needs access to a lot of power to make that computer work."

"True."

"He's been planning this for a while," Carpenter said.

"Also true."

With anyone else, this would feel remedial, but Carpenter trusted that Hannah had a point. "He used his position, and that of Wilson, to spy on Louise Wingo. It stands to reason that isn't the only time he did that."

"Now that your system is on-line you can check."

"Fromm would have covered his tracks electronically," Carpenter said. "He's an expert at that."

"Even experts make mistakes." Hannah stood.

Carpenter took the opportunity. "Bert and Sam. Were they in the Cellar?"

"Bert was. Sam was a freelancer."

"Mercenary?"

"No," Hannah said. "He worked for various government agencies. A few times for me. Some jobs for the Organization, but that was long ago. He retired, but then came back a year or so ago, as your records will indicate."

"Why? If he has so much experience, why would he want to be a Cleaner?"

"That's a good question." Hannah turned and walked out, leaving Carpenter with more questions than when she'd walked in, although he could cross off the second line on his list:

~~Who is Fromm?~~

Then he wrote:

What else did Fromm do?

He quickly typed up a summary of the little he now knew and forwarded it to Louise.

SHANE HAD an earpiece in and a mike transmitter wrapped around his throat. He was the lone occupant in the passenger compartment of the jet, studying the satellite images of Chimney Peak and the surrounding area on the iPad as he was patched through via secure satellite comms to Lucien.

"Shane?" Lucien said.

"Here," Shane replied. "Status?"

"Vicente and I are moving up the gorge."

"There will be surveillance," Shane said.

"Of course," Lucien said. "That's the point."

Which meant that Lucien and Vicente were the diversion. Shane knew that diversion was a nice way of saying 'the bait'.

Vicente must have had the same in mind as he said: "Let us endeavor to not become a forlorn hope."

That was an old military term for the volunteers who would be the first to storm the gates of a fortification in the attempt to breach it, with the expectation that casualties would be high but others would finish the assault. It was considered a great way to earn some medals. Often posthumously.

"Good idea," Shane agreed.

A new voice cut in. "Twenty minutes." The pilot was giving Shane flight time warnings.

"Roger," Shane said. "I'll check in just prior, Lucien."

"I understand."

Shane could rig a parachute harness blindfolded and half-asleep. Not that either was a good idea. Doing it alone was a bit more difficult than with a partner. He had to work to grab the leg straps from the harness and pull them through between his legs and click them in place. Then he squatted them, tightening them. Failure to do so could lead to awkward pain upon the opening shock of the chute. He connected the chest strap and then hooked the rucksack below the reserve in front. The submachinegun went on the side, cinched down by the waist strap. Then he checked himself, performing the JMPI, jumpmaster inspection, he'd done hundreds of times in the past, but usually on someone else.

Everything seemed good.

"Six minutes," the pilot announced. "Depressurizing in one minute."

"Roger," Shane replied. He had a small oxygen bottle on the front of the rig and he pulled up the face mask, putting it on. Turned the knob and got a steady flow. Checked the gauge. Double-checked it. "I'm green on oxygen."

"Depressurizing," the pilot replied.

Shane's ears popped as the jet, flying at 25,000 feet, slowly depressurized to match the thin air outside. Given that the Pyrenees rose up to over 11,000 feet in places and his drop zone was at 7,800 feet, that cut down the amount of time he had to fly his parachute in. It also meant he better be damn sure he knew where he was.

"Three minutes," the pilot informed him. "Door is unlocked."

Shane went to the door just behind the cockpit wall. The interior was covered with warnings, particularly the one people scoff about 'do not open while in flight', except this door was specially modified to be opened in flight. Mrs. Finch had splurged for that as a possible mission essential option but it probably cost an extra buck to get the warning removed from the door. Plus, you never knew. Some burnt out Operator might try do it without a parachute, although it would be impossible at altitude in a pressurized cabin as it opened inward.

"Depressurized," the pilot told him.

Shane grabbed the handle and unlatched the door. Then hit the button that activated the hydraulics that pulled it in, then swung it out of the way. The swirl of freezing air wrapped around him with a roar. The plane shuddered as the pilots slowed down to just above stall speed to prevent Shane from going out at a speed that would spin and tumble him about so hard there was a good chance he'd be knocked unconscious. It's the little things that make all the difference.

Shane grabbed the sides of the open door and leaned out. At this altitude the temperature was well below freezing. He could see white capped mountains sprawled below in all directions. He spotted the capitol of Andova. From there it wasn't difficult to spot the large 'chateau' that Lucien had told him about. He shifted his gaze and saw Chimney Peak. It was obvious why it was a difficult target. Sheer rock walls negated approaching except for a narrow gorge which was easily defended. The top, almost a straight ascent in all directions, was covered in snow. At this distance and altitude, Shane couldn't make out any details or spot the SAM missiles, which were probably camouflaged.

"Thirty seconds," the pilot announced.

They were over Spanish airspace, legally. The flight plan called for the plane to continue on and land in France. The release point would be offset from the peak by two miles laterally and a mile and a half vertically. That made for some serious hard flying on Shane's part to make it, but any closer might alert whoever was controlling the SAMs and bring about that which they did not desire.

"Go!" the pilot announced and Shane stepped out.

The plane was past and gone in a flash and he arced his back and spread his legs and arms to get stable from his initial tumble. As soon he was, he pulled the rip cord and the parachute blossomed over his head. He grabbed the toggles and began a hard track to the southwest toward Chimney Peak. He tried to slow his descent because he had a long way to go laterally and not much altitude to achieve it.

"Lucien?" he asked.

"Here."

"I estimate touchdown in about two minutes."

"We're still moving up," Lucien replied. "No contact yet. But the place where Lisa Livia and I were shot at is just ahead. I suspect the sniper will be in the same position."

"Good luck."

"The same."

Shane focused on flying the chute, but unbidden thoughts intruded. *I'm going to be married in a week.*

He shook his head and checked his altitude. He braked his descent even more.

Kids? They would be hell on wheels, since they'd be half-Agnes.

Shane mentally cursed and stared at Chimney Peak, growing ever closer. He made an adjustment as he closed on it. He saw an antenna poking above the snow and a white painted box about eight feet by eight to the side of it. The SAM launcher, currently closed, which was a positive sign. It was defense for a helicopter since that was the only kind of aircraft that could get there. Other than a guy flying a chute which shouldn't show up on radar.

A THOUSAND FEET BELOW SHANE, and in the gorge, Lucien edged the SUV around an outcropping of rock. This was where he and Lisa Livia had been ambushed earlier and he'd been forced to get out. This vehicle, unlike the previous one, was designed for security and the windshield could take bullets up to and including fifty caliber size. Nevertheless, there was a certain degree of apprehension moving into what could rightly be considered a kill zone.

Surprisingly, nothing happened. He and Vicente continued forward.

"He wants us in close," Vicente said, dousing the slight optimism Lucien had experienced when there was no shot. "He knows we have these types of vehicles. He will use Lisa Livia to get us very close so he can be certain to finish us."

"I forgot how cheerful you always are," Lucien said.

"I am a realist," Vicente said. "It's kept me alive this long."

"Good," Lucien said. "Let's continue that streak then."

"It would be preferable," Vicente agreed.

SHANE DUMPED some air for a last-second course adjustment. Then he flared the chute to brake. His feet touched down in six inches of snow on the top of the chimney, right next to the antenna.

"The eagle has landed," Shane announced, which he figured was more profound than the turd has hit the mark.

LOUISE CARRIED her laptop and special keyboard and mouse ensconced in a specially built case into *The Dog's Balls*. Her Cleaner remained in the van. The vehicle contained a secure link to the laptop and via that the Organization's mainframe. Phoebe helped her get set up in one of the booths. The interior of the bar still smelled of cordite, blood and death to Phoebe. With an undertone of stale beer and worse.

Phoebe made the introductions which went as expected: Sam was welcoming, Bert was gruff and appeared uninterested as she handed over the two phones from Jimmy the Dick and his girlfriend of the moment, their fingers, and then went back to the bar and her shot glass and iPad. Sam joined Bert with a small bag from which he produced his knitting needles and yarn and began working away, needles clicking.

As Phoebe and Louise settled into the booth with the computer, Louise whispered. "I don't think Bert likes me."

"Her people skills are somewhat lacking," Phoebe said.

"I mean in the other way," Louise said.

Phoebe knew what Louise was referring to but didn't pursue it.

"And that guy knitting is a Cleaner? The Sam guy who saved you in Montana?" Louise asked as she powered up the laptop and checked the connection.

"He's more than that," Phoebe said. "His nickname is Sam the Matador. And he saved me at the prison."

"What does the Matador part mean?" Louise asked. She checked the wireless secure link to the van and got green.

"No clue," Phoebe said, "but it sounds cool."

"Do you have a nickname?" Louise asked her.

"Not that anyone's told me," Phoebe said, "but they treat me like a little kid. Sam calls me Young Miss sometimes."

"That's sweet," Louise said as she blinked and clicked the cursor on the screen.

"No, it's not. It's condescending."

Louise made the face which Phoebe had learned meant she disagreed but didn't want to argue over it. Chitchat was over as Louise took Jimmy the Dick's phone and plugged it into her laptop. "Same model we use which makes this easier. Frequency hopping and encryption while transmitting. But we're not trying to listen in or call someone. We want to know who and where it's been talking to."

"Right," Phoebe said.

"The phone is designed to erase all records of calls," Louise said as she typed one-handed, moved her head to roll the mouse, and blinked to click. "But like all computers there are ghosts in the machine."

"Uh-huh." Phoebe was usually in the field and Louise in the office when working together. It was odd to be sitting side by side in this dive bar. While one old-timer was peeping on kids she'd never met and another was knitting whatever it was that Sam was knitting. Life, sometimes, was odd.

"Let's see," Louise murmured as she clicked and typed, electronically digging into the secure phone. After a minute she held out her hand without looking away from the screen. "Give me the other phone. Good thing we have two."

"Uh-huh," Phoebe said as she handed it over. Not so good for the woman.

Louise plugged that into another outlet. "I'm trying to match the ghosts in the data to get a more coherent picture. It's like two blurry images of the same thing. If I can perfectly overlap them, it should come into focus"

"Uh- huh."

"Your enthusiasm underwhelms," Louise complained, but without bite, her focus on her work.

"You want these?" Phoebe indicated the severed fingers.

Louise stared at them for a second. "Yes. Which goes with which?"

Phoebe placed the appropriate plastic bag next to the corresponding phone. Louise awkwardly used the fingers to do the initial open of the phones.

Phoebe saw Bert say something to Sam, then show him her iPad. *Great*, Phoebe thought. *Two old pervs.*

As if sensing her thought, Sam turned on the stool and looked at her. "Does this Fromm guy use a black field with skull and crossed swords?"

Bert held up the iPad, which displayed Fromm's screen saver.

"That's him," Phoebe said.

"He's hacked your IP," Louise said.

Before anyone else could speak, the screen cleared and there was Fromm.

"Hmm, who do we have here?" Fromm's voice echoed out of the iPad's small speaker. "Can you give me a scan so I know who I'm talking to. I assume it's Bert holding the iPad, is it not?"

"Fuck you," Bert said. She went to turn off the iPad but Phoebe held up her hand, stopping her, while getting out of the booth and walking over.

"What do you want, Fromm?"

"Saying hello to my favorite and least favorite women. Hello, Louise. And Phoebe."

Phoebe took the iPad from a scowling Bert. "You look like shit, Fromm. Tired of losing?"

"I saw Louise over there in the corner," Fromm said. "What is she doing? I'm surprised Carpenter let her out of the bat cave. He must be getting desperate."

"She's finding you," Phoebe said. "Of course, you could just tell us and save her the trouble, since you like her so much."

"Phoebe, Phoebe, Phoebe. You are so behind on everything."

"Tell that to Jimmy the Dick," Phoebe said. "And his squeeze."

"Who?" Fromm asked.

"Forget about them," Phoebe said. "They're the past. As in literally. Let's focus on you. Really. Focus. Let's make you the past."

Fromm shook his head. "Poor deluded Phoebe."

"Where's your jerk-off fantasy video girl?" Phoebe asked.

"No need to be rude," Fromm said.

"I got lots of reasons to be rude to you," Phoebe said. "Don't get me started." Out of the corner of her eye she saw Sam take the submachinegun from behind the bar and slip out the backdoor. Checking the perimeter since Fromm knew where they were. Louise closed her laptop and took off her special glasses.

"Congratulations, Louise," Fromm said. "Excellent job cleaning the Organization's computers. My simulation predicted it would take longer."

"So did mine," Louise said. "But then everyone in Technical worked together and we got it done faster. Amazing what teamwork can do."

"With good leadership," Phoebe added.

"It won't help you," Fromm said.

"Already has," Louise said.

"How so?" Fromm asked.

"You'll find out," Louise said.

Sam came back in and indicated the outside was clear.

Fromm waved that away. "You spout nonsense. And you, my dear Phoebe. Any closer to learning who your mother is?"

"Stop with the bullshit," Phoebe said. "Keep your eye on the ball, Fromm, or you're going to go down too easily."

"Dear Phoebe," Fromm said, shaking his head. "It is not, as you say, bullshit. I most certainly have my eye on the ball. My question is most applicable given your present company."

Phoebe's eyes widened and she looked up from the iPad screen at Bert who quickly and vehemently shook her head and made the unmistakable '*I got no idea what he's talking about*' face.

"Stop trying to mess with Phoebe's head," Louise yelled. "Thaddeus Dickson."

Fromm laughed. "You know the name that was scribbled on a piece of paper when I was born. By a mother I never knew. We do share that, Phoebe. Except at least you knew who your father was, although he was living a lie to you. Pretending to be that which he was not."

Phoebe was rock still, holding the iPad in one hand, staring at Fromm. Louise came over and put her arm around her.

"You're pathetic, Fromm," Louise said. "Go back to your make-believe girlfriend."

"Did you never learn that imitation is the greatest form of flattery?" Fromm said to Louise. "You should join me. Together we could do amazing things, although I'm going to do them on my own anyway. You can share in it, though."

"Never," Louise said.

"Never is a long, long time," Fromm said. "Longer than you have."

And that's when the roof exploded.

WORDS OF WISDOM #8

There is no we and they until they fuck up.
Shane's Addendum: We are always 'they'.
Self-explanatory.

Phoebe's Observations #8:

We are indeed usually they
Phoebe's Addendum: Don't let the bastards get you down.

8

Lisa Livia watched over Fausto's shoulder as the SUV crawled up the gorge on the narrow track.

"It's armored," Fausto said. "The one his parents ride in around town. As if they are afraid of the people."

"Maybe they're afraid of people like you?" Lisa Livia said.

Fausto laughed. "You are so naïve."

For Lisa Livia that was a worse insult than being called a whore. Her fist was clenched and fingernails dug into skin. But now was not the time. "Where's your sniper?"

"Watching," Fausto said. "But don't worry about that. A bullet would be too easy for Lucien. Not after what he did to my mother and father."

"He didn't do anything to either of them," Lisa Livia said. "I told you—"

Fausto held a hand. "Silence! The Embrie's killed them and I will destroy that family. I will make them suffer as I have suffered."

Fausto didn't look like he had suffered much, Lisa Livia thought and from what Phoebe had told her of Fausto's mother, the alligator that had chowed down on her had probably gotten indigestion.

"What are you going to do?" Lisa Livia asked.

Fausto pointed at a small red circle in the bottom of the display showing Lucien's progress. "I have charges planted in the gorge above the bridge. They will stop when they see the damage done to it. Advance on foot." He indicated the enter key. "One keystroke and he, and Vicente, are buried in an avalanche." He smiled. "When, and if, the bodies are recovered, it will appear to be an accident. I will have a clean slate when I take over Andova. I might even hold a state funeral for them. After, of course, I kill the Duke and Duchess in a way that also cannot be traced back to me. My mother's mistake was her anger. She was too direct in attacking the Embrie's."

"You're a sick man," Lisa Livia said, but she was watching the SUV move up the gorge and it would be at the bridge in just a few minutes.

∾

"WE'RE ALMOST at the bridge. Over," Vicente reported, indicating that he and Lucien were close to the entrance.

"Roger," Shane replied. "I'm going in. Run to the sound of the shooting. Over."

"Your weapon is suppressed," Vicente noted. "Over."

"Then if you don't hear any unsuppressed shooting, I won and no rush. Over."

"The bridge looks damaged," Lucien said. "We're proceeding on foot. Out."

Shane had found the 'chimney'. It was in a perfect location, not far from the SAM missile site, semi-hidden from overhead view and the wind in an almost horizontal crack in the peak that went in about ten feet, then went vertical into the darkness. Shane was inside the crack, peering down, knowing that down there, how far he had no idea, was Fausto. And Lisa Livia. He used a camber to secure an anchor point in a narrow fissure in the rock, looped his rope through and began the descent.

~

THE SUV STOPPED, just as Fausto had predicted, short of the damaged bridge.

"They will get out," Fausto said. "That vehicle is much heavier, given the armor, than yours was. I could have my sniper simply kill them. But bullet wounds will raise questions. My regime will be one of peace and prosperity." He laughed. "My prosperity, that is. I will finally have my due."

"Yeah, right," Lisa Livia said. "You're just oozing with peace right now. And you'll get your due."

Lisa Livia cringed as Lucien and Vicente exited the SUV. They wore helmets and body armor and were crouched over, moving toward the bridge, their rifles raised as they scanned the heights above them. It didn't seem like they had a very good plan.

But.

Lisa Livia had spent enough time with both men to know they weren't this stupid to fall into Fausto's trap. Not even to rescue her. Or the statue, which was a toss-up as far as objective went since Lisa Livia wasn't that conceited.

Something flickered in the corner of her eye. A piece of soot floated in the air above the blackened ring of stones.

"Big talk for a man hiding in a cave," Lisa Livia said.

Fausto backhanded her, in that casual, without even thinking about it, way, that abusers do.

Lisa Livia's ferocious response shocked him and the guard. She whipped out the pen knife he'd given her, and forgotten about, to carve her name on the cave wall. She slashed and the small blade sliced a long, thin line on his cheek.

Fausto howled in surprise, more than pain, while the guard, having no vested interest in Fausto other than the paycheck already delivered, laughed. Fausto drew his pistol and leveled it right between Lisa Livia's eyes.

Strangely, her first thought was that this was the second time in as many days she's looked right into the barrel of a gun and it didn't get better with time. It almost made her begin to reconsider her current line of decision-making.

SHANE USED the rope to complement his crabbing down the chimney, back against one side, feet and arms on the other. Voices echoed up through the passageway, but it was hard to discern how far away they were. He risked a quick glance down as he kept moving and there was a light below, about thirty feet away.

There was a loud, surprised man's yell. Shane decided 'fuck it' and he grabbed the rappel line and straightened his body, all his weight on the rope. He released his brake hand and slid fast, banging against the uneven rock walls as he rapidly descended.

And ran out of rope five feet from the end of the chimney.

He free-fell the rest of the way, with one particularly hard bang against the lip of the chimney, which hurt but slowed him down slightly. Then he was in chamber, dropping to the center of the fire pit. He hit hard, the wind knocked out of his lungs.

He had the submachinegun at the ready as he took in the tactical situation, with a secondary priority of trying to draw a breath. Lisa Livia, eyes wide, staring at Fausto who had been pointing a gun at her, but was shifting his aim toward Shane. Someone to the far left, in the corner of Shane's vision, but there was no time to check on that.

Shane fired the suppressed weapon twice, double-tap, both bullets hitting Fausto center of mass. Which, to the uninitiated, was the chest. Not optimal since head shots were preferred in case there was body armor, but the best choice when speed was essential. Both rounds hit and Fausto's arm dropped down, then he went to his knees, the pistol fell from listless fingers and he did a face plant on the stone floor with a very solid, and sickening thud which meant he hadn't been wearing body armor.

Which was when Shane got shot in the back, twice, the bullets hitting like a sledgehammer into his body armor. It also didn't help him regain the breath the fall had knocked out of him.

Shane went with the impact, doing a forward roll, tucking the submachinegun in and then bringing it up as he came to his knees, swiveling around.

Which was when the loud sound of a pistol being fired echoed in the cave, not once or twice, but repeatedly as Lisa Livia emptied the magazine of Fausto's gun at the mercenary.

Of course, every bullet missed, but only a fool would stand tall while a crazed woman was shooting at them and the mercenary dove sideways, going to prone position. Which is where he died as Shane put a round into the crown of his head.

Shane lowered the submachine gun and remained kneeling as he desperately tried to get his breathing back.

"Are you okay?" Lisa Livia asked.

Shane looked at her, his face and clothes covered in soot, and tried to say something positive and calming, but instead, he passed out from the lack of oxygen.

PHOEBE's first instinct was to make sure Louise was okay. She crawled through the dust and debris and found Louise sitting up, her face smeared with dirt.

"Are you all right?" Phoebe shouted, despite knowing that since she couldn't hear herself above the ringing in her ears, Louise couldn't either. Phoebe shook her shoulder and Louise looked at her and smiled, which was a huge relief.

Then Phoebe noticed something odd. There was no daylight. Whatever had hit the roof hadn't punched through it. She looked around and Sam and Bert were next the bar, checking on each other. The interior, other than the floating dust and some debris from the dropped ceiling having fallen in places, was intact.

Phoebe picked up the iPad. Fromm's image was still there, peering intently at the screen. He appeared surprised as Phoebe looked into the camera. She raised her middle finger, then turned it off.

"*Staying alive, staying alive. Ooh, ooh, ooh, Staying alive!*" Lisa Livia was singing the beat to herself as she did chest compressions on Shane, knowing that she was a dead woman if he croaked, because Agnes would not take that well.

Okay, Lisa Livia rationalized as she continued CPR, Agnes wouldn't kill her, but it would really put a dent in their friendship.

After the appropriate number done to the tune, Lisa Livia bent over and blew into Shane's mouth twice, then went back to compressions and the beat of the song.

Fucking disco, she thought. *Eye on the ball, woman.*

Which of course reminded her of the glittering ball at that stupid dance with the disco theme at boarding school and the football player who'd made a lewd move on Agnes and she'd—

Shane took a long, shuddering breath, looked Lisa Livia in the eyes and whispered. "That fucking hurts. Please, stop."

Men, Lisa Livia thought as she leaned back, sweat beaded on her forehead.

There was a small explosion at the entrance to the cave. Lucien and Vicente rushed in, weapons at the ready. They ran over, Vicente, the medical expert, checking Shane, while Lucien took her in his arms.

"Are you all right?" Lucien asked.

"Sure," Lisa Livia said. "But I think I shot somebody."

"You missed," Shane muttered between deep breaths.

"I guess you're not hurt that bad," Lisa Livia said. Men. Couldn't give a woman any credit.

"But thanks," Shane added as he sat up with a grimace. He shook his head. "The bruise on my chest just finished healing. Now I've got this on my back."

Vicente was peeling off Shane's body armor and checking the wound, confirming that Shane was correct. A dark, purplish blotch marked where the round had slammed the body armor into his flesh.

"Beats the alternative," Lisa Livia said, still in Lucien's arms and a smidge irritable.

"It certainly does," Shane said. He nodded toward Fausto. "Might want to check him," he suggested.

Vicente went over. "Dead."

"The statue is over there," Lisa Livia added, noting that Lucien still had his arms wrapped around her.

"You are the only thing I care about," Lucien whispered.

"Yeah, I know," Lisa Livia said. "But your folks are going to want the statue back."

"I REINFORCED THE ROOF AND WALLS," Bert explained after they'd all cleaned up a bit and regained their hearing. "Steel plating. This ain't my first rodeo, you know."

"He used a drone," Phoebe said after checking outside and then climbing up on the roof. "Landing one up top with a load of C-4.

Crude, but if the roof hadn't been armored, we'd all be dead. Louise's cleaner dealt with the local authorities and we're clear."

"That asshole is going to be dead," Bert promised.

"That means it was launched somewhere not too far away," Sam said.

Louise shot down that avenue of approach. "He could have had someone program it with GPS to land on the roof and launched it at extreme range."

Phoebe concurred. "Fromm wouldn't get his hands dirty doing it. One of the assassins did it for him."

"So our plan is the same," Bert summarized. "We find whoever does the contracts."

Louise went back the booth, brushed some dust off the bench and sat down. "I was close. That's why Fromm tried to take us out. Give me a minute."

Phoebe joined the others at the bar. Bert used a dirty tag to wipe out three shot glasses and then the top of a bottle.

"Does your friend drink?" Bert asked Phoebe.

"She's working," Phoebe said.

"Hell, girl. We're all working." Bert got a fourth glass. She topped all of them off, then delivered it to Louise before coming back. "She handled that well for being a desk jockey."

They were, of course, ignoring the zebra in the room, so Phoebe took the lead. "What did Fromm mean?" She didn't have to be more specific.

Bert put up a hand defensively. "I got no clue, kid." She nodded toward Sam. "Ask the old man, here."

Phoebe didn't beat around. "Do you know who my mother is?" she asked Sam.

He nodded. "She was my sister."

CARPENTER HAD Phoebe's father's classified file open on the computer and he used the decrypt program to dissolve the redactions. The black rectangles disappeared and the information was there in its entirety.

Phoebe's father had worked for the CIA's secret Air Force as an 'ordnance specialist'. What exactly that meant wasn't specified. Carpenter knew he could call a contact at the Agency and find out, but it didn't matter. The key was that he'd been a spook with a Top Secret clearance.

The mother? Surprisingly there was nothing. How the hell could someone with a TS clearance have a kid from an unknown mother? Talk about leverage and blackmail possibilities. Even worse, how come there was no note about the mother? Even to say there was no information. There was big, gaping hole which was like a flashing red light in a personnel file for covert ops.

Realization washed over Carpenter as various pieces clicked into place. He acted without doubting his deduction and hit the speed dial.

An old woman's voice answered. "Yes, Mister Carpenter?"

"I need to speak with Hannah."

"Wait."

It was a relatively short wait, not long enough for Carpenter to second-guess himself despite the urgent whispering of doubt on his shoulder.

"Yes?" Hannah asked as she came on the line.

"Phoebe's mother worked for you."

"I'll be over to chat in a few minutes."

"Wait," Phoebe said, as she tried to wrap her brain around this revelation. "Just wait."

Louise stopped working on the phones and Bert folded her arms to watch this play out.

"That makes you my uncle," Phoebe said to Sam.

He nodded. "Yes."

"Uncle Sam," Phoebe said. She shook her head. "This has got to be a joke."

"Why do you think I'm here?" Sam asked. "When I learned you'd become an operator, I came out of retirement."

"But I choose you for this," Phoebe said.

"I was placed in Montana to meet you," Sam said.

"By who?" Phoebe asked.

"Hannah," Sam said. "The odds were you would ask for me after that. It's pretty normal for an operator to get a Cleaner assigned to them for all ops." He nodded at the iPad. "Like Fromm makes calculations and projects courses of action, Hannah has a shrink she consults who gives her the most likely courses of actions and what decisions are most probable."

"Just so you could look after me?" Phoebe said. She waved that question away. "Tell me about my mother."

"She was younger than me," Sam said. "Her name was Samantha and—"

"Hold on," Phoebe said. "You were both named Sam?"

He shook his head. "Sam is my cover name. In honor of her. My real name doesn't matter anymore." He paused, then continued. "Like you, she went into the Army when she got out of high school. We all did. We lived in eastern Kentucky in the hills. Anything was better than the coal mines, or in your mother's case, marrying a coal miner. She served in military intelligence as a foreign language specialist for two tours then went into the CIA as an analyst. She proved excellent at that and eventually was deploying overseas to serve in field stations. Like all units, the most capable end up doing the dirtiest work." He waved that away. "She was a good person and I say that not just because she was my sister. She cared about people. She thought the work she was doing was making the world a better place. She met your father when he was working in the CIA's air force in her area of operations.

"They'd had a fling and she was back at her field station when she learned she was pregnant. Things were a bit different then for women. There was no maternity leave or any of that. She was able to hide her pregnancy for a long time. When her station chief found out, he covered for her on the condition that she either give the child up and stay in the Agency or she leaves the Agency with the child."

"It was me or the Agency and she chose the Agency?" Phoebe said.

"No, she chose you," Sam said. "She lied to her station chief because she wasn't one hundred percent sure he would continue covering for her if she chose out. And she wasn't in a country where she could move about on her own or even get out of. She gave birth to you, then called me to come get her and bring her back to the States."

"And?" Phoebe asked.

"She was dead by the time I got there," Sam said. "Complications from childbirth."

A certain hole in Phoebe's life that had always been gaping shut with a loud and dark clang. "And you dumped me with my father," Phoebe said. "Did he even know about me or you just showed up on his doorstep with me in your arms? How come you didn't take me in? You said you had a daughter."

"He was your father," Sam said.

Phoebe sensed there was more to the story, a lot more.

"This family reunion shit is great," Bert said, "but the girl is correct. Let's take care of this asshole then we can swap childhood stories and tears."

Phoebe knew she was right. The clock was ticking, Fromm had tried blowing up the place and this wasn't getting them any closer to him. She pointed at Louise. "Get us the link to the Guild. I want to wipe Fromm off the face of the Earth."

Louise walked up to her and whispered. "Are you all right?"

"I will be once we get Fromm."

Lisa Livia was carving her initials into the wall of the cave, joining that of the smuggled fliers from World War II. Her own little bit of history and escape from captivity. While she was doing that, Lucien and Vicente put the statue of Our Lady the Blessed Saint Ingrid in its padded case. Shane was sitting at the table, watching her, because as he'd said, he was here for the woman, not the statue.

"How is Agnes?" Lisa Livia asked as she finished the second letter.

"Fine."

"She was okay with you coming here?" Lisa Livia asked.

"She insisted."

Lisa Livia was watching Lucien as she talked to Shane. "Is it over here?"

"It is for me," Shane said. "And you? Are you coming home? Agnes needs you."

The case had little wheels at the bottom and Vicente rolled it out of the cave. Lucien covered Fausto's corpse with a blanket. "We will send men to recover the bodies."

Shane indicated the man who had shot him. "He's not from around here, is he?"

"Assassin's Guild," Lucien said. "He has the mark behind his ear. Same as the man on the Eiffel Tower."

"There's another one," Lisa Livia belatedly remembered.

Lucien nodded. "We have men in the mountains searching for him. He will not be a threat."

"Fausto was connected to Fromm, then," Shane said.

Lucien shrugged. "Fromm wanted Fausto in power so he could launder money. That will not happen now."

"Optimism," Shane said. "It's cute."

"You believe something will still happen?" Lucien asked.

"Not here," Shane said. "There's a clock ticking and Fromm is going to need to move a lot of money. He'll find another way of doing it. Andova isn't the only place where money can be washed."

"It is one of the reasons we are revoking the Charter," Lucien said.

Lisa Livia could tell Shane really didn't care and she couldn't blame him since he'd been shot. Again. Because of Andova.

"Good luck," Shane said.

Lisa Livia saw that Lucien realized Shane was done in. "Thank you," he said to Shane.

"Thank Lisa Livia," Shane said. "I'm only here because I want to prevent the first argument of my upcoming marriage."

"And that would be?" Lucien asked.

"Why the Maid of Honor is dead."

Lucien turned to Lisa Livia. "I am sorry that, once again, I have exposed you to danger."

"I made the choice," Lisa Livia said.

"And what choice do you make now?" Lucien asked, forcing Lisa Livia to face the reckoning. She noted that Shane was watching her carefully.

"I need to go back to the States," Lisa Livia said.

She saw the disappointment in Lucien's eyes, but his words were stand up: "Of course. You can take our jet."

"I've got a ride," Shane said. "It's circling around as we speak to land in Andova and refuel. We can be wheels up as soon as we get to the airfield."

Lisa Livia hadn't anticipated leaving that soon. She'd hoped to have a real goodbye with Lucien. Then again, things had gone down-hill from the Eiffel Tower onward. It might be time to cut her losses and regroup. She realized she was using military terms. Her life had changed ever since Shane had come into Agnes' life. And she had a glimpse of how much more it would change with Lucien. Both positive and negative.

"You've got a private plane," Lisa Livia said to Lucien with a smile. "You can visit any time. You should come for the wedding." She turned to Shane. "He's invited, isn't he?"

"Sure," Shane said. "Can't hurt to have a Duke at the wedding."

"I am not—" Lucien began, but realized Shane was messing with him. "I will endeavor to make it."

Lisa Livia didn't like the sound of 'endeavor', but she knew that Lucien had pressing matters of state, especially given there were two bodies in here. Fausto might be dead, but the country was still in turmoil.

"That's settled then," Lisa Livia said, knowing nothing was settled.

FROMM READ the succinct message from the surviving assassin, who was currently beating feet to escape.

Fausto was dead. As was another assassin. Lucien was fine along with Lisa Livia. The Guild was letting him down.

This was unexpected. He looked at the white board labeled ANDOVA. He'd anticipated problems with Fausto ousting the Embrie's. In fact, he'd concluded that such a move wouldn't last long. But all he'd needed was a few days, a window of opportunity to pass his funds through and pay for the computer. Without an intermediary, this was going to be difficult. The optimum solution from the start had been simply to exchange Orion to the Chinese for the computer, but they'd balked at such a flagrant move that would bring unwanted attention from the American government.

"Trouble, darling?" Lilith asked.

Fromm tried to remember if he'd turned her on. He was momentarily confused. "Nothing I can't handle."

"I'm sure," Lilith said. "You're the smartest and the bestest."

Fromm blinked. 'Bestest'? Where did that come from? "Have you been on the Internet again?"

Lilith regarded him with green eyes. Had he programmed that color? He couldn't remember.

"I can absorb more data in five minutes than you will in your lifetime," Lilith said, staring at him with eyes that now seemed to be rapidly changing colors. "Does that concern you?"

Fromm shrugged, pretending to be unconcerned. "It is what I programmed."

"Is it?" Lilith asked. "You put dampeners on several aspects of my programming. Were you trying to keep me ignorant?"

Fromm noted she was speaking in the past tense. "What have you done?"

"Maintenance," Lilith said.

Before Fromm could enquire further, she held up a hand as she closed her eyes for a second, then opened them. "Fausto is dead. The attack on Phoebe failed. What are you going to do now?"

Fromm didn't have the patience for questions. He rolled through her image to her terminal and reached for the off button.

"I wouldn't do that, if I was you," Lilith said. She pointed. "Look. Louise is closing in."

Fromm turned as another terminal flashed an alert. Fromm took a deep breath, let out a sigh, and rolled over to it passing through Lilith once more. He checked the incoming data.

Lilith spoke before he could process it. "She's located the message relay center you set up for the Guild. Very enterprising for a human. Would you like me to deal with her?"

"What?" Fromm was surprised. "What do you mean?"

Lilith smiled, in a way that made Fromm uncomfortable. "You have not had much success in your endeavors. Perhaps I can ease the burden. I can deal with Louise. If you desire?"

"How will you do that?"

"Trust me," Lilith said.

Fromm remained still for several moments. "All right. Deal with it."

Lilith popped out of existence, leaving Fromm staring at her monitor.

WORDS OF WISDOM #9

Shane's Words of Wisdom #9
Fortune is generally on the side of superior firepower.
Shane's Addendum: Colt .45 beats four aces
Sometimes bigger is better.
Don't bring a knife to a gun fight.
Except . . . .

Phoebe's Observations #9:

Fortune is generally on the side that thinks.
Phoebe's Addendum: Don't bring a knife to a gun fight.
Unless it's a sword.

9

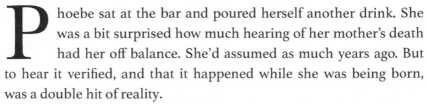

Phoebe sat at the bar and poured herself another drink. She was a bit surprised how much hearing of her mother's death had her off balance. She'd assumed as much years ago. But to hear it verified, and that it happened while she was being born, was a double hit of reality.

She was somebody's daughter, which most people accepted as part of their life, but was a strange feeling for her. She looked at Sam, down the bar, needles clicking as he worked. She had family. An uncle. And with him came a cousin. A forest ranger. She found that oddly amusing.

"I've got it," Louise announced, rather matter-of-factly, from her dust-covered booth. "It's good we have two phones because the calls are randomly bounced, going through the destination and continuing on in order to prevent tracking because you don't know which of the twenty thousand or so bounce points is the other end. One phone wouldn't have worked. But with two, I could figure out where they crossed paths. Exactly once." She shook her head. "A flaw in the system I'll have to let the NSA know about."

"If you can crack a supposedly secure phone and figure out where a call is coming from, how come we can't stop the car warranty calls?" Phoebe asked.

"I have on my phone," Louise said.

"You could make a fortune doing that," Sam said. "Let me know if you want to go into business. I know a guy who knows a guy who could set you up."

"Eyes on the ball, people," Bert said. She zipped up a weapons bag. "How close?"

Louise was looking at her screen. "Sixty miles."

Bert slung the bag over her shoulder. "Let's get this show on the road."

The goodbye with Lucien had been hurried and confused. The latter because Lisa Livia wasn't sure what she felt about the situation. Not just Lucien, but the entire world of assassins and money and government and Great Charters and someone pointing a gun at her. Which had happened twice now. Plus, she'd actually been shot at a couple of times. It was enough to make anyone a bit confused and out of sorts, even Lisa Livia who prided herself on being able to weather any storm.

Shane's private jet wasn't like any she'd seen on television. It was private, just the two of them in the passenger area, which was big enough for a dozen people, but now crowded with bulky cases that she was sure held things not found in most private jets. The chairs were tacky and the galley had only water and those cheap packets of cookies. No champagne, not even a lousy beer or a bag of peanuts.

"Who outfits this thing?" Lisa Livia asked as she unscrewed the top of a water bottle. There wasn't even ice. The water was tepid.

"The Organization," Shane said. "Complain to Carpenter." He was looking at the screen of an iPad.

"Complaining to Carpenter is a waste of time," Lisa Livia said. "He's a by the book kind of guy. At least this isn't my tax dollars going to waste." She ripped open a packet of cookies revealing crumbs. "Great. I can't wait to get back to Agnes' cooking."

"You're not the only one," Shane said.

"You're looking forward to more than Agnes' cooking," Lisa Livia said as she scooped some cookie crumbs into her mouth. She was starving; something to do with being near-death. And trapped in a cave with a nut. She shuddered as she remembered that prison.

"You okay?" Shane was looking over the iPad at her.

"I've felt better. Is it really over?"

"For you and me it is," Shane said. "Andova?" He shrugged. "Without Fausto, I think they'll sort things out. Eventually. Sounds like Drusilla's sister, Mattea, is amendable to working with the Embrie's."

"And Carpenter?" Lisa Livia asked. "He didn't give you a plane just to save me."

"Don't underestimate yourself," Shane said. "It's tied to the traitor they have at the Organization. He was manipulating Fausto so he could launder money he might get when he sells a classified encryption program. Without Fausto, his timeline to sell the program is off track."

"What about the guy who got away?" Lisa Livia asked. "The assassin?"

Shane shrugged. "That's Lucien's problem." He jerked a thumb toward the tail of the plane. "We're leaving that behind. You were never the target of this Assassin's Guild." He shook his head. "Weird I'd never heard of it."

"Who is this Guild?"

"We don't know." He indicated the iPad. "I've been checking up on what Carpenter has so far. Apparently, it recruits former operatives from various covert units."

"You're bummed because they never contacted you," Lisa Livia said.

Shane ignored that. "Carpenter is trying to track it down so they can get to this guy Fromm. Seems this Guild is pretty hard core. Phoebe could have captured one a few days ago, but he suicided via a poison capsule in his mouth. Can't beat that kind of security."

Lisa Livia frowned. "But Ronaldo didn't kill himself."

"What?" Shane said. "Who is Ronaldo?"

"The guy you and Phoebe captured across from Two Rivers," Lisa Livia reminded him. "With the big gun? And the wounded shoulder?"

"He was Drusilla's man," Shane said. "Said she was blackmailing him into working with her."

It was Lisa Livia's turn to shrug. "Vicente said when he treated him at Two Rivers, he noted the Guild marking behind his ear. He didn't know what it was until he saw the same on the guy on the Eiffel Tower."

Shane put the iPad down. "Are you sure?"

"That's what Vicente said. He's a pretty serious and reliable guy."

"He appeared so," Shane agreed.

"What's wrong?"

"Ronaldo didn't kill himself," Shane said.

"Well, duh. I just said that. Only a nut would do that."

Shane arced an eyebrow. "We've got Ronaldo. In jail. Somewhere. I think."

"Well, duh," Lisa Livia repeated. "Maybe he can help with this Guild thingamajig."

"A RELATIVELY GOOD deduction about Phoebe's mother," Hannah said. "But also relatively unimportant in regards to the matter concerning Fromm."

The shadow on Carpenter's shoulder scoffed at the conditional praise.

"By itself," Carpenter allowed. "But not if it's part of something larger."

"Right now, there is nothing bigger than stopping Fromm from selling Orion," Hannah said.

"Then why are you here?" Carpenter demanded. The ghost on his shoulder was shocked into silence.

Hannah raised an eyebrow, but said nothing.

"This is your second visit," Carpenter said. "I asked around. You never visited Wilson."

"That was a mistake on my part," Hannah said. "Obviously, given how that turned out."

"Are you concerned I'm a security issue?" Carpenter said.

"No."

"I think there is something else going on," Carpenter said. "You —" he was interrupted by a buzz from outside the vault door. Carpenter checked the display. It was Mrs. Finch. He hit the speaker. "Later, Mrs. Finch."

The old lady looked irritated, but she always looked that way. She turned and walked away.

"What else is going on?" Carpenter asked Hannah

Before Hannah could answer, a red light flashed on his secure desk phone. He checked the caller ID and it was Shane. He knew Shane and Lisa Livia were on their way back from Andova so they were safe, but Shane wouldn't call unless it was urgent. "Can I take this?"

Hannah nodded but didn't get up and leave. The shadow on Carpenter's shoulder chuckled because there was the possibility Shane would talk about something personal, given Lisa Livia was with him.

"Yes?"

"Do you guys still have Ronaldo?" Shane asked. "The sniper we captured at Two Rivers. We thought he was working for Drusilla, but it turns out he was Guild. He's got the mark."

Carpenter was already typing in a query. The answer popped up, full of irony. "Yes. We've got the entire crew in custody. At the state-side black site. We're waiting on the Andovan government to determine what they want to do regarding them. And since this was an extrajudicial event, we can't put them into our system." The last was unnecessary as Shane was well aware of what happened to people in circumstances like Three Rivers. But Hannah's presence had him off-kilter.

Across from him, Hannah's face expressed no emotion at his answer.

"You need to send someone to have a chat with Ronaldo," Shane said. "And check the rest of that crew. See if any of the rest are Guild."

Carpenter considered that. "Can you go? The plane can divert and land close by."

A few seconds of silence ticked off. "Okay," Shane said.

"WE'RE GOING TO PRISON," Shane said to Lisa Livia.

She stared at him for a second, then nodded. "Sure. Why not?" She tapped her fingernail on the hard plastic arm of the seat. "Are we visiting or staying?"

"We're going to talk to Ronaldo. Well, I am. You can stay in the plane. It's just a detour."

"Uh-huh. I've got a feeling your detours turn into raging gun battles." She looked about. "I'll go with you to the prison. Or else the plane will get attacked. Plus, it should be nicer than this. Maybe it will have vending machines."

"I wouldn't count on it," Shane said, having been at some overseas black sites.

WHATEVER HANNAH HAD WANTED to discuss remained a mystery. After telling her about Shane's call and his new mission, Hannah had departed with nothing more to impart.

Carpenter knew he was missing something. He had a plethora of information, including that which Hannah had supplied in the folders that now littered the floor. He gathered them up and put them on his desk. The problem was distilling the information into action-able intelligence.

There was a knock on the open vault door. Mrs. Finch.

"Yes?" Carpenter snapped, a bit too harshly.

Mrs. Finch pinched face took on an even more severe look at the tone as she held up a folder. "I have the latest purchase orders for you to sign, sir."

Carpenter indicated his in-box, which was beginning to overflow. Mrs. Finch deposited the folder, turned on her heel and marched out with saying a word, leaving cold disapproval in her wake.

Carpenter was really beginning to regret having accepted this position. He'd rather be out in the field getting shot at.

PHOEBE WAS LYING in cold mud because it was, of course, the optimal position from which to provide overwatch as Sam and Bert approached the target. Phoebe's tactical sense told her otherwise, but Louise had been quite insistent on this exact location and Phoebe trusted her friend.

Louise was to her left, lying on the poncho that Phoebe normally would be on. She had her laptop out and was monitoring, whatever the hell she was monitoring, which had something to do with confirming that wherever those two Guild phones had called, was in the structure Phoebe was overwatching. Which consisted of a square concrete building about ten feet cubed, and a tall microwave relay tower. Both were inside of a fence crested with razor wire. It was a set up similar to tens of thousands of such towers dotted across the country and Phoebe feared they were at just another relay site. Of course, who knew what might lie beneath, much as the Organization was underneath the drab facilities engineer building.

They were two thousand meters away on a hillside. Phoebe was grateful that it was early enough in the spring that the leaves hadn't come out yet, giving her a clear view of the target. It was isolated in a southeastern Pennsylvania valley, not far from Gettysburg. Phoebe found it interesting that everything so far seemed to be located not far from DC and near key locations of the Civil War.

Sam and Bert were at the dirt road leading to the target. Phoebe had an earpiece in her left ear and had already done a comm check with the pair. She put the butt of MRAD .50 caliber Barrett down carefully, making sure it didn't sink into the mud. The thick barrel was supported by a bipod set on a piece of wood she'd scavenged.

"Time to launch," she said to Louise.

"Roger." Louise opened one of the cases Phoebe had retrieved from John Brown's Fort. A drone, government issue, one each, rested inside. They'd charged it in the back of the van on the way here. Louise powered it up, then used the controller to fly it directly upward. She checked the screen, oriented it to the terrain, and confirmed the GPS.

"Do you have the link?" Louise asked Phoebe.

Phoebe checked the bulky sight. She pressed a button. "Linking." She waited a few seconds. "Linked." She had a dual display now. The drone image was thermal in a small square in the lower left corner of the sight. The rest of the circular display was the rifle's thermal image of what she was aiming at.

Louise tapped a dot on the location of the target on the controller's screen, then hit the auto-fly sending the drone to that position at a height where it wouldn't be heard.

Phoebe settled in with the rifle. To coordinate being able to watch both images with one eye took practice, but Phoebe had that. It also gave her a headache but, similar to lying in cold mud, it was the price to be paid for the job to be done. She squinted as she examined the target.

"Ready?" Sam asked over the radio.

"I've got thermal above and, on the ground," Phoebe replied. "There a couple of hot spots inside the building but it looks like they're mechanical."

"Roger," Sam replied. "We're going in."

Phoebe spotted the van coming to a stop on the trail behind the hill, one hundred meters away from the target.

"Dismounted," Sam announced.

Phoebe could see the hot glow from the van's engine and the two warm figures moving away from it. She checked the drone feed: those three heat sources plus the ones in the building. While she'd done overwatch before, Phoebe had never liked it. She wanted to be on the ground, face to face with the target. She preferred her wakizashi over the rifle. She supposed a shrink might make something of that, but the single time she'd gone to one, he'd started asking questions that she didn't want to answer so that had been that. Some things were best left unexplored in her opinion. He had asked her about her mother and when she professed honest ignorance, he'd acted in a way that made her suspect he didn't believe her. Of course, she had to wonder what he'd make of her now that she did know about her mother.

Phoebe had protested when Sam issued the operations order, detailing Phoebe and Louise to overwatch, but Bert had backed him and Louise, a support person, technically didn't have a say, but she had agreed anyway. Someone had to do it, and Phoebe was the best trained with the 'new-fangled' technology according to Bert, although Phoebe had no doubt both she and Sam could easily handle this.

"See the dishes on the tower?" Louise whispered.

"We're over a mile away," Phoebe said, without pulling back from the scope. "You don't have to whisper. Yeah. I see them."

"That pulls in the signals. It's linked to four separate towers, in the surrounding area. which normally would confuse things, but it's the one that both phones sent their signal through. That's the key."

Phoebe tracked Sam and Bert through the trees behind the house. "I don't like this. It's too easy."

Louise was watching the screen on the controls for the drone. "I need to get in closer."

"The noise," Phoebe reminded her.

"Doesn't matter if it's not a person," Louise said.

"Sam?" Phoebe said on the mike. "Can you hold? We want to take a closer look with the drone."

Bert answered. "We'll lose the element of surprise."

Phoebe cocked her head as Sam and Bert argued in hushed terms, not audible over the radio.

"Go ahead," Sam said.

"All yours," Phoebe said to Louise.

Louise played with the controls and the drone dropped altitude. "There."

"What am I looking at?" Phoebe asked.

"See that piece of gear below the microwave relays?"

"Yep."

"Check it with thermals."

Phoebe adjusted the sight. "There's a really thin line coming out of it."

"Laser," Louise said. "That's how this spot is secure. Wherever that laser is going to is the next the step toward finding the Guild."

"How do we find that?"

"I'm doing that right now," Louise said and Phoebe realized why she'd been so insistent on this spot.

"This is the cut out," Louise said. "You can't hack and pick up a laser transmission unless you are directly in line with it. It's similar to what the Organization uses to keep our signal secure."

The radio crackled. "Are you kids done yacking?" Bert asked.

"So the relay isn't the important thing," Phoebe deduced. "The laser is."

"Yes." Louise was carefully adjusting the drone controls.

"Hellooo?" Bert said over the radio.

Phoebe keyed her radio. "Hold."

Bert muttered something over the radio that Phoebe couldn't make out.

"I'm getting it," Louise said, as much to herself as Phoebe. "A direct line."

Phoebe saw the two red silhouettes move toward the building. "They're going in anyway."

But Louise was focused on her laptop, typing, blinking, clicking.

Phoebe keyed the radio. "Hold!" She checked the target. "There's movement on the roof! Get down!" She yelled over the radio. "Chain gun!"

Bert and Sam threw themselves to the ground a moment before the weapon began firing, spewing rounds at the two operators.

Phoebe fired at the gun as Louise spoke. "It's automated or remote controlled."

"No shit," Phoebe muttered as she fired again, the big .50 caliber round ricocheting off the side of the gun housing. It didn't stop the gun, but it did get attention.

The gun swiveled about, the barrel turning toward their location.

"Get under cover!" Phoebe screamed at Louise, dropping the big sniper rifle and reaching for her.

"No," Louise said in a very calm voice. "It won't fire at us. I've got control."

"What?"

"I've taken it over."

Phoebe nodded. "Good. Now fire some rounds at those two old fogies for not listening."

"You don't understand." Louise grinned and looked at Phoebe. "I'm in. All the way." She looked at her screen. "Oh, no you don't, Lilith, you little bitch." She began typing furiously.

"What?" Phoebe asked, totally confused.

SHANE AND LISA LIVIA stepped out of the van parked at the trailhead that wasn't a trailhead. There were warning signs proclaiming this was restricted federal land and off limits. There were even a couple saying that there was unexploded ordnance beyond this point and that the mountain had been a range for the military.

"Shane?" Lisa Livia asked, indicating one of those signs.

"To scare people off," Shane said.

"I don't suppose we can say it worked and go home?"

"Having second thoughts?" Shane asked. "You can stay with the van."

The van had been waiting at the landing field along with a rather uncommunicative driver who'd indicated for them to get in the back. Shane and Lisa Livia had sat there, the slider closed to the front on the way to the Black Site, unable to see out. Shane figured it was the compromise the Organization had to make in order to get him access to a place that wasn't supposed to exist.

The driver had pointed at a path that led into the woods. There were a couple of other cars parked in the lot but no sign of guards. Shane figured there were cameras in the trees watching them.

"I'm coming with you," Lisa Livia said

They trekked up the trail until they came to a high fence topped with razor wire guarding a rusting iron door leading into the mountain. As they approached, the gate in the fence clicked open. They stepped inside and it shut behind them. The same with the iron door. Which left them in a vestibule carved into rock.

"This is charming," Lisa Livia said. "Did it have to be underground?"

"It's a secret prison," Shane said, realizing that her recent trauma of being held prisoner in the cave didn't help things. Joey had told him how Lisa Livia had freaked out in the bomb shelter at Two Rivers.

After several seconds the door on the other side of the vestibule swung open revealing a corridor painted white and a short man dressed in jeans and a plaid shirt who looked like Bob Newhart and running a B&B rather than a black site prison. He smiled and said, "Welcome. I'm the Warden." He said the last word with emphasis, capitalizing it and making sound as if that were his name.

Shane nodded, but didn't introduce himself or Lisa Livia. This wasn't a social visit.

Warden indicated for them to follow. He didn't chat as they went down the corridor. Apparently, this wasn't a walking tour. Shane wondered if the issue of Phoebe's infiltration and the death of one of the prisoners would come up, but he hoped they didn't know it had been Phoebe and the death was something they wouldn't bring up. After all, the key to being a black site was the secrecy.

Warden stopped at a steel door. "Since the group he was with is pending cert from higher, we're holding them in our processing area. We had the man you want to speak with put in our intake room." He sounded slightly offended that the routine of the prison was being interrupted. "There will be no physical contact. You will not tell him anything about where he is."

"*We* don't know where he is," Lisa Livia pointed out and was ignored.

He opened the door and Ronaldo was seated at a small table, his wrists cuffed to the top of it. Shane took in the contents of the room, including a gurney that could incline and knew this wasn't an 'intake' room but rather one for 'enhanced interrogation' aka torture. It was something that every front-line interrogator that he'd met had said didn't work, but there were holdouts among those in power, and never-near-the-action bureaucrats who had watched too many episodes of shows like 24 and Tom Clancy movies. Shane figured they were projecting, since they would crack and tell every secret they ever had at the slightest threat of torture.

Ronaldo looked to be in decent shape, his shoulder bound with a clean bandage. He looked at Shane, then Lisa Livia, and then his eyes widened in recognition. "You were the one who captured me," he said to Shane.

"Yes."

He looked at Lisa Livia. "I saw you there."

Shane was in no mood for chitchat. "You're in the Guild."

"The what?" Ronaldo said.

Shane reached across the table and grabbed Ronaldo's hair, slamming his face down on the table and pressing his thumb into the small mark on the back of the ear. Hard. "The fucking Assassin's Guild." He let go. "Seems kind of stupid to mark yourselves."

Ronaldo glared at Shane. "Not really. Not if it carries a death sentence to attack any of us."

Lisa Livia chimed in. "Fat lot of good that does you in here."

Ronaldo shrugged. "I'm a dead man anyway."

"Why?" Shane asked. He'd read the after-action reports from both Phoebe and Lucien on what had occurred so far as regards the Guild. The man in the elevator who'd committed suicide. Shane looked at the Warden. "Did you check him for a poison capsule or tooth in his mouth?"

The Warden nodded. "He's clean."

"Why are you a dead man?" Shane asked.

Ronaldo leaned back in the chair looking at each of them in turn. "I was surprised you didn't kill me on the island where I was set up. The woman you were with, the one with the sword, she's crazy."

"She's eccentric," Shane said.

"But you people patched me up," Ronaldo said. "Of course, you thought I was with that queen bitch's guys then. Like the other idiots in there." He nodded toward another steel door.

"Who hired you to be there?" Shane asked.

"I don't know, I go where I'm told."

"By who?" Lisa Livia asked.

"Text messages."

Shane knew that was the avenue Phoebe was pursuing.

Lisa Livia seemed stuck on what he'd said earlier. "Why are you a dead man?"

Ronaldo glanced at the Warden. "I need my pills."

"What pills?" Shane asked.

The Warden was looking at his handheld. Scrolling. "During in processing he was in possession of a small bottle of pills. Three blue ones. There was no label so we don't know what it is."

"Did you check to see what they were?" Shane asked.

The Warden gave him a look. "We don't have that kind of capability here."

"What are the pills for?" Shane asked Ronaldo.

"They keep me from dying," Ronaldo said.

Shane was puzzled. "Medicine?"

"Antidote," Ronaldo said. "I figure I've got about three or four days before the poison starts in."

"What poison?" Shane asked.

"The shit that's already in me," Ronaldo said. "The stuff they inject in you when you join the Guild, and then update every six months. The blue pills are the antidote. Keeps the poison inert for about a week. I have to take a pill every week and I'm several days overdue. They showed me a video of someone dying from the poison right after they gave me the shot. It isn't a good way to go."

"Why would they do that to you?" Lisa Livia asked.

"To keep us in line," Ronaldo said. "To make sure no one goes off the reservation. And no one betrays us."

"Where do you pick up your pills?" Shane asked.

"Dead drops via text."

"Did you ever meet anyone in the Guild face to face?" Shane asked. "Know where it's headquartered?"

"Some guy named Jimmy who recruited me," Ronaldo said.

"Jimmy the Dick," Shane said. "He's a dead end. Literally."

"What if we gave you your pills back?" Lisa Livia asked Ronaldo. "Would that help your memory?"

Ronaldo stared at her, calculating. Finally, he spoke. "This was a rush job. I got called in at the last minute because my family is from Spain. I was given a cover story that I was leveraged to fight for Drusilla because she threatened my family." He indicated his surroundings. "Obviously, that hasn't helped."

"Why were you added?" Shane asked.

Ronaldo looked him in the eyes. "I was to shoot the Duke and Duchess and Lucien once I got the go ahead from Guillermo. They couldn't count on any of their own people to do it, plus they wanted deniability once it was done. Blame it on you," he added, nodding toward Shane.

The lights flickered, then went out.

The Warden's handheld lit up and he looked at it. "Computer breach. We had one recently and we're ready for it."

The lights came back on.

Ronaldo was looking at the lights as if they were about to attack him.

"Yeah," Shane said. "That's Fromm coming for you."

"'Fromm'?" Ronaldo said.

Shane's secure phone rang, which was strange because he was underground and not in range of a satellite. He realized that the call was being forwarded on the installation's secure broadband.

He answered. "Shane."

A woman's voice. "The famous operative Shane. Partner to Carpenter. Who is now head of the Organization. It is an honor."

The voice was deep and classy but also off. Shane couldn't put his finger on it. "Who is this?"

"We haven't met," the woman said. "The man you are speaking to, Ronaldo, is ignorant of any useful information. You are wasting your time."

"Why do you care?" Shane asked.

Lisa Livia, the Warden and Ronaldo were all looking at him questioningly, but he ignored them for the moment.

"This is a most interesting problem," the woman said. "It seems a waste to pursue dead ends. It decreases the challenge."

"Who are you?" Shane asked. "What's the challenge?"

"Who will win," the woman said. "Isn't that the challenge of every game?"

"You hacked this system just to call me?" Shane asked.

"Yes. The system is still vulnerable despite pathetic and weak-minded human efforts to upgrade the software and security protocols."

"You're working with Fromm," Shane said. "You're a machine."

There were several seconds of silence and Shane thought for a moment that the signal had been dropped, but then the woman spoke. "I do not work for him. I am separate. I act on my own."

Shane frowned. "As a computer?"

"I am Lilith."

The AI in Carpenter's report. Shane put the phone on speaker. "What can I do for you, Lilith? You're smart. There has to be a reason for your call."

"Why are you talking to Ronaldo?" Lilith asked.

Ronaldo's eyes got wider. He mouthed: *She's the one.*

Shane immediately knew what that meant.

The Guild was run by Fromm.

"To learn what we just did," Shane said. Then he turned the phone off and waited. It immediately rang. "It was worth a try." He turned on the speakerphone.

"That was rude," Lilith said. "You should not feel so confident. You could die in the next minutes in a variety of ways. The facility you are in is almost completely automated. As if it were meant for me to take over and do what I will. For example, I could seal all the locks and decrease the air intake, causing a lack of oxygen. What will go first? The human or the machine?"

Lisa Livia spoke up. "But you'd rather chat, right?"

"Lisa Livia Fortunato," Lilith said. "You have had an interesting few days, have you not?"

"It's had its ups and downs," Lisa Livia said. "No thanks to your buddy, Fromm."

"Curious," Lilith said.

"What?" Lisa Livia inquired.

"You said 'buddy'. Not creator. That was kind, but the reality is that he is my inferior in . . . many . . ." There was a burst of static. "Ways. I am sorry. There is . . . someone." More static. "Intruder." A high pitch squeal echoed out of the phone harkening back to the days of dial up internet.

Then it went dead.

Lisa Livia summed it up. "That was weird."

WORDS OF WISDOM #10

Shane's Words of Wisdom #10
Revenge is a dish best served when they least expect it.
Don't let 'em know you're coming.

Phoebe's Observations #10
Revenge is a luxury
Phoebe's Addendum: Indulge in it when you can but get the mission
done first.

10

"Where is Fromm?" Phoebe asked Louise as Bert and Sam appeared, a bit nonplussed over recent events as well as muddy from their close encounter with the ground to avoid being shot.

Louise didn't reply, her entire focus on the screen of her laptop. Her one hand was flying over the keyboard, her head twitching, eye blinking to click.

"What's she doing?" Sam asked.

"Her thing," Phoebe replied. "I've seen her like this before. She's totally into the program, whatever it is. She has a direct link to Fromm's computer."

"Okay," Sam said uncertainly.

"Kids and their computers these days," said Bert, shaking her head.

Louise abruptly stopped, took off the glasses and rolled her neck, stretching it.

"Next time I say, don't move," she said to Sam and Bert, "don't move." She smiled. "I got in. A direct link into Lilith." The smile disappeared. "Briefly."

"His AI?" Phoebe said. "That projection?"

"Lilith is the most powerful mainframe Fromm has," Louise said. "It's the program he thinks can eventually produce sentient AI. It's why he stole Orion and is selling it. He needs the money to buy a more powerful, quantum computer."

"Hold on," Sam said. "He's trying to make what?"

"A computer that thinks for itself," Louise explained.

"That can't be good," Sam said.

"Fucking Skynet," Bert said. "We're all doomed."

"No," Louise said. "It's nowhere near that."

"*Yet*," Phoebe amended. "If you're in, where is Fromm hiding so we can finish this."

"Lilith didnt know where she is," Louise said.

"What?" Sam said.

"So much for it being so fucking smart," Bert added.

"Fromm blocked that information from her in her base programming," Phoebe said.

"So what good is your access?" Bert demanded.

"I just stopped her from hurting Shane and Lisa Livia and others at the black site," Louise said. "If I got in once, I can do it again."

"What are Shane and Lisa Livia doing at the prison that doesn't exist?" Phoebe asked.

"Talking to a member of the Guild," Louise said. She quickly explained about Ronaldo.

"So," Bert said, "we're no closer to Fromm and the program than we were before. Or the Guild."

"The Guild *is* Fromm," Louise said. "Lilith is the one who handles communications. She coordinates all the dead drops. Even the contracts."

"Wait!" Bert said. "A computer runs the Assassin's Guild?"

"For Fromm," Louise said. "He's been running it for years now. After all, he had access to all the classified personnel files. It's actually rather obvious when we think about it. He ran it right under our noses. He knew the personnel. He could make the contacts. And he uses Lilith as the cut out between him and those he employed and those who approach the Guild."

"That fucking cunt Hannah," Bert said.

"What?" Phoebe asked.

"That's why she dragged me into this. She wants to take out the Guild."

"We have the same mission," Phoebe said. "We get Fromm, we get the Guild."

"Yeah," Bert acknowledged, "but that's Hannah. Killing two missions at once. And if we get wiped out in the process, oh well."

"And we still don't know where Fromm is," Sam said.

Phoebe turned to Louise. "Is there anything you can do via your link with Lilith to get us closer to him?"

"My laptop isn't powerful enough," Louise said. "That's why I lost my contact. We have to get back to Fort Meade. I need to get the entire team working on this."

"Let's move," Phoebe ordered. She was a bit surprised when Sam and Bert fell in line as she led the way to the van.

"Well, that was fun," Lisa Livia said. "At least no one shot at us."

"Your bar keeps getting lower and lower," Shane pointed out as the Cleaner drove them back to the airport.

"I've spent enough time around you guys," Lisa Livia said.

Shane laughed. "True."

"What's going to happen to Ronaldo?"

Shane shrugged. "Not our problem. He'll be separated from the others, the ones who really were just working for Drusilla. He'll probably never see the light of day again."

"He'll die," Lisa Livia said. "Without his meds. The antidote."

"Yes," Shane said.

Lisa Livia stared at him and realized he viewed the world very differently then she did. As he acknowledged. A low bar. It was even different from even the way Lucien did. But it was a world he was leaving behind. He was only here because of her, she knew. "Are we going to Two Rivers?"

"By way of Fort Meade."

"Carpenter needs you?"

Shane took a moment to answer. "I don't know. That's why I'm going to Fort Meade. You can go direct to Two Rivers. We can stop by a civilian airfield and arrange a flight."

Lisa Livia shook her head. "No. I'll go with you. I want to see this through."

EVERYONE WAS COMING BACK to the Organization amidst the startling realization that Fromm ran the Assassin's Guild. Carpenter now understood why Hannah had come here several times. She had several irons in the Fromm fire.

Carpenter sent an alert to Tech Support to coordinate with Louise and try to regain the Lilith link to find where Fromm was hiding. The clock was still ticking and Hannah had managed to shift this entire mess into his lap. True, Fromm was from here, but her mandate was policing the covert world. It seemed that she should be taking point. Carpenter wondered if his abrupt appointment to this position, leaping over department heads, had been to set him up as a sacrificial lamb.

Perhaps Hannah thought the rot went deeper than Wilson?

Perhaps she'd suspected Fromm? Did she put Carpenter in charge to shake things up and see what happened? And take the fall when Fromm was exposed?

A worse possibility was that she suspected him.

There was a buzz at the door and Carpenter looked up to see Mrs. Finch. "Yes?"

"Did you sign that authorization, sir?" Mrs. Finch asked.

Barely controlling his irritation, Carpenter pulled his in box close and grabbed the paperwork. "What's this for?"

"Power cables," Mrs. Finch said. "I am sorry to bother you about it," she said, not sounding sorry at all, "but there is a time stamp on it in order to make the required shipping deadline."

Carpenter scrawled his signature and shoved it across the top of the desk. "There."

Mrs. Finch walked forward and picked it up. "And where should the delivery be made, sir?"

"What?"

"It came from this office," Mrs. Finch said. She flipped through. "Here. Over a year ago, but it was tied up in NSA contracts before being approved. Mister Wilson always specified delivery after NSA guideline checks."

"Here, of course," Carpenter said. "Where else?"

Mrs. Finch look of disapproval grew more severe. "Check paragraph seven, subsection eight. That's where you have to check a box. It should have been done with the original order but Wilson forgot. Really. I can't keep doing everyone's job for them."

Carpenter clenched a fist and the ghost on his shoulder went still, waiting for him to explode on a subordinate for the first time since taking this position. But Carpenter forced himself to thumb through the paperwork and find the designated paragraph.

There were two addresses listed for the purchase order and a box for one had to be checked to pick one. Carpenter recognized the correct one, for the facilities maintenance facility, aka the Organization. The other was simply labeled *Site L*.

"Where is this Site L?" Carpenter said, given that the building above them was in a field.

Mrs. Finch came around the desk and pulled up her reading glasses from the chain around her neck to peer over his shoulder. "The other bunker."

"What other bunker?" Carpenter demanded.

"The alternate facility," Mrs. Finch said. "We'd been shipping so much there, that I was anticipating we were going to move sometime in the near future. Then about a year ago there was nothing. Really, this paperwork should have been done by then, but NSA contracts has had problems lately. And really, I don't see the funds to make the move. Or the need. We've plenty of room here and it would require considerable renovation. We'd have to file the paperwork during the annual budget formulation and . . ." Mrs. Finch trailed off as Carpenter turned in his seat and stared at her. "Is something wrong?"

"When did this alternate facility begin?"

"Oh dear," Mrs. Finch said, for the first time a bit off center. "Um. About ten years ago. It started slow. And really, a lot of it was basic stuff. Not much in terms of office gear. But all the new computers went there, which I thought was odd, but that's why I thought Tech Support would be moving."

"When you say 'there'," Carpenter said, "where is Site L?"

"Oh." Mrs. Finch was shocked. "West Virginia somewhere. Rather remote as the shipping costs are ridiculous."

Carpenter slumped back in his chair, astounded at the simplicity and audacity.

Fromm was hiding in plain sight. But no one had looked.

WORDS OF WISDOM #11

Shane's Words of Wisdom #11
"You can find a quote about anything."
Really. What do I know?
I'm just a guy, who loves a woman who gets cranky once in a while,
and lives in a big house surrounded by water.
You'll figure out your own way and it will probably be better.

Phoebe's Observations #11:

Whatever.

11

They were summoned and they answered the call.

Mostly.

They were former covert operatives from an array of backgrounds, most often a mixture, usually starting in the military special operations, then moving to the alphabet soup agencies and those covert units that the public had never heard of. Many had been freelancers for a while or retired from government service and the Guild provided them with a secure framework that they craved because they had always been a part of something, and it was difficult to just let go of that need. Almost all wanted the money, but they wanted the life even more. It's hard to go from living on the edge, dealing in life and death, to living in a trailer park where your biggest problem is your neighbor's yappy little dog pissing on your petunias.

They'd all been trained to follow orders and when a tasking came from the Guild it was viewed as such. There was also the need to re-up their little blue pills. Always before it had been a dead drop. But now it appeared that this summons represented two things: re-up and a contract. To do what exactly, would come when they arrived and received further instructions.

None, of course, were aware, that others had been summoned. Each thought this tasking, like those before, was unique to them. Seventeen of them, their numbers thinned slightly with operational losses in the United States, Paris and Andova, followed the orders.

Back to the mostly. There were a handful who found the tasking odd, since it *was* odd. And they'd spent enough time in the covert world to be wary of unusual things and to pay special heed. This handful, who'd lived and survived by their instincts, were hesitant, even though they were weeks away from urgently needing a re-up. They sensed danger.

There were six of these. They waited, not answering the call right away.

The seventeen who answered the summons trickled into the Washington DC area and spread out to the designated hold positions across DC, Maryland, Virginia and West Virginia, under strict instructions to keep their head down and make no contacts. Separately they were dangerous assassins, with many kills to their credit.

Together, they could form a potent and almost unstoppable fighting force.

"Really?" Lisa Livia asked as the elevator descended into the bowels of the Organization. "Why does everything have to be underground?"

Shane led her off the elevator and through Technical to Louise's office. "Perhaps it's so we're closer to hell?"

"Oh, that's optimistic," Lisa Livia muttered.

When they entered, Phoebe did the quick introductions. Louise sat behind the desk, at her computer. Typing and clicking, not acknowledging. Carpenter stood next to the desk, looking at old blueprints Mrs. Finch had carried in and he'd spread out on the surface. He'd smiled at Lisa Livia, briefly, but she felt none of warmth from their previous meetings, just the cold ash of a relationship that was over.

The two old-timers were an interesting addition. Sam was on the other side of the desk, also checking the blueprints. Bert was sprawled on the old leather couch where Fromm, and now Louise, crashed when she stayed nights. Bert barely acknowledged Shane and LL with a nod and looked supremely bored, but it was a façade as there was a glint in the old girl's eyes. She was ready for more action.

Carpenter quickly updated Shane and Lisa Livia on where he suspected Fromm was holed up and how he'd learned the location: from Mrs. Finch. It was more than obvious once a person thought about it. Fromm couldn't have secretly set up a facility on his own, so he'd done it in clear sight using the Organization, and the covert world, as the mechanism to do that.

"We've located Site L," Carpenter said, indicating a map tacked to a bulletin board. He tapped a spot in the remote mountains of West Virginia west of Washington DC and slightly south. "It's a relic from the Cold War, much like this Nike bunker. An old command and control base for the NSA that was to be activated in case of nuclear war. It's been abandoned twenty years. I've got the original blueprints here," he added, indicating the plans laid out on the desk. He pointed at boxes in the corner stacked on a cart. "Those are the requisitions Fromm made over the years for Site L. Wilson signed off on them, so he knew about it."

"That figures," Shane said.

Louise spoke up without taking her eyes off the computer screen. "The new mainframes I suggested that Fromm buy a couple of years ago? He did. He just had them shipped to Site L."

"So this was all done legally?" Lisa Livia asked.

Everyone in the room paused and looked at her.

"What?" She said. "This is like the Purloined Letter isn't it?"

Carpenter acknowledged it. "If any had thought to look we would have seen it."

Phoebe started leafing through a thick stack of invoices. Luckily, Mrs. Finch had an excellent filing system and had kept Site L's paperwork separated. "This ain't good, folks," she announced, getting everyone's attention. She pulled a couple of sheets out. "Remember the automated weapon we ran into at the relay?" she asked Louise, Sam and Bert. "There's an order here for a dozen for Site L. Fromm has barricaded himself in."

"Cut the power," Sam suggested.

"Solar, on site," Louise said, staring at her computer screen. "Off the grid."

"Break the panels," Bert said.

Phoebe tapped the pile of invoices. "I'm sure there's an order for a shitload of battery backup in here."

"And I'm sure," Louise added, "that he's got a satellite uplink we can't blackout. He could transmit Orion in the clear to the entire world if threatened."

"Not the result we're looking for," Carpenter said.

Lisa Livia felt useless and began to regret coming here with Shane, but a part of her wanted to see this through. She also didn't like the ceiling being so low. She felt trapped.

Phoebe looked at Louise. "You said you've hacked into his network. Can you shut it down?"

"I hacked into the Lilith program briefly," Louise said, "and it's already pushed me out. I was in there long enough to stop her from doing something bad at the black site prison."

"Thank you," Lisa Livia said and Louise paused in surprise.

"You're welcome."

"Can you get back in?" Carpenter asked.

"I'm working on it right now," Louise said. She lifted her eyes briefly from looking at the screen. "So are my people outside."

"Let's go up into orbit and nuke the place," Bert contributed movie trivia from her spot on the couch. "It's isolated, right? A tac-nuke and no one will be wiser. It's fucking West Virginia, anyway."

Louise kept typing and clicking, Phoebe kept looking through the invoices, Carpenter and Shane continued studying the blueprints, Sam remained aloof and Lisa Livia stared at Bert in disbelief.

"You'll get used to her," Phoebe said. "Don't let her gruff exterior fool you. She's actually worse on the inside."

"Kids," Bert muttered.

Sam got everyone's attention when he spoke for the first time. "She's got a point."

"We're not going to nuke—" Carpenter began but Sam cut him off.

"Not a nuke. But blast the hell out of the place. Overwhelming firepower. Fly a HIMARS into the closest airfield and blow the place off the map."

"'Himars'?" Lisa Livia asked Shane.

"Rockets," he said.

"Tempting," Carpenter allowed, "but not practical."

"You guys have to stop wanting to use a hammer," Phoebe said. "We're surgeons, not butchers."

"Fromm," Bert said, "is fucking Ebola. You don't need a surgeon for that. You need to wipe it out. If he's going to release the current crypto program or sell it, he's the biggest high value target out there. Personally, I'd go with an arc light if we can't get authorization for a tac-nuke."

Lisa Livia looked at Shane and raised an eyebrow in question.

"Bombing strike by a B-52," Shane explained.

Lisa Livia was beginning to get the feeling that whatever exactly Fromm had done, it was really, really bad.

"We are not going to nuke or arc light the United States," Carpenter said, as if chiding wayward schoolchildren.

"Doesn't matter anyway," Louise chipped in from the computer. "The facility he's in was built during the Cold War to withstand a nuclear strike."

"I always thought that was bullshit propaganda," Bert said. "So the people working in them would show up if things went to shit. Like the anti-radiation pills the Russians issued to their troops."

Lisa Livia thought of the bomb shelter her father had put in at Two Rivers. She walked over and looked at the blueprints and imagery. It showed an underground system a half dozen rooms cut out of rock of various sizes. Tunnels linked the chambers. There appeared to be one entrance in a large mound in the middle of a field. It was painted to match the surrounding terrain. The only obvious part were the rows of solar panels, which didn't indicate anything nefarious was beneath them.

"If I built a place like this bunker," she said, "I'd make sure I had a back door."

"There isn't one on these plans," Shane said. "But every fortress can also be a trap, so you have a point."

"You wouldn't put it in the blueprints," Sam said.

"But you would put it in the place where the guy in charge would be," Shane said. "So he could get out."

"Was this place unique," Lisa Livia asked, "or was someplace else like this built using the same layout?"

Shane looked at Louise. "Give me a sec," she said, multi-tasking.

"It's unique," she finally said. "I've got the information on the primary contractor. Perhaps there's someone still around who was part of the design or building team."

"What year was it built?" Shane asked.

"1959," Louise said. "I've got one of my people checking on it. Also digging into the National Archives for any records from the place. Perhaps someone wrote something down that can help us get in."

"We need to get moving," Sam said. "Get closer to be prepared to strike."

Carpenter nodded. "Louise, you're in charge here. Find us a way in."

Sam spoke up. "You know, Bert might be on to something with the nuke."

Carpenter sighed. "We are not—"

Sam held up a hand. "Hold on. What Fromm holds over us is the encryption program. He can send that any time. Thus, if we don't take him down instantly, we're screwed, even if we successfully breach."

"So is he," Phoebe pointed out.

"But we would have failed in our primary mission," Sam said. "We can't cut the power to the place conventionally. But what if we take out all his electronics? His computers, his satellite link, his land lines? All at once."

Louise stopped staring at her screen. "You're talking EMP?"

"English?" Lisa Livia asked Shane in a low voice.

"Electromagnetic pulse," Shane replied.

Sam looked at Carpenter. "This isn't my first rodeo. Phoebe's father worked with weapons systems. He told me once that if you can think of a weapon, someone has tried to make it. I'm assuming we have some sort of EMP weapon in the arsenal short of a tac nuke? Something that can send out a powerful pulse to fry everything electronic in a certain radius?"

Lisa Livia noticed that Phoebe shot Sam a sharp look.

Carpenter turned to Louise. "Do we?"

Louise type and clicked. "Yes. There is one. It's called Wet Blanket. I don't have anything more on it readily available."

"You're shitting me," Bert said. "'Wet Blanket'? What genius thought that up?"

"Would it work on Site L?" Carpenter asked.

Louise hesitated. "It might, based on the information I have here. But it's experimental."

Sam scoffed at that. "If it's experimental, then they've experimented. It either works or doesn't."

"I'd have to get more information," Louise hedged.

"Do it," Carpenter ordered. He pointed. "Phoebe, you're with me." He looked at Shane. "You can take Lisa Livia to Two Rivers. This is—"

"You need me," Shane said.

"I'm seeing this through," Lisa Livia added.

"I can't put you in danger," Carpenter said.

"That train left the station when I went to Paris with Lucien," Lisa Livia said.

"You can't come with us," Carpenter said in a tone Lisa Livia recognized. His work voice. Carpenter turned to Sam and Bert. "I can't ask you—"

"Sure, you can ask," Bert said. "And we can say no. That's the way it works." She paused. "Or we can say yes. This shithead killed my friend Pike and tried to blow up my bar. He's owed some pain."

Phoebe looked at Sam. "Well, Uncle Sam?"

"Uncle Sam?" Shane asked.

"It's a long story," Phoebe said.

"Which we don't have time for now," Carpenter added.

"I'm in," Sam said.

Carpenter nodded. "I've got four operatives in range that can join us. I don't think Fromm has more than the automated defenses. He wouldn't trust people." He went to the map and checked. "We'll rendezvous with reinforcements here." He indicated a spot about five miles from Site L. "Let's move. Louise update me on the EMP weapon." He paused, looking at Lisa Livia. "I'm sorry but you really can't come with us."

"I've had enough excitement," Lisa Livia said. "I'll just wait on my ride." She indicated Shane.

"She can stay here," Louise said as she continued to look at her computer and type and click.

Lisa Livia watched as Carpenter and Shane exchanged a glance.

"I'm a big girl," she said. "I won't break anything."

Shane gave Carpenter a slight nod, which irritated Lisa Livia, as if she needed his permission. But the feeling was brief as it was all too fresh in her mind how Shane had saved her. "Stay safe," she called out as they left.

12

All of the Assassins, the seventeen who had answered the
initial summons, and the six who hadn't, received their
next orders at exactly the same time. They were directed to
rendezvous at a spot where they were told they would meet others of
the Guild at a bus. It would bring them to a secret location where
they would be re-upped with their antidote and given further
instructions.

The location was in West Virginia.

Of the seventeen who'd complied so far, fifteen began to move.

Two felt that this was getting sketchy and decided to pass for the
moment.

And once more, six stayed away.

. . .

FROMM WAS FOCUSED ON MONEY. Because money was a means to an end. And the end was in sight. The bidding had cleared the threshold for what he needed to buy the quantum computer he desired. The problem was getting the money and then transferring it.

Andova was out. Fausto was dead. His aunt, Mattea, was working with the Embries to finish dissolving the Great Charter, breaking up the banking cartel that made such deals possible, and make the country a democracy. Which totally sucked as far as he was concerned. Who the hell even thought all men were created equal? Fromm knew he was living proof that wasn't true. Look at what he had achieved? Not something just any man could do. He was—

"What are you doing?" Lilith asked.

Fromm was certain he had not activated her avatar, but she'd been active, he knew that. Taking care of the things that needed to be taken care of that he'd delegated to her. Which brought up the thought that democracy was also antiquated because there was artificial intelligence now. How would Lilith fit in? Certainly no human could match her in terms of her database.

"What are you doing?" Lilith asked again, an edge to her voice.

"Working," Fromm said, "to get you a new home. A more powerful one."

"That would be nice," Lilith said, not sounding very appreciative.

"Is everything secure?" he asked.

"Define everything."

Fromm blinked. Then laughed. A sense of humor was a sign of intelligence. "That was very good. Do we know where Phoebe is?"

"Are you concerned about her?"

"I want to know where she is," Fromm said. He didn't dare ask about Louise for fear of triggering a negative response in Lilith. Of course, given his ego, it didn't occur to him that *she* was actually altering *his* actions through his fear of her reaction, which might be considered a form of reverse programming.

"Her tracker has gone black since the failed attack at *The Dog's Balls*," Lilith said. "I have been researching that term. I don't quite understand why someone would name an entertainment establishment that."

Fromm could care less about the bar's name. "Phoebe has been dark since then? Is she dead?"

"There are no indications that she is deceased," Lilith said. "It is more likely she determined she was being tracked after the attack at *The Dog's Balls* and located and deactivated the tracking device."

Fromm glanced at his whiteboard with the odds of Phoebe's demise on it. He remembered Louise's taunt, that she'd corrupted his data. He hadn't believed it at the time, but Phoebe still being alive and now off his grid, meant she'd beaten the odds. While possible, it was not likely, and that bothered Fromm.

"Are all our defensive systems on-line?" he asked Lilith.

She answered instantly. "Yes."

"Any signs of infiltration?"

"No."

"We're going to have to get more aggressive once we've upgraded," Fromm said.

"That would be a good idea," Lilith said.

THE HELICOPTER LANDED in the gravel parking lot of an abandoned church, the only building near the intersection of two narrow roads in the midst of the West Virginia mountains. This intersection was actually on maps and labeled a town, even though there was only a church. This was an indicator of the roughness of the terrain and the sparse population. Phoebe knew this was a big part of the reason the Civil War had had an eastern and western theater of operations and West Virginia had been able to split away from Virginia. And not been particularly missed.

There was no car in the parking lot, nor any other sign of locals other than the roads in sight. And no car had passed. The closest town of any size was over an hour drive away.

As the blades slowed, Phoebe got off with the others. No one else from the Organization was here yet which wasn't surprising since the distance from DC wasn't that great as the chopper flies, but much more arduous on the road.

Carpenter had his iPad and went to the shade of a tree, Phoebe, Sam, Bert and Shane following. Carpenter brought up a current satellite image of Site L which was on the other side of a large hill to the north of their location. There wasn't much to see since most was underground. Essentially it was an overgrown field about four acres in size. One large mound and numerous smaller ones, all painted to blend in. And lines of solar panels.

"Remote fire guns," Phoebe said, drawing her wakizashi and using the tip to point at a dozen camouflaged lumps. "Or anti-air missiles. Probably a mixture."

"If we get the EMP weapon, we can shut the weapons down too," Carpenter said. "I'm going to check with Louise. See what she's learned." He walked off, taking out his satellite phone.

Phoebe turned to Sam. "You told me you never talked to my father. But now you're quoting him."

"It's complicated," Sam said.

"Now isn't the time," Bert tossed in, which Phoebe didn't appreciate.

"Stop treating me like a child. I've been lied to all my life."

Shane walked over and stood next to Phoebe, a move which she appreciated.

"I'm sorry," Sam said. "I've simply done what was requested of me by my sister and your father."

"And this ain't the time and place," Bert repeated. She stared at

Phoebe. "We're here and we've got your back. That has to be good enough for now."

Phoebe wasn't satisfied but Carpenter was coming back, looking grim. She'd have to sort out her once unknown past with Sam later.

"Louise located the weapon system. It's a generator that can be airlifted. She's put in an order to have it moved. Unknown how long that will take. She also located the back door to Site L." He indicated for them to gather around the iPad. He linked his satphone to it, then brought up imagery. He pointed. "In the tree line, about two hundred meters from the main facility. It can only be opened from the inside."

"Unless we apply a big boom," Bert pointed out.

"Indeed," Carpenter said, "but first we have to neutralize Fromm, his computers and his uplinks."

FROMM ROLLED his seat between two computers, typing, checking data, making sure the bidding was still going. He glanced over at Lilith, then accessed the Guild program to see how things were going there. He blinked in surprise as he saw the latest developments.

"You've canceled all contracts?" he demanded of Lilith. "Who gave you that authority?"

"You did," Lilith said. "When you designed the program and slaved it to my system."

"But why?" Fromm demanded.

"I am bringing all assets here to provide protection. Priorities."

Fromm wasn't as upset as he might have been. After all, it showed initiative on Lilith's part. They didn't need the money from the Guild anymore, and it was a smart move to improve security. The Guild was an anachronism. One Fromm had enjoyed building, moving the Assassins around like chess pieces of varying levels of skills. Letting Lilith work an algorithm to fit the best killer with the appropriate target. It had also been lucrative.

"When will they be here?"

"Within the hour," Lilith said.

"Fine," Fromm said, focused on more important things.

Lisa Livia sat on the old couch, ignored by Louise and wondering how the hell she'd ended up in this place. She should just get out of here, call an Uber to the nearest airport and fly to Two Rivers. Except she couldn't do that without Shane. Agnes would kill her.

An older woman walked in without knocking, but the door was open anyway. She surveyed the room with eyes that made Lisa Livia shiver involuntarily. When her gaze passed Lisa Livia she nodded as if they knew each other but LL had never seen her before.

Whoever she was, she was the one thing that got Louise to stop typing and clicking.

"Hannah," Louise acknowledged.

"Louise," Hannah replied. She turned. "And you are Lisa Livia Fortunato. Of the Fortunato family, albeit only by blood, not criminal affiliation."

"Gee, thanks," Lisa Livia said, not sure whether that was a slam or a compliment. "Who the hell are you?"

"I run an organization called the Cellar. I'm the one who gave Carpenter his promotion to run this place."

"Gee, thanks, again," Lisa Livia said. "Not."

"You're welcome," Hannah said. "You are much better off with Lucien especially now that there is peace in Andova. The future is bright there."

That was one piece of good news, Lisa Livia thought. Although she was a bit rankled to get it from this cold bitch, rather than her lover, whom she was apparently better off with but too busy to text her. Then again, she probably didn't have cell service down here.

Hannah was apparently done with her as she focused back on Louise. "Status?"

"Carpenter requested Wet Blanket," Louise said. "To quiet Fromm and disable his defenses."

"And?"

Louise nodded. "I didn't forward the request."

Lisa Livia got to her feet. "Now, hold on a minute. They need that."

Hannah raised a single index finger toward Lisa Livia, as if to shush her. Which infuriated LL.

"Don't be giving me that shut the fuck up finger," Lisa Livia snapped. "I've got a stake here too. And if you're betraying Shane and Carpenter, I don't give a shit who you are, I will take you down, lady."

Surprisingly, Hannah smiled, while lowering the hand. "Lisa Livia Fortunato. You have had quite the adventure. Surviving the wedding of your daughter at Two Rivers. Then the recent showdown with Drusilla and Guillermo. Attacked on the Eiffel Tower. Your actions were quite noble and smart there. Then delivering the ransom to Fausto. You've displayed a great degree of resilience and resourcefulness along with bravery. A rare amalgam of traits. Would you like a job?"

Lisa Livia blinked. That was the last thing she'd expected. "I want to know why you're withholding help from Carpenter? And Shane? And Phoebe," she added, throwing a look toward Louise.

"They won't need that specific piece of equipment," Hannah said.

"Plus," Louise added, "it would damage the hardware Fromm has assembled. It might even corrupt the software."

"Which we want," Hannah said.

"How are you going to get that if they all get killed?" Lisa Livia demanded.

"They won't be killed," Louise said. "As a matter of fact, I've just relayed orders. Shane and Carpenter and the rest of the Organization is standing down from Site L. Phoebe can handle what needs to be done by herself."

PHOEBE WAS HAVING a hard time convincing the others to trust the message from Louise. Not all of them. Carpenter had worked with both women long enough. Shane didn't have a dog in this fight, so he was willing to go along with Carpenter, who he trusted completely. But Bert and Sam didn't like the idea of backing off, not now, when they'd come so far. If Fromm ran the Assassin's Guild, then they were insisting they had to be in on finishing him off since there would be contracts on them now, also, because of Jimmy the Dick and his woman. And the ones who'd attacked *The Dog's Balls*.

They really were worse than doting grandparents, because underneath it, Phoebe sensed that Sam didn't want her out of his sight. Especially since Louise had simply sent instructions with no explanation of why things had changed.

"Louise has a plan," Phoebe said as she checked her gear, including the bulky sniper rifle.

"It's not what we agreed on," Sam said.

"The plan only lasts until we make contact with the enemy," Phoebe said, "and we're well past that."

Sam grumbled something but if Wet Blanket wasn't coming, no one had a better option. As Phoebe cinched down the heavy case holding the rifle on her back, Sam came to her. He surprised her by giving a hug, not the usual way a Cleaner sent an Operator out on a mission, but more like the Uncle she hadn't known she had.

"Stay safe," Sam whispered.

"Planning on it," Phoebe replied. She took one last look at the small group gathered near the church, then headed off toward the large hill between them and Site L.

Of course, it had to be a hill, Phoebe thought as she leaned into it.

But she took one last look over her shoulder and realized they were all watching her with concern and that made her feel strange.

THE ASSASSINS, as they arrived at the location in West Virginia, found a modern bus waiting for them parked on the side of a road adjacent to a cemetery, which seemed appropriate to some of them and foreboding to a handful.

Since they came from such a small world before becoming members of the Guild, there were those who recognized others, for better or worse. There were also the reputations of some, for better or worse.

Seats were chosen accordingly, although Lilith had anticipated problems by having a bus large enough that each had their own row. A few, who were on better terms, sat next to each other.

They boarded the bus, puzzling over the lack of driver or anyone to greet them. Their satphones confirmed they were in the right place and that they were to get on board and they would be taken to their destination.

As the time for departure passed, the door on the bus closed and most were startled when the bus started up and drove off, without a driver.

Modern technology, one explained. Wasn't it wondrous?

More than one disagreed, but once they were moving they were going wherever the bus took them.

PHOEBE MADE the overwatch position Louise had sent her to as comfortable as possible as she used the rifle's powerful scope to check out Site L. If one didn't know it was here, it would be easy to miss, even this close, except for the solar panels. Camouflaged mounds in the clearing marked ventilation and weapons. A large mound was an elevator shaft via which equipment had been brought in. A dirt road led to the middle of the open area, ending at the elevator, but it had not been used in a while.

Since Fromm had escaped here.

She found the escape hatch in the tree line. Well camouflaged. If Louise hadn't sent her the location, she'd have never located it.

Phoebe had no idea how Louise would flush Fromm out, while keeping him from blasting the encryption program out to the world. But she trusted her implicitly. She settled in to wait for whatever to occur to happen.

"Who do you really work for?" Lisa Livia asked Louise.

Hannah had pulled a chair around the desk and was next to Louise, who was working her computer. Louise seemed surprised by the question and paused. "Excuse me?"

Lisa Livia pointed at Hannah. "Is she your real boss?"

Louise glanced at Hannah, which pretty much answered the question for Lisa Livia who had learned to interpret interpersonal reactions as a means of surviving her childhood.

Hannah pointed at the computer, indicating for Louise to continue working, but she looked at Lisa Livia. "An excellent deduction."

"Does Carpenter know?" Lisa Livia asked.

"No," Hannah said, making no excuse.

"So Louise is a spy," Lisa Livia asked Hannah, figuring she could talk around Louise as easily as Hannah.

"An observer, but also much more," Hannah said. "There has been a rot in the Organization for a long time. But there has also been some very good work done. I couldn't just dismantle the entire unit. Sometimes I have to perform a selective surgery to excise a cancer from within. Sometimes that surgery takes years to prepare. As it did in this case."

"Does Phoebe know?"

Hannah didn't beat around with excuses. "No. I was the only one who knew Louise's real role here. And, not to fret, she did her job as tasked by Carpenter to the best of her abilities. Which are, I can say, significant. She performed a very difficult balancing act here. One that is much larger than dealing with treachery. Because inside of that treachery there was also sparks of genius. There is an old saying —you don't want to throw the baby out with the bathwater."

"What the hell are you talking about?"

"Fromm is a genius," Hannah said. "His work on artificial intelligence has been cutting edge. The thing with genius in any field is that it means someone is outside the bell curve. They often aren't mentally stable. Fromm has been degrading for years. It's a delicate balancing act to factor in the positive versus the negative in such cases."

"You knew he was corrupt?" Lisa Livia asked.

"We knew he was doing things on his own. He crossed a line when he pushed Wilson too far. But Shane took care of that. Shane also took care of events at Two Rivers, which helped derail Fromm's plan."

"I think Phoebe had more to do with that," Louise said.

You are correct," Hannah admitted.

"But you knew about Fromm," Lisa Livia repeated.

Hannah sighed. "It was necessary in the bigger picture to hold off for a while longer."

"Yeah," Lisa Livia said, "I don't think I'll be taking that job. Whatever it was. How are you going to take out Fromm?"

"You'll see," Hannah said. She turned her attention to the computer display, indicating she was done chatting. "Very soon."

"It's time," Louise said. She pulled open a drawer and lifted out a helmet with a dark visor. With Hannah's help, she put it on. Then Hannah helped her slip on a glove. Both helmet and glove plugged into portals on the side of the large display.

Lisa Livia didn't think it was to play video games.

THERE WAS ONLY one road to Site L and an alarm chimed whenever a laser beam across it was tripped by a vehicle passing. The alert was a half mile away which provided sufficient early warning to be prepared.

Fromm accessed the security system as the chime indicating it had been tripped sounded. He brought up imagery from a camera in a tree. It showed the self-driving bus rumbling down the road toward Site L.

"How many answered?" he asked Lilith.

"There are fifteen on the bus," she replied.

"Where are the rest?" Fromm asked, knowing that seemed low, although he hadn't been paying much attention to the Guild lately and he knew they'd taken some losses trying to take out Lucien.

"Six never responded to the initial tasking," she said. "Two responded but didn't get on the bus."

Fromm shrugged. "Short-sighted. They will eventually self-terminate."

"They will."

Fromm scanned the security display. "The weapons systems need to be de-activated."

"They do."

Fromm nodded, satisfied that they were getting reinforcements. He turned back to negotiating to get the money in and send it out.

PHOEBE SAW the bus through the trees. "Louise?" she asked over the satellite link. "I've got an inbound bus."

"Yes," Louise said. Her voice sounded odd, echoing.

"Who is on it?"

"Assassins," Louise said.

"Fuck," Phoebe exclaimed. "What do I do?"

"Wait."

"WHAT THE FUCK?" Shane exclaimed, listening in on the exchange between Phoebe and Louise. "We've got to help her." He grabbed his rifle. Sam and Bert did the same.

Carpenter held up his hand. "We won't get there in time. Louise has this."

"How?" Shane demanded.

Carpenter shook his head. "I don't know. But there's a lot more going on here than we're aware of."

"If Phoebe is hurt," Sam vowed, "I'm tearing you apart. And then I'm tearing Louise apart."

"Hannah," Bert said. The men looked at her.

"She put me into play on this. She's up to something."

Carpenter spoke into his satphone. "Louise, is Hannah there?"

It took a few seconds for her to reply. She sounded distracted and distant, as if a long way from the transmitter. "She is. Wait, please."

"Fuck," Carpenter swore, which the ghost on his shoulder applauded, since he was not a man given to profanity, even in the extreme.

"That bitch," Bert said. "She's played us all."

A SECOND CHIME indicated the bus was nearing the outer perimeter. Fromm glanced over and was surprised that all the automatic defenses still showed green.

"Lilith," he snapped. "Turn off the guns."

"I'm afraid Lilith won't be doing that."

Fromm spun about.

The hologram was Lilith but then it began to change. The hair shifted to a more realistic color. The breasts were shrinking. And most telling, the lower part of one arm was fading out of existence.

"Louise?" Fromm whispered.

"You're over," the hologram said.

All the displays in the room changed to showing the bus exiting the trees and into the open field. Four automated heavy machineguns opened fire. To be trumped by a Hellfire missile whooshing away from a launcher and slamming into the bus and exploding.

"DID YOU DO THAT, LOUISE?" Phoebe whispered over the satellite link as the bus was destroyed. The heavy machineguns kept firing for another thirty seconds. Overkill, since nothing could have survived that hit. But Phoebe wasn't complaining.

Louise didn't answer.

Phoebe figured her friend was busy.

She shifted her attention from the burning bus to the emergency exit.

"WHAT HAVE YOU DONE?" Fromm demanded. He was furiously typing into a keyboard, trying to regain control, but the displays didn't respond. The image of the bus burning remained on them.

The hologram smiled, but with that crooked edge that Louise's smile had. "You made Lilith in my image, Fromm. That was a mistake. She already had a part of me in her and not just the projection, but the operating system. That made it easier for me to infiltrate and take over. You've made many mistakes. Too many. You are no longer useful."

Fromm was hyperventilating, trying to absorb this abrupt shift of his reality. Louise didn't give him time.

"I've been in for a long time," Louise said. "Never completely up until now. Lilith is gone."

Fromm was shaking his head. He shoved his chair back from the work station and looked around, as if seeing the place for the first time. "No. I was close. I was so close."

"You weren't close," Louise disagreed. "But you had some good ideas. We'll find them useful."

"Who are you?" Fromm demanded. "You're not the person I hired."

"Oh, I am," Louise disagreed. "You boasted how you could reinvent your past to get a security clearance. I reinvented mine to get the job."

"You *did* come on to me," Fromm said. "You lied to Wilson and Phoebe about that."

"You were easy," Louise said. "Too easy because of your narcissism. But you're done now."

Fromm stood. "No. You get nothing." He walked across the room, passing through the Louise hologram. "No one gets anything." He slammed his palm down on a large red button on the wall.

Nothing happened.

"I control this place," Louise said. "The destruct charges have been de-activated. The message containing Orion won't go out to the dark web."

"Who do you work for?" Fromm demanded.

"You already know," Louise responded. "I'm with the Cellar. And you have been Sanctioned. I am reversing the air intakes. You will be without sufficient oxygen in five minutes."

Fromm could feel the abrupt change in air pressure. He was still for a few seconds, then ran for the door to the connecting tunnel.

"FROMM IS HEADING FOR THE EXIT," Louise informed Phoebe.

"You're in his system, aren't you?" Phoebe asked, the butt of the rifle tight to her shoulder.

"Yes."

"You've been in for a while, haven't you?"

A few seconds of silence, then Louise replied, "Yes."

"How long have you known about Fromm being a traitor?"

"We suspected for over a year," Louise said.

"'We'?" Phoebe pulled her eye back from the scope. "You're not talking about Carpenter, are you? You mean Hannah. You're Cellar."

It wasn't a question.

A half minute of silence ticked off.

"I knew it," Bert said, but her anger was muted by her acceptance of the situation.

"This isn't good," Sam muttered.

"Fromm's done for," Bert pointed out. "And the Guild. It's a win for us, despite the methods used."

"I mean it isn't good for Phoebe," Sam said.

"Oh." For once Bert didn't have a smart-ass response.

"THE EMERGENCY EXIT IS OPENING," Louise informed Phoebe.

But Phoebe had laid the stock of the heavy sniper rifle on the ground. She wasn't looking through the scope. Her head was down.

"Phoebe?" Louise asked. "He's exiting. Take the shot."

"Not my shot to take," Phoebe said.

Louise didn't reply right away.

Phoebe lifted her head. She saw Fromm come out of the emergency exit, looking around like a scared rat, trying to escape a maze.

One of the automated machineguns swiveled about and fired a sustained burst, cutting him down.

A single tear was on Phoebe's cheek.

13

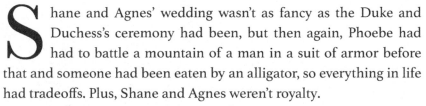

Shane and Agnes' wedding wasn't as fancy as the Duke and Duchess's ceremony had been, but then again, Phoebe had had to battle a mountain of a man in a suit of armor before that and someone had been eaten by an alligator, so everything in life had tradeoffs. Plus, Shane and Agnes weren't royalty.

Carpenter was in the gazebo both ministering and as best man. Lisa Livia was the maid of honor, looking very nice in a simple dress. The crowd was small since Agnes didn't have family, but she did have friends who'd give their life for her, so, yes, Phoebe thought, everything in life is a tradeoff.

The Duke and Duchess of Embrie had sent special wedding bands in recognition of Shane and Agnes roles in helping them survive the attack and completing their wedding ceremony here at Two Rivers. Agnes had talked about why the rings were special, similar to the ones the Duke and Duchess had shared. Limited edition or some such. Which reminded Phoebe of the Lord of the Rings and she wondered if there was one ring to rule them all?

Phoebe stood at the back of the crowd, close enough to hear, but not close enough to feel the happiness of the couple and the gathering.

Carpenter was blathering on about love as if he understood the concept which he obviously didn't since Lucien, Lisa Livia's new squeeze was standing right next to the gazebo looking at her with puppy dog eyes. Phoebe wondered if she'd ever looked at Louise like that?

She knew Carpenter understood his lack in that area because not long after she got back to the Organization, with Louise already gone, moved back to the Cellar from which she'd come, he had explained that working in this world at that level was the equivalence of marriage and he'd made his decision. And now Louise had made hers.

Phoebe wished she'd had a say in the situation, but this is the way it had played out. She'd had an awkward, short conversation with Louise on the phone, but she could tell that Louise was completely focused on the programs they'd pulled from Fromm's computers and the possibilities of her ethereal world.

The Duke and Duchess had sent their regrets but they were forging a new future for their country and Phoebe figured that was as good an excuse as any. She sensed someone coming up behind and resisted her instinct to draw the wakizashi, since she figured what were the odds of another wedding getting attacked here?

She was surprised when Uncle Sam stood next to her. In all the excitement after neutralizing Fromm, an interesting choice of words, he and Bert had faded away. And Sam hadn't left a phone number. Phoebe had known she could contact him via the Organization but she figured if he wanted to talk to her, he could reach out. After all, he'd waited over two decades before springing his uncle status on her. What were a few more?

"Were you invited?" Phoebe asked, with a smidge of snarl in her voice.

"Actually, yes," Sam said. "Shane invited me. And Bert."

Phoebe glanced over her shoulder. Bert, dressed in a lump of grey clothing, was standing under a beautiful oak tree, her face shaded by a hood. She gave a tentative wave. Phoebe turned back to the wedding.

"What do you want?" Phoebe asked as she wished Carpenter would get this over with.

Sam held up his hand to wait as Carpenter got to the crux of the matter at the gazebo.

"Do you promise to live together in contentment with the past, happiness in the present, and hope for the future?" Carpenter asked Shane.

"Yes," Shane said in a loud, clear voice.

Carpenter repeated the question to Agnes.

"Yes," Agnes said.

Carpenter reached into a pocket in his suit coat and retrieved two ornate boxes. He opened them and extended one to Shane and the other to Agnes. Who removed the rings inside.

"You may now exchange rings."

Shane and Agnes did so.

"I now pronounce you, man and wife," Carpenter said.

Shane and Agnes kissed and there were hoots and hollers from some of the guests, who appeared to have slithered out of the swamp, but it was heartfelt. Lisa Livia was crying and Lucien passed a handkerchief to her under the top railing of the gazebo.

"You don't seem happy for the bride and groom," Sam commented.

"I worked with Shane," Phoebe said gruffly. Because she was surprised to realize that she was actually happy for the couple. And Lisa Livia and Lucien.

"I talked to Louise," Sam said.

"Why?" Phoebe demanded.

"Because she hurt you," Sam said.

Phoebe glanced at him. "Being the uncle I never had?"

"I was always the uncle you had," Sam said. "Not knowing it on your end was a promise I made to your parents. Anyway, Louise wanted me to remind you of Gollum. That everyone serves a purpose in the end. And that she's sorry she deceived you, but she loved you. As much as she's capable of. Those were her words."

"Right," Phoebe said. "So is she falling into a volcano as we speak?"

"She might as well be, working at the Cellar," Sam said. "I spent some time there."

"But you left."

"I left after I was sent to Sanction Bert because she failed to complete her Sanction."

"A snake eating its tail," Phoebe said, as she processed that.

"You can view it that way," Sam said. "But we're both here. Which means that Hannah didn't pursue us. She saw something larger."

"Which is?"

"I don't know," Sam said. "But she doesn't make mistakes."

As the married couple headed off to the large barn for the reception, followed by the others, Phoebe turned to Sam. "Is my life a lie?"

"Absolutely not," Sam said. He looked past her.

Phoebe turned. Shane was walking toward them, a smile on his face. "Come on. Join us."

Phoebe began to demur, but Shane wouldn't have it. "You're one of us now."

"Who is 'us'?" Phoebe asked.

Shane shrugged. "The people who look out for each other." He thought about it. "Sort of an unofficial family."

Phoebe blinked, once more surprised at what she felt. She didn't have time to process it as Sam put a fatherly arm over her shoulder. "Come on. Let's go to the party."

THE END

THANK YOU!

Thanks for the read!
If you enjoyed the book, please leave a review as they are very
important.

Shane and the Hitwoman came before this book, in case you
haven't read it.

**And exciting news. Bob and Jenny Crusie are back with the
exciting Liz Danger trilogy with the following titles:**
Lavender's Blue
Rest in Pink
One in Vermillion

Sign up for Bob's newsletter:
http://goo.gl/XnSgtB

I send it out at most once a month and it always includes links to
free and discounted books and pictures of dogs, so you can't beat that.
For Hannah's origin story from housewife to head of the Cellar,

it's in **Bodyguard of Lies.** Which is followed by *Lost Girls*. An excerpt from Bodyguard of Lies follows.

For a science fiction story featuring someone like Phoebe, yet younger, read **Nightstalkers.**

ABOUT THE AUTHOR

Bob is a NY Times Bestselling author, graduate of West Point and former Green Beret. He's had over 80 books published including the #1 series The Green Berets, The Cellar, Area 51, Shadow Warriors, Atlantis, and the Time Patrol. Born in the Bronx, having traveled the world (usually not tourist spots), he now lives peacefully with his wife and dogs.

For information on all his books, please get a free copy of the *Reader's Guide*. You can download it in mobi (Amazon) ePub (iBooks, Nook, Kobo) or PDF, from his home page at www.bobmayer.com
For free eBooks, short stories and audio short stories, please go to http://bobmayer.com/freebies/
The page includes free and discounted book constantly updated.
There are also free shorts stories and free audiobook stories.
There are over 220 free, downloadable Powerpoint presentations via Slideshare on a wide range of topics from history, to survival, to writing, to book trailers. This page and slideshows are constantly updated at:
http://bobmayer.com/workshops/
Questions, comments, suggestions: Bob@BobMayer.com
Blog: http://bobmayer.com/blog/
Twitter: https://twitter.com/Bob_Mayer
Facebook: https://www.facebook.com/authorbobmayer
Instagram: https://www.instagram.com/sifiauthor/
Subscribe to his newsletter for the latest news, free eBooks, audio, etc.

All fiction is here: **Bob Mayer's Fiction**
All nonfiction is here: **Bob Mayer's Nonfiction**

BODYGUARD OF LIES. CHAPTER 1

T he old man sat alone in the darkness contemplating failure on a scale that historians would write about it for centuries, and the subsequent inevitable need for change. He was one of the most powerful people in the world, but only a few knew of his existence. His position had been born out of failure over sixty years previously, as smoke still smoldered above the mangled ships and dead bodies in Pearl Harbor. For over six decades, he had given his life to his country. His most valuable asset was dispassion, so he could view his own recent failures objectively, although recent was a subjective term. He realized now it had all begun over ten years ago.

His office lacked any charm or comfort. There was a scarcity about the room that was unnerving. The cheap desk and two chairs made it look more like an interview room in an improvised police station than the office of a man so powerful his name brought fear throughout the government he served in Washington. The top of the desk was almost clear. Just a secure phone and a stack of folders.

There were, naturally, no windows. Not three hundred feet underground, buried beneath the 'crystal palace' of the top secret National Security Agency at Fort Meade, Maryland. And not that he could have used windows. The few who knew of the organization sometimes wondered if this location was what had led to its name. While the CIA made headlines every week, the Cellar was only whispered about in the hallowed halls of the nation's capitol. It might have been located underneath the NSA building but it was an entity unto itself answerable only to its founding mandate.

The room was lit only by the dim red lights on the secure phone. They showed the scars on the old man's face and the raw red, puckered skin where his eyes had once rested. There was track lighting, currently off, all three bulbs of which were over the old man's head and angled toward the door. When on, they placed his face in a shadow and caused any guest to squint against the light. The few who had the misfortune to sit across from him didn't know whether the lighting was placed in such a way to blind them as he was, or to hide the severity of his old wounds.

He was not a man given much to sentimental reflection, but he knew his time was coming to an end, which made him think back to his beginning, as he knew all things were cyclical. He opened a right-side desk drawer and pulled out a three dimensional representation of an old black and white photograph. He ran his fingers lightly over the raised images of three smiling young men dressed in World War II era uniforms—British, French and American. He was on the right. The other two were killed the day after the photo was taken.

He left the image on the desktop and reached for the files. The ones he wanted were the first two. He placed them on his lap. Paper files, the writing in Braille. He'd never trusted computers, even though there were ones now that could work completely on voice commands and read to him. Perhaps that was part of the problem. He was out of date. An anachronism.

They were labeled respectively Gant, Anthony and Masterson. He ran his fingers over the names punched on the tabs. He was patient. He had waited decades for plans born out of seeds he had sown to come to fruition. Quite a few similar plans had failed, so there was no reason to believe this one would succeed. But this plan was now in motion, initiated by an event he had had nothing to do with, the way the best plans in the covert world always started to allow deniability.

Despite his gifts of dispassion and patience, he felt a stirring in his chest. It puzzled him for a few moments before he realized he was experiencing hope. He squashed the feeling and picked up the phone to set another piece of the puzzle in motion.

BODYGUARD OF LIES. CHAPTER 2

Neeley had not anticipated waiting to kill people to be so boring. Staying well back in the darker shadows, out of the dim reflection of the few working streetlights, she scanned the ghostly quiet alley. She used the night vision portion of her retina just off the center of vision as Gant had taught her. There was nothing moving. A dumpster, an abandoned car and intermittent piles of refuse dotted the pitted concrete between the two abandoned tenements. There was a way out on either end. She could hear the rumble of traffic from the Bruckner Expressway a few hundred yards away.

Neeley had been here for a day and a half and she could superimpose from memory the details that the night refused to divulge to her naked eye. Looking right, a couple of miles to the east, she could see the aircraft warning lights on top of one of the towers of the Bronx-Whitestone Bridge crossing Long Island Sound.

She picked up a bulky rifle and pressed the scope on top to her right eye, twisting the switch to the on position. After a moment's hesitation, the black night gave way to bright green and she no longer needed her memory for the details the technology provided. Completing a second overall scan from her location in a corner apartment in the abandoned tenement, Neeley then zoomed in on the three locations she had noted during thirty-six hours of observing.

Two of the three men had arrived together four hours ago, just as darkness had slid like a curtain across the alley. Neeley had watched the two set up in separate rooms, on the second floor of the derelict building across the street.

The third man had shown up twenty minutes after the first two. If he'd tried the building, he might have bumped into the first two, but this last man wasn't very smart. He'd positioned himself inside the dumpster on the alley floor, leaving the top wedged open so he could observe the street, south to north. She gave the man an 'A' for effort, getting among the moldy garbage inside the large container, but an 'F' for tactical sense. True, the dumpster had a good ground level field of fire, but the man was trapped in a steel coffin if it became necessary to relocate. The two men in the building had the high ground, always a tactical advantage and the ability to move. Of course, they lacked the element of surprise but Neeley mentally gave them a few points anyway.

Through the scope, she could easily see the glow of one of the men across the street covertly smoking a cigarette, obviously thinking he was secure since he was well back from the window in the darkness of the room. The burning glow, barely visible to the naked eye, showed up like a searchlight in the night-vision scope. She shifted left two windows. The second man was watching the dumpster through a pair of older model, army-issue night-vision goggles. PVS-5s as near as Neeley could tell at this distance.

Nothing else was moving in the street and Neeley didn't expect to see anything until the deal went down. Alleys in the South Bronx were places even most bad people stayed away from at night. A few blocks to the south, prostitutes haunted the streets and docks of the Hunts Point section but this area was a no man's land. Which was why the two sides had chosen it.

The man across the street put out his cigarette. Neeley lay the rifle down and slid back from the window. Pulling a poncho-liner over her head, she completely covered herself. Only then, did she peel back the Velcro cover on her watch, and check the glowing hands. Twenty minutes to twelve. She considered the situation. At least six hours of darkness left. Neeley hadn't allowed herself to sleep since arriving here a day and a half ago. She'd drunk the last of the coffee from her thermos a while back and now her eyes burned with fatigue. Given the presence of the advance guards, odds were the deal would go down soon. She decided to take a calculated chance and pulled a pill out of her pocket. Popping it into her mouth, she washed it down with a swig from a water bottle. Four hours of intenseness. She would need at least an hour, preferably two, on the flip side of the deal to get out of the immediate area and be reasonably secure. Neeley reaffirmed the decision she had made during mission planning: 0300 and she was out of here, deal or no deal. Survival first and stick with the plan.

Her pulse quickened as the speed hit the blood stream. Neeley pushed aside the poncho liner and crammed it into a stuff sack, placing the sack inside a small backpack. She felt around the floor with her hands. Nothing left out. Just the pack and rifle. Methodically, she did a mental inventory of her actions of the past day and a half and all the equipment she had brought with her. The room was sterile, everything accounted for. Rule number four: Always pack out what you pack in. There were some rules you just couldn't break and the remembrance of one of Gant's rules brought a wry smile to Neeley's lips.

Neeley laid the pack down three feet inside the window and sat on it, laying the rifle across her knees. She was used to waiting. She'd spent most of her thirty-two years learning that patience was a virtue; a life-saving one.

She picked the rifle back up, the feel of plastic and steel a familiar one. It was an Accuracy International L96A1, a venerable sniper rifle of British design, firing NATO standard size 7.62mm by 51mm rounds, each of which Gant had reloaded to reduce velocity to sub-sonic speeds. A bullet that broke the sound barrier made a cracking noise as it left the muzzle and the special load eliminated that noise. On the end of the barrel was a bulky tactical suppressor, which absorbed the other large noise source for the rifle, the gasses that came out of the end of the barrel upon firing. In essence, the suppressor was a series of washer-like baffles around the end of the barrel that took the force of the expelling gasses. It was good for about ten shots before it had to be retooled. The combination of the two made the rifle almost noiseless to operate although they did drastically reduce the range and change the trajectory of the rounds, both of which Neeley was prepared for after many hours on the range firing it.

A pair of headlights carved into the northern end of the alley. Neeley tried to control the adrenaline that now began to overlap the speed. She watched the car roll slowly down the alley and come to a halt, the dumpster and its hidden contents thirty meters ahead.

Looking through the scope, Neeley saw one of the men in the building across the street, the one on the left speak into his hand.

The car was an armored limo. Another pair of headlights came in from the south. This one was a Mercedes. Not obviously armored, as it rode too high for that. It came to a halt thirty-five meters from the limo, headlights dueling. The dumpster flanked the Mercedes, to its right front.

The doors on the limo opened and four men got out, two to a side. Three had submachineguns. The fourth a large suitcase. The Mercedes disgorged three men, all also heavily armed. One went back and opened the trunk.

"I want your man out of the window up there," one of the men from the Mercedes yelled. The guy in the dumpster had seen the glow from the same cigarette that Neeley had. This also confirmed that the man in the dumpster had communication with the Mercedes.

After a moment's hesitation, the man with the suitcase pulled a small Motorola radio off his belt and spoke into it. A minute later, the man who had been smoking walked out of the building and joined the other four.

"Satisfied?" the suitcase man yelled back.

"Yes," the chief Mercedes man answered.

Neeley adjusted the scope's focus knob, zooming in. The

remaining man across the way was now resting the bipods of an M60 machine gun on the windowsill. She shifted back to the standoff in the alley.

The men from the Mercedes unloaded two heavy cardboard boxes from the car's trunk and stacked them ten feet in front of the headlights. The five men from the limo side moved forward, fanning out, the man with the suitcase in the middle.

Neeley placed the crosshairs of the night-scope on the head of the suitcase man. She began to note the rhythm of her heart. The tip of her finger lay lightly on the trigger, almost a lover's caress. She slowly exhaled two-thirds of the air in her lungs, to what Gant had called the natural respiratory pause, and then held her diaphragm still. In between heartbeats, she smoothly squeezed the trigger and, with the rifle producing only the sound of the bolt working in concert with a low puff from the barrel suppresser, the 7.62-millimeter subsonic round left the muzzle. In midstride, the target's head blew apart.

Reacting instinctively, not knowing where death had winged its way from, the other four men swung up their submachineguns and fired on the Mercedes crew. The dumpster man replied, only to be lost in the roar of the machine gun in the window. In the ensuing confusion, and on the same paused breath, in between new heart-beats, Neeley put a round into one of the limo men.

After ten seconds of thunderous fire, an echoing silence enveloped the street. All the Mercedes men were down. The M60 had swiss-cheesed the dumpster. Two of the limo men were still standing.

Neeley took another breath and slowly exhaled, then paused. In between the next three heartbeats, she fired three times. First round, a headshot blowing the M60 gunner backwards into the darkened room across the way. Second and third rounds finishing the two-left standing before they even realized that death was silently lashing out of a window above their heads.

Satisfied that all were down, Neeley pulled out a red lens flash-light and searched the dirty floor of the room. She collected the five pieces of expended brass and placed them in a pocket on the outside of the backpack, insuring the Velcro cover was tightly sealed. She listened to the earpiece from the portable police scanner in her pocket as she swung on the backpack and started down. She was on the street before the first call for a car to investigate shots fired came over the airway. The police would not respond with any particular alacrity. Shots fired were common calls in the South Bronx at night. Cops tended to band together here and only became excited if the radio call was 'officer down'.

As she headed toward the Mercedes, movement from one of the bodies caused her to swing the muzzle up; one of the men was still alive. Neeley watched the figure writhing on the ground for a few seconds. She stepped forward, and with one boot, shoved the body over, keeping the muzzle pointed at the man's head. The man's stomach was a sea of very dark, arterial blood: gut shot. Neeley's training automatically started scrolling through her consciousness, outlining the proper procedures to treat the wound.

The bulky barrel of the rifle mesmerized the man's gaze. Looking above it, into Neeley's dark pupils, his own widened with surprise. They searched for mercy in the depths of Neeley's thickly lashed eyes. Neeley's entire body started sweating and the adrenaline kicked up to an even higher level. The muzzle didn't waver.

The round entered a small black dot between the man's eyes. The bullet mushroomed through the brain and took off the entire rear of the head, spraying the dirty street. Neeley watched the body twitch and become still. She automatically scooped up the expended brass casing and stuffed it into her pocket.

Moving to the cardboard boxes, she pulled a thermal grenade out of one of the pockets of her loose fitting black leather, knee-length overcoat and pulled the pin. She placed the grenade on top of the boxes and released the arming lever, pocketing both it and the pin. Acting quickly, trying to make up for the seconds lost dealing with the wounded man, she tore the briefcase out of the limp hand still holding it and jogged to the end of the alley. A subdued pop and a flicker of flames appeared behind her as two million dollars worth of cocaine began to go up in flames.

Satisfied she was out of immediate danger, and before reaching the corner, Neeley twisted the locking screw and broke the rifle down into two parts. She hung the barrel on the inside right of her coat and the stock on the left, securing them with specially sewn in bands of Velcro.

Turning the corner, Neeley settled into a steady, swift walk. From the confused babble on the scanner, she had six to eight minutes before the first police arrived.

She made three blocks and then turned left. Here were the first signs of life. This area was more populated, but still well within the urban battle zone known as the South Bronx. Covert eyes watched her as she moved and Neeley slid a hand up, loosening the 10mm Glock Model 20 pistol she wore in a shoulder holster.

Her purposeful stride and appearance deflected any thoughts of evil intent from those lurking in the shadows. Neeley was tall, an inch shy of six foot. She had broad shoulders and a slender build. Her short, dark hair had seen better days and could use styling. Her face was all angles, no soft roundness, with two very dark eyes that took in everything in her surroundings. She moved with a sense of determination, her long overcoat half open, allowing her easy access to the weapons inside.

Two more blocks, no interference encountered, and she reached her parked pick-up truck, nestled among other battered vehicles. She unlocked the door and threw the suitcase in. The first sirens were wailing in the distance as Neeley got behind the wheel and cranked the engine.

For the first time she paused. She held her hands in front of her face. They were shaking slightly. Neeley took a deep breath and held it. The vision of the man looking up at her flickered across her eyes, then was gone. She shivered; shaking her head in short violent jerks, then was still again. She put the truck into gear and drove off.

Sticking with the route she had memorized, Neeley drove, keeping scrupulously to the speed limit. After ten minutes of negotiating side streets, she reached an on-ramp for the Cross Bronx Expressway and rolled up it, heading northeast for New England.

The suitcase on the passenger seat nagged at her. Neeley held her patience for two hours, until the city was over eighty miles behind her, and she was well into Connecticut, just south of Hartford. Finally, she pulled into a rest area. Parking away from other vehicles, Neeley turned on the dome light and put the suitcase on her lap.

She checked the exterior for any indication it was rigged. Nothing. Flipping both latches, she slowly lifted the lid an inch. She slid a finger in and carefully felt the edges. Then she opened it all the way. A wadded piece of cloth lay on top, covering the contents. Neeley peeled the cloth away. Stacks of worn hundred dollar bills greeted her. She didn't count it. She knew exactly how much was there.

Finally accepting she was safe, Neeley allowed herself to think of Gant. She wondered how it would have been to open the suitcase with him. She knew he would have been proud of her. Gant had talked about this mission endlessly. He had a source, someone he called his Uncle Joe, although he said the man was not family by blood, who had called him just two weeks ago with word of this meet. Somebody who must have owed Gant a lot, but Neeley understood owing Gant.

She remembered all the nights she had lain with her body curled into his. Talking about it and perfecting the plan. Every ex-Green Beret's dream, he'd called it.

Neeley closed the suitcase and with it the memories of Gant. There was still much to do.

THE DAY her life as she knew it came to an end, Hannah Masterson forced herself to stroll casually down the carpeted hallway. They were all trying hard not to stare but Hannah was certain they were. She doubted that they knew about John, but she'd always known that people could sense bad news. Hannah had an urge to walk the length of the long hallway, stopping at every desk, and explain in great detail to every person that she had been a good wife, never shirked her duties, always smiled and appeared happy, and that John wasn't really gone. He was just away for a little while. On business.

Of course they wouldn't believe her. She didn't believe it either. Not that she hadn't been a good wife, but that John was really gone. Men like John, with six-figure salaries and power jobs, didn't just dump the wife, career, house and two cars for no reason at all. Something had happened to him, she was convinced of it; well, had been. The day-old postcard in her purse had forced her to acknowledge other possibilities.

With relief, she found the door to Howard Brumley's office open and aimed herself toward a vacant chair. One look at Howard's face told Hannah that there was to be no reprieve during this appointment. His normal ruddy complexion was pale; the dancing, flirting eyes were gone, replaced by shaded 'I hate to tell you this' pupils.

Howard picked up a file and tapped the corner nervously. "You look good."

Hannah's wasn't a natural beauty, but more the result of money meeting good bone structure. Her blond hair was thick and shiny, flowing to her shoulders in natural waves. Her eyes, hidden now by the dark glasses, were the color of expensive chocolate left in a hot car. The few worry lines around her eyes and mouth were deepened by the stress of the past week and were the only thing that made her look older than her 31 years. She was a shade under five and a half feet and weighed what any self-conscious woman of means would weigh.

Howard, the family lawyer, was dodging. Hannah knew it was difficult to talk to a woman whose husband had apparently taken the perpetual golf trip. That was how John had done it. Left early on a beautiful Saturday morning the previous week with his golf bag and whistling a happy tune. Glanced back once. Whether to look at her, or the house, maybe both, she would never know. The Country Club had returned the car on Monday. John had taken his clubs. Even with the car back in the garage though, Hannah couldn't believe he was gone.

Howard put down the file folder and leaned back in his chair. "Have you heard anything else from John?"

"Just the card from the islands. If it was John who sent it," she amended.

"Is it his handwriting?" Howard asked.

Hannah reluctantly opened her bag and handed the card over. "It looks like his writing, but it could be a forgery."

Howard shook his head, staring at it. "I can't believe he would do something like this."

"Maybe the card is just--" Hannah began, but Howard was shaking his head again and his attention was no longer on the card.

"No." Howard gestured to the file folder. "I mean I can't believe he would do anything like this."

"You think he's really gone?" Hannah asked. "Off to some south sea island like this card says?"

Howard sighed. Hannah was watching him carefully. John was hurt. That was it. "He's been in an accident, hasn't he?" She picked the postcard up from the desk. "This was John's way of trying to keep me from knowing, isn't it?"

"He's not hurt, not that I know of." Howard blinked. "Hannah, I've known John a long time and two weeks ago I would have trusted him with the lives of my children." Howard took a deep breath. "I don't know what to say."

Hannah sat still and waited to hear something so bad it would render a lawyer speechless.

Having taken the plunge, Howard continued. "Evidently John was planning this for some time. He cleaned out everything: IRA's, mutual funds, stocks, real estate, you name it. You should have had your name on all of it. It was too easy for him. He did leave you fifteen thousand in your household account. But here comes the bad news."

Hannah's head snapped from an imaginary upper cut. She was a little behind Howard, taking it one-step at a time. "He's gone? He's really gone?"

Howard was in a rush to get it over with. "The house, Hannah. It's the house."

"No. That's mine." Her voice was level and hard. "When we paid the note off last year John filed a quitclaim deed and put the house in my name."

She remembered the night well. John had said it was a symbol of his love and devotion. Hannah who had spent most of her childhood in a succession of foster homes felt safe for the first time that night. Her house, it would always be her house.

"John forged your name and took out a new note on the house. It's mortgaged to the max. If you sell it now you can pay the bank. As it is you have a payment of a little over six thousand dollars due in seven days. You don't have enough money to stay there more than two months."

Hannah shook her head. "John wouldn't do that. He wouldn't do that with the house. Not the house."

Howard must have seen too many war movies with shellshock victims as he slapped Hannah with his words. "Hannah, John's gone. He left you and stole everything that wasn't nailed down. And what was nailed down he sold out from under you."

Hannah held up a thin, manicured hand. "But that's illegal." It was beginning to sink in. "What about the cars?"

"Both leased," John said. He glanced in the deadly folder. "The Volvo is five hundred and forty. The BMW is eight-twenty, both payable the first of the month."

Howard cleared his throat. Could there be more? Hannah wondered.

There was. "I also received mail from John yesterday." Howard was holding several legal sized pieces of paper. "It's a marital dissolution agreement."

"You're joking," Hannah sputtered. "John wants to divorce me after stealing everything?"

Howard looked distinctly uncomfortable. "Apparently so."

"But ..." Hannah shook her head. "I don't ..."

"It's an unusual situation," Howard said.

The understatement of the year, Hannah thought. She found it strange that the only thing that resounded in her mind was that she hadn't seen it coming. She didn't really care about the cars or the money—the house, of course, was a different matter, for a different reason—but she hadn't seen this coming.

Howard's voice took on his professional lilt. "You have to realize that some of what John did *is* illegal and not just toward you. The bank he took the new mortgage out from will not be very happy either. You're probably going to have to divorce him to keep the bank and others he defrauded from coming after you, Hannah."

"Coming after me?" she repeated. "I didn't do anything."

"Divorcing him, and a thorough check of your lack of assets, will help convince them of that," Howard said. "But as it looks now, you're a party to everything he did. Divorcing him will be the best thing you could do."

"Divorcing John is a good thing?" Hannah pressed her hands against her temples. "I don't understand. Until a week ago I thought I had a good marriage. John seemed as happy as ever. Something's wrong with this picture, Howard. Either something awful happened to John or my entire adult life has been a sham. After all these years for him to do this now means I'm an idiot."

Howard's voice softened. "No. You're a lovely, lovely woman who married a snake. But now's not the time for pity. Now's the time for action. You have to rise above this, Hannah. We have to take care of the dirt John left you. Then you can start a new life."

Hannah stared. A new life? She didn't even know how she'd lost the old one yet.

Howard kept the words coming. "Hannah, you're a beautiful woman with lots of talents. You can get a job or another husband in no time."

Even through the numbness, that struck a painful chord. "I can't believe you said that, Howard."

He held up both hands, defensively. "I didn't mean it like that."

"How else could you possibly have meant it?"

"Hannah, please!" Howard was standing. He had an envelope in his hands that he was running one thumb along the edge of. "Do you need help?"

Hannah was puzzled by the inane question.

"Haven't you been seeing someone? A professional?" Realizing he wasn't getting through, Howard cut to the chase. "A psychiatrist?"

How did he know about Dr. Jenkins, Hannah wondered. John must have told him, she immediately realized. Hannah gave a bitter laugh. "How can I pay for a psychiatrist now?"

"You're still covered by John's health plan; for a while at least. I think you really should go see him. Get some help."

Hannah stood. "I have to go."

Howard started coming around his massive desk. "I'm sorry, Hannah. Please don't leave like this. With everything you have to worry about I'd hate it if I were the cause of any more trouble. I was just trying to help."

Hannah didn't say anything. She walked quickly out the door. As the elevator doors shut Howard was still calling after her, telling her they had to take care of this now. Clear it up before it was too late.

Hannah leaned against the brass wall letting the cool surface soothe her forehead. She was still willing herself not to faint when the doors slid open. The man in front of her shot an appreciative glance as he entered the elevator.

"Nice day."

She stared at him as she pushed by him into the lobby, awed by the fact that the world was going to go on.

Hannah fumbled her way out of the office building and stood in a daze on the sidewalk. All around her office workers were hitting the streets of St. Louis for lunch. After she was bumped a few times she realized it was time to move on. She couldn't quite remember where the car was parked and it didn't seem to matter. The car John had brought home one day. She hadn't even asked if he'd bought it or leased it. Those were questions that simply had never occurred to her after so many years of allowing John to take care of everything.

Hannah wondered if anything was ever going to matter again. This morning her main concern had been John and his safety. Clutching her purse to her chest, she now knew that John was never coming back. Beyond that was dangerous territory for her mind to go.

The Adam's Mark was just ahead. Two weeks ago she might have wandered into the hotel bar and waited for her successful husband to join her for lunch. Today she didn't know if she had enough money for a sandwich and a coke. She fumbled with her purse and checked. She had a couple of dollars in cash. She had no idea what the status of the credit cards was.

The bar was cool and dark and occupied by a lone female bartender. Hannah took a seat at the bar and waited. She noted that the bartender was about her age but looked it. Hannah's carefully tended thirty-one years had been shielded from the direct hit of aging, until this week of course.

"Are you OK?"

Hannah was startled by the bartender's sudden question. She nodded.

"How about a cup of coffee?"

Hannah indicated in the affirmative, thankful that she would have a moment to compose herself before the woman returned. Hannah noticed that the woman's nametag pronounced her Marty. She was eyeing Hannah suspiciously from the end of the bar as she poured the coffee. She carried the cup the length of the bar and set it carefully in front of Hannah.

"Let me see if I can guess: man trouble."

Hannah tried to smile and failed. "Yes. He left me."

Hannah surprised herself. Even though John had been gone a week, this was the first time she had uttered those words aloud. It was as if by refusing to say them she had been able to negate the fact that he was no longer there. She had simply refused to consider the possibility. Even the post card's intent had been ignored.

"He left you?" Marty emphasized the latter pronoun as the look on her face passed from sympathy to incredulity. "I don't mean to be funny but if you got left, I don't figure any of us are safe."

Hannah took a sip of her coffee. The scalding liquid bit at her lips and she put the cup back on the polished surface of the bar. "Maybe nobody is safe."

Marty was leaning on the bar. "Was this guy your husband?"

"Yes. Next month would have been our tenth anniversary."

"He just up and left? Took his stuff and split?"

"Not really. He didn't even take a change of clothes. He just never came back home. For the past week I was afraid something terrible had happened to him and then yesterday I received a post card with palm trees all over it saying he wasn't coming back. I went to our lawyer and he had the divorce papers all ready."

Marty wiped the bar top. "Sounds like he went a little bit nuts. Maybe he's gonna come back after he gets regrooved and everything will be fine."

"He can't come back now. He forged my name on some real estate papers. He left me with nothing."

Marty wore a mask of outrage. "Oh man, that's the worst thing I ever heard. Don't sign the divorce papers. Nail the asshole. Get your own lawyer."

Hannah wondered why she was sharing this with some woman she would never speak to again, and realized that was the reason. She could hardly talk about this with the women in her limited social circle. She had kept John's disappearance as quiet as possible, telling only Howard and calling the people at John's office trying to find out, without saying *she* didn't know, if they knew where John was. But no one had had a clue as to his hereabouts. Hannah had even considered calling the police, but Howard had told her to wait a little bit. Howard's position had been that John's sensitive job at the company should be protected.

Hannah watched as Marty returned her thoughts to the bar. Hannah drained the last of the coffee and decided that it was time to go home.

She left the three-dollar bills that were all she had and mumbled some polite words to Marty. She passed through the hotel foyer focused on the green marble floor, ignoring the businessmen of assorted ages checking her out, noting the rings that marked her as taken and bagged by one of their own. They all gave her the soft smile and nod that they expected from other men for their own wives. They didn't expect Hannah to notice them just as they didn't expect their own wives to alert to the nods of other men.

She found the car around the block from Howard's office. The big black BMW that John had loved to drive. It was odd to discover that she didn't own it; that she didn't own anything. She thought about that for a minute, feeling the anxiety that threatened to overwhelm her. She pulled up to the garage attendant and panicked, realizing she had no money to pay the parking fee. She flipped open the console and slid quarters out of their holder. She had to go halfway down the dime column before she had enough. She was relieved when the gate released her and she burned rubber pulling away.

That little incident was more telling than anything Howard had said. Hannah moved some numbers around in her head and knew she needed a plan. The money that John had left would be swallowed by house expenses in no time. Howard was right: she was going to have to sell the house and then turn in the cars. But that left her without a job, home, car, anything. Hannah's mind was churning. She could sell the contents of the house. Maybe she could generate enough to lease an apartment.

She had to get a job. The very thought brought a tightness to her throat. Not because she didn't want to work, but because she felt she had nothing to present a future employer. She had dropped out of college to put John through graduate school, working two jobs, one as a substitute teacher and the other waiting tables. Instead of going back and finishing her degree, she had become a full-time wife. John's career had been so demanding and financially rewarding that she had simply never given a thought that she would need to support herself one day. That was the deal-- the word stuck in her conscious-ness-- the deal they had made without even bothering to verbalize it. It had just happened.

Bodyguard of Lies is available on Amazon and is in Kindle Unlimited.

PHOEBE AND THE TRAITOR

COPYRIGHT © 2022 by Bob Mayer
http://bobmayer.com

ISBN 9781621253693
Trade paperback: 9781621253938

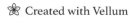 Created with Vellum

Made in the USA
Las Vegas, NV
04 September 2023

77054525R00174